Maya

An Irish-American History

by

Michael Boylan

PWI Books
Bethesda, Maryland

Published in The United States of America

ISBN-13: 978-0692-961636

ISBN-10: 069-296-1631

Library of Congress Number: 2018900674

Copy edited by Joanna Jensen
Proof read by Lydia Johnson

THE DE ANIMA NOVELS

Rainbow Curve

The Extinction of Desire

To the Promised Land

Maya: An Irish-American History

In the Beginning

Right away, let me tell you that I am a liar. Moksha. That's right: straight as a rail, a liar. Keep this information in mind as you read the story. I'm about to tell you of four generations within a particular family. Kama. The time-span is around a hundred and fifty years. But I won't go in order—no, I'm too clever for that.

Get me straight—I'm not impugning my characters. They aren't necessarily liars. They have their own lives to lead after a fashion. And I'm not saying anything about the author of this book. I can generally keep him out of it. After all, I am the mise-en-scène of the project while he acts like a producer getting me what I need to complete the presentation. *Artha.*

I am reasonably skillful in my deceit. You'll have a bit of work to do in order to trip me up. But I will hoodwink most of my readers. And I mean this—honestly! Dharma.

Prologue[*]

In the forest, a certain holy man was making his way. In the midst were wild and ferocious animals that were waiting to feed on human flesh. The snarls and guttural intimidations of the animals would be enough to frighten the dead! Still, the sadhu kept walking, but then a tiger sprang out at him and the holy man jumped aside to the safety of a slender tree that he began to climb in order to save himself. He shimmied to the top and smiled as he saw the tiger jumping in vain to get at him.

Then, in his self-satisfaction, the holy man looked up to the sky. What he saw there was the image of a giant woman who held an enormous fine-meshed net that contained all the forest. She held the drawstrings at the top, but kept them somewhat loose. Her hairs were snakes, slithering and spitting their venom. Her visage was frightening, as her eyeballs were hollowed out to the eye sockets. She sang a song of dissonant tri-tones that so unhinged the sadhu that he fell backwards from the tree into a giant pit. Only his quick mindedness allowed him to grab onto some vines to break his fall.

There he was: upside down in a giant pit. He looked up and saw at the top of the pit a large elephant with six faces and twelve feet who was stationary at the opening of the pit. Then he heard the sounds of giant snakes underneath him—not unlike the snakes that

---

[*] Adapted from the *Mahabharata*.

formed the hair of the net-keeper above. If he let go of his grip on the vines, he would perish among the vipers in the bottom of the pit. His hands ached: the vines were cutting his flesh. Drops of blood descended to ravenous reptiles and gave them hope.

The holy man was then aware of another noise. It was the sound of bees. He looked about him and saw a hive just above him. The sadhu reached out his other hand and grabbed some honey from the hive. It tasted sweet and gave him so much pleasure that he immediately wanted more. He gorged himself so that the vines began to strain with his added weight.

Then he smelled the foul odor of rats. He looked up again and saw two gray, lazy rats who were slowly gnawing at the very vines to which he was clinging for his life. The sadhu shut his eyes and smelled the rodents for a while before he reached up again for some more honey.

PART ONE

CHAPTER ONE

The Self slays not and is not slain.
   Katha Upanishad 2.19[*]

The news of the day: Bandit for a Night/Soldier a Suicide: After a swift series of robberies, private kills himself to avoid capture. His two companions escape. McBride, in a letter to a girl, threatened to do something desperate.

Death agreement seen in girl's murder: note to Elizabeth Johnson, 15, from suspect, reveals plan to die together. Slayer believed to have lost his nerve after he had shot his victim.

Davis denounces Republican tariff, saying that it favors the few over the good of the masses.

German American held as rum-fleet-pirate. He is accused in Paris of an attack on a French Ship.

The New York Times front page for September 18, 1924

JAMES looked down. The cool mist of the night collected with the sweat on his skin. He held on tight with both hands to the metal supports of the bridge. The tendons in his gaunt arms rose up. Then his right shoulder began to twitch. He tried to grip tighter. Below, the streaking water of the Ohio River was punctuated by uneven currents that swirled and ebbed in sections amidst the relentless rush of the greater body away — away to the sea. The noise of the water seemed to coalesce into an audible signal that called to him.

---

[*] Translated by Robert Hume, *The Thirteen Principal Upanishads* (London: Oxford University Press, 1921).

Wolf didn't want to give him the money he needed to continue. This was *family*. And still James felt Wolf wanted to twist him. Put him in his place. James thought he'd left all that behind when he had departed Louisville for St. Paul and his own pharmacy. But circumstances and his son's death had made everything wrong. The center no longer held. It was all falling apart. Swirling like the water. Robbed of everything by Niall. Bankrupt. Disgraced. That was why he came back to Louisville to work things out with Wolf. The man had the money to give him another chance. When that hadn't worked, he tried to find his former partner. He was reputed to be here.

The wind began to pick up and made the mid-September day seem cooler than it was. The howling furies made his ears sing. Why had he returned to Louisville? He relaxed his grip and stepped back. The noise was unbearable. He took three steps back to walk away.

James looked down at his sixty-four-year-old hands. The skin was rough and spotted with brown blotches. He rotated his hands to stare at his palms and then, suddenly, he edged forward again, and looked into the abyss. The swirling waters were so beguiling. Then it began to rain.

CHAPTER TWO

Darkness was hidden by darkness in the beginning; with no distinguishing sign, all this was water. The life force that was covered with emptiness, that one arose through the power of heat.*
  The Creation Hymn

The news of the day: The *Theatre Royal* will present Italian Operas sung by Mr. Harris and Mr. William Beale.

£100 Reward by the Constabulary
Whereas on the night of the 6th, a man cut the farm gates and thus broke into the barn of Miss Georgina Byrne in County Dublin. The thieves stole apples and set fire to the barn.

Irish Missions to the Roman Catholics:
Roman Catholic friends: Come to a discussion at Coombe class in Skinner's Alley on Thursday evening of March 15th at half-past Seven O'clock. Subject—"Are Adoration of Relics and bowing down to images lawful for Christians?"
Roman Catholics are earnestly and affectionately invited to attend.

Total Abstinence Question
This evening will be the first meeting at the Metropolitan Hall. Speakers will be the Rev. G.W. Dalton and Geoffrey Pope, esq. After the meeting, members will be enrolled. Tickets 3s. Tickets are transferable.
  The Irish Times, front page for March 15, 1860

SEÁN O'Neil was sitting on the stairs of the tenement in the city of Cork. The dark wood smelled dank with mold and was combined with the wafting acrid urine smell from the common toilet down the hallway. The small man with jet-black hair and pale skin was slumped over and holding his head in his hands. Then he tried to scratch his temple, but the nail on his index finger was broken from the accident at work. The nail cut into the skin of his face. He started to curse, but didn't have the energy. He was exhausted.

---

* Translated by Wendy O'Flaherty, *The Rig Veda* (New York: Penguin, 1981).

Mary had gone into labor six hours ago. That's when he left for the midwife. She was a woman in the building who had had thirteen children of her own and knew exactly what she thought of everything. She generally looked on the fair side of things. Was it those years in the convent?

Rose came almost immediately, even though it was midnight when Seán knocked on her door.

"Whatcha be wanting me for?" said Rose through the door. Rose was a short, stout woman whose husband worked at the same factory that Seán did.

"It's Seán O'Neil, Rose. It's about Mary. Her water's burst out everywhere."

"Why didn't you say so? I'll be right there."
And she was. That was six hours ago. Seán was dozing on the stairs. Every so often he'd awaken by the cry of a child or woman who was being slapped around by her husband. Seán would be alert for a moment and then return to his trance.

In another hour, Seán would have to leave for work to be there by 7:30. He was hungry and tired. It would be a very bad day.
The church bell chimed fifteen minutes after the hour. The door behind him opened up and little Tommy, just turned two, toddled toward his father. "Da, Da, Da!"

The little boy in his short pants and dirty shirt came forward. As he walked, his bare feet squeaked over the hard-aged carpet whose pile had long ago been beaten down to a flat plane by mud and filth and vomit.

Tommy walked forward with his broad oval face that exuded unrestrained joy. "Da! It's a boy! I'm a brother!"

Seán smiled a half-smile, grabbed the handrail and pulled himself up. He lifted little Tommy in his arms and walked back to their flat. The door was open and he walked into the room where his wife, Mary, lay. Rose blocked the view of his wife. She was holding the bawling red baby boy. He looked up at Rose. "Is everything all right?"

The midwife nodded her head and held the boy forward for the father to see, then she turned around and went back to the exhausted wife who was lying on the straw tick, and put the child to her breast.

Seán knelt on the floor next to the straw tick. The sight of his new son gave him a sense of energy. He kissed Mary. The church bells chimed. It was seven o'clock. He had to leave for work.

***

It was lunchtime. Seán had wrapped four biscuits in his handkerchief and had just purchased a ha'penny cup of tea to wash them down. He sat next to his mate, Patrick. The long wooden benches in the lunchroom were partially empty due to the recent lay-offs.

"My missus just had my son this morning."

Patrick nodded his head and gnawed at a thick piece of black bread. His brother worked in a bakery and got him day-old bread for a song.

"Have you thought of a name yet for the little stranger?"

"We've several we've been tossing around, actually. You know, boy names and girl names. If we can't make up our minds, we'll ask Father McGinnis before the christening. He has an opinion about everything."

Seán put the last biscuit in his mouth and then picked up the lukewarm, weak tea.

"I like the name Patrick, I do," said Patrick as he took another bite of bread. Even though it was a couple days old, the grains in the bread gave off an odor that made Seán's mouth water.

"Patrick's a fine name, it is. Too bad they wasted it on you!" said Seán as he lifted his forearm and gave his mate a jab. Patrick smiled and jabbed back.

Then there was the work whistle. Seán downed his tea and Patrick stuffed the rest of the bread into his mouth.

***

Seán came right home after work. No stopping at the Green Dragon tonight. He opened the door and smelled the aroma of boiled cabbage. Tommy was playing with some small sticks that Seán had roughly carved so that they resembled people. Each one had a recognizable head, body, and legs. The biggest drawback to the toys was that they had no arms. That's what the imagination is for.

"Whatcha playing, Tommy?"

"Red Branch."

"Which one is Cuchulain?"

Tommy lifted up the tallest stick figure. His father clapped his hands.

Michael Boylan   11

Then Seán walked a few steps past his son to his wife who was holding her baby close to her and under the stained, blue cotton blankets that had been made in the factory that Seán worked in. Mary's usual ruddy complexion was redder than normal. The tenement was drafty and, this being the middle of March, it was a damp-cold. Seán took off his coat and put it over his wife and baby.

"How was work?" asked Mary.

Seán shrugged his shoulders and knelt next to the pair. "He's a beautiful lad. Have you thought of a name yet?"

"He has your eyes. Blue eyes. What kind of Irishman has blue eyes?"

"The damned handsomest one on his shift." Seán inhaled and stuck out his chest. Then he exhaled and shook his head, "But what about a name?"

"Well, both of our fathers were named 'James.'" The infant popped off the breast he was feeding on.

"But I hated my father," said Seán, turning away and addressing the wall.

"Well, you had good reason to. But this little stranger would never hurt anyone."

Seán rubbed a small scar next to his left eye. He stared at a roach that was emerging from a crack in the plaster.

"Let's ask Father Mac about it," put Mary as she used her free hand to brush her light brown hair out of her eyes.

Seán turned back to his wife, smiled, and gave a kiss to Mary and their child before walking over to the stove to ladle out what was left of the boiled cabbage. The fire had long since gone out. Tommy was engaged in a battle of the Red Branch—including sound effects.

"So there's nothing new at work, then?"

"Nope, just the same. Another couple guys made redundant."

"More firing?

"Yeah. The place is contracting, that it is." Seán walked back to his wife and lowered himself to the floor. "Some of the guys are getting shorted, too. A dozen hours work and they only pay you for ten. It's not like we are lace Irish and don't give a damn: bloody awful place to work. But what choice does a lad have? We know it. They know it. And they use that knowledge to keep us down. Bloody English way of commerce."

"And how safe are you?" asked Mary as she transferred the baby to her other breast.

"Don't know. But there was another bloke at the plant today to round up workers for America."

"Free passage?"

"Yeah, but you have to work three years at their factory or pay the full price of the passage for the family."

Mary smiled and reached out her hand to her husband. "Don't worry, Seán. I've always said you were my protector. I mean it, honey, until the day I die." Seán leaned forward and took Mary's hand.

"Bam!" yelled Tommy, as Cuchulain killed ten English soldiers who were trying to invade Belfast.

Seán smiled, shook his head, and ate his cabbage.

***

Two years later, the O'Neils were riding steerage on their way to New York and then to Philadelphia. The American Civil War had depleted much of the working-class population for the army. A clothes company wanted to replace the lost skilled workers who knew the cotton and wool business from the ground floor and could deliver cheap cloth to the female work force that were fettered to their sewing machines (a good portion of which was going to the war effort). The pay was half of what was promised but an apartment was included that had its own toilet and bath. Even though the ceiling leaked and there were roaches, the O'Neils thought they had died and gone to heaven.

Their parish was mostly Irish, German, and a few Italians. Tommy was a year away from attending public school and James was just a toddler. The family made some friends in the apartment building that was populated mainly with people from the clothing factory (as the building was owned by the same man). They were paid daily in cash and they were never shorted. It seemed that life was beautiful.

***

One night Seán woke up coughing. The factory in Philadelphia was smaller than the one in Cork. There were fewer windows and there were more cotton fibers in the air. Sometimes it became hard for Seán to breathe. He had to get outside for a few minutes. However, if you left the work floor (even to go to the bathroom) you were docked a half-hour. But better a few bob short than to fall over dead.

**

Seán walked over to the faucet near the oven. He picked up a ceramic mug and filled it with water. Then he had another coughing fit. When it had subsided, he took a few sips of water, walked over to the window and opened it up. It was November and getting cold, but the air felt good even though it prompted another coughing fit. He wished he had enough money to buy tobacco. A good smoke would soothe his lungs. He was sure of it.

Then Seán went back to bed. The straw tick seemed to poke him like needles as he drifted into a dream about Tommy and James. They were all members of the Red Branch and were on their way to report to Cuchulain, who was protecting Dublin against an attack of the British. Tommy carried a long sword and James had a dagger (he fought on the sly and caught you when you were unprepared). Seán was the attendant. He led a donkey that carried what they needed for battle. Suddenly, they were lost. How had it happened? It was Seán's job to lead them to their destiny, but somehow he had lost his way and the family honor would be forsaken forever.

Seán awoke in a sweat and began to cough.

It was the beginning of March in the middle of Lent when Seán went to find a midwife. They did things different in America. In Cork, people just helped each other out in the tenements. There was no talk of compensation because people simply helped each other out when they needed it. But here he had to take the midwife and her children into their apartment for meals until the child was born. This arrangement made everyone a bit uncomfortable. Tempers were a bit frayed when Mrs. Bernadette Coughlin and her brood of five came for lunch and supper each day. Seán often came home a little late so that he might avoid the cacophonic circus.

Bernadette's husband was in the army, and she hadn't received a letter from him in over a year. The last she'd heard was that he was fighting in the army of General Sherman.

Mary made the fire in the oven with the scant coal from the factory allowance that was augmented by scraps that Tommy picked up around the neighborhood. The food was mostly vegetable-based soup with bread washed down by tap water.

Mrs. Coughlin was a short, stout woman with black hair and dark brown eyes. The features on her face seemed to have been pushed to the middle by her puffy, rosy cheeks. Bernadette's teeth were not good. She'd lost two in her smile plus a molar. Her children (two boys and three girls, aged six to twelve) were terribly thin and had to use the toilet a lot.

On Thursday, the thirty-first of March, when Seán came home from work at eight o'clock, he found the house in disarray. Mrs. Coughlin's children were bouncing off the walls and occasionally knocking James over, who was sitting by himself toward their outside window. Tommy ran to his father. "Mommy's having her baby!"

Seán looked over to the side of the room where the bedding lay. There was a bucket of water and some rags hanging over the side. James could smell the coal fire in the oven. Both of their lamps were burning at high wick.

The blue-eyed, pale skinned, black haired little giant of a man strode toward his wife without thinking. When he had taken three steps, Bernadette Coughlin twisted her head around and screamed at him, "Get everyone out of here! I need some decent space about me now."

The remark puzzled Seán, but he instantly obeyed. He picked up James and rounded the other children out into the hall and deputized Martha, the oldest Coughlin child, to control the group. The hallway was wide—ten feet or so. There was a carpet that covered the seven feet in the middle. The plaster walls were in good condition thanks to the occupants having painted them last summer. (Free paint from the factory owner. They provided the labor.) The only light they had was from the gaslights outside. The dim corridor smelled of dank and dried vomit. At the end of the hall was the staircase. Martha posted herself there to prevent any children from venturing that way.

For seven hours they waited. One by one the Coughlin children went to sleep. Even Tommy went to sleep holding his brother, James's, hand. Only James and Seán remained awake. The trio was positioned together when the door to their apartment opened and Mrs. Coughlin emerged holding something.

Seán pulled himself up, lifting little James and nudging Tommy awake with his left foot. Coughlin moved her head in an impatient way. The O'Neil clan proceeded on cue.

"This is your new baby sister," said Mrs. Coughlin. The baby was red and bawling: this resonated in Seán's consciousness as a memory confirmed. He smiled and took the baby in his arms. "Smile at your father, Lucy," intoned Mrs. Coughlin.

Then Tommy blurted out, "Lucy?"

Even Seán was confused. Something was amiss.

Bernadette sensed the confusion and took the baby back and with a flip of her hand dismissed Tommy and James. Then she lifted her free hand and motioned Seán to follow her. It was only then that Seán noticed that Bernadette's hand was dripping blood. Unconsciously, he followed Mrs. Coughlin to the doorway where his eyes were captivated by the form of his wife lying in a bloody mess. Seán rushed to Mary. "What's the matter? What has happened?" Seán's voice was squeaky high. His hands were shaking as tried to wake her up. He kneeled down and lifted the unconscious body into his arms.

"Wake up, Mary. It's Seán, your protector."

But Mary didn't move. Her body was still warm.

***

Tommy O'Neil finished his schooling at sixteen to take a job in the factory with his dad. Tommy had been a passable student, but he didn't really see the point of learning math and English grammar—to say nothing about the Greeks and Romans! Tommy was a very practical fellow and he didn't like to go into abstractions such as are taught in high school.

James was fourteen and liked Latin in particular. He was partial to Virgil's *Aeneid.* "I sing of arms and men!" What could be finer? One day when Tommy had come home from work with his father, James was strutting about the room reciting lines on the death of Dido.

"What do we have here?" queried Seán as he entered the room and began coughing.

James and Tommy helped their father to his armchair for rest. The great protector needed a little protecting himself. When he had stopped coughing, the patriarch renewed his query. "What is this prancing all about, James?"

James slunk back and hid his book behind his back.

Tommy put his hand on his father's shoulder. "That's all right, Da. Jamie was just role-playing from Virgil. He's a great Latin poet."

"Damnation boy, don't you think I've never heard of Virgil? Just because I never went to school doesn't mean that I don't know a thing or two."

Tommy smiled and went over to the sink to draw his father a glass of water. It was dark outside and there was only one kerosene lamp lit. Seán's vision range did not extend to the sink, so to him Tommy disappeared and then re-appeared with the cool elixir. The father took a long drink and then set the glass on the floor. James furtively slid closer to his father. He wanted to touch his father as Tommy had, but he was afraid.

As Seán's youngest boy stepped forward into his lamp-lit field of vision, the father reached out his arm. James eagerly bounded forward and grasped his father's hand. "Since I don't know the Latin tongue like your learned brother and you (though I did learn a spot of Gaelic in my youth), please tell me the scene that you were going through when we came home." Seán looked up with a smile.

James grimaced. "It's not a really good scene, Da. It's just a lot of military stuff. You know it's a book about war."

Then Seán frowned. "When I ask you a simple question, young man, I expect a simple answer and not a lot of shenanigans. Now tell me, what was the scene about that prompted your prancing and dancing?"

James looked to Tommy, who lifted his hand to his brother and answered for him. "James was reading a very sad part of the story in which a woman in love with the hero of the story, young Aeneas, becomes despondent when her love deserts her for his exploits."

"Why did he do a damned-fool thing like that for?" inquired Seán.

"Well, the short story was that he had a mission to accomplish that required him turning away from the personal. His duty as a king was bigger than his private life."

"And who was this fair lass who he treated so wrongly?"

"Her name was Dido," put James (emboldened by his brother's largesse).

"Dido? What kind of name is that? County Donegal?"

"It isn't an Irish name, Da," said Tommy, caressing his father's shoulders. "It's from the Mediterranean area, in a city called Carthage."

"So what does this woman do?"

"She's a princess, Da. She's very important. She loves Aeneas, another royal soul, and when he leaves her she throws herself off a cliff."

Seán began coughing very hard. Blood came up and the boys tried to lay him onto the floor. They both alternately caressed him and gave him a few sharp jabs to the back. Soon he stopped hacking. The fifty-one-year-old factory worker seemed to go to sleep.

The boys retreated a few steps when Seán awoke and said, "I don't want this talk about death around here: especially self-inflicted death. Don't you know that you go to hell when you kill yourself?" Then he seemed to breathe in a very labored way. The boys started forward again but he resumed speaking. "That's what keeps the likes of me going. And don't you forget it. It's not enough that your blessed mother, Mary, and your dear sister, Lucy, are no longer with us, but do you have to read stories about—" and then Seán fell immediately into a deep sleep.

The boys checked their father's breathing and then went and covered him up with a thick wool blanket that his factory had produced and had been given to him last Christmas. Tommy walked over and picked up the book James had been reading and handed it to his brother. "Now, once again, read me the passage and put your soul into it."

***

Seán's health was getting worse. Tommy found that he hated factory work. It was too repetitive. He was forced to work with a team of five in a very small space for long periods of time. This wasn't pleasing to him and he wanted to get out. The trouble was James. He was a delicate soul who couldn't stand very much conflict. James liked to be by himself. James didn't play with the other boys, but preferred studying for school. He got high marks, but the family couldn't eat his high marks. If Tommy left, then James would have to go to work because they couldn't live on the contracted hours that their father could still perform. He was only working a six-hour half-shift, and that for only five days a week. If Tommy quit, his brother and father would founder.

It was the beginning of Advent in 1876. Tommy tossed the fish and potatoes he'd purchased for dinner on top of the black cast iron oven. The temperature was cold and the humidity was high. The combination was particularly uncomfortable to Tommy. He washed his hands and unwrapped the fish from its newspaper covering. It was then that he saw a large font advertisement for policemen in New York City:

> **Wanted:** Young Men Strong and True to be Policemen in New York City. High Wages, Job Security, Career Opportunities—Especially Interested in Immigrants: Irish, German, Polish. Contact Padreig Conley . . . .

The advertisement set Tommy's mind on fire. It was like an omen from God telling him where he should go. The only drawback was getting James a job so that he could help support their father. That would not be an easy task. James was not cut out for the harsh indignities of the factory floor. In America, a man in a factory had to be prepared to fight at the drop of an insult. Tommy had protected his father. But then even the young punks weren't really out to get a man with one foot in the grave. But James was too delicate for all of that. He needed a different sort of job.

After Easter, Tommy took a hike to central Philadelphia. His first idea was retail sales. There were a myriad of little shops with so many people who wanted work that the task daunted him. It was important to get to a part of town where people with some money shopped. If he stayed in south Philly where the O'Neils lived, any job Tommy got for his brother might be gone the next day.

So Tommy headed to the area of town that had streetlights, just a few blocks from the waterfront in the beginning of the old capital area. An unusual sign of a top hat with a white handled cane arrested his eyes. Tommy stopped and took in the haberdashery. It was not too fancy, but not working class either. The merchandise in the window was respectable but not ostentatious. At the far end of the window was a little placard that said, "Help Wanted." He took off his own Irish tam and proceeded inside. The interior was dark wood, probably walnut. It was the afternoon so the lamps inside were not lit, but the atmosphere was very dim.

Tommy had been inside no longer than a half a minute when a scrawny man wearing a gray waistcoat and broad tie approached him. The man was very old—sixty or more! He carried his hands in front of him and was constantly rubbing them as if he were washing. "Excuse me, can I help you?" said the high crackling voice. It was a question that was phrased like a veiled threat.

Tommy cleared his throat. "Yes sir, you can. You see I was walking down the street here and I saw your help wanted sign in the window."

The scrawny man stopped rubbing his fingers. His eyes took on a focus and then he raised his right arm and pointed his index finger right at Tommy's face. "You Irish trash. Why don't you stay where you belong? Do you think I'd dirty my shop with your filth? Why, I wouldn't even sell you a hat unless you paid me in gold."

As he spoke, the scrawny man jabbed his finger closer and closer to Tommy's face. Tommy knew that he could take out this little bigot in thirty seconds or less, but he also knew what it would cost him. So he pursed his lips, pivoted, and exited the shop.

When he was outside, Tommy gave in to his urges and spat on the outside wall of the shop under the plate glass windows. He continued on his journey.

After a dozen or so attempts, Tommy called it a day. He was sick and tired of all the anti-Irish sentiment in the English part of town. For a moment he began to question his interest in becoming a copper in New York City. Maybe they would treat his kind in the same way. At least at the clothes factory they didn't hold his blood against him. But that was probably because the owner was Irish and most of the workers were, too. Tommy began to think about how he might take some short cuts on the four-mile walk home when he stopped in his tracks. A gray-haired man dressed in a black frock and white shirt was in the process of locking up his store when a horse that was pulling a cab knocked down a young boy, who had been crossing the street.

The black-clad man rushed to the boy. Tommy didn't think twice: he also rushed to the boy. The lad was probably around eleven—just a few years younger than James.

The gray-haired man was in complete command. He saw Tommy's approach and directed him to lift the legs while he took the torso. They walked him over to the shop the black-clad man had exited. "Set him flat," directed the elder man. The sidewalk was brick and was reasonably even. When the boy was down the man took out some keys from his coat and opened the door to the shop. Tommy kneeled near the boy's head. He stroked the boy's face and the child opened his eyes.

Tommy smiled. "Tell me where it hurts."

The boy didn't reply.

"You took a nasty fall there. A horse ran into you and sent you sprawling backwards. I need to know where you hurt so we can help you."

The boy's gaze was now clearly focused upon Tommy's face. It had an imploring air of helplessness.

Then the man in black returned with a dark brown glass bottle and a spoon. He unscrewed the cap and poured out a teaspoon full. "Open your mouth, son. This is medicine that will help you." The boy turned his gaze to Tommy. Tommy nodded his head in accord and the boy opened his mouth and accepted the proffering.

The man in black then turned his gaze to Tommy. "Can you stay with him an hour? I have to go to a meeting and will be back to get this lad on his feet."

"Sure," replied Tommy as he sat down next to the sleeping child. It was forty-five minutes after the hour when the man left and twice fifteen minutes after the hour when he returned. Tommy was very tired. It was his day off, but the combination of everything took all that he had. He passed the time by making note of the way various people made their way around him on the sidewalk. No one offered any assistance or asked him what had happened. It was just as if a pile of sand had been dumped on the sidewalk and everyone had to negotiate around it.

"Ha! There you are," said the man. "I told them so at the meeting."

Tommy tilted his head quizzically.

"The meeting," he said with more volume, as if that would solve the problem. "Sister Catherine and Brother Mark were certain that I had been wrong to leave you with the boy and that you'd be gone when I returned. I told them that I was an uncommonly good judge of human nature. But I didn't convince them."

Tommy looked down at the sleeping boy.

"Has he been calm?" asked the man in black.

Tommy nodded, his eyes half-closed.

"Well, then let's get him inside my shop to have a good look at him."

Tommy reacted almost mechanically to the command. He instinctively took the feet as they carried their charge inside through the main shopping area to the back room where there were several tall wooden tables. They set the boy down and the man in black undressed the boy and examined the body. Even with all three lamps lit, there were many shadows. Shadows frightened Tommy. He felt that no good came from them.

The man in black turned to his young assistant and said, "There are no broken bones. The boy has some severe bruising that can be eased by this herbal extract that is rubbed on the affected area. What I want to do now is to wake the boy and have you take him home with the salve."

They managed to wake the child and get a sense of where he lived (about two miles away). Tommy would assist his walking and see to it that the boy got home. As the trio exited the shop, the man in black reached out his hand to Tommy. "Young man, you are a person of character. If there is ever a boon that I can bestow upon you that is within my power, please let me know. I am Charles Quincy, trained chemist."

Tommy shook the man's hand and started home with Johnny, the waif they had rescued. Tommy couldn't see it but Charles Quincy tipped his hat to the pair when they were but fifty yards into their journey.

When James graduated on June 15, 1876 on a Saturday, the sixteen-year-old was taken to the park. They sat on a bench and chatted about the future.

"Well, James, my boy, you seem to have followed the course of your brother and graduated from high school. You are a scholar and a gentleman." The now gray-haired blue-eyed little giant teared a bit when he talked. He had recently gone down to a third-shift (the lowest shift allowable).

"Yes, Da." James shared many of the same physical characteristics of his father while Tommy was a mix of their mother and father.

Tommy put his arm around his brother that was followed by his father. The scene was set: James sat in the middle of his brother and father. As they sat there frozen for a minute in time, there was a gaggle of geese that had been walking about in some non-descript pattern that suddenly decided to fly up in the air, flapping their wings and emitting a cacophony of loud squawking sounds.

The cascade of sounds revived the frozen pair to the moment at hand.

"So, what do you have to say to the future?" asked Seán.

"Future?"

Tommy cuffed his brother on the head. "Don't be daft, Jamie boy. You understand English."

"Of course I understand English. What do you mean by that?"

"Your Da asked you a question."

It was June. The black-capped chickadees in the park were swirling about. It was a partly cloudy day. There were insects a-buzzing and in the center of the park a band was setting up in the circular white bandstand to begin a concert.

"I don't know," replied James. He didn't look at either his father or his brother.

"YOU DON'T KNOW!" screamed Seán. "Don't you know that only losers talk like that? Life doesn't just come after you like we've always given you. You got to have the balls to go after it in order to survive. There's no room in the world for 'I don't know.' You've *got* to know or you will go under." The patriarch lurched forward, but the exertion was too much. He retreated in a paroxysm of coughing that caused him to fall off the bench onto the turf.

Tommy quickly moved to retrieve his fallen father. James was frozen and didn't know what to do. When they had placed the patriarch back into position on the park bench, James began to talk.

"Listen, Da, it's not like I don't think about these things. I think about quite a bit, actually. It's just that—I mean that I'm not sure how much good it does."

Seán looked at his younger boy and listened.

"You know there is so much out of our control."

"What are you talking about, James?" asked the father.

James fidgeted a bit. He was now sitting on his hands and moving his shoulders up and down. "Well, for one I'm talking about moving from home."

Seán nodded.

"And for two, there was Ma. I don't know why she had to die giving birth to Lucy. I mean why did that have to happen? We never talked about it much. It was like an unspoken sin—except it wasn't any of our faults."

Seán's hands began to shake. Tommy tried to calm his father, but the elder man brushed him away.

"And then all that for a sister who goes and dies of the measles three years later. I mean. What was the point of Ma dying? She brought something into life that quickly made her exit."

"Lucy didn't make an exit," said Seán. "She was given the hook. She would have stayed if the good Lord would have let her. But it wasn't in His plan."

"Damny the plan, Da. I want my mother and sister!"

The older brother and father froze again. Then their attention went to a thin, young mother walking with her little daughter in front of them on the bench. The father and older brother patted James on the shoulder before standing up.

Seán turned and said to James as the trio exited the park, "You shouldn't say 'damny' son. It makes you sound like Irish scum."

They had walked a few blocks aimlessly when Seán directed the group toward South Street. Seán and Tommy had decided to take young James to a show at the new Ravioli Theater. It was a gay time watching comics tell bawdy jokes, singers present popular tunes, and dancing numbers here and there.

It was a high school graduation that James would never forget.

A few weeks later when Tommy took in the mail after work, he found a fat brown envelope addressed to him from the New York City Police Department. The letter offered him a probationary job in the force. If he showed his stuff in the first six months, his job would be permanent. There was also a brochure that set out all the particulars. Tommy took the letter outside to read. The evening was warm and the sun lingered on the horizon.

The following Saturday, Tommy took off from work at noon and walked back to central Philly to the chemist shop of Charles Quincy. Tommy opened the door and took off his tam. The store was very simply arranged. Over the door was a small window that could be opened with a pole that had a hook on the end. To either side of the door were large-paned glass windows that provided light for the interior. When one walked inside, he would see a shop with light red mahogany walls, the two flanking walls each sporting a large picture.

On the wall to the left was a picture of the staff and snake of Asclepiad, the symbol of the medical profession. To the right was a painting of William Penn. In front of Tommy at the center was a red cherry counter with an opening on the left side, and behind the counter was an entry to the back room, where he could see countless stoppered bottles sitting on little shelves that rose to the ceiling and a ladder that moved on a metal track for access.

When Tommy had opened the door, it hit a little bell on a string that signaled the entrance of a visitor. The noise prompted a scurry in the back room and the appearance of Charles Quincy without his black coat.

The elderly man appeared a bit flustered. His face was flushed and his sleeves were rolled up. "Can I help you?" said the man, adjusting his spectacles.

Tommy walked forward. "Excuse me, Mr. Quincy. I made your acquaintance quite by accident a couple of months ago. Do you remember? There was this little boy who was violently knocked down by horse pulling a cab—"

"Oh," began Quincy, pulling out his shirttail to clean his spectacles. "Yes, indeed I do." The chemist reached over the counter and shook Tommy's hand. "You know the mother came by on the Monday after and thanked me. She wanted to thank you too—especially for taking her boy such a long ways home. But unfortunately, I knew neither your name nor where you lived."

Tommy grimaced. "I'm sorry sir. That was very stupid of me. You see I'm just a simple lad who works in a clothes factory. I've not a lot of experience in the manners of this part of the city."

"You're an Irish immigrant, aren't you?"

Tommy grimaced again, and looked down at the cherry counter. He prepared himself for the worst. "Yes, sir."

"C'mon, boy. It's nothing to be ashamed of. We're all immigrants here. This country is full of immigrants—everyone except the Indians, you know. That's the beauty of America. You know, I'm a Quaker. We weren't wanted in England. They thought we were stupid simpletons because we weren't part of the Anglican Church. So we got up and left and lots of us landed here after our patriarch procured a land grant from the Crown." Quincy gestured with his left hand to the painting on the wall. "Now, why don't you come in the work room with me and I'll fix you up a cup of tea. I've invented a device that can make a quick contained fire under a special pewter pot that I also designed. I can get us hot water in fifteen minutes. Have some tea with me, and tell me your story."

And so they went into the back room. It was there that Charles Quincy did all the hard work of curing and preparing his herbs and salves for medicine based upon the tried and true recipes of his forefathers and mothers. Everywhere were little gadgets that Quincy had invented himself to make the job more efficient. In his modest way, he pointed out most of these to Tommy.

Before Tommy could make his request, Charles Quincy offered him a job in his shop. "You see, this is too much for one man. I used to have a nephew who helped me out, but he got big ideas and went to St. Louis. Why anyone would want to go to St. Louis is more than I can fathom. Anyway, I'm not getting any younger and I need an assistant. Do you want the job? I'll match your pay at the factory and the work is lighter and uses your brain more."

"Oh, dear Mr. Quincy. What you are saying moves me deeply. But let me give you some facts about my family, first."

And so, two cups of tea later, Tommy O'Neil had procured a job for his brother, James. The way was now clear for New York City and an exciting career as a cop!

CHAPTER THREE

When they divided the Man, into how many parts did they apportion him? What do they call his mouth, his two arms and thighs and feet? His mouth became the Brahmin, his arms were made into the Warrior, his thighs the people, and from his feet the Servants were born.
The Hymn of Man[*]

The news of the day: Spiritualism Extraordinary. To go from the Beecher-Tildon Trial to lunatics and idiots, and then to drift to spiritual affairs seems to show a degree of continuity of thought and deference to the connection about up to my usual mark. Pope and Foster sat opposite to the American skeptic. This evening we were in a dark parlor. We were all in gay spirits when Foster dropped his cigar. "That man has conjured up a man who drowned and is at this moment hovering over Pope."

Hamburg Embroideries: Wholesale and Retail French and Domestic Underwear.

Agnes Booth stars in Shakespeare's *King John*. It was the first time the play has been produced in St. Louis or if it has nobody can remember it.

In due time Mrs. ____ became a widow. She called upon her idiot son and recalled how her husband had deserted her, but he had always come back one day a year with his mistress to pay his respects. And now he would never return.
The St. Louis Republican. February 14, 1875.

IT was a cold. Cold makes the catgut strings contract, therefore affecting their pitch. The Mississippi river was flowing slowly on its long journey to New Orleans. Cedric Smith was tuning a violin that he had made on commission for a sale to a wealthy family from Bellefontaine. He was sitting in the large room of his three-room apartment while his wife, Barbara, was in labor with the doctor. It had been over 24 hours since he had summoned Dr. Wilson, who

---

[*] Translated by Wendy O'Flaherty, *The Rig Veda* (New York: Penguin, 1981).

lived only a few blocks away. The good doctor went to their church and when Barbara was in the family way, Cedric naturally thought of him. In payment Cedric was working on a small hand instrument of his own creation. It had five strings and a moveable button that acted like a fret for strumming very simple melodies. Dr. Wilson had three children of his own who were still young enough to enjoy making live music.

Cedric didn't mind spending long hours awake. He lived for the pure tones that the violin, viola, and cello produced. He could also tune and repair pianos. He manufactured, on commission, violins, violas, cellos and dulcimers. For twenty hours each week, he also gave music lessons on almost any instrument known to man. And in addition to that, he was the church organist and choir director. The music of the spheres resonated with the manufactured musical instruments and afforded him the backdrop that made life possible. His concentration was broken by a loud cry. Cedric put down the hand-sized auto-harp and ran into the bedroom. "What's the matter?" managed the musician, struggling to find the measure for his own pitch.

Dr. Wilson turned and smiled. "You've got a healthy boy, Cedric. Come on over and hold him before I give him back to Barbara."

Cedric inched forward. This was his first child. Since Cedric had grown up as the youngest child, he had had little experience with babies. Babies were mysterious. But the moment he held little Malcolm in his arms, something natural took over and he was overwhelmed. Dr. Wilson had to break the trance in order to return the baby boy to his proud mother.

Cedric moved over to his wife and kissed her.

"Barbara's been through a lot, Cedric. Why don't you go make her a cup of tea with a teaspoon of sugar? I think she needs to get her strength back. Why, she's been in labor for over a day. It's just as important, you know, to take care of the mother as the child."
Cedric went back to the big room and lit a fire to boil the water for tea. His mind was hearing Beethoven's *Sixth Symphony* with heavy timpani.

Little Malcolm was the apple of his father's eye. His father built him a wooden cradle and rocked him with his feet while he constructed musical instruments. Barbara nursed Malcolm for ten months and then transitioned him to solid foods—mainly administered by Cedric. Barbara spent a lot of time at their church, the Third Baptist Church. She was always involved in one project or another. Cedric used to joke that she spent more time at church than many men spent at their full-time jobs. Barbara would simply laugh and get on with cooking the dinner. Barbara loved to cook (Cedric always said so). She generally made stews that lasted three to four days. They'd buy a fresh loaf of bread each day for breakfast and lunch and use the remainder to sop up dinner.

Since Cedric's income went up and down according to how his students paid him and whether he had a commission for new instruments, they had to be creative and live rather in the present. The church paid the rent on the apartment in return for Cedric being the organist and choir director. When they got a little money, Cedric would bring it home and place it in a carved wooden box with a lock on it. The wooden box had been in Cedric's family since they came to Massachusetts in the late seventeenth century. Cedric's early family had been farmers then lawyers then musicians—three generations teaching at the Boston Latin School. They had changed their name from 'Smith' to 'Smythe' in the mid-eighteenth century because they thought it more refined.

It was Cedric who bolted from this bastion of old blood and little money for the West in order to make his own way. In the process 'Smythe' returned to 'Smith.' Cedric came into his job because his aunt (a Baptist) was married to Cedric's father's brother (an Episcopalian) and they were living in St. Louis and went to the Third Baptist Church. Cedric saw it as his destiny.

Three years after establishing himself in the area and building up a clientele for lessons, the renegade WASP found his true calling as a builder of stringed musical instruments. Cedric had always been musical. Cedric had always been handy. But it was wood and catgut that he loved most of all. Soon his instruments were renowned in the area. They were mentioned in the paper. All the parishioners paid him particular attention—especially one Barbara Jones. Barbara had light brown hair and blue eyes. She was a husky five-foot-six with strong arms and large hands. But most of all Cedric was taken with her beautiful skin and delicate features. It had been an odd courtship that was carried on mostly at the Church, at the reception after Sunday morning service and at the potluck before Sunday evening service. Sometimes Barbara even baked pastries for the choir at Thursday evening choir practice. The church had a wonderful kitchen and a social hall that could be arranged with portable tables and chairs.

Cedric proposed to Barbara just after the Easter picnic that was held in the park. Barbara announced the news to those who were cleaning up the tables. Everyone said it was the perfect match!

They were married in July and they honeymooned on a steamboat that went all the way to New Orleans. It was approximately a seven-day trip, depending upon the current of the river and how long they stopped at local hamlets along the way. Their boat was named *River Belle*. It was a steam powered wooden paddle wheel vessel with accommodations for two hundred souls that included most of the economic classes. Rooms with a view and a private toilet & bath were the most expensive. Those rooms below the waterline that shared toilets were much more reasonable. On the main deck was a restaurant and saloon with live music. It portrayed a wholesome, family atmosphere. On the upper deck was a seedier bar with a single musician and men playing poker. The lights were low and the stakes were high. Cedric and Barbara always went to the main deck.

On the first night, they were having a simple dinner of fried catfish and potatoes. Their table was pine and covered with a red and white checked rough cotton tablecloth. Their utensils were smooth cast iron. Barbara drank beer while Cedric drank wine. They sat near the stage where a Dixieland band was playing old favorites. Cedric was in heaven.

When the set was finished, Cedric began tapping out the syncopated rhythms of the last song on the table. His eyes were closed. A smile was on his face.

"What are you doing?" asked Barbara.

Cedric finished the musical phrase and opened his eyes. "The rhythms. They are so different, don't you know? They drive me crazy. So take the rhythms in our hymn book at church, they go: bum, Bum, bum, Bum or Bum, bum, Bum, bum or Bum, bum, bum, bum—or a few minor variations on the same. But these guys are mixing things up entirely: Bum, Bum, Ba, Ba, Ba, Bum. It breaks all the old rules and re-writes the score."

Barbara laughed, "Cedric, the music is a distraction. What do they have in the other restaurant on the upper deck?"

Cedric's stopped. His expression was changed as if he'd been slapped in the face. Then it darkened. "Barbara, that's no place for family folks: just a lot of drinking and card playing upstairs and low, lewd blues on a honky-tonk piano. That's no place for us."

Barbara screwed up her face. She looked at the stage in front of her, now vacant because of the set interval. Then she turned her attention to the ceiling and heard the pounding of shoes above, along with vibrant laughing and cursing. Barbara grimaced and shut her eyes. Obviously, she was happy where she was. "Cedric, can I have another beer?"

During the day, Cedric enjoyed sitting out on the main deck on a chair reading sheet music for a concert he was having at the church in October. Barbara was not a sedentary person, so she liked to prowl about the boat trying to understand just where everything was. On the lower deck there was a smoking lounge frequented by young men. Were these the forbidden souls who listened to honky-tonk piano? Why were they on the boat at all? Were they professional gamblers? Card sharks? Traveling salesmen? If a few of them could make a pitch to her, she might listen.

What freedom men had, she thought. Women were restricted to the family room while men could go anywhere they chose. Why was this? Just because Eve ate of the apple? The penalty seemed a bit harsh.

Barbara turned away and decided to fetch Cedric for lunch.

"So what did you discover in your journey about the boat?" asked Cedric as he dipped his spoon into the gumbo.

"Oh, it's a mighty big boat. If you go real high near the smoke stack it makes a lot of noise. Also if you go on the paddle deck right up to the rail, you can get sprayed with water."

Cedric chuckled. "That's one experience I will forego, my dear. You can be both Lewis and Clark. I'll be Jefferson and stay in my library."

Barbara tilted her head and then proceeded to tell Cedric a story about a group of birds that was following the boat. One of the birds veered out of formation and was sucked into the paddle wheel. "A terrible price to pay, Cedric."

"Shouldn't have left the group. Serves her right."

"Her?" inquired Barbara, putting the napkin to her mouth.

"Just a figure of speech, my dear. Just a figure of speech."

When they arrived at New Orleans, they looked up an aunt of one of the members of the church. The lady was married to a banker, so they were given a guest room of their very own. During the day, Barbara took Cedric on long walks to see the various sights of the town. During the night, Cedric and Barbara went to music houses to listen to Dixieland and other new music.

Cedric preferred syncopated piano and banjos while the trumpet-playing soloists delighted Barbara. The music houses were racially mixed—a fact that was invisible to Cedric but which fascinated Barbara. She felt the whole atmosphere to be *exotic*.

After their four-day stay it was time to return. The trip back was generally a couple days longer because the boat was fighting the current. Cedric had finished his concert planning and allowed himself to be led by his wife around every square inch of the boat—more than once!

On the seventh night coming home, Barbara asked Cedric to explain the concert he was planning. The couple was in their cramped double bed atop a sawdust-filled mattress atop sagging ropes. Cedric was so happy that he went over his general plan of the musicians who would be invited and guests that would be invited. "The Church will make money on this one and maybe they'll pay me a salary in addition to the apartment."

"Oh that would be wonderful," cooed Barbara. "How many people do you think might come?"

"We'll fill the room at fifty cents a ticket," replied Cedric.

"Fifty cents? That's mighty steep." Barbara inched closer to her husband.

"That's nothing. I'm also planning on holding a music master class—admission one dollar!"

"What's a master class?"

"It's where other, aspiring musicians from rich homes come to get advice on best practices in music. They get some personal attention and a chance to rub shoulders with the performers."

Barbara closed her eyes and grabbed her husband. She was adding up all the money and it made her giddy. "And you know, I could do a cash reception afterwards. We could really clean up!"

Cedric smiled.

Barbara kissed him passionately. It was then and there that they consummated their marriage.

The newlyweds spent a pleasant summer planning the upcoming October concert. Barbara took the lead and was very successful by incorporating her culinary offering plus a printed program that would be sold and commemorative pencils embossed with the name and date of the concert on panel one and the name of the Church on panel four. Barbara wanted to come front and center and show the congregation that she was the brains and the driving force in the new partnership she had forged with Cedric. This event would make money and even grow the church.

For example, there was a sign-up sheet printed, to be placed in every pew with a place to record residence addresses so that the canvassing committee could make a call on all newcomers the following week to try to convince them to become members. Barbara put the whole thing together and sent out all the orders (along with deposits) by September 10th for delivery by October 1st. The concert was scheduled for Saturday the 4th. Congregation members dreamed about what attendance might be like in church the following day. The Church Board was excited — though their name was the Third Baptist Church, they might transform to the number one congregation in town! The local community was excited. Several newspapers from the St. Louis Globe-Democrat to the St. Louis Post-Dispatch had agreed to send art critics to review the event. It all looked grand.

Then the news of Jay Cook & Company hit the papers on September 18, 1873. It was a dark Thursday. This major bank (like others) could not market railroad bonds necessary for capital lending. The result, everyone said, was very dim. A chain reaction followed and the New York Stock Exchange was closed on September 20th. And the next week in St. Louis, several firms notified the papers that they might have to lay off workers.

Suddenly everyone was concerned. People who had purchased batches of tickets wanted to send back all or most of them. Others who had signed the congregation pledge sheet for support were suddenly no longer coming to church. On Sunday, September 21st the ushers counted the congregation at 60 per cent its usual amount. On Sunday, September 28th, that had dropped to 40 per cent. Euphoria had dissolved into panic. The concert was cancelled. The food orders, the programs, the pencils, and all the sundry extravagances were cancelled—though the deposits already paid were lost. Since it was Barbara Smith who was the public face on it all, she became the bête noir and took the brunt of criticism. Needless to say, she did not attend church on Sunday October 5th. The post-service reception (that Barbara ran with coffee and freshly baked pastries) was cancelled. People just went to church and headed home. Some went out the fire door so that they didn't have to shake Pastor Philips' hand.

The currents of the Mississippi River were affected by unusually light rainfall. The effect was that the water level dropped significantly. Now, normally straightforward currents began to be affected by boulders and fallen trees on the riverbed. This created a swirling effect in the water. And still there was no rain.

The financial crisis hit the country differentially. The big cities: New York, Boston, Philadelphia, Chicago, and San Francisco took the biggest hit. The smaller cities in the middle were stretched, but the effect wasn't devastating. In St. Louis at the Third Baptist Church, the congregation started to come back, as did Sunday tithing. One year after the disaster, things were back to normal. Barbara was baking pastries and brewing coffee for the social hour after the morning service and refreshments before evening church. However, there had been a change. There was no longer any talk of making music the centerpiece of the social program. The organist played so that the congregation could belt out their soul-felt convictions before the sermon and offertory.

The old routine began again like soldiers marching in lock step. Hitting shoes on the pavement in regular 4/4 time. When Malcolm was born, the family had a resurgence of vigor and communication. Cedric constructed a cradle that he could rock with his foot while he made a new instrument. Barbara went back to long hours at the church. And all was right with the world.

Cedric lived on Malcolm's development: his transition to solid food, learning to walk, learning to talk, and toilet training. It was like a symphony unfolding from movement to movement—romantic period, of course. Barbara got a job outside the church at a catering company. It paid good money. That cash went into a metal cache that she kept locked in a far corner of their armoire.

When 1880 came around, Malcolm was five years old and could already read books and sheet music. Cedric dreamed of a future in which Malcolm and he could work together making the best violins, violas, and cellos in the Midwest.

One day when Barbara came home from her catering job, Cedric asked her to stop and listen to Malcolm play an arrangement of Mozart on the violin. It was clear that a child was playing as Malcolm hit most of the notes and kept going no matter what. At the end, Barbara clapped and kissed her boy.

"Now honey, you've played for Mommy, let's see you help her make dinner. It's time you were with me and *my* work. We've got some good coal here so the heat will be very even." Malcolm skipped to his mother and helped her as much as a five-year-old could. (Cedric had made his son a two-step ladder so he could help his mother on times like this.)

Dinner usually took Barbara ninety minutes (give or take an hour if she were making pastries). Tonight it was a beef stew made from a big thigh bone with considerable meat still on it, and carrots Barbara had canned over the summer in glass jars with copper lids. She had also made biscuits that she had just rolled out and placed on a metal sheet. When she was at a point of pause, Barbara turned to her husband and said, "You know, Julie down at work told me about a new mattress that is coming out. It uses metal springs instead of sawdust, feathers, wool, or horse hair to fill it up." Cedric had been sanding a piece of wood over a bucket. He stopped and tilted his head.

"Springs?" responded Cedric skeptically. "How could a person possibly sleep on springs? Wouldn't the springs just pop them out of bed onto the floor?"

Barbara picked up her rolling pin and walked over to her husband. "Look, you dinosaur. The future is changing rapidly. Look at all the new machines they have in the factories: assembly lines, mass production, the works. This is big stuff. I think we must get on the train or get run over by it."

"You are talking about mattresses?"

"I'm telling you that I want one of those new mattresses."

"How much do they cost?"

"I don't know. Fifty dollars, I think."

"Fifty dollars! For a mattress?"

"They say you spend a quarter of your day in bed. Why not be comfortable?"

"But wouldn't you get so nervous about being bounced out of bed onto the floor that you couldn't sleep? Then you have to go to the doctor, except you don't have any cash because you just spent fifty hard-earned dollars on a mattress!" Cedric set down the wood and the sandpaper. He got up and approached the rolling pin.

"Many men would be happy to invest in a nice bed for their wives. You know, there might be some pay-back for you." Barbara winked and then retreated to the stove. Cedric followed. Barbara made some key assessments of the stew and then put the biscuits into the oven on the upper rack.

When Barbara had shut the oven door, Cedric gently took hold of her shoulders and turned her to him. "You know, I've always wanted a companion for Malcolm. Perhaps a spring mattress might make it happen?"

Barbara smiled. "Tomorrow can you give me fifty dollars before I leave for work?"

"Absolutely," replied Cedric.

During the night on their horsehair stuffed mattress, Cedric felt the ropes that supported the mattress against his back (he was a back sleeper). He thought about their (he and Barbara's) recent life together. First there was Malcolm and his incredible progress in music and reading. Then there was the plan that Barbara had for a re-try concert. The first time had turned out so badly that Cedric had consigned the very thought to the dust heap. But Barbara persisted.

There was a new musician that had started coming to Third. His name was Gavin Smart. He was a trumpet player who worked on the riverboats. Though trumpet was never a favorite instrument for Cedric, he could objectively appreciate what it did in the musical ensemble. Mr. Smart said he could bring five musicians to do a concert at Third, and they would be paid on a percentage of the take (rather than the standard 'kill-pay' contract that gave you money in the event that the concert was cancelled). The kill-pay provision had cost the church a pretty penny last time, so this new proviso made it more appealing. Still, it was quite a risk given the history. But like most questions in their marriage, Cedric gave in.

The concert date was set for Saturday June 5th: three weeks away. There was no high-powered hype this time. It was very low key. There would be a concert. The programs would be hand drawn by the children of the church during Sunday school the week before. The posters advertising the event would be made in the same venue two weeks before. The reception afterwards would be no more special than the social hour after church. With this simple scheme, the church board approved.

Everything worked like a fine watch until Friday, June 4th. On that day, Barbara didn't come home after work. She had skipped town with her trumpet-playing paramour, Gavin Smart. The concert was cancelled, and the spring mattress never came.

CHAPTER FOUR

On departing from this world become immortal.[*]
Kena Upanisad

The news of the day: Shooting at his Landlady. It appeared from the examination in Justice Walsh's court, yesterday, that James T. Walker, when he fired two shots from a revolver while holding his landlady, Mrs. Barbara A. Davison, of No. 14 Willow-street, Brooklyn, by the arm, in her bedroom.
The New York Times, January 31, 1880

A Wife's Property Rights. A very interesting case was decided yesterday by Justice King, affecting the question whether a wife's property can be taken for a husband's debt, even though that debt be for rent.
The New York Times, March 15, 1880

The Graves of the Union Dead. GETTYSBURG, Penn., May 29.—The usual beautiful honors of Decoration Day were this afternoon conferred upon the nation's dead in the National Cemetery. The ceremonies drew large crowds, and people from the surrounding country early began to pour into the town, bringing generous contributions of flowers.
The New York Times. May 29, 1880

The Draft Riots Reunion. Ten survivors of the old Twenty-sixth Precinct Police, who saved the Tribune Building from destruction by the mob which overran this City during the terrible draft riots of 1863, held a reunion last evening at Delmonico's, it being the seventeenth anniversary of the attack upon the newspaper office.
The New York Times. July 14, 1880

A Christian Woman Becomes a Jewess. This morning, at the synagogue on St. Joseph-street, was performed the imposing ceremony of receiving a Christian woman into the Jewish faith.
The New York Times, August 1, 1880

---

[*] Translated by R. E. Hume, *The Thirteen Principal Upanishads* (Oxford: Oxford University Press, 1954).

TOMMY O'Neil woke up before dawn in his studio apartment in University Heights, Bronx. He knew he would have a long day. He lived on West 188th Street. The hours of a policeman were very much like that of a fireman. Once you went on duty, you stayed attached to the job for around 48 hours. This schedule didn't do much for his social life. Tommy had dated two girls, but neither relationship went anywhere because of his crazy schedule. Tommy walked over to his white ceramic-covered metal washbasin that sat on his chest of drawers, the only furniture (besides a bed) that he had in his apartment. He bent over and splashed his face with water, worked up some lather in a cup and shaved in the dark (except for the faint illumination that came from the gas street lamps). Tommy didn't shave too closely so that he might avoid cuts. (He also didn't sharpen his razor except for every other day—when he was home.)

Then it was time to hit the streets and walk to the precinct by way of a little bakery that opened at 5am. Tommy looked forward to the routine.

There had been a long dry spell with only work—no socializing. Tommy walked his beat and tried to keep on good relations with the people who lived there. It was the beginning of June and the world seemed very much alive.

Today, while he walked his assigned beat, time seemed to race by. By the time it was late morning, Tommy just happened to be looking up when he saw the child. The child was in diapers held on by two shiny pins that reflected brightly in the summer sun.

Soon there were several people on the sidewalk, looking up and gasping. One woman started to sob uncontrollably. Tommy knew these buildings and didn't hesitate a second. He went to the alley and jumped high in order to pull down the metal fire escape stairs. On the third try he got it and the rusted joints yielded to his efforts so that he could climb up the stairs to the fourth floor, where he got down on all fours and crawled onto the ledge (that wrapped all around the building at every floor). When Tommy turned the corner, he was only ten feet away from the child. The baby was very pale and had light brown hair. When he saw Tommy, the baby stopped moving.

Instinctively, the policeman increased the speed of his crawl. The baby seemed confused and didn't like this change of situation. He didn't know this strange man and decided to turn around. The trouble was that there wasn't enough room to execute the maneuver. As the child twisted to his right his hand slipped off the ledge, putting him into an unstable gravitational situation.

Tommy lunged forward and snatched the child with his left hand and brought the baby to his breast. The crowd that had gathered below broke into loud cheers. Traffic stopped and another policeman was soon on hand. By the time Tommy had re-traced his route (crawling backwards with a wiggly child in his arm), there were people below to greet him as he got off the stairs.

His fellow officer came by to give him a *well done*. But Tommy wanted to find the mother. The pair of police found the live-in custodian who was one of the many people on the sidewalk. He gladly took them to the apartment where they found the mother, sound asleep. When the mother awoke she cried, "What are you doing with my baby?" She got up and ran toward the officers. "I want my baby. I'm going to call the police."

"Ma'am, we *are* the police," said Éamon, Tommy's colleague. "Then I'm going to file a report against you, damn Tammany Hall blaggards." The woman proceeded to pummel Tommy with punches to his face, even as he was holding her son. The other officer physically restrained her.

"Ma'am, while you were asleep, your child climbed out of his place in the dresser drawer there and got up on the chest and crawled out the window and onto the ledge. If he had fallen he would be dead now. This brave officer risked his life to save your child. You owe him thanks and not this ingratitude."

The woman became calm and took her child from Tommy. The two policemen turned to go when Tommy stopped, pivoted and said, "Ma'am, it would be advisable for you either to close the window when you go to sleep or move your dresser away from the window. You don't want this to happen again. Next time the little tyke might not be so lucky."

The mother turned her back to the police officers and walked to the far side of the room, muttering under her breath.

***

Back on the sidewalk, an attractive matron approached Tommy and gave him a hug. Tommy was a little confused. "Young man, that was truly an act of heroism. And we could hear most of the conversation you had with the mother down here. Your behavior was very commendable. I'll bet you're a Catholic boy?"

Tommy smiled. He certainly was, but his job didn't really allow him to attend services. The matron didn't wait for an answer. "You know, we have a really good Irish Church on 37th Street in Manhattan, St. Gabriel's. We're having a festival next week and we're especially honoring our fine Irish city employees. Would you be free any evening next week? It'd mean a free dinner and a chance to meet a lot of folks." Then she leaned forward and whispered, "You know, evening mass is a spoken mass without any folderol. The priest goes through it in seventeen minutes!" This was an offer he couldn't refuse. Tommy said he'd talk to his sergeant about it.

When Tommy left, he began to regret his promise. His superiors were very much against granting personal requests that altered the work assignments. Luckily, Billy Pierson, his sergeant, took kindly to him.

"I heard you did good today, Tommy." Pierson was a big man, five-foot-ten and broad chested. His skin was ruddy and there were broken blood vessels around his nose. The captain used to say, "You've got the map of Ireland on your face, Billy-boy." But Billy was no boy. He was nearing sixty and was a grandfather.

"Oh, it was nothing," replied Tommy. He started rubbing his hands together in front of him.

"It wasn't nothing, me boy. Your mate, Éamon, told me all about it. I think there's a medal in this for you and a chance to take the sergeant's exam."

Tommy was ecstatic. "You mean it, the sergeant's exam?"

Pierson smiled and slapped Tommy on the shoulder. "Absolutely. I've already talked to Monahan about it and he's got someone doing the paperwork now. They've got some sort of event after Mass at St. Gabriel's in Manhattan. I think he'll probably give you the award then. Lots of people, you know, who will applaud all the good work we do."

Tommy was giddy. He wasn't really himself until the next morning (when he got to his bakery and bought a pastry and some coffee) and he came to see how fortunate he was. Just days before he had been a person ground down by his arduous job. His life had been about having enough endurance to make it through another day.

But now, suddenly, things were different. He was a small-time hero of sorts who was about to be given a whole lot of attention. He wasn't sure how he felt about this. It was very pleasurable. He might pass the sergeant's exam and become a leader on the force. Tommy had a lot of ideas on how he might improve things. And he might connect to an important parish in Manhattan. Who knew what else might be in store for him!

***

When Tommy finished his shift, he headed over to a bar for a beer and some free happy hour food that sat in little bowls: peanuts, wee sausages, and potato pancakes. Tommy could fill up for a dime. As he sipped the brew and chomped down on the light fare, his thoughts turned toward May 1st two years before, when he received a letter from James informing him that their father, Seán, had died of emphysema. He was 53.

At first Tommy was mad at James for not telling him sooner so that he could have been there for the end. But when Tommy arrived for the funeral on the express train from Penn Station, he realized that their father had been sick for a long time at roughly the same level. He had coughing fits and then had to lie down and inhale some camphor (from Charles Quincy) to clear up his lungs. Generally, James would bring him a glass of whiskey and a bread roll and wait by the bedside until his father fell asleep. The two had adjacent beds so the younger son could keep track of his father. On the night of his death, Seán woke up in the middle of the night and asked James to take him to the toilet. It was a regular ritual. James complied and held his father's left arm with a grip under the armpit. That night, Father took much longer than usual—so much so that James could not maintain the general semi-somnolent state that would permit him to quickly fall asleep once he'd deposited his father in bed again.

The awakening in James led him to be more observant. From the dim light that came from the gaslights outside, a pale portrait emerged of a visage that James hardly knew. It frightened him.

When James climbed into his own bed, he turned to look at the silhouette of his Da's labored breathing for an hour or two, and then the rhythm transformed into a paroxysm that ended in the rattle of death.

***

Tommy regretted that he was not there, too. But he had been in New York pursuing his career as a cop. Why does one choice disallow the other? Why couldn't he have had both? Well he could have—*if* he'd been in the Philadelphia police force. But then, they weren't hiring when he wanted to start his career, and there was not sympathy in Philadelphia for hiring Irish in key jobs like the police. Tommy accepted these facts. This intellectual act also required him to accept other facts that he wasn't keen to encounter. These included the death of his mother, in childbirth, and his sister who died of the measles when she was three. At the same time, there had always been a pall over the Irish, or so his father, Seán, had said. It came with a vengeance in the potato famine that many said was a punishment from God meted upon the Irish—but for what? Not being good enough Catholics, or for having been the slaves of the British for hundreds of years? These were thoughts that his father had ranted about after the death of Mary, his wife. Mary had started out as a novice nun when she was just a lass. She was always the dreamer in the family who sought for the very best of all. She never spoke of the potato famine.

When Mary died, Seán's silence and his optimism died, too. Tommy thought about all of this as he walked home and threw himself in bed. Then he shut his eyes and thought about his imminent change in life. When he fell asleep, Tommy was smiling.

***

As he slept, Tommy dreamt of being awarded a medal at St. Gabriel's Church (a place he'd never been). In the crowd were some tough looking characters with unshaven faces, smoking cigarettes. In the front row was the woman who he had met on the sidewalk after saving the baby. Seated next to her was her husband and two grown children: a boy and a girl. The siblings were beautiful. Tommy immediately fell in love with both of them. He wanted to run up to one of them for a congratulatory hug and kiss—but he didn't know which one.

Tommy again looked to the hooligans. They were going to make some trouble. Tommy was sure of it. But there were more of them than Tommy could handle. It was then that Tommy woke up shaking. He went over to his porcelain basin and plunged the washcloth into the water so that he could wash his face. But even the water couldn't wash the nightmare away.

***

When the big day came, Tommy was driven to St. Gabriel's in a horse drawn patrol wagon. It was a good trek from University Heights in the Bronx. The ceremony was scheduled for a Sunday after the eleven o'clock solemn mass (*not* the small evening mass). The police commissioner and the archbishop would be there. It was a big deal.

Tommy arrived just after ten. He went into the large social hall and found a chair to sit down. That's one thing walking a beat does for you: it makes you aware of when and where you can sit down. Fourteen hours on your feet makes you long for a seat.

As Tommy stretched out his legs, a familiar face approached. It was the woman from the sidewalk. She was walking toward Tommy, accompanied by a retinue. Tommy shot up from his chair.

"Tommy," said the woman as she gave him a big hug. "I am so glad you came. I want you to meet my family. This is my husband, George—you may have read about him. He's on the City Council. Then there's our daughter, Catherine and her older brother, Michael." Tommy did the hand shaking, smiling, and nodding. It was uncanny. The people were nothing like the dream characters in appearance. The wife and children were Scot-Irish with light brown hair and blue eyes (just like his brother James). But in some inexplicable way, Tommy immediately felt drawn to both of the Walsh children.

The patriarch was black Irish with straight hair and brown eyes. He was a portly fellow of medium height and wore a three-piece black suit with a bright red tie and pinstriped gray vest. His bushy moustache was neatly trimmed and waxed at the ends. There was a perpetual smile on his face that accented the turned-up waxed ends so that the effect made Tommy apprehensive.

Before Tommy could get into the small talk, the police commissioner (walking with the archbishop) approached and said a brief hello before moving on. Tommy turned to return to the small talk, but was interrupted by an officious assistant who took over and before Tommy knew it, he was sitting in the front row of the well-appointed church. Next to him were seated the Walsh clan: Michael, Catherine, Mary, and George (in that order from nearest to farthest). Tommy was sitting on the aisle.

There was much commotion. Tommy looked about and his gaze stopped at a statue of the Blessed Virgin Mary. Tommy was always attracted to the BVM, probably because his own mother, a novice nun (who never took the vow), was also named Mary. But maybe also because the gift of being able to love another without reservation was always held high in Tommy's consciousness. His greatest heroes were women—like the BVM and Dido (from the *Aeneid*). Tommy gazed at the statue. The gaze of Mary was downward in humility. Her arms were reaching outward. The marble was so smooth that it magically reflected the smoky gas lighting.

***

The next thing that Tommy remembered was that he was at the Washington Square home of the Walshs amidst many people. Standing right next to him was Catherine. She had sat next to him on the cab ride after the ceremony. The clickity clack of the horses' hooves on the paving stones put Tommy in a trance that was only broken when he realized that he was standing next to Catherine as she planted a kiss onto his cheek.

Suddenly Tommy looked at this fair lass with new eyes. Her gaze and voice captivated him so that he was her prisoner. "You know, Tommy, that our family came over with Daddy—probably just before your family did. We were from Dublin near St. Stephen's Green."

"I've never been to Dublin. Our family was from Cork," replied Tommy.

"Ah, and that's near Waterford Castle where they make all the beautiful glassware."

Tommy smiled. He was obviously out of his league here. "Have you ever read the *Aeneid*?" was all he could muster.

Catherine's eyes widened. "*The Aeneid*? How quaint. Is it a poem or a novel?"

"A poem written by the Latin poet Virgil. He was a poet in the Roman Empire. He gives a sort of third book to the epic of the Trojan War. It's a second odyssey—this one concerning the people of Troy in their search for a new home in Rome."

"Oh, I've heard of that. My governess read me a version of it with hand-painted illustrations."

"*The Aeneid*?"

"No, I think they gave it another name." Catherine scrunched up her face while she tried to think about it. After a minute or two she changed her expression. "I think they called it the E-lad or something like that."

"The *Iliad*?"

"Yes, that's it." Catherine felt very happy. She gestured the servant to re-fill their wine glasses.

Tommy thought about discussing this further, but decided it wouldn't be productive. "What do you do, Catherine?"

"What do I do? I don't have a job—if that's what you mean. I stay at home mostly. I like to sketch and play the piano. Grandmamma is teaching me needlepoint. It takes tremendous patience and all of my free time."

"I'll bet it does."

"But I'm getting better at it."

"Needlepoint?"

"No, patience."

"I see. You seem very patient to me."

"That's because you are very kind. And you are so learned with all this Latin. I'm sure if I put in a word with Daddy, I could get you a very important job."

Tommy looked down. "That's not necessary, Catherine. I'm scheduled next week to take the sergeant's exam."

"The sergeant's exam?"

"Yes, if I pass I become a sergeant."

"That sounds important," said Catherine putting her hand on Tommy's right arm (the one that was holding the glass of wine that hadn't been sipped since it had been refilled). Tommy's hand shook slightly, but nothing spilled.

"It is. If I'm successful I can manage a team of men at the precinct and try to make our little grid of the city one of the safest and happiest in New York City."

"That sounds wonderful. I will most certainly tell Daddy."

"Oh, you don't have to do that. I don't want to look as if I am after any favors."

Then Catherine giggled and touched the tip of Tommy's nose with her index finger. She then turned to get another glass of wine.

Tommy stood alone in the center of the room that was bustling with activity when Michael Walsh came up and put his arm around Tommy's shoulder. Catherine's older brother smiled. "You're a stout Irish lad, Tommy O'Neil. I heard your conversation with my sister just a few seconds ago. You don't know how many come through the doors and try to cozy up to Catherine in order to procure favors from father."

"Really? I didn't know."

Michael gave Tommy's shoulder a squeeze. "I know you didn't. That's as clear as Waterford Crystal."

Tommy smiled. The phrase sounded different from a man.

"The truth be told, we have a lot of bounders after Catherine and her wealth. After all, she's eighteen and the parents are looking to get her engaged."

Tommy took a long sip of wine. "Engaged?"

"Of course. That's the way they did it back home." Michael took his arm away from Tommy's shoulder.

"My mother married at seventeen and she'd been a convent for three years."

"A novice?"

"Yes. She never made the vows."

"And does she live in New York, as well?"

"No, she passed sixteen years ago giving birth to my sister, Lucy."

Michael took Tommy's free hand. "I'm terribly sorry. Is your father still alive?"

Tommy shook his head and teared up just a bit. "Died two years ago in 1878. May 1st, it was."

"So it's just you and your sister? Do you have any other family?"

"Yes, I've a brother, James, who lives in Philadelphia and works in a chemist shop. He's learning the trade from a dear Quaker man. My sister, Lucy, died when she was three, of the measles."

"The German measles?"

"I don't know. Maybe it was the English measles. They have certainly been a plague." Then a waiter carrying a tray bumped into Tommy and almost made him spill his half-filled glass.

Michael smiled. "Say, Tommy, what do you say that I take you for dinner at my club tomorrow night? I think I'd really like to have a longer conversation with you in quieter circumstances."

Tommy thrust his jaw forward a bit and squinted his eye. He retained this posture for fifteen seconds or so before he replied. "It would have to be a different day. I go on a thirty-six hour shift tomorrow."

"Well, I could ask the commissioner—"

"No, please don't. I'm taking the sergeant's exam next week. I don't want any extra help except what I can do for myself."

Now it was Michael's time to be silent for a moment. Then Michael over-dramatized a pretend punch to Tommy's stomach. "Well, we'll have to make it the day after you finish, then. I'll have a cab pick you up at your apartment at five." Tommy turned to go when he was stopped by Michael's coda, "You *are* a Mick, and *I'm* proud of it."

True to Michael's word, a swanky cab waited in front of Tommy's shabby building on the appointed day at five. The sun was starting to slant a bit, but this was June with its abundance of sunlight. Tommy had never ridden in such a comfortable carriage before. It had strong springs that absorbed most of the bouncing about. You could hold a glass of water in your hand and not spill a drop.

Tommy was greeted curbside by a doorman in elaborate uniform that resembled a medieval nobleman. Tommy was taken to a man inside who wore a tuxedo. The interior was divided into three rooms. The maître d' escorted Tommy to Michael, who was sitting in a booth along the wall near the corner. The room was dimly lit with candles on the tables and large kerosene lamps in the corners. Michael was smoking a cigar. The two exchanged small talk. Michael liked to make sweeping gestures with his cigar. Tommy listened, smiled, and took occasional small sips of the whiskey aperitif that Michael had ordered for him.

"You know, Tommy," began Michael as he set down his cigar in the cut glass crystal ashtray, "I talked to Father after you left the other day. I told him that I really like you." Michael paused and reached out for Tommy's forearm. Tommy felt confused. He would have reached for another sip of whiskey but Michael's grip kept his hand where it was. The grip was firm but affectionate. "Mother was there, too. I told them that I had asked you to dinner to talk about the future. And they agreed to everything."

There was a long pause when Michael looked Tommy straight in the eye. Tommy became a little nervous. "I'm sorry, Michael, I don't follow you."

Michael smiled, released his grip and slapped Tommy on the bicep. "Of course you don't! That's the beauty of the whole thing. Like I told you before: you're the real thing, Tommy O'Neil. That's why I want you—" Michael stopped. He had something in his throat and had to cough to clear it, followed by a couple long sips of whiskey. Tommy followed suit with one short sip. "What I'm trying to say is that we want to bring you into the family."

Tommy forced a smile. "What do you—"

"What I mean is that you are to marry Catherine, naturally."

"Catherine?" Tommy's voice was suddenly high pitched.

"Of course, Catherine. Who else could I mean? I've only got one sister, you Mick."

Tommy took a long sip of whiskey. He looked into the glass in the dim light and saw the viscous spirit dancing around the water in lines of constant motion. Then Tommy looked up again. "Have you asked Catherine what *she* thinks of this?"

Michael slapped the table in front of him and smiled. "That's just exactly what Mother said you'd reply. She saw you save that child while she was doing charity work in the Bronx, remember? She also heard how nicely you treated that awful slum mother. You know that most of the rich folk in New York marry other rich people. But the real character comes from those who've risen up from adversity. And that's you, Tommy O'Neil. You are Irish through and through."

"I don't know what to say, actually. I think that I need to get to know your family better—and you need to get to know *me* better."

"Already in the works. When's your next day off?"

"Saturday."

"Then you're invited for the afternoon and dinner. A deal?"

The two men shook hands.

***

The courtship of Catherine Walsh went rather quickly. Tommy came by the house once a week for six weeks. Each time he spent almost as much time with the parents and Michael as he did with Catherine. Tommy got word that he'd passed both exams (the Walshs' exam and the sergeant's exam) on the same day. The dual success was observed by the ecstatic Walsh family with a family dinner that now included Tommy: a whole new life lay ahead.

Tommy came back to his simple apartment and lay down in bed. Normally he set his bed away from the gaslights, but that night he did a 360-degree turn so that he might gaze into their artificial luminescence. He dreamt his earlier dream over again, but this time each person in the drama turned against him and he was all alone. Tommy woke up in a sweat.

***

It was the middle of September when they finally set the wedding date for January 8th, near the beginning of Epiphany, 1881. Tommy had received his letter on passing the sergeant's exam weeks earlier, but the news did not hit his precinct until now. Billy Pierson was the one to celebrate with him. Billy's large smile betrayed his happiness. His ruddy skin became even redder as he gave Tommy a bear hug. "I'm hoping that they keep you in the precinct. We have an opening and you'd be perfect for it."

***

Tommy was kept in limbo about his new assignment for over a month. It was early November when he got a letter asking him to travel to police headquarters in Manhattan. It was a long trip and there was no Walsh luxury taxi to take him there. But make it he did—and on time.

Tommy was ushered into a large room. The room was functional. The walls were white plaster with a smooth coating. There was one strip of wainscoting on the walls, six inches below the twelve-foot ceiling. The floor was pinewood two-inch tongue and groove that had turned black. At the left-side of the room were several large windows.

In the center of the room were seven chairs, six of which were filled. At the front of the room was a wooden lectern. Tommy decided that the empty chair was his, and he took it. The other men looked at Tommy, but nobody talked to anyone. The atmosphere was tense. After a half-hour, a short black Irish man came trotting in, cursing under his breath. He had a bunch of papers in his arm that he deposited on the lectern. One more curse, and then he took his left hand and pulled back the black hair from his olive tinged skin and addressed the audience. "Gentlemen, my name is Charles Yancy. And from this time forward, I own you. You are here today because you are all sergeants or lieutenants who have served the city with distinction. You are the best of the best. You are the cream that sits atop the bottle of milk.

"Manhattan has a problem. We've got some Irish and Italian gangs out there who are tearing up the city. They've got to be stopped so that decent people can call New York home and live in peace.

"We've tried to stop them before. This has been going on for years, but now the commissioner named me to head a special task force to eliminate this scum from our city. I have devised a scientific approach to the problem that cannot fail. All I need are men of courage to execute it. And you men have the balls to get things done. That's why you're here. We're after some of the worst people in the world: Eastman Gang, Bowery Boys, Dead Rabbits, and especially the Five Points Gang and that young hooligan, James Ellison, who goes by the name of 'Biff.' As you are probably aware, the leadership in these gangs is primarily Irish and Italian. That's why I chose a team of four Irish and three Italians. You guys know the score and I'm confident that you can help us take these guys out.

"Here's the plan: I want you to recruit a few men from your home precincts who are just like you—Irish or Italian. And then I want you to go plain clothes into the neighborhoods like in the 6th Ward and act like you want to join the gang. Then find out as much as you can so that we can prepare a battle plan to wipe the sons-of-bitches off the face of this goddamn earth. If you have to commit a robbery or something like that, make a note of it and the department will reimburse the victims. The only thing you cannot do is to kill a civilian. Kill the trash you're working with, but no civilian deaths."

Yancy took out a handkerchief and wiped his brow. "Understand that this plan requires the utmost secrecy. Only choose men you can really trust to work with you. And don't tell nobody else—not even your wives. This is a dangerous mission.

"We all meet here in this very room on Friday, November 19. At that point we will have an all-day session to discuss your information with an overall plan of attack that will send blood down those newly constructed water-sewer drains. We will purge this city of the disease that threatens to kill it. And you are the men to do it."

Yancy paused and pulled back his overly long hair from his forehead once again. He tried to look every man in the eye. Then he said, "Well, are you up to the task? Are you man enough to save the city of New York from filthy Irish and Italians?"

The cadre of Irish and Italians stood up and declared in unison, "Yes, sir!"

Yancy smiled. His grand plan had just begun.

Tommy decided to head down to Washington Square. Only Catherine and her mother were in. Tommy sat down and had tea with the two Walsh women.

"I'm so happy you stopped by, Tommy," began Mary as she stirred some sugar in her tea. "But aren't you supposed to be at work?"

Tommy smiled. "Well, I'm on a special assignment, Mrs. Walsh. The hours will be very irregular for a while."

"How long will that be? It won't interfere with the wedding, will it?" Mrs. Walsh lifted her teacup delicately with her thumb and forefinger only as she took the smallest of sips.

"I'm sure my participation in the project will end long before the wedding, Mrs. Walsh."

The matron smiled and began a discussion of the details of Catherine's dress and the imported lace that was coming in any day from Belgium to adorn the perimeters of the gown. Tommy just smiled and drank his tea. He really didn't understand any of it. He just shot a glance at Catherine when he could. She was looking at him the entire time.

When tea was done it was time to go. Catherine walked Tommy to the door without Mommy. The demur Irish-American lass kissed Tommy lightly on the lips and grasped his strong hardened right hand in between hers. "This mission, Tommy; it isn't dangerous is it?" Catherine reached her hand up and pulled up the silver Celtic cross that she had given Tommy at their engagement. On the back were engraved the words, "From Cathy, with Love."

"Well, Cathy, there is always danger in police work: part of the job. But I'm a careful fellow. I've got a lot to take care of." He smiled and planted a kiss on the lips of his fiancée.

***

Tommy picked his back-up team of Éamon, Randy, and Paedrig. They had been assigned to infiltrate the Five Points Gang. They created a back-up story of Tommy coming from Philly and then meeting up with a few local toughs and looking for some action. They were accepted into the group and helped commit an armed robbery of a jewelry store on Little Water Street. Then they went to meet their contact, Ken Carney, near Collect Pond and delivered the loot.

Ken was impressed and invited them to a meeting in a flop on the corner of Mulberry and Anthony Streets on Friday. The money was divided, and Tommy and his mates split up (only to rendezvous back at their home precinct in the Bronx).

Tommy's crew turned in their shares of the ill-gotten gain and in return were given a small amount of spending money, compliments of the City of New York.

***

Tommy's team went to the Five Points event. They arrived a half-hour late and were ushered into a large room in the derelict building that was ablaze with candles fatter than your thigh set on high stands that were scattered about, along with some tall kerosene lamps. In the front of the room was a group of musicians playing a Céilidh. The dancers were wild and whiskey flowed freely. Tommy and his crew jumped in and twirled some comely young women as the fiddles quickened the pace until a final climax followed by one bow on E minor that seemed especially plaintive after the commotion that went before.

Then a wild-faced thin young man with unkempt hair stood up on a soap box and said there would be a break while the women set out the food and the men clustered to talk business.

The gents formed a semi-circle around the wild-faced James Ellison. Though the night was young, he already seemed to be on another register. "Gentlemen, we've got a few newcomers from Philadelphia. They made us some money this week doing professional work. Ken, why don't you introduce these young degenerates?"

Ken Carney stepped forward and turned so that he was standing next to his chieftain. Ken was neat and controlled—just the antithesis of Ellison. "Yeah, this is Tommy, Éamon, Randy, and Paedrig. They robbed a jewelry store: one, two, three. No fuss. No drama. Must have ice water in their veins." There was a murmur of approval.

Then Ken called out various names (including Tommy) to meet with him in the corner about jobs for the following week. Ellison ranted for the rank and file.

Then there was more dancing as the Céilidh got serious. They danced and drank past midnight. When it was over, Ellison came up to Tommy and put his arm around him, "If you're as good as you seem to be, I'll make you a rich man."

Tommy smiled and gave Ellison a hug.

***

When the elite task force met on November 19th, Charles Yancy asked each team leader to step forward and give a report. Three had made significant strides, a couple were ostracized and not admitted, and two were on probation, just like Tommy. Yancy then had a session with each to tailor an individual strategy. Before the group left, Yancy addressed them: "I'm very impressed. We've got five real leads here. If you're as good as you seem to be . . . well, I'll get you a promotion."

***

The plan for Tommy was this: There was another Céilidh scheduled for Sunday November 28th. Tommy and his team would go and when the meeting was just about to start, Tommy would step outside, ostensibly to urinate. This would be a signal for the police to raid the place and kill or capture most of the gang. It would be a feather in his cap and mean a promotion. Tommy was on the way to his destiny!

***

The Céilidh began just as before. Tommy and his crew were a half-hour late. They came in and danced with the crowd and had a drink or two. Then when the music was over Tommy, who was standing next to Ken Carney, moved toward the door.

"Where are you going?" asked Carney.

"Got to make water."

Carney nodded his head.

Tommy went to the exit and unbuttoned his fly. But before he could open the door, he felt an arm across his throat and the raspy voice of Ellison—no longer out of control. "Thought you could put one over on us, did you? You stinking copper."

"No, Biff, you've got it wrong—" But Tommy couldn't finish his sentence. James Ellison raised his other arm and with one fast motion put a gun to Tommy's head and blew his brains out.

The noise of the gunshot brought the police contingent of two hundred onto the derelict building in force. They outnumbered the Five Points Gang 4-to-1.

The gunshots brought shrieks from the women, who dropped everything to run. Candle stands were knocked over, as were the kerosene lights. The tinderbox was ablaze. The police descended into the inferno. Guns fired without regard to targets. People were fleeing and the flames spread to the buildings on either side. The fire brigade was notified.

Soon there was total pandemonium.

***

When it was over, Éamon, Randy, and Paedrig escaped—as did the leaders of the Five Points Gang. Twelve male gang members and twenty-five sisters, female cousins, and wives of gang members were also killed. The bodies were all burnt beyond recognition.

One charred body contained a Celtic cross that inspectors picked up and sent onto police headquarters. It read, "From Cathy, with Love." After six months, Yancy was fired. His commission was a failure, and there were rumors of bribery.

CHAPTER FIVE

Nature (*svabhava*) they say, is what appertains to the self: /Creative force (*visarga*) is known as "works" (*karma*)/ For it gives rise to the [separate] natures of contingent beings.[1]

The news of the day: Momentous battle of ballots in Germany to-day. Revolt of the people against the Emperor's Army Bill. A contest of great significance to all of Europe.

THE END IS NEAR. An unexpected event in the Borden Murder Trial. Baffled in its line of prosecution the state rests its case.

Milk inspector Sullivan has inaugurated a crusade against mixing milk with water.
The St. Louis Post Dispatch, June 15th 1893

CEDRIC Smith was sitting in his apartment, opening up his mail. He was finishing a commission for a violin and a viola. His son, Malcolm, would be home soon from one of his part-time jobs unloading and stocking vegetables for the green grocer down the block. Every time the mail came, it was Cedric who would look it over first. He harbored unrealistic fantasies about who might be writing and how it might change their lives. But today, there was a letter that *would* change their lives: a letter of acceptance to St. Louis University's medical school. Malcolm had just graduated from high school—something that Cedric had never accomplished— and now there was the possibility of medical school! Cedric carefully re-read the letter and then returned it to the fine linen paper envelope with raised lettering.

Part of Cedric was ecstatic. Part of Cedric was saddened. He had half-imagined that Malcolm would take after him. After all, he

---

[1] From R.C. Zaehner, ed. *The Concise Encyclopedia of Living Faiths* (Boston: Beacon Press, 1959).

was already the assistant organist and assistant choirmaster at the Third Baptist Church. The church had grown and Malcolm was actually paid for his duties.

It was true that Malcolm was often a little too abrasive to the choir members. He didn't smooth their feathers, but ruffled them. He possessed a bit of an attitude that wasn't at all agreeable to the congregants. Why, if it weren't for Cedric's long service and the sympathy that was felt for him by all when his wife left him, Malcolm would have been sacked. But Cedric attributed his son's shortcomings to the impetuosity of youth.

Also, Malcolm wasn't very good at constructing musical instruments. He wanted to rush through everything. But a violin or cello could not be rushed. The wood had to be cured, and that took time. The bending and molding also required great patience and a supreme attention to details. Malcolm was a boy with a short attention span. But patience was a virtue that could be learned.

Cedric knew that if Malcolm were to give himself over to his father's wise direction, that he could gradually take his place. By the age of thirty, Malcolm might marry just as Cedric had—only this time the marriage would work because he would take his time to find a really quality person. It was just like finding the right wood to construct a violin. The keen eye can spot the perfect product. The rest follows a time-tested routine.

On the positive side, Malcolm could play the organ well, and also the violin and cello. He had a gift for putting emotion into his playing—which sometimes got him in trouble with the congregation of the Third Baptist Church (who felt that musicians should be heard but not noticed in any way). Playing with emotion makes one noticed. But this was also the character of a virtuoso performer. Malcolm might just be that.

Cedric felt so elated at his vision for his son as a musician that he dropped the mail on the floor and went over to the file cabinet and took out his Mass in C: *The New Beginning*. It had been a project that he began thirteen years ago when Barbara left. He was almost halfway done with it. He was convinced that when he was done with it and it was performed at several churches around town, his reputation in the world of music would be made and the Smythes of Boston would know him for what he really was: a man of genius.

***

Malcolm started classes at Medical School. He told his father that while he was in school he would live near the campus in a little garret so that he'd spend less time commuting. He got a job on campus in the admissions department and all seemed to be fine. His job paid his room and board while his assistant organist position contributed half of his $500 annual tuition.

The medical program was pretty straightforward. There was a year of anatomy and basic science followed by three years of experience on the wards in levels of increasing responsibility. There were various tests that had to be passed in order to graduate, to do a year of internship, and then go into private practice. Physicians were generally well regarded—just like ministers (and above teachers and lawyers).

Parts of the process were quite interesting, such as carefully dissecting a cadaver in order to learn anatomy first-hand. (There were many discrepancies between the dead body before them and their textbook, but the teachers said to always trust your own eyes first.) But much of the process left Malcolm cold. It was too much drudgery and routine memorization—much of it Latin terms. Malcolm had stopped Latin in grammar school and switched to Italian because his father said that it would be more useful for his career in music. Therefore, Malcolm was at a disadvantage.

***

It was by happenstance that Malcolm met Ray. Ray Carver was a professional clarinet player who played on the riverboats. They met in a bar called *The Renaissance* as Malcolm was downing a cup of late afternoon coffee before going to eat some raw vegetables at his hovel. Malcolm liked going to this particular bar because it was close to campus and on a direct line with the chapel. The bar's large windows and kerosene wall sconces gave the place a sense of space. The floor was swept clean, and there was only a small bar. Most of the seating was at petite square tables that could be pushed together for groups. *The Renaissance* had a full menu to complement the drinks. About a quarter of the patrons were drinking tea or coffee at five o'clock. It was late October and there was already nippiness in the air.

Ray was nattily dressed and wore cologne. The place was pretty full, so Ray asked if he could sit down at Malcolm's table.

Malcolm said, "Sure."

"What are you drinking there, coffee?"

"Who's asking?" replied Malcolm.

Ray laughed and took a long swig of beer. "Ray Carver's my name. I play the licorice stick."

"The clarinet?"

"None other."

"What sort of music do you play?"

"The only music, that is, the music of the river."

"I'm afraid I don't know much about that. My tastes have always revolved around Church music. I'm the assistant organist and choirmaster at the Third Baptist Church. My father's the chief."

"You mean the minister?"

"No, the head organist and choirmaster."

Ray leaned his head forward and with an intense expression on his face, he gazed into Malcolm's eyes. "So, what sort of instrument do you play? The church organ?"

"Oh sure, the organ. I can play the usual stuff: Bach, Vivaldi, Beethoven—you know, the classics." Malcolm smiled and almost finished his coffee.

"Do you play any other instruments?"

"My best instrument is the violin, but I'm also pretty good at the cello. I write some music, too. And I can construct musical instruments from scratch."

"No shit," said Ray in amazement. He then drank three-quarters of his beer at once.

"It's the truth." Malcolm finished his coffee and started to pull out his chair to leave. But Ray put out his hand to stop him.

"Don't go yet. Let me buy you a beer."

"No thanks. I don't drink."

"Don't drink? What do you do?"

"I play beautiful music."

"Well, so do I. We may have more in common than you know."

Malcolm tilted his head, "I don't know what you mean."

"Look, whoever your name is, I have this band, see? And we've got lots of fluidity. I'd like to hear you play something—anything. If you're as good as you say you are, then I've got $10 a night for a soloist."

"Ten dollars a night?"

"Yeah. We're a good band: *The River Rats*. We get top dollar on the riverboats."

"The riverboats?" Malcolm barely got out the words. His voice cracked.

"Yeah, you know about them, don't you? They go up and down the Mississippi with their paddle wheels, just like a Dixieland riff."

Malcolm got up and headed for the door. Ray was quicker and caught him by the shoulder. "No wait. You can't go now. Say, look, there's a piano in the corner there. Why don't you play me something?"

"I don't think so," said Malcolm, turning away.

Ray twisted Malcolm around so that they were looking at each other face-to-face. "You know what I think? I think you're full of shit and you can't play a single note. You're no musician. Look, there's a piano. Prove to me that you're not a goddamn liar."

Malcolm twisted up his face. He couldn't look Ray in the eye. The two stood there for a moment, fixed in time. Then Malcolm pulled Ray's hand off his shoulder and went to the out-of-tune upright piano and played "The Moonlight Sonata" without a flaw and with sensitive emotion.

After Malcolm was through, Ray ran to him and put twenty dollars into his hand. "I want you to go with me right now to the pier. I need for you to meet my band. We're about to practice. You keep the twenty if you go with me—whether or not you decide to join us. What do you say?"

Malcolm paused and then agreed.

As they were leaving, Ray asked Malcolm, "By the way, what *is* your name, anyway?"

"Malcolm."

"That's no name for a musician on the riverboats. From now on, I'm calling you Mac."

And the two men left together.

***

Malcolm (Mac) really took to the *River Rats* and they to him. At first he played fiddle and piano music to accompany the band. But then Mac picked up the trumpet, because the trumpet was the most revered solo instrument on the riverboats. Mac Smith was a wonder at the trumpet and the pay was very good. In no time, other bands were bidding on Mac Smith to play with them.

Mac's wallet was becoming fatter, but his grades in medical school were barely passing. He was in school four days a week and on the river three. When he was in town Malcolm was trying to keep up appearances at the Third Baptist, go to classes, do the minimum in admissions (and fake the rest). Except for choir practice, he never saw his father. Sundays were out for him (Malcolm said he had obligations in the medical school. His real obligations were to the *River Rats*.) Mac's passions in music had always been a hindrance to Malcolm the church organist, but here they made him a minor celebrity.

Then, near the end of his first year in medical school, Malcolm had a conference with the dean. Dean Krank was a short, thin man with a bald head. He was a surgeon who was making a great name for himself as he pushed to the limit what might be done with the general anesthetic, ether, and strict obedience to Lister's rules of hygiene. But Dr. Krank was a hard man to please, and he had called for a meeting with Malcolm Smith in his office.

Malcolm showed up to the appointment on time. Dr. Krank had a large office on the corner of the second floor of the hospital. Two walls were almost floor to ceiling windows. On one of the free walls were Dr. Krank's diplomas framed by wood and glass. There were two candle sconces on each of the free walls. Dr. Krank's desk was a flat piece of dark wood that was set atop two metal file drawers.

Dr. Krank came around from his chair once Malcolm had seated himself, and Krank perched himself atop the desk no more than three feet away from the medical student. There was an exceedingly long pause in which Krank stared at Malcolm until the latter broke the gaze and looked downwards.

"You know why we called you here." Dr. Krank's voice was flat and conveyed a slight German accent.

"Yes, sir."

"You are on the edge of being expelled. You know that?"

"Yes, sir."

"What do you have to say for yourself?"

Malcolm started playing with his hands. "I don't know, sir."

"You don't know? That's not a very good answer, young man."

"I know sir. You see, I'm working several jobs to pay the $500 tuition and my living expenses."

Krank pursed his lips. "Well, that's honest at least. I've heard that you're not to be found for three days each week. But that's something that we all have to live with. The world doesn't owe you a living, son."

"I know that, sir."

"Well, I want to see what you can do. For one month, starting June 1st, I will wave your monthly payments to the medical school if you will give us seven days a week. I want to see what you can do."

"That's very generous of you sir."

"Damn straight that's generous. You can eat in the hospital cafeteria for free, but you'll still have to pay for your apartment. Can you manage that?"

"For one month, yes I can."

"One month is what I ask."

"I won't let you down, sir."

"I hope not, Malcolm." The dean got off his perch on his desk. Malcolm stood up immediately. The two shook hands. "You may go now." Malcolm turned to leave when the surgeon added, "Please don't call me 'sir.' I am a doctor and a surgeon. You may call me 'Doctor Krank.'"

Malcolm turned and tried to smile, "Yes sir, Doctor Krank."

***

Malcolm's trial month started well. He finished his first-year test and passed. Now he was moving to the wards. This meant a peak in hours. It wasn't unusual for him to work a thirty-six hour shift. Malcolm had cut ties with Third Baptist and the admissions department, but he couldn't handle the stress he was getting from the *River Rats*. Near the end of June, a buddy of his in the program, Paul Pilgrim, asked Malcolm what was wrong. Malcolm told him that he was on a one-month probation and might be kicked out of the program.

"But why?" asked Paul.

"I need money to pay tuition, living expenses, and—" Malcolm cleared his throat, "—to take care of my invalid father."

"What? You have all those obligations? You cannot possibly work the sorts of hours that they're demanding and do what you must. You need an angel."

Malcolm burst out laughing. "Yeah, sure. I need an angel."

Paul shook his head and put a finger to Malcolm's mouth. "Don't say another word. I'll be your angel. I'll save you, Malcolm."

Malcolm looked amazed.

***

In the succeeding days, Paul created a scheme whereby Malcolm could work "outside" when he needed to while Paul would create phony paperwork to cover him. Paul also supplied Malcolm with a wonder drug, cocaine, which could allow Malcolm to stay awake and alert for an absurd amount of time.

The combination of the false paper trail and the cocaine allowed Mac Smith to return to the stage and play the riverboats for a day down the river and two days back. The band always shifted one day down and two days back. The *River Rats* never went the entire trip to New Orleans.

It was a very trying schedule: three days on the river from noon to 5am. Mac was up all night during his time on the river and his four days in the hospital were more of the same. Soon, Malcolm found that he needed more and more of the wonder drug to keep up the pace. He began falling asleep between sets and had a hard time waking up. It was Ray that began laying down the law to Mac. "Listen, young man. You're good. Very good. We make a lot more money than we used to because of you. But *success* is a blink of the eye, got it? We've got to go out there and prove ourselves *every day!*"

Mac was drifting in and out of consciousness. "I'm not going to let you bring us down, understand? Now you have a double shot of whiskey to get your blood a-rolling so that you can do the third set."

Mac began to form the words, "I don't—" but he couldn't finish. He let Ray pour some firewater down his gullet. The result was predictable. Within a few minutes, he was ready to play the third set. And so it went.

***

On July 10th, 1895 Malcolm collapsed at the hospital. His vital signs were poor so he was admitted to a ward for observation. When he came to, he was incoherent and showed positive signs of mental instability. The diagnosis was *nervous breakdown*. The therapy was involuntary commitment to the St. Louis County Insane Asylum. The main building was five stories with a copula atop that was attended by two side buildings of four stories that held the main wards. The medical offices constituted another square cap of four stories at each side. It was a beautiful institutional façade. It was rather different inside.

The patients in the asylum were variously diagnosed with: furious mania, erotomania, imbecility, dementia, chronic mania, incoherency, delirium of grandeur, raving mania, melancholy, and dipsomania. There was moaning and screaming—almost all the time. But Malcolm had snapped. He no longer existed. When his father, Cedric, came to visit, Mac did not recognize him. Now if you ask me, I think that Mac—Malcolm—or whomever you choose, was putting on a bit of an act. I'm not quite so sure about all these Freudian theories of the time. But then, I'm just the narrator. I don't want to make waves or the producer might fire me.

Be that as it may, Malcolm Smith was discharged from the hospital in care of his father on Christmas 1899. When they got home, his father had a cooked goose and all the trimmings, compliments of the congregation at the Third Baptist that had been praying that the devils that had taken over poor Malcolm would leave him just as Jesus had chased away the devils in the Bible. Cedric served his son some goose, sweet potatoes, and string beans. They prayed before dinner and then Papa took the first bite. It was a pantomime of a drama that was once their lives. But Mac would have none of it, and Cedric knew this. Malcolm was dead and Cedric grieved for his lost son. Just after the New Year, Mac picked up a spot on a riverboat headed to New Orleans. This time he went the whole way—never to return to St. Louis.

***

Once Mac arrived, he went to a band member's house near Algiers. The family took him in and nurtured him. The family, headed by Gabriel Alva, a Creole, worked in a small shoe factory, *Quality Shoes*. The factory was very successful, but Gabriel wasn't being paid very much compared to other regular men working in similar jobs in New Orleans.

At a dinner of yesterday's gumbo and yesterday's bread, Cecilia (Gabriel's wife) began to rant on how the northerners were exploiting the poor folk of the city in order to build another fancy wing on their northern homes. The words 'white' and 'northern' were used interchangeably. But the word 'white' was never used in relation to the European-descent individuals working for generations in the city. They were in a different category all together.

"When you first arrived," began Gabriel, "we thought perhaps that you were from the unions."

"The unions?"

"Yeah. You know. They organize plain folk like us so that we can step up to the owners and be important—just like they are."

"You mean powerful."

"Sweet."

"You mean powerful."

"You know that I do. And we know that you are our man."

"Do you know where I can talk to a union person?"

Gabriel tilted his head a moment and then smiled. "Of course I do. I've been writing them to help us for over a year. I'll walk you there tomorrow before work."

"Fine. When do I have to leave?"

"Four-thirty in the morning."

Mac thought a moment. He was used to finishing his last set around five. His time clock for sleeping in the asylum had thrown everything askew. Then he fixed his expression and looked Gabriel in the eye. "Four-thirty it is. Can someone wake me up at four?"

"We'll wake you earlier. It's when they close the Lucky Seven. Three o'clock. City ordinance. There's always a commotion. Just like a clock. We'll get you then."

***

The next morning, Mac awoke and drank a couple cups of the most unusual coffee he'd ever tasted. It did the trick. He was ready to go and out the door at four-thirty. The walk to the union hall was about an hour. Gabriel walked him most of the way and then pointed him forward. Mac got there at five forty-five. There was already a line of men waiting. Mac got in line.

Nobody talked much in the line. There were people of all shapes and sizes—though mostly men. They were sleep walking—waiting. At six-o'clock a very thin, white man came outside the hall accompanied by a boy with a candle under a glass atop a narrow wooden platform.

"All right. We have forty-two jobs right now. Jeremiah here will take the jobs in construction and I'll take the factory jobs. Sarah will be out in a minute to take those in janitorial. That's all we have today. We'll have another call at noon."

Then Sarah came out. She was a very old, wizened lady who wore a white cap on her head and had a white apron atop her dark smock dress.

In less than half an hour, the crew had vanished—except for Mac. The three functionaries were about to leave when Mac stepped forward. "Excuse me, I need to talk to someone."

"Sorry, mac, but the job call starts at six. You're too late." The men pushed aside Mac. But the musician started to run after them. "You're mistaken. Please, I promised the people who are looking after me."

Perhaps it was the tone of his plaintive request, but the men stopped and turned. All three were rail thin, but one was tall and bald (though he appeared to be still in his twenties). "Okay, mac, spill it." The men were on their toes, poised for a quick exit.

"I don't have a set speech. I promised Gabriel that I would try to help them unionize their factory."

"Unionize their factory?" the trio said together as they dropped down from their toes to their heels. "What factory is this?" asked the tall bald man.

"*Quality Shoes*, have you heard of it?"

"Sure have. A hundred and fifty or so hard-working slugs who get paid crap. We tried to unionize there once, but the ownership figured us out and fired our guy." The tall bald man approached Mac.

"So you say you work there?"

"No. I'm a musician. I'm staying with a family and the father works there. He's very unhappy with the place. We got talking about unions so I agreed to come by to see whether I could help them out for putting me up."

"So you just want to return a favor for a favor?"

"That's right. It seems only fair."

The tall man pursed his lips. Then he put his arm over Mac's shoulder. "You've got to come with us. Things are much more complicated than that. Most of the unions in this town are down at the docks. We offer the jobs service for the working man, though we don't make a penny out of it."

This wasn't exactly true, where the union guys really wanted to go was to a new factory that was producing patent medicines for distribution around the country. The boss-man, Wolf Sullowald, was a nut about efficiency. Thus, the union men wanted a piece of a very lucrative operation. But they didn't want to share such visions with this new kid in town.

***

And so Mac followed the trio for the morning wherever they went (but not to the new plant that was being built). He learned a little bit about union organizing. It wasn't easy. And he could clearly see that he was not cut out to be a grassroots union organizer. At the end of the day the obvious didn't need to be said. Mac shook hands with the trio and turned to walk away. That's the way you've got to play it, and Mac was in tune.

But the tall bald man told him to stop. Mac did as he was told.

"You say that you play a musical instrument?"

"Sure I do. Several instruments," he said over his shoulder.

"Do you know how to play the trumpet?"

Mac turned around, a bit surprised at the question. "Sure I do. Why?"

"Well, the unions in the town—especially the Central and the IWW—have been trying to put together a band to build spirit and comradery. The result hasn't been very good. I'd like to see what you could do with the group."

"Well, I don't know," began Mac. The prospect of playing with a bunch of amateurs did not appeal to him.

"There's money attached to the job: ten dollars a day when you're working."

That was not as much as he had been making on the boats, but it would allow him to live on his own until he decided where life was heading. He agreed. The first practice was in two hours.

***

Quality Shoes once was unionized, but had not been for ten years. During the same decade of 1900-1910, Mac built a band of temporary musicians who played on the boats and went all the way to New Orleans, and who were willing to wait a week or so and play for Mac until they caught a spot on the return trip going back up-river. This allowed Mac a high-quality group that played at union events and strikes. They were forced to play some of the emerging repertoire of labor folk songs along with a short list of other rousing melodies that they jazzed up a bit. Mac was the bandleader, but he often played as well: trumpet, fiddle, and piano.

The band was an important part of the labor movement in New Orleans, and Mac was the point person for the pan-union operation. Mac sometimes attended meetings at the various unions in town as the poor cousin (a member of the team but not a "real" worker—is playing music really work?). Nevertheless, Mac was there and he became a known commodity. This was during a period of consolidation cooperative agreements that made the unions more powerful. There was even talk of a musicians' union!

From 1910 to 1915, Mac continued to be brought into more venues within the labor movement. His band began to become more permanent and traveled to other cities to support union activity. People liked his mix of folk labor tunes, rousing melodies, and intoxicating jazz. This versatility and his ability to mix singers effectively made Mac a hot item.

One day in March of 1915, Mac Smith was approached by a Mr. Murray Tupman of the Great Northern Railroads. Mr. Tupman was a man of diminutive stature. He wore a bowler hat and sported a bushy black moustache. He always sported a three-piece suit that seemed too small—even for his petite build. Even though Tupman was physically tiny, his voice was big. They were in Chicago at the Palmer House Hotel. Mac's band was playing for a convention of union leaders. Tupman had made arrangements for a late-morning breakfast in the exclusive dining room.

The dining room was small but tastefully decorated with thick white linen table cloths, fresh cut flowers, and silver cutlery. This was the highest level of hotel that Mac had ever been to—the floor of the barbershop was tiled in silver dollars. Mac felt very underdressed in his worn coat and flashy red tie.

The two men shook hands and Tupman did the ordering. Murray handed Mac his business card. Mac glanced at it: Regional Vice President! Mac put on a forced smile.

"I guess you're wondering why I asked you to breakfast?"

"Yes, sir," replied Mac.

"Hey, don't call me 'sir.' You may call me Mr. Tupman."

"All right, Mr. Tupman."

The railroad vice president folded his hands in front of him and smiled beneficently. "Well, as you know, Great Northern Railroad is one of the two premier lines in the northern Midwest and West.

Our main competitor, the Northern Pacific, is not really well positioned for the twentieth century. We are the future."

The waiter brought coffee and scones.

"Yes sir—I mean Mr. Tupman."

Tupman smiled and then continued, "We have a vision of acquisition for the upper Midwest and West. We want to pick-up small lines that are no longer as viable as they once were. We can bring them under our management and make them profitable."

"That sounds like a good plan," replied Mac.

"It's a dynamite plan, and it's going to work."

"I'm sure it will," replied Mac as he buttered up his scone, added some jam and drank some strong coffee.

The two men finished the sweets with careful preparation until the eggs, sausage, and toast came. Murray was watching his quarry attentively. Sometimes the senior vice president would pull up his right lower lip so that he could catch his moustache hairs. When he was successful, Murray would lightly chew on them while at the same time moving his eyebrows up and down.

Mac was oblivious to the machinations of Murray. At the moment, Mac felt that he was being fêted and preened. Mac's consciousness was on the luxurious quarters he was in and all the little details of life that he had never observed. He was overwhelmed.

When they were on their eggs and sausage, Murray leaned forward and pointed his finger at Mac. "Mac, I have a proposition for you,"

Mac tilted his head.

"I think you could work for the Great Northern Railroad."

"You do?"

"Of course. You bring a lot to the table."

"Like what?"

"Well for starters, you've shown organizational skills in forming your traveling union band. There never was a band like this before. It is a mainstay of the union movement at present and you are to be congratulated in creating such a well-working organization."

Mac smiled. "Thank you."

"Great Northern needs men who know how to innovate. We think you've got what it takes."

"Are you offering me a job?"

"Yes," said Murray, leaning forward and grabbing the back of Mac's hands. "We want to make you a regional director in the Dakotas for Great Northern."

"What would that entail?"

"You'd assist us in our acquisitions program in the region. You'd be stationed in Fargo but you'd go all around the two states, finding out which rail lines we might purchase and then beginning the deal."

Mac pulled his hands away and began smoothing back his very fine hair that was thinning at the peaks. "But I don't know anything about the railroads."

"I think you're smarter than you make out."

"Oh really?"

"Yes, really. We've investigated you thoroughly and we're convinced that you are bright and talented."

Mac pursed his lips and began nodding his head in short jerks. "But then I'd have to give up my band."

"Yes and no on that one. I'd like to start a Great Northern Band. It could be a union band, too, but it would be under the banner of the Great Northern Railroad."

"A union band under the banner of the Great Northern Railroad? Perhaps it's too early in the morning, but isn't that a conflict of interest?"

Murray smiled and put the last piece of sausage into his mouth. He chewed thoroughly and washed it down with the strong coffee. "Not at all. Mac, part of your job as regional director would also be as the union spokesman for all Great Northern employees. You would be their liaison to upper management. You could contact me directly by telegraph if there was ever a union problem in your region, the Dakotas, and you would have significant discretion on setting out the resolution."

Mac thought a minute. But the surroundings, the opulence, the powerful presence of Mr. Tupman made it difficult for him to concentrate. "Let me get this straight: I'd be the representative of the union while I worked for Great Northern?"

"In your region. It's been a region in which we've had a lot of labor problems and we think you could solve them even as we expand in that region."

"So you want me to solve your labor problems since I am a fixture in the labor movement and will be trusted?" Mac pushed aside his plate. He was only half-done.

"Exactly! You can be our man to turn around the Dakota operations."

"But what about my friends in the Labor Movement? Won't they feel betrayed?"

"We're willing to pay you $10,000 a year plus a housing and travel allowance."

Mac was taken aback. He was making around $1,000 a year at present. It was all right, but he had dreams. Like many Americans, he dreamed of becoming a Rockefeller and putting an end to the day-by-day penny-pinching that characterized most people's lives. Ten thousand dollars was a fortune! Why, if he maintained his present lifestyle and invested his money, he could become really rich. Sure, he'd have to give up his present friends, but then he'd done that before. Ten thousand dollars: the thought captivated him.

"You say $10,000 a year?"

"Plus a housing and travel allowance. You'd also have your band under the Great Northern name and maintain your union ties."

The Fates were with him. It seems like a deal made in heaven.

The two men shook hands.

***

Mac began his new job immediately. On Easter Monday, April 4, 1915, Mac Smith moved to Fargo, North Dakota. The company gave him enough money to rent an entire house on his supplementary allowance. The white wood-framed house he chose with a wrap-around front porch was a very fashionable house for the town. Mac got to work setting up his schedule of travel. First on the list was Deadwood, South Dakota.

Deadwood, South Dakota was a town that saw its moniker as a display of realism. The "dead wood" referred to the gulch that was largely stripped bare in the gold rush that ensued after General Custer declared that there was gold to be found. 'Gold' was certainly one way that a person could move from rags to riches very quickly. One family that took the bait of gold fever was Arne and Freya Moe, who moved from Minneapolis for the allure of the yellow metal in 1885. That was a decade too late for the first claim settlers, but just in time for the real action. In the space of a year, legendary lawman Wild Bill Hickok was gunned down in Nuttal &

Mann's Saloon. Wild Bill, they say, had an eye problem—probably from looking at all those lovely Saloon gals.

There were major fires in 1877 and 1899 as the dry climate turned the flimsy construction into tinder. Some say that the fires were due to the rather rowdy frontier ways that always accompany a gold rush. But the native population, the Lakota Nation (largely invisible to the European immigrants and second generation explorers), had a different account: The 1868 Treaty of Laramie guaranteed the Black Hills and the surrounding areas to the Lakotas. Custer's clarion of gold made a necessity of violating such treaties. After all, if it was legal for European immigrants to shoot native peoples from a train just as one might shoot birds and rabbits, then why would one bother about treaties? Aren't all treaties made to be broken?

Amidst the turmoil of the region, Mac had been sent to buy a small gauge mining rail line. It was still profitable, but it was rather inefficient with the private line owned by one company, the hook-up owned by another, and the end producer being Great Northern. If Great Northern could own all the levels, they could cut costs and increase profits.

This is where Mac stepped in. He had an appointment with Swen Jorgensen, who was the president of the mine that had a controlling interest in the small-gauge rail line. Mac left his room at the Grand Hotel (which was anything but grand) in time for the two-mile walk to the office of Swen Jorgensen.

The one-story wood-frame structure was typical of Deadwood: the original plain, rosy hardwood with a coat of varnish that once brimmed with vitality had now worn off in the frigid Dakota winters and transformed the starting structure into a dried, shriveled gray shell that was waiting to catch on fire.

Mac opened the door and saw a small waiting room that had a dozen or so functional wood chairs that had weathered their age better than the exterior structure. In the far wall to the left was a beautiful door that couldn't have been more than a year old. It was light oak with all the grains of the wood in sharp relief against the light yellow-orange background of the core wood. The handle of the door showed strength unlike any handle that Mac had ever seen. Above the door was a mounted bison head.

The keeper of the door was a young woman, sitting behind a desk that had a telephone atop it. She was a thin lady with dark brown hair and brown eyes. She was at the far cusp of young—

perhaps twenty-five, but she had a firm attention and command of her sphere of influence. "May I help you, sir?"

"Yes," began Mac, who was a little off his game by the presence of this receptionist. "My name is Mac Smith. I have an appointment with Swen Jorgensen."

"Oh yes, Mr. Smith. I have you on the calendar. The trouble is that Mr. Jorgensen was called out to the mines. I'm not sure when he'll be back. You are certainly welcomed to a seat to wait or you can go back to your hotel."

Mac looked at the receptionist, smiled, and decided to stay put. What he discovered during the ensuing six hours was that the receptionist was named Florence Moo (pronounced Moe). She was the daughter of Arne and Freya Moe (who changed their name to Moo because there were so many people named Moe in South Dakota). Florence (who also went by Flo), was twenty-five and was the receptionist, accountant, and pretty face of the world of Deadwood mining operations. Flo didn't care a hoot about mining. She only wanted to earn her pay and split it with her parents who were less able to work these days.

In the next two weeks, Mac succeeded in his contract negotiations: he purchased the mining train line and the secondary connection. In addition, he proposed marriage to Florence Moo and was accepted. By July 12th they were married and the two returned to Fargo, North Dakota. Mac settled an allowance for Flo's folks and they started saving their money.

***

Malcolm performed as the company hoped on the various projects that they wanted him to execute. Upper management considered him to be a model of middle management. This led to a promotion: Montana. The next move the couple made was to Havre, Montana. They procured a house at Wolf Point. The house was at the edge of an Indian reservation. Florence had spent some time with Native Americans as she grew up in Deadwood. But it was there that their two children were born: Moira and Mac, Jr. (that Mac delivered himself—after all, according to him he was almost a doctor).

The early years in rural Montana were financially successful to Mac, but he was not able to keep up a band in the geographic isolation. He was nowhere, according to the music world. The Mississippi River was hundreds of miles away.

Sweet river run softly as I begin my migration to the great sea.

CHAPTER SIX

No one can buy immortality with money
  The Brihadaranyaka Upanishad[*]

The news of the day: These Kids Won't Have Small Pox.
Hundreds of children take advantage of a school holiday to get vaccinated at City Hall.
  St. Paul Pioneer Press November 6, 1924

JAMES opened the envelope with trepidation. He slid out the bad news and opened it flat. Another of his suppliers was changing the terms of payment. Instead of net 90 to 180 days for payment, they were demanding payment in full or the return of merchandise. James had called the last supplier who said that someone was spreading a rumor about his financial instability so the companies wanted to move quickly to get back as much as they could. This was a reasonable strategy from their point of view, but it was all based upon a lie someone was spreading about him. And James thought that he could see Wolf fangs all over this one. If Wolf had been spreading rumors about the soundness of James's pharmacy, then a panic could ensue that would turn a balanced operation into one that could not pay its bills. One cannot run a business that way. It would mean the end.

There was no one in the store just now; Mollie was out for her early lunch. James sat on a stool behind the counter. All the prescriptions had been prepared. He could sit and think about his options. James had tried to set up his pharmacy on the basic principles of store organization that he had learned at Charles Quincy back in Philadelphia when he was still an apprentice.

James went to the backroom to the safe where they kept the accounting book. Niall Mullins, his partner, did the accounting and tax stuff. James ran the day-to-day operations. Niall was the

---

[*] *The Brihadaranyaka Upanishad* from *The Upanishads*, tr. Eknath Easwaran (Tomales, CA: Nilgiri Press, 1987).

backroom of the business. Today Niall was gone. He had not come to work. Probably sick, thought James. But when James had a look at the books, it was James who began to feel sick. The books said one thing about the weekly receipts while the bank statements were telling a quite different story. James did daily tallies so that he had some rudimentary check on the books. The books seemed correct, but the bank statements starting in July showed only a quarter of what should be there. A terrible thought entered his mind. It was time for James, too, to take an early lunch.

James went to the door and put up the sign that said he was out. At the bottom of the sign was a mock clock with hands that could be moved to show customers when he would return. James fixed the hands to say he would return by 12:30.

Instead of going for food, James headed for the bank. His worst fears were confirmed: His partner, Niall, had been making short deposits for over a month and just today drew out most of the money from the business account. James was ruined.

***

On the way back to the pharmacy, James' mind went back to the beginning with Charles Quincy. James had gotten that apprenticeship because of his brother, Tommy, who then moved to New York City. When his father died in 1878, James was quite alone in Philadelphia. He gave up the apartment and slept in Quincy's back room, rent-free. He was also an effective night watchman (pharmacies had to be very careful about the theft of certain jugs, like laudanum). It was a deal that helped both of them. When his brother Tommy was killed in his police job in 1880, Charles Quincy and the Friends were very supportive.

James had been happy with Charles Quincy. He even went to a Meeting with him at the Quaker Meeting House. Things had been steady for nine years. James had completed his apprenticeship in three years and had been an assistant for six years. His duties included all but the most intricate pills and potions. Quincy was very knowledgeable, having been taught by a man who knew some chemistry from school. Everything was done according to the highest standards. Charles had learned the four-humour approach to medicine and the appropriate herb that would counter phlegm, blood, black and yellow bile. They had two delivery devices: syrup in a bottle mixed with herbs and a pill making machine that took inorganic compounds mixed with the herbs to create a pill that the patient might swallow whole. The prescriptions were made to order in case the physician had any special orders—such as "high phlegm: no citric acid, but a mixture of sugar and coffee bean." The normal prescription would have been lemon peel extract. It was important to be able to address each patient's particular needs through the careful opinions of the physician. Only when there was a case of acute pain did Quincy create a syrup containing laudanum.

Charles Quincy had regular customers who paid a small premium for his superior product and service. Charles earned more than he spent and lived frugally. In short, James longed to be like Charles.

But Eden was also made for intruders from the dust. In this case the serpent adopted the guise of a canine: Wolf Sullowald was his name. Wolf was a man of medium build and short stature (like James). His hair was black and his eyes were blue. One might look at Wolf and declare that he was a relative of James (they even both sported full straight moustaches). The biggest superficial difference was in attire and the way each carried himself. James was shy and wore simple clothes. Wolf wore expensive clothes and smoked a cigarette from a long varnished wooden cigarette holder. His fedora was always pushed back a bit, and he sported colored scarves that accented his neckties. You might say that Wolf glided into rooms. The first time that James met Wolf was when Wolf came in to buy some powder for a headache. Wolf declined the first two remedies that James suggested. Then Charles Quincy came forward. It was clear that Wolf knew what he wanted: he wanted laudanum. Charles Quincy was loath to dispense the drug without a note from a physician. It was such an addictive medication. But Wolf was very insistent, and there was no law against it. So Charles made him an elixir that was intended to last for a week. Wolf paid and left. He glided out the same way he had magically appeared.

***

Soon Wolf was a regular client. He continued to buy the same medication and made inquiries about morphine and cocaine for a pain in his foot. Charles Quincy wouldn't sell him both. The two got into a bit of a row, and Wolf left the shop.

That was the end of Wolf's patronage, but not the end of Wolf. James used to take a walk to a bakery for a cheese roll for lunch. He liked talking to the daughter of the owner who ran the cashier. 'Mary' was on the nameplate she wore on her white uniform. James was rather fond of the name as it had been his mother's. James would take his roll into the park and eat it slowly to extend his lunch break.

One day when he was almost to the bakery, Wolf Sullowald called out his name. James turned around and Wolf invited him to lunch at a sit-down place. James accepted. They went to the Book Binder's Restaurant on Walnut Street. They sat in a booth next to the window. James was very impressed. He'd never eaten in such a fancy restaurant. He didn't know the prices, because his menu only showed the dishes. But Wolf ordered for both of them.

"I am guessing zat you war wondering about why I to lunch inwited you?" said Wolf. He had just put a cigarette into his fancy cigarette holder.

James smiled. He wasn't sure just what to say. Wolf lit his cigarette and pulled and straightened his tie.

"Vell, let me a kleine geschichte, a history, tell you. Und it might zee explain much. You see, mein bruther, Klaus decided to America travel mit his children when after his frau died. But his son, Johann, didn't vant to go. He had his mind on career in army, and school first he had zee to finish. So I became his guardian. Vhen he finished (third in his class), he enlisted und he vas sent to the country Togo in zee Africa. Zere caught he a bad case of malaria and he died. Wery sad, really. It made me want to leave aus Germany to travel. Zo as zoon as I his life insurance from the army collect, I vent to America, auch. I moved in mit Klaus mein brother und his Tochter, Frederica, right here in zee Philadelphia.

"Vell, I vanted zee American vay to follow und my Geld to make. Zo I kept mein eyes open to zee opportunities. I thought to myself: vhat do people need really? Zee first thing zat came to mind vas 'shoes.' Not zee neu Schuh, but zee shoe repairs. Shoes are zo expensive zat everywon is always zee shoes repairing."

Wolf paused as he drank some of his beer. James sipped on his soda water.

"But I am not ze impulsive mensch. I have less than ze year here been (zo I speak ze perfect English as you can see)." Wolf made a broad and winning grin (or so I think James thought).

James told Wolf that a shoe repair store might work well. The placement of such a store would mean a lot. Location was the success of Charles Quincy and his pharmacy. Wolf perked up when James talked of Charles and his store.

"Zo you are a partner or zee employee?"

"I was an apprentice. I became a full pharmacist myself after three years. He is obviously more skilled than I am, but I am qualified to grind and mix the general herbs and medicines that most people need. But it is true: I work for Charles."

Wolf smiled. He had very white teeth.

***

In the months ahead, Wolf increasingly made contact with James. He took him to lunch at least once a week. Each time it meant that James returned late. These changes in behavior were not lost on Charles Quincy. But the Quaker maintained his silence.

***

When Wolf had softened his prey, he sprang a surprise upon his young charge (James was ten years younger). "I zinks tzats I have found zee house of tzee geld. A pharmacy to buy I must."

James started coughing. He dropped his knife on to the fish atop the pewter plate.

Wolf laughed, "Zeen bones in zee Fisch sind not zo good, right? Est is ungesund."

But it wasn't the bones in the fish.

For a fortnight James considered Wolf's offer. James would be the head chemist in his own pharmacy. James would be considered a partner and earn a salary of $700 a year. Since James had no real capital to speak of, he would have to earn his share in the business by a formula of overtime hours. The entire endeavor made his head spin. But there was the inconvenient reality of Charles Quincy. This caused James to put off agreeing to Wolf's offer. Over the next month, Wolf kept upping the ante until he was now offering James $1,400 a year (though the ownership stake would not be earned until he had been in the business ten years and it maxed out at 20%). This was beyond belief! James accepted on the spot and shook Wolf's hand on it. The Fates were smiling.

***

"I see," said Charles as they were cleaning up shop on a Friday afternoon near closing time. "You are giving up nine years of service for this German drug addict." Charles took out his cleaning cloth and began scrubbing the place down. James took out the duster and performed his task.

"He's not a drug addict. At least, I haven't seen him take any narcotics."

"I base my assessment upon what he did here for a month or so before I cut him off. He was addicted to laudanum. It is a powerful drug that can sap your soul. The man wants his own pharmacy to feed his drug habit. And he wants to make you his patsy. Are you really that stupid?"

James finished his cleaning without another word. Before he went he said, "I think you're being unfair to Wolf. He's an immigrant, you know."

"Of course, I know by his speech. But before you finalize things, I want to let you know that if you are patient enough to wait five to seven years, I'll be retiring. I'd pass on the store to you and you could pay me for it in time with the profits. In ten to twelve years or so you would be your own boss of an established and proven business. I can't see how that offer can be bested."

James pursed his lips and left.

***

James was a young man of twenty-five years old. Ten to twelve years seemed like a very long time: it was half his life. He had to think about his future. But this wasn't easy. His whole life had been one of radical changes. First was their move to the United States when he was two and the tumult that caused it. Second was moving to Philadelphia when he was three. Then there was the birth of his sister that resulted in his mother's death—and all for nothing: his sister, Lucy, died when she was three and he was seven. He really loved his little sister (though he did blame her in his heart for his mother's death). Then he got his job from Tommy's good deed, but then Tommy went away, too. Then his Da died. Then Tommy died. There was very little left except Charles Quincy and his friends at Meeting. But these weren't *his*.

Wolf Sullowald was of the old country like himself. James liked this. He had always viewed the Germans as a clever lot who were boisterous enough to get their way. It was how he wanted to live his life. It's true that Charles Quincy had saved him from economic ruin and given him a trade. He had trusted him and brought him into his family, which was the Quaker community. Charles had no living family.

Was this a proper way to repay such love and kindness?

It wasn't about love and kindness, decided James. It was about his own future.

***

James opened Wolf's chemist shop on 3ʳᵈ Street heading toward Society Hill. Wolf had purchased a three-story town house that housed himself, brother, and niece in the upper two stories and the pharmacy on the street level. Wolf gave James a rather free hand to choose what to order. He also gave him an assistant, Frederica Sullowald, his niece. Frederica was a tall, young woman around five-foot-seven. She had excellent posture that made her seem even taller. Frederica's hair was dark auburn and pulled straight back and tied in a bun. Her skin was pale and unblemished. Her eyes were piercingly blue. She normally pursed her lips.

The task was to see how fast they could get stocked-up. Wolf, himself, promoted the establishment to a high society crowd that he had successfully gained entry to. I'm not sure how he did it and neither did James. One can ask too many questions. But the quantities of cocaine, laudanum, and morphine were about half of their inventory.

One day a woman around twenty who was dressed as if she were in service came for Cheryl Audley's regular cocaine refill. Charles Quincy had limited the amount of the painkiller to ten grains for a daily dose and no more than one week at a time to stave off addiction. But under their regime, 25 grains was given for the daily dose and they would dispense a monthly supply.

"Excuse me, ma'am. But we filled this for a month. It is not due to be refilled for over two weeks. Our intent is to give you a one-month dosage." James pulled on his bushy top lip moustache to make his point more effective.

"Yes sir. My name is Molly. I am a servant and I do as I am told." Molly was an Irish girl who had probably been bought and paid for through some newspaper advert. Her teeth were black and her pale skin was blotchy.

"Well, I don't know," began James. Then Frederica came out from the back room and declared, "We can certainly help you out if you have money today. We don't do credit on accounts past their normal due dates." Then Frederica seemed to rise above her five-foot-seven inch frame to address the four-foot eleven-inch servant. "Do you have the money?"

"No ma'am. The misses told me to put it on the bill."

"Well, then tell the misses that she'll have to wait until the first of the month. We will refill upon demand with cash up front." Frederica was rather imposing with her dark auburn hair that was pulled straight back. She had a wide forehead and broad shoulders. Her Baptist ancestors, in Oberhausen Germany, gave her the conviction to speak her mind and bring everyone to her side.

When Molly left, Frederica said to James, "It's important to run this place as a business. That's what Wolf says. You know he lives with me and my father."

"Yes," replied James. He didn't dare challenge the ire of the clan from Oberhausen.

Two hours later, just before closing time, Molly returned with enough money to pay the past bill and two more monthly installments. James dutifully did the deed and Frederica tallied the money and quickly took it to the safe.

After James had dealt with two more customers with more conventional needs, he went back to Frederica. She was furiously writing letters. The table she was working at was a large secretary with fifteen cubbyholes. On the top of the secretary was a large kerosene lamp that illumined most of the back room. Her dark auburn hair was falling out of its clips and cascading over her concentrated brow with the result of blocking her vision. In her furor, she didn't reset her hair, but instead kept tossing it back with her left hand.

James approach Frederica with the intent of telling her how things had been handled at Charles Quincy's chemist shop. But he was arrested: first by the realization that he was rather attracted by the furious positive energy that Frederica exuded, and secondly by the high level of concentration she possessed. For some reason, he thought of his late brother, Tommy. It was at that time that James semi-realized that he was attracted to the intense light of the obsessed. It compelled his moth-like character forward in ways he could not explain.

Then Frederica, noticing for the first time that James was standing five feet from her, shot a glance over her shoulder and focused her eyes. All the features of her face were in high alert. "What do you want?"

James smiled and turned back to the shop. A few seconds later the little bell attached to the door announced another customer.

***

In the weeks that followed, the Halcyon Chemist shop (that had been misspelled as Halcion on the first sign delivered from the painter) became largely a shop that dispensed laudanum, cocaine, and morphine. There was very little of the legitimate principles of Galenic medicine and its herbal treatments of deficiencies in the four humours. Instead, real science was supplanted by the drugs of happiness: it was three-quarters of their business. However, this emphasis was hidden behind a façade of sundries such as fine cloth, needles, and thread. There were also supplies for needlepoint and yarn for knitting. The walls were bright and there was a healthy, family atmosphere about the place. (There was even a small supply of little dolls from Oberhausen, Germany.)

Because of the nature of their real business, Wolf and his niece, Frederica, made very clear policies about payments up-front. They also employed Wells-Fargo to empty their safe every other night. Wolf purchased several pistols and two shotguns for their defense in case of robbery.

On Sunday, the only day the shop was closed, Wolf went out with James to the park to practice shooting. They took some empty boxes from the back room and drew targets on them and went through a dozen shots each. "If zere is und problem a second shot ve may not have."

It was these dark aphorisms that disturbed James the most about his outings with Wolf.

***

One day, Frederica was pounding a nail into the yellow plaster wall.

"What's that for?" asked James. Frederica didn't answer but went into the back room. James gripped the counter edge. He held on tight with both hands. The tendons in his gaunt arms rose up. Then his right shoulder began to twitch. He tried to grip tighter.

Frederica returned with a long rectangular sign that had picture wire on the back. The sign said, "In God we trust, everyone else pays cash." When she hung the sign, Frederica turned and gestured with her left hand, smiling. "What do you think?"

James relaxed his grasp. It was a sign of something else.

***

For the next four years, the Halcyon was a big success. Profits were huge. The upper class clientele enjoyed getting their drugs without going through any unpleasant individuals. At the Halcyon, a client could come in wearing long white gloves and buy her laudanum along with a toy for her child without getting her gloves dirty (an Italian maid came in with James each day at 6am to be sure that everything was very clean).

James's bank account also began to rise. He had moved into the top floor of a duplex house. The change in situation was acute for James: it was as if *he* owned a home. The owner lived on the bottom floor and rented out the top floor to James. His square footage moved from 400 sq. feet to 1,000 sq. feet. He felt like the squire of his second floor domain. Wolf had procured James's place. It was only two blocks from the pharmacy. This allowed James to arrive at 6am and to grind the compounds for the clients who would be coming by that day. He could supervise Claudia, the maid, and check the shipment log for anticipated arrivals.

The chemist shop opened at 7am and stayed open until 6pm. After it closed, James stayed an extra hour to make sure everything was in order. Frederica (who generally started around noon) also stayed until 7pm to work on the books and to hand the money over to the Wells Fargo men.

One day in the late morning, there was a short man in a dark suit sporting a thin moustache who was purchasing some cocaine along with some yarn for his wife. He wanted the purchase to be put onto his bill. James pointed to Frederica's sign. The man shook his head. "There was a woman with red hair. She said it would be fine so long as I paid my bill at the end of the month."

"Well," began James, "that is not our general policy. I can find her and bring her down."

The short man in the dark suit and thin moustache smiled and shifted his weight to a black lacquered cane with a silver ferrule. James turned to the back room, shut and locked the door and proceeded to the end of the room where the stairway to the second level was located. It was probably around ten o'clock (late enough for even Frederica). He opened the door that blocked the stairwell and called up to Frederica. The vibrations of his voice seemed to echo up the narrow, dark, wooden stairwell to the second floor that was illumined by a gaslight. He knew that at the top of the stairs to the right was Frederica's room. Her door was a white, painted six-light door with three-tiered molding. He had on other occasions interrupted her repose to assist him with critical duties in the shop. James started to ascend the creaky stairs. Because of the high rise of each step, James moved slowly. With each step, the old wood sang of his impending arrival.

When he was thirteen steps up the twenty-five-step staircase, the bedroom door flew open and Frederica came running out. She was disheveled and was fixing her hair as she ran towards James. Frederica knew that she had to attend to a problem that was beyond James. Therefore she rushed past him and bumped him into the wall. In the process she dropped one of the long hairpins that held her bun together. The metal pin dropped to the step and made little noise. Frederica was already down the stairs and heading to the main shop to confront events. James turned to follow her when he paused to pick up the hairpin. As he straightened up he heard another sound from upstairs. James turned his head and saw Wolf sneaking out of Frederica's bedroom. He was also disheveled and pulling his hair back with both hands and tucking in his shirt tail. Part of his concealment was to not look down to the staircase as he disappeared to the far end of the hallway.

James was frozen. He stared at Frederica's white six-light door with three-tiered molding and saw a black stain near the handle. The door remained open. James grabbed onto the handrail as he turned to return to the shop.

When James got to the front counter, Frederica was writing up an order form. The short man in the dark suit and thin moustache was gone. "So what was that all about?" asked James. Frederica had a look of terror on her face. The placid judge of the universe was visibly shaken.

James repeated his query, "I thought you never wanted to credit anyone. What gives? We only use those order forms for credit accounts."

The query sent steel into the auburn-haired Fraulein. She straightened herself and mechanically checked her bun. It was askew with rebellious strands of hair out of place. James instantly responded and handed her the prodigal hairpin. "I think you're missing something. I have what you need."

***

Three months later James and Frederica got married, June 6th, 1890. On December 16th of the same year, their first child was born and christened Marie in the Roman Catholic Church.

The money kept rolling in. Halcyon was a big success. Then one day a man came in, dressed like a dandy wearing a black cape over a light brown suit and a freshly cut flower in his lapel. His wide brimmed fedora bowed rakishly at an angle. He was smoking what smelled like a Turkish cigarette.

James walked up to him. "Can I help you?"

The man tilted his head, removed the cigarette from his mouth and said, "Are you the owner of the shop?"

"The owner? No. I'm not the owner. I hope to become a partner someday, but for now I'm just the hired help."

The man turned and spat on the floor and used the sole of his shoe to rub it in. "Too bad, sonny. I need to talk to the boss man."

Just then Frederica came in from the back room. "Do you have a problem, sir?" she said in her most intimating voice (the one in which her straight posture made her seem to rise an inch). She was the tallest person in the room.

The stranger walked forward and bumped into her. James was startled and scurried to the aid of his wife, but the stranger turned and delivered a sharp blow to James' chin that laid him out cold on the floor. The man continued to press forward until he had Frederica against a wall. The intruder took a long drag on his cigarette and then gestured with it towards Frederica's unblemished skin as he blew smoke in her face. "Now listen to me, lady. I need to talk to the boss and I need to talk right now. Is he upstairs?"

"Oh, no! He's out."

"Is that a fact? Well, then, I suppose you wouldn't mind if I went upstairs on my own to look for him."

"Yes I do mind," retorted Frederica with renewed vigor as she pushed the intruder away with both of her hands. The man moved backwards two steps and then reached into his coat pocket and pulled out a derringer. He stepped forward and thrust it right against Frederica's forehead. "Now bitch, you take me to the asshole who owns this shop or so help me God, I'll blow your fucking brains out."

"Okay." Frederica was transformed. She didn't even look at the unconscious figure of her husband, James, lying on the floor. Instead, she was an automaton who took the man to the staircase, up the stairs and to the far end of the hallway where Wolf had his suite of rooms: parlor, office, and bedroom. She opened the door and led the man in.

Wolf was sitting at his desk in his office. His secretary desk was cluttered with papers, dark brown glass bottles, and dirty spoons. He swiveled on his chair when he heard the door open and got up when he saw Frederica.

"Was machst du—" then he stopped. He saw the man behind Frederica who had a gun. Wolf moved down to get his own firearm when the intruder arrested his action. "Do that, asshole, and she's dead and the next person to take the fall is you."

Wolf stopped. "Who sie?"

"Put your hands in the air so that I can see them."

Wolf complied.

"Now the bitch lies face down on the floor with her hands extended."

Frederica complied.

"All right. Now that's better. I need to engage in a conversation with you. First, what is your name?"

"Do you vant one of my cards? On the side of my desk there in the black case they are."

"Why don't you get one out and hand it to me *slowly*."

Wolf did so.

The man looked at the card. "Wolf Sullowald, eh? Sounds like a German name."

Wolf didn't say anything.

Then the man said, "Well, Mr. Wolf Sullowald, I've got a business proposition for you. I work for a man named Biff who runs the Five Points Gang in New York. Well, we're expanding our operations. My name is Carney. You might say that I'm one of his lieutenants."

"Vhat mit uns do you vant? Only a little shop here do vee habben."

"What a stupid question. Don't they teach you to think when they teach you English? You German dogs aren't too bright, are you?"

Wolf looked terrified. James Carney held his gun pointed straight at Wolf's forehead. Wolf started to shake. He began crying a little. Carney smiled. "So look, I'm not going to close your shop. Instead, *you* are going to start working for *me*."

"Vhat do you mean?"

"I mean this, boxhead. Biff is interested in keeping the peace around these parts. We've done the same in the Five Points neighborhood in New York and now we're branching out. We're targeting Irish areas like this, but sometimes we get a surprise like you, sauerkraut. Our deal is this: you pay 25% of your profits and in return we will make sure that nobody else shakes you down for money. Do you understand?"

Wolf regained his composure. He didn't like giving up 25% of his profits. That was a lot of money. The thought of losing so much of his dream in life gave him courage, "Und vhat if I refuse?"

"Then you're dead along with this tramp on the floor."

Wolf looked at the gun. Then he looked at James Carney. Wolf hadn't seen an Irishman like this before. It seriously unsettled him. He paused over a minute before replying, "Ya, ya. Okay."

The man went over the details with Wolf on how and when he would be contacted. In fifteen minutes, James Carney walked out with a signed piece of paper. He didn't even notice the still unconscious body of James O'Neil on the floor as Carney stepped over him on his way to the exit.

***

The Five Points Gang began making further and further inroads into the neighborhood in Philly. Wolf brought in an apprentice and had James teach him. The apprentice's name was Swen. He was a Norwegian lad in his late teens with a strong back and a willingness to do as he was told.

Frederica for a time was different. She walked about and kept the books, but she was no longer a force in the running of the chemist shop. Each month on the third day, a runner from Carney would come by to pick up their share of the money. Periodically, Carney, himself, would stop by and go over the books and square that with the money that they had received. Frederica was always present to answer questions, but there were few errors. She knew what might happen.

But what *did* happen on December 4th in the middle of the night was the birth of James, Jr. Dr. Byrne delivered the child at home without complication. Though it took Dr. Byrne twelve hours to deliver Marie, James popped out in just under two hours. Frederica was getting into the rhythm of having babies. The laudanum wasn't bad, either.

The event was the high point of James's life, so much so that he got Father Cleary of St. Mary's parish to christen the boy within a month of his birth. "You know, James," Father Cleary said, "when you baptize a child, a metaphysical change occurs and that child belongs to Jesus Christ forever."

James didn't know what a metaphysical change was, but he did know that he'd given the good Father a good deal of change to go through the ceremony quickly. James Jr. came home to their upper floor duplex apartment with mommy and big sister, Marie. The baby now had a name and an ontological change (or was that a diaper change?).

***

The newspapers were beginning to run stories about the Prohibition Party and the Women's Christian Temperance Union. Halcyon wasn't the only chemist shop selling patent medicine and other forms of opium, cocaine, and morphine. It was catching on to all those who could afford something beyond basic existence. Even some medical doctors touted the restorative powers of these medications.

One day in 1892, a policeman came to call. His name was Tomas. He was a sergeant in the local precinct. He wanted to talk to the "man in charge." James looked quickly to Frederica, but decided himself to lead Tomas upstairs to Wolf.

Within less than a minute after Tomas left his hour-long conference, Wolf came storming down. He told Swen to go out and buy some groceries. The smooth-faced boy left with a song on his lips.

Inside, Wolf gave his critical assessment of what was happening. The police now wanted protection money, too. They claimed that bad things might happen to the shop if they didn't get 5% of the take. Along with the Irish gang's 25%, this would amount to a forced taking of almost a third of the money. Wolf declared that he was going on a trip to see what other prospects were on the horizon.

He bought a special circle train ticket that took him through the heartland to the Mississippi from St. Louis to Minneapolis/St. Paul and back again through the upper Midwest.

***

Wolf called a family meeting. Remarkably, his English was very much improved. "Mein family. This city is no place to be. I have decided that we move. We will go to Louisville in six months. I have sold this place to the General Holding Corporation, GHC, and they will employ our Swen and a bookkeeper to run the operation. We will have in Louisville our own store and vill not have to pay these extraordinary gang/police taxes."

"When do we move?" asked Frederica.

"Around June. I have to get things ready."

"But we make a lot of money here," began James.

"You forget zee taxes to police and thugs."

"But why should we bother about the taxes if we make enough money?" replied James.

Then Wolf cuffed James on the head. "You are really a dumkopft. We want what is ours. Why should we share it?"

What neither Frederica nor James asked about was who the General Holding Corporation was. If they had, they would have discovered that its stock was solely owned by Wolf Sullowald. But because the shop was legally changing hands, the equity share in the shop that James (20%) and Frederica (10%) would have gained upon the completion of their probationary period was now forfeit: with only one and a half years to go. Now they had nothing. In the new store they would be employees only.

James looked at his two children. Their family net worth had declined and they had a jarring move ahead of them. In the process, James starting criticizing Wolf, but Frederica would have none of it. "Were you half the man he is we'd have our own house by now. Since you aren't, we must live as his slaves. He owns us."

"Well, he certainly owned *you*—maybe he still does," was James's reply.

Frederica turned and left without a word.

James sat down and picked up the paper and read that Charles Quincy had just died. He was seventy-two.

***

Wolf had purchased a building on West Magnolia near 3ʳᵈ Street. He came upon a real bargain because prices were still rock bottom after the Flood of 1890. The three-story structure afforded a central location near the park and the college and not too far of a walk to the Ohio River. The store was about twice as large as their Philadelphia establishment. This meant more retail space for a general store with popular sundry items. The new store would be called *The Owl* because they stayed open late. There was an intermediate level atop the store that Wolf rented to Frederica's family, and the top floor was all Wolf's. The staircase leading upstairs had two doors installed: the first a hollow core door with a flimsy lock to protect the O'Neil's. The door to Wolf's level was a metal door with a slide bolt lock that went three inches into solid oak to protect the privacy of Wolf. Wolf also had a fire escape installed for himself that retracted to the top floor and could only be lowered by someone on the top floor.

The clerking duties in the new store design separated the general retail sales from the pharmacy. Wolf hired a fifteen-year-old boy, Niall Mullins, to run the retail sales. Niall was a Welsh-Irish lad whose father had recently died in a factory accident. Niall and his brother, Rory, had taken to work to support the family. Rory had taken the job his father had in the factory. (And after five years, Rory lost his left hand in a work-related accident and with his hand he also lost his job.)

***

By the beginning of July, Wolf, James, Frederica, and the children had moved in to the new place in Louisville. Except for a few trunks, Wolf left their old furniture in Philadelphia. He rented out the upper floor to Swen (the chemist that James had trained) and Max (an immigrant from Bavaria who was a trained accountant). An outside firm of Schmidt and Steinhoff was retained to audit the books every three months.

It was meant to be a clean start. The beginning was to be of a new life away from the claustrophobic East Coast. This was truly one of the frontiers of America, thought Wolf. If he could make things go here, he had some relatives from Oberhausen who might like to start another shop in St. Louis (where Wolf *almost* had moved the clan). The basic idea was to change the concept of shopping from a small specialized shop, like a chemist shop, into a more general store where one could purchase a wide variety of goods from cloth, to hats, to shoes, and a variety of miscellaneous sundries that were positioned in a cubbyhole shelving system that was behind the counter and ran to the ceiling. A ladder, that was moveable on a track, allowed Niall to navigate to the appropriate spot to locate needles or thread or yarn. Prices were set. There was no bargaining. From the perspective of someone entering the shop, she might think that the pharmacy business was a small sideline. The percentage devoted to Niall's space covered 90% of the visible area. But when Frederica tallied up the profits, 90% came from the drug trade. Wolf kept the general store prices low to draw in customers, but charged top dollar for the narcotics. Limited credit was allowed in the general store, but the 'in God we trust' motto was applied to the chemist counter.

Business boomed. The general store brought in customers on account of its prices and selection. It branded the store as being principally about notions and dry goods. But then gradually customers would migrate to the far corner and consider the house-prepared patent medicine, cocaine, laudanum, and morphine.

One day in 1895 at the christening of James's third child, Catherine, Niall brought a little doll as a present. The doll was made of a wooden core with layers of cloth wrapped around for softness. It was dressed like a little girl with a red and white checked frock over a white dress. The face was painted in bright colors with enamel.

After Mass at the St. Louis Bertrand Church, Niall made a point of presenting his gift to little Catherine. Of course the infant was oblivious to the whole event, but Frederica quickly took the present and thanked their office mate.

The party went to the noon-day dinner that Wolf was throwing for family and business associates at Mrs. Toll's Chop House. Wolf had rented a back room and a two-course meal for thirty. Niall was invited.

Niall happened to sit next to the left of James while Frederica and baby Catherine were on the right. The fare was beef and cabbage with jacket potatoes.

"So, the family is okay, I guess. At least with the death of Papa, we won't have any more children to support," said Niall.

"You have six in the family, eh?" asked James, who had few times to chat with his office mate even though they had been working together for two years. Niall was all business. When he was at work he wanted to immerse himself in that world. James was the same way. It was as if they became different people when they signed in at the time log each morning. It was to them a profanation of their working roles to discourse familiarly while the store was open. Thus, when they were alone together at a table filled with guests, the opportunity arose to speak in a different voice.

"Yeah, seven if you count my mother. But Rory, me brother, and I make the whole thing work. It isn't easy. We often have to find a way to cheat at the corners, if you know what I mean." Niall laughed. James laughed, too (but he didn't know why). Irish blokes just like to minimize conflict whenever possible (though sometimes conflict rears its ugly head).

James took a fork to his last potato and finished his glass of beer. It had been a grand day. Wolf paid the bill and the party exited the restaurant. Niall clumsily bumped into a recently vacated table, knocking over a glass which he quickly turned up as he consolidated the change that had been left on the table: all in one smooth move that sinisterly transferred the receipts to his left hand as deftly as a magician. No one was the wiser—at least that was what Niall thought.

When the O'Neil's arrived home, James decided to walk to his favorite view of the world: the Big Four Railroad Bridge that went across the Ohio River. James could gain access via a service ladder and walk on the emergency walkway to about half-way where he would gaze at the motion of the mighty river. Its motions captivated him and stimulated feelings of pity and fear.

***

As the O'Neil clan continued to grow, the celebrations became fewer. Mollie (1898) was feted, but not Ruth (1901) nor Ellen (1905) nor Jeanette (1908). There was a large celebration for Gertrude (1910) that corresponded with Wolf opening a department store in St. Louis. The idea of a department store was a gigantic general store that offered as many goods as all the local stores put together. The concept had been pioneered via large physical stores by luminaries such as Sears and Roebuck. Wolf Sullowald wanted to see how far he could go. The new store in St. Louis only had a very small chemist's window. The business model was changing.

When Doris O'Neil was born on March 25th in 1912, Wolf was in Chicago negotiating a new deal. Niall was now working very long hours, spelling Frederica from her accounting duties now that the family was expanding. His own siblings were now on their own, so Niall had no one to account for except himself. He lived frugally and gave James and Frederica reason to know that he was a man to be reckoned with.

They went to Mrs. Toll's just as they had for Catherine (the first child to be born to the O'Neil's in Louisville). The party was small, just James and Frederica and their eight children—along with Niall, the host.

Doris had been born with a caul. During the baptism, the priest was delivering the "salt of wisdom" to the child. Doris chomped down on the priest's finger and ingested immediately all of the salt (instead of one or two grains that the service called for). When the child was walked up and down the aisles of the cathedral by the priest, the baby raised its arms as if it were acknowledging the applause that welcomed the new child into the bosom of Christ.

At the restaurant, Doris would occasionally wail in order to remind the group whose occasion this was! When the group was on to dessert, Niall leaned over to Frederica. "I have to be gone for two weeks on a trip. It is of vital importance that I leave. I need you to cover for me in the store."

"But I've been phasing out of working at the store. I barely work ten hours a week anymore and you work sixty. I don't see how this can be possible. I also have to look after this bawling brat."

"Look, hire a girl to help you for two weeks. I'll pay the cost out of my pocket."

Frederica pursed her lips and tilted her head. These were the sorts of power words that captivated her. Of course she'd accept. But before she said 'yes,' Doris set forth a plaintive cry of her own. When the deal was done, so was Doris. The baby fell asleep.

The two-week trip ended on schedule. Niall was a changed man. He had new energy and scheduled a meeting at the *Lucky Seven* (a local bar) with James.

The *Lucky Seven* was one large room with the bar to one side and small square tables on the other. The tables could be shifted so that more people could sit together. There was also one long table that sat ten. The dark-stained pinewood floor was covered with sawdust in case patrons exceeded their limit before they could make it to the toilet.

The bar served light food (nothing cooked), draft beer, and the area's famous bourbon whiskey. Niall and James sat down at one of the small square tables in the far corner of the room. Niall was in a generous mood and he ordered two bourbon whiskeys and some peanuts. The bar had electric lighting but was still quite dim, even though it was late April. When the drinks and peanuts arrived, Niall looked down and began shelling the nuts at a furious pace: crack, snap, pop into palm, drop shells onto floor, wash it down with whiskey. Niall was on his third whiskey before he presented his marvelous vision. "St. Paul, Minnesota, James. It's really the place to be. It is populated by Germans and Irish. And what are you?" Niall made a light laugh.

"You'd love it. They have streetcars that will take you anywhere in St. Paul or over to Minneapolis (that's where the Swedes and Norwegians live). It is a booming urban center. The future is in St. Paul."

James tilted his head and took his third sip of his first whiskey. Then he took his first peanut and carefully broke the shell and awkwardly decimated the shell to procure the two fruits of his labor. For a moment, James considered removing the thin brown skin that covered the prize, but decided he'd just go for it and swallowed them, skin and all. "Are you telling me this, Niall, because you are planning on leaving the store?"

Niall finished his drink and leaned forward on the table so that he was only eighteen inches from James's nose. "Damn straight, my boy. I'm cutting out, but I want *you* to come with me."

"Me?" James dropped the peanut in his hand upon the floor.

"Yes," said Niall, signaling for another drink. "I've got enough money to set down a deposit on the property near the corner of Snelling Avenue and University, but I need you to help me with the cash to stock the place and your expertise with the pharmacy to mix and sell the patent medicines that could make the place a gold mine that you and I share in, *without* Wolf."

James started to choke, even though there was nothing in his throat. He finished off his first drink. Niall ordered him another with a wave of his left hand. James shut his eyes and tried to see what was proposed. When the second drink arrived, James was oblivious to it. "You mean that you've put down a deposit on a property that could contain a general store with a pharmacy and that you want me to be your partner?"

Niall reached out his hand and grasped James's left hand. James opened his eyes.

"Is it a deal?" inquired Niall.

James looked out at the street through the plate glass window that was darkened according to local ordinance. But darkened or not, James saw the light of hope, and he committed his fate to a bargain with Niall.

James then walked alone to the Big Four Railroad Bridge to look out at his future.

***

"You did WHAT?" screamed Frederica. They were in bed together. It was one of the new metal spring mattress beds that was so much more comfortable than the beds they had previously had.

"Yes, we have to separate ourselves from Wolf. He takes everything for himself while we do all the work. It isn't fair. Now we have a chance to make real money."

"But what if we fail? Wolf has so much that he can look after us."

"Yes, as his slaves. Do *you* want to be a slave? I don't. I can tell you that. My father came to this land because Ireland was dying. He wanted to define his *own* future. That is the Dream. Well, if we live under Wolf, then it's just like the old world. It's not like America." Then James moved to his wife and pulled up her nightgown. "We've got to make it, Ticky. Now is the time." And that was the time, as they consummated the deal.

***

On July 4th, 1912, James O'Neil and Niall opened their store, *The Peoples' Store*, near to the corner of Snelling Avenue and University. The O'Neils rented a house with the option to buy on Thomas Avenue only a few blocks away. The house was a white frame house with a wrap-around front porch.

Marie took a job at the store. James Jr. decided that he wanted a job in construction. Since the town was booming, there was plenty of work. Catherine stayed at home and took in mending clothes from an advert at the Church of the Assumption (that was far enough away to prevent weekly attendance at Mass). Mollie was somewhat addle-headed and took on the chore of looking after

Jeanette, Gertrude, and Doris. Ruth and Ellen enrolled at St. Luke's School on Summit Avenue.

On the train ride up to St. Paul, Frederica frequently took her husband to the smoking car so that they could hash out just what had happened. Wolf had been glum when James told him his plan. But he didn't hit the ceiling. Wolf was opening a new store in Chicago and was now in the employment management business. He really didn't need James or Frederica any longer. Indeed, because they were family and might call on him to act contrary to strict business practices (beneficial to himself), he was now totally free to run things the way he really wanted to.

Wolf had three stores in Philadelphia, Louisville, and St. Louis (all under the official name of the General Holding Corporation). He was ready to open a store in Chicago and planned on another in Cleveland. There was no limit to Wolf's ambitions. He even owned farms that were largely dedicated to poppy production in the United States for opium and morphine, and a plantation in Brazil that produced coca leaves for cocaine. This cut his costs down enormously. Wolf had opened a manufacturing plant in New Orleans several years before that really lessened his need for someone like James, who had apprenticed in mixing drugs.

Yes, Wolf really rather enjoyed James and his wife moving to St. Paul, but Frederica didn't see things that way. She ushered her husband to her favorite abode, the smoking car. It was a car like no other. It was largely inhabited by well-to-do types who also bought drinks at the bar. At the far end of the car was a door that opened up to a small platform that was surrounded by guardrails. One could look back on the track they had just passed: it was a window to where the train had been. Generally the platform was free, but at other times the brakeman would go there to hang out.

At this moment in time, Frederica was well into a harangue against her husband. They were seated in a plush double seat, but Frederica made sure that each party sat as far as possible from each other. The room was half-full. A steward came by and asked James if he wanted a drink. Frederica declined for both of them. She then produced a cigarette case that James never knew about. It was silver with an inscription that James couldn't read. She lit her cigarette with a wooden match that she kept in the small pocket on her vest. After the first three long drafts, she exclaimed, "You dick head, *was machts?*"

"Don't give me any of that German crap," replied James. "You're in America now."

"Do you know how rich Wolf is becoming? He could take care of us forever."

"Has he ever offered? I see that your cigarette case has an inscription. Is that also from him?"

"None of your business."

"For services rendered?"

Frederica slapped James. In the process, her cigarette fell to the floor. She watched the burning embers for a moment before snuffing them out. "You are so stupid. Why would you walk away from a man who could have guaranteed permanent success for your family? Why is it so *important* to make it on your own? This sounds like a little child trying to learn how to use the toilet. It makes no sense for an adult."

James did not reply. He lit a cigarette from a paper package in his breast pocket. When he had inhaled the smoke, he offered one to Frederica. She refused and left the car.

James decided to smoke his cigarette on the rear platform of the train. He opened the door and looked backward. The vision of the past frightened him. He swayed in a brisk gust of wind. The cool mist of the evening mixed with the sweat on his skin. He held on tight with both hands to the metal supports of the short deck on the last car. The tendons in his gaunt arms rose up. *Then his right shoulder began to twitch. He tried to grip tighter. And then it began to rain.*

***

The transition into their new home went smoothly. They only shipped their cherished items. Wolf owned most of the stuff, anyway. He would let his next cadre of hired help use it for their tenure. So when the O'Neil's first moved into their rented house, it was rather bare. First on the agenda was to procure beds to sleep in. With nine children, this was no easy matter. Luckily all but one were female (so that they could share beds), but before the bed purchases the strategy was lots and lots of blankets on the floor.

Once their basic furniture problems were solved, Frederica immediately took to St. Paul. She appreciated the German neighborhood into which they moved. It was a mixed neighborhood with Bavarian Germans (Catholic) and northwestern Germans (like

Frederica) who were Baptist. Up until that point in their married life, Frederica had attended Catholic Mass and taken communion. But she was always uncomfortable. Her new surroundings gave her new courage to speak out against the Papist mumbo jumbo to her friends and her children. The older children, Marie, James, Jr. and Catherine would have none of it, but Frederica had a sympathetic ear from the younger girls (Mollie, Ruth, Ellen, and Jeanette) who chafed under the nuns' strict discipline at St. Luke's parochial school.

Niall and James employed Wolf's business model, creating *The People's Store* as a general store with a small pharmacy attached. As it had been with Wolf, there was no emphasis upon the scientific Galenic medical principles but instead upon the popular drugs (laudanum, morphine, and cocaine) with the addition of hemp extract that was increasingly in demand with the clientele. It was marketed as a health food.

The first two years went exceedingly well. The money was pouring in and James bought the family house they had been renting. Then one day in 1914, soon after their second son, Andrew, was born (March 13th, a Friday), Wolf came calling. He was met by his niece, Frederica.

"Oh Wolf, what a surprise," she said as she opened the door and beheld her uncle. Wolf smiled. "May I come in?" he inquired. Frederica blushed and stepped aside from her position blocking the doorway. In his hand, Wolf was carrying a small leather handbag. Frederica showed her uncle into the parlor. Wolf sat down on their new blue damask-covered divan.

Frederica sat in a wooden rocking chair that had belonged to her father, Klaus. "So, what brings you to St. Paul?"

"What brings me to St. Paul, you ask? I read in the newspaper (you know, I have a subscription to the *St. Paul Dispatch*) that you had another child. It is a son and that he would be baptized tomorrow. I got onto the first train I could. I was hoping to take the clan to a restaurant, like Mrs. Toll's back in Louisville."

"Why that is very friendly of you, Wolf. Why we'd be delighted. There is a restaurant we rather like, *Oberhausen Haus*. It's only a short walk from here. Well, of course, I like the name!" Wolf and Frederica laughed at the restaurant named after their hometown in Germany.

"When does James get home?" asked Wolf.

"Oh, around nine. This area has long hours: eight to eight. Of course, his hours are a little longer at each end."

"And you're no longer involved in the business?"

"No. Niall does the books and supply ordering. There is nothing really for me to do there. Marie works there, you know. She's got strong legs."

Wolf laughed, "That's one advantage for the big family. Put them to work for free."

"Well, they *do* get room and board."

"Spoiled kids, these days."

They both laughed.

"Do you suppose that James would mind if I stopped by the shop?"

"Of course not. Why don't I take your bag? You can sleep in our bed."

"Okay. I hope that doesn't put you out?"

"Of course not. We're younger than you. We're happy to make you comfortable."

***

James and Frederica were fifty-four and forty-four, respectively. Wolf was sixty-four. James didn't like the arrangements. The two were standing in the kitchen of their home. James muttered in audible tones as he turned away from his wife, "The man's got enough money to buy his own hotel to sleep in. Why does he always want to sleep in my bed?"

"Always?" replied Frederica incredulously.

***

When the baptism and christening were completed at the Cathedral of the Assumption on the other side of town, the party returned to a special room of the *Oberhausen Haus*. Niall was invited but he couldn't make it.

As they sat around the table, Wolf tried to talk to each of his grand-nieces. He particularly took a liking to thirteen-year-old Ruth. She was a very practical girl. Ruth told a story from school: *There was a young maiden in Germany. She was engaged to a boy from a wealthy family. The boy had given her a very expensive engagement ring with diamonds and precious stones carefully* laid. *After the wedding ceremony, the couple was walking to their new home. On the way, they were accosted by a robber who wanted to steal from them. The robber pulled out a long knife and held it to her husband's throat as the robber demanded her expensive ring. Then the maiden looked about and lifted a large piece of wood with a nail sticking out of it. The robber told her to drop it or he would kill her husband. She struck first, hitting the robber with quite a blow. The robber's knife slit the bridegroom's throat even as he tumbled to the ground. Both men died. Now Sister Mary-Katherine asked us whether the bride acted wisely. Most of the class said, 'no' but I said, 'yes' because a husband will die on you some time anyway, but a beautiful ring will last forever!*

Wolf clapped (as did Frederica). James scowled.

***

The real reason that Wolf had come to St. Paul was to first inform James and Niall of the Harrison Tax Act that was being debated in Congress. If it were enacted, the sorts of profitable drugs that they had been selling as patent medicine and the like full of cocaine, morphine, opium, and hemp extract would be made unviable via the tax laws. An era of making money was over.

"What if we sold it on the sly?" inquired Niall.

Wolf peered at Niall. "Of course you could, but if they found out that you didn't pay your taxes properly, they could confiscate all you own to pay the taxes."

Niall smiled. "You're right. Of course that's too much of a gamble for anyone to take."

Wolf nodded. The two men understood each other.

***

Wolf's next move was to attempt to buy into their operation. With the new law, they'd need new lines of business to make up for the lost revenue. Wolf was prepared to help. His new store had opened the year before in Chicago. It was a big success, and Minneapolis-St. Paul was a logical next step. Niall said they needed to think it over. When they did, a month later, the answer was 'no.'

This resolution did not go over so well with Frederica. "If our income stream is going to change, we need capital to make up the difference or we'll become bankrupt."

"But Wolf's not to be trusted. Look what he did to both of our shares of the business in Philadelphia. That man is a crook. I took a deep breath of relief when we moved up here to run a clean operation with people we can trust."

"Wolf is family. If we were ever up against it, he wouldn't let us down. I know he'd look after us."

James shook his head, "Humph. A real considerate guy he is; he'd screw every one of us if he thought it would make him happy."

"At least he's wealthy."

"Yeah. Tell it to Ruth."

***

For two years, Niall tried to ease their dependence upon the newly-taxed drugs by selling them clandestinely to their regular customers after closing time in the back parking lot. Niall's rule was never to sell to anyone new (they could be revenue agents). If the client list decreased, then so be it. To compensate himself for the added risk, Niall and James agreed that Niall's split would be 75% and James's 25%.

They started selling more clothes and shoes. The pharmacy took on a new line with aspirin and cough medicines that James created with trace amounts of codeine (a legal drug). These were popular, especially among mothers with small children.

The store wasn't as profitable as it had been. But they were paying their bills and putting a little aside.

***

Andrew and Doris were a pair. They were two years apart in age and seemed to have a mystical bond between them. In 1916, when Andrew was two and Doris was four, the latter used to take Andrew on walks around the yard. There were more and more motor cars, so Frederica made Doris promise not to take the toddler into the street. She did not want her children to be run down by the obnoxious, four-wheeled joy riding machines, as Frederica liked to call them.

When the young pair needed a chaperone, it was always Ellen. As it is in most large families, the middle children raise the younger children after the parents lose their energy.

Catherine and Mollie enrolled in secretary school to learn shorthand and bookkeeping (Mollie lasted only a couple of months before she dropped out). Ruth, Ellen, Jeanette, and Gertrude were still at St. Luke's parochial school.

The odd one out was James, Jr. On August 1st, he confronted his parents with some important news. It was 9:30 pm. James had been late at the store.

Frederica and James, Jr. were in the kitchen. James was eating the dinner that the family had consumed two hours before. His wife lit a candle, poured him a glass of beer, and gave him his meat and potatoes that had been kept warm (though now hard and chewy). James Jr. had made his entrance when his father was half done. He glided into the room and turned a dark-oak spindle-back chair around so that he could rest his chin on the back of it. Then he told his parents that he had enlisted in the army.

It was Frederica who reacted first by standing up and screaming, "YOU DID WHAT?"

"I enlisted in the army, Mom. I'm going to serve my country."
"You dunderhead," she replied, and tried to slap James, Jr.'s head, but he was too quick for her. He grabbed her arm and pulled her over with one arm, and twisted the chair to its normal position with the other so that she sat in his lap. With his right hand, James Jr. began stroking his mother's long, curly auburn hair.

"It's going to be all right, Mom. Look, I'm twenty-four. I've never caught on to what I want to do, and so I thought that this would be the perfect opportunity. I could make a break with my past and find out who I really am."

"And you need to make a break from your mother who gave you birth?"

"It's nothing against either you or Dad. It's something everyone has to do: to take personal responsibility for one's life." Frederica still had a scowl on her face. James, Jr. continued. "Look, Mom, *you* made a break when your father took you to the United States when you were ten. You made another break when you moved to Louisville and then to St. Paul—"

"—That was your father's idea."

"But you went along with it. You could have stayed with your uncle, but you kept with the family. We made a change and bought our first house and have a stake in our own business. It's the American way."

There was a pause in which Frederica kissed her son on the forehead. Then she was overcome with emotion and hugged him harder than he expected and almost toppled the chair.

"I have to tell you my fear; my brother Johann was just a young boy when he joined the army. They sent him to Togo where he was killed in an uprising. He was seventeen—two years older than I was. He refused to go to America. He stayed in Germany. Wolf raised him then and took care of him." Then Frederica lifted her gaze to the ceiling. She was somewhere else, "The young men, they are so stupid. They fertilize the graveyards."

James, Jr. chuckled, "That won't happen to me, Mother. Look, we aren't at war and we've all been reading in the papers how President Wilson is putting his reputation and his re-election on staying out of the European war. The only thing that could happen to me is to get my thumb caught in the breech of a gun during target practice."

"He's right, you know," repeated James. "Wilson promised we'd never go to war. And I think he's a man of his word."

Frederica shot a gaze at her husband and then spat on the floor and stepped on it with her shoe, twisting the spittle into the wood. "When did the word of a politician ever mean *anything*? I don't want my son to go into the army. I want him to live."

"Mother, it's my destiny. I know it is."

"That's what I'm afraid of."

***

A year later, America did enter the war. James, Jr. was among the first to deploy since he was fully trained and had already risen to the rank of corporal. Mail took a long time from the front. But Frederica and James, separately, hung on news of the war. Frederica started clipping articles from the newspaper that she intended to put into a scrapbook.

Together, the couple began attending the movie houses to watch the newsreels that ran between the films. They saw footage of fighting, of gas attacks, of barbed wire, trenches, and terrible new engines of war. It was more than either of them could stand. After the newsreel, they often left the theater (skipping one or both of the movies). James rued his earlier cavalier attitude about the army, but he couldn't tell his wife that.

On June 9th of 1918, Marie announced that she had accepted the marriage proposal of Harold Stevenson, a deliveryman (to the store) who was also a carpenter. Just as in the case with James, Jr., the news was communicated in the kitchen when James was eating his cold, hardened dinner. Frederica threw her arms around her twenty-eight year old daughter. "Oh, Marie, that's wonderful!"

"Is this the same Harold who makes deliveries to the store?"

Marie nodded. She was still in the grasp of her mother.

"How can he afford to keep you on his salary?"

"Oh, Harold also earns money from the furniture he makes. He's such a handy carpenter." Frederica hugged Marie and the two of them giggled.

James edged forward in his chair. "I've barely said, boo to this guy. How do we know he's square?"

Frederica shot a glance at James. There was fire in her eyes, "Our lovely *twenty-eight* year old daughter is mature enough to think for herself. I trust her judgment entirely."

James scowled. Then Ruth came to the doorway of the kitchen. She was all aglow and wanted to share her happiness over her impending graduation from high school the next day. She was the first of the O'Neil children to do so. She was very proud. James got up and left.

***

Ruth graduated and immediately got a job at the local patent office in Minneapolis. Marie was married in a simple ceremony five weeks later and moved in to her husband's apartment just off Hennepin Avenue in downtown Minneapolis.

Catherine had to put aside her home sewing and mending business to work in the shop in the place of Marie. It wasn't long before she met a customer who took a fancy to her and proposed within a month. The lad's name was Krister Bykvist and he sold automobiles with his father in St. Paul.

The ceremony on October 1st was more lavish than Marie's. The groom's family seemed to have some extra cash to burn on the proceedings that included a reception afterwards with abundant food and refreshment.

***

Mollie was the next in the shop but she was plainer and less mentally acute than her sisters. Neither customers nor deliverymen made advances to her, and at church socials she generally clung to her younger siblings for comfort.

***

Then there was terrific news on the war front. Several specific victories were taking place, culminating in the German's general surrender in a railway car in the town of Compiègne in North East France. The day was one of celebration in the O'Neil household. James went out of character and purchased food for a family banquet, complete with wine and two buckets of beer. Marie and Catherine, along with their husbands, were of course invited to fête the end of the *War to end all Wars*. There were also cakes and sweets for the children: Ellen, Jeannette, Gertrude, Doris, and little Andrew.

The family awaited a letter from James telling of his date of arrival. These things didn't happen overnight. It could take six months to return home from the war zone. In their last letter from James, he had been fighting in the northeast of France near to where the Armistice was signed.

***

Three months went by and there was no news. As each week went by in the early months of 1919, the parents became more anxious. One Sunday morning before Mass, the family was eating pancakes around the table. Little Doris wasn't eating a thing.

"What's the matter, Doris? Don't you want your food? I'll take it if you don't want it," intoned Frederica.

Doris didn't respond.

Frederica grabbed the six-year old's head and twisted it so that she was looking at her mother. "Did you hear me, child? When I talk to you I expect a response."

"You won't like it," was Doris's reply.

"You let *me* be the judge of that, young lady. Now you tell me why you aren't eating."

"A dream, Mommy. I had a bad dream. It took away my appetite."

"Now you tell me your dream, you silly child. Dreams mean nothing."

"I won't do it."

Frederica then slapped her child across the face. The impact of hand on flesh made a sharp snap. James started from his chair and moved to his youngest daughter.

"Doris, can you write down what happened in your dream on a piece of paper and then you can be excused?"

Doris looked into her father's eyes for an extended interval and then nodded. Her father got a pencil and some foolscap. Doris hovered over her writing, folded the paper, and flew out of the room.

James unfolded the paper for all to see:

I dreamed my brother died in the War. It was real.

The next week the family received notice that James, Jr. had indeed died in the war not twelve miles from where the Armistice was signed—*two days after the war had ended.*

Frederica was stone faced. "I'm going to punish that child."

James tried to hug his wife, but she would have none of it.

"Doris didn't do this. Some German bullet did it," said James.

Frederica left the house for eight hours.

***

The death of James, Jr. affected everyone in the family. Frederica bought herself a twin-sized bed that she decided to sleep in on the far side of the bedroom. Communication between the couple came to a standstill. Frederica even started attending the local Baptist Church instead of the Church of the Assumption. The war in Europe was over but the war on Thomas Avenue was well underway.

Business was declining. The clothes and notions were down a bit. The tonic pills, aspirin, tooth powder, toothache soap, and James's herbal concoctions were very slow selling. Niall even claimed that the other shadow drug business was off. James was skeptical, but he didn't want to stick around after hours to find out.

Then there was the outbreak of the Spanish Flu. James created an aspirin-based herbal syrup that would help with the severe fever and relieve chest congestion. He labeled it "Flu Away." It was selling faster than he could manufacture it. Frederica encouraged James to bring Wolf in. He had a manufacturing plant in New Orleans and could meet their supply needs. James turned instead to a lead obtained from Catherine's husband, Krister Bykvist. Krister's uncle also ran a factory in Mankato, Minnesota. The distance was shorter and James felt as if he could trust Krister.

The effects of the flu were very severe. It was the battle after the War—a battle that incurred many causalities. But for *The People's Store* it was salvation. They were able to pay off the note on the store and put themselves into a three-month positive capital position (an emergency fund). Niall and James even gave themselves bonuses.

***

In 1921, Otto Munson approached Ruth O'Neil one day on her job at the patent office. He wanted to submit a patent to modify the dial phone and to link it to another patent he had pending on telephone switching. If successful, this new patent would interface with the other and allow mechanical calling and begin to eliminate the need for operators to connect telephone calls. Ruth took Otto's application and processed it according to the normal procedure.

Otto was German, from Berlin. He had served in World War I on the American side. He was very much anxious about his patent, so Otto took to visiting the patent office once a week. He finally decided to ask the attractive Ruth O'Neil to lunch. Otto was tall and thin. He possessed a high and ample forehead and slightly receding hairline (though he was just thirty years old). There was no hint of an accent in his speech, and he affected a suave nature that included a gold-plated cigarette case. Otto lived only a half-mile away in a house with his mother—she had a small amount of money from her husband's life insurance and his bank account. Otto lived meanly with few extravagances. He made side money doing various odd jobs as they came up. (He had a spend-thrift brother who lived in Minneapolis who had been kicked out of the house by his mother for frivolous spending habits.)

Ruth accepted his invitation and every other invitation that occurred weekly. Otto wondered whether Ruth had it in her power to speed his patent application along. Otto asked solicitous questions about the O'Neil family. Ruth answered in a fashion that exaggerated the positive points—such as family wealth, and ignored the bad points—such as the family war between her parents.

Otto began to become intrigued. He initially started asking Ruth to lunch in order to expedite his patent application, but he now found that he was falling in love with Ruth. Her practical way suited his own nature. Soon, Otto was taking Ruth out to the movie houses on the weekends. They would take public transportation. Otto met James and Frederica, and Ruth met Otto's mother, Frieda. Otto's strategy paid off. Ruth did everything she could as a mid-level clerk in the regional patent office to move Otto's claim along. On October 15th, 1922 Otto Munson's patents were approved in almost record time. Otto bought a train ticket to New York to talk to the people at the Bell Telephone Company.

Otto rode coach and stayed at the YMCA. He made his pitch, but was careful about not revealing too many details (even though he had two patents from the U.S. Patent Office). Six months later, Otto received a telegram summoning him again to New York—this time at company expense. He rode first class and stayed at the Waldorf-Astoria Hotel. When he returned home, he held in his hand a cashier's check for one million dollars!

Otto kept to himself for a few days. He deposited his money in the bank. He then went to the library to check out books on stock investing. Otto was a very thorough man. When he felt ready, he showed up at the patent office and asked Ruth whether he could come by for her on Saturday. It was their routine, so she agreed. Otto then went out and bought a new Packard Twin-Six automobile painted in yellow (instead of the standard black).

Otto Munson pulled up in his new car and fancy clothes in front of the O'Neil's place on Thomas Avenue. He was transformed. Frederica, Mollie, Ellen, Jeanette, and Gertrude greeted the new millionaire. They all scampered out to look at the fancy new car as they listened to his story of success. They wanted to touch the shiny yellow finish. (Doris and Andrew listened from an open window in the attic where they had been playing. It was Andrew's bedroom.) James went outside but stayed on their front porch and watched from afar. James was in shock. Frederica was in heaven. She had always wanted to live in Berlin.

Ruth went out with her beau for a spin in the car and she came back engaged. Nobody was surprised nor upset. The couple took an eleven-month honeymoon in Europe—mostly in Germany, Switzerland, and Italy. Before they left, Otto made some strategic stock investments based upon insider information. When he returned in July of 1924, he found himself a richer man than when he had departed. Otto continued to wheel and deal for three years in the stock market and then transferred half of his money into a lifetime annuity with Aetna Insurance, and he put the remainder of his cash into U.S. government bonds.

***

On August 1st, 1924 James O'Neil came back from the bank and re-opened the store. He had a small crowd waiting and he accommodated them with the help of his daughter, Mollie. When they closed the shop at 8:00, James told Mollie to go home alone. He had to reconcile a few things. Niall had stolen 75% of the money in the store. James could go to the police. But then people would find out that the store was in trouble and they would no longer go there. James had established an emergency fund that would cover three months of expenses. It was in his name, and his trip to the bank verified that the account was intact.

The only way that James might be able to get out of this jam was a quick infusion of money. Perhaps he could sell the illegal drugs that Niall had been dealing? Those clients were due to come around 10pm. James kept all the highly regulated drugs in a special safe in the back that only he and Niall had the combination for. James went back and found that most—but not all—of the stash was gone. James decided to wait until 10pm.

The back lot of the store stood for deliveries and parking for those few patrons who owned cars. There was one street light that came on just after 9:30. James kept a gaze out the window. He saw no one. Then just before 10 he saw someone walk up and stand in the lot. It was a policeman. Niall's operation had been found out. James sat in the back until midnight—waiting. The cop stayed until 11, but no one came by.

When James returned home, there was no one waiting up for him. Frederica was in her bed, snoring away. James lay down atop his bed in his clothes and tried to relax. Around two, he went down to eat cold, hard dinner. There wasn't much left.

James could go to the bank for a loan, but then he'd have to expose his terrible financial condition. No one would lend to him.

Anyone who was honest could see that his business was heading for bankruptcy. That shut out taking out his hat for handouts from Catherine's or Ruth's husbands. James had a ten-thousand-dollar life insurance policy, but the cash value was less than a thousand. That wouldn't do. The only hope was Wolf.

James got up and went to the kitchen to pour himself a cup of cold coffee and presently went to sleep, slumped over in his chair. In the morning, Frederica came down. James told her what had happened. She agreed that going to Wolf was the only answer. Jeanette, Mollie, Gertrude, and Frederica would work the shop. James bought a train ticket to Louisville.

Wolf knew that James was coming. Frederica had telegrammed him of the facts of the case. When James arrived at his office, Wolf seemed very friendly. "Come in. Won't you sit down?" James did so. Wolf lit a cigar.

"So you've found out that without your uncle-in-law, you're a total failure."

"My partner stole from me."

"I knew he was a crook from the time he worked here. You know I've been selling him illegal drugs for years from my plant in New Orleans."

"You have? I thought that he was only selling what we legally purchased for prescription and which we were adulterating and selling short."

"No. He threw that shit away. I gave him top quality crap. The kind I use myself. No addict wants anything less. He was doing fine until the police caught on. He got away one step before the law."

James had been cheated even more than he had realized. His 25% was merely a payoff like the payoffs that they used to make in Philadelphia. But then why had Niall stolen profits from the legitimate business?

"You're a dumkopft, James. You don't check on your employees or your partners. They steal you blind. You'd have been gone a long time ago except you hire family. But Niall, he's a player. We did business since the baptism of your youngest boy, Andrew."

James weakly nodded his head.

"You're a chump, James. You're a loser in the competition of life. Who's that Englishman, Spencer? I think his name's Spencer, who said that life is a competition to see who is the fittest. Those who are, deserve to succeed. Those who aren't, deserve to fail. James, my boy, you are a loser."

"But you can give us a loan so that we can succeed."

"I *could*, but why should I?"

"We're family."

"You're not my family. You're a Mick."

"I'm married to your niece."

"That's her problem."

"I worked for you for twenty-seven years. You promised me a partnership to leave Charles Quincy, who had offered me his whole business if I'd waited for him to retire. I gave you *everything!*"

Wolf smiled and extinguished his cigar. "What can I say, James. You're a loser. You should have never listened to me. You had a better deal. That means that you're soft in the head. Why should I invest with a guy who's soft in the head? I think our interview is over. I want to go to dinner."

"Can I at least stay here for the night?" asked James.

"What do I look like, a hotel?"

***

And so it was over. James lugged his case as he walked to his cathedral of contemplation, the Big Four Railroad Bridge. It was early evening and time to decide what to do.

As James walked toward the bridge, he felt as if he were being followed. He stopped to buy a pack of cigarettes from a small wooden stand that carried newspapers, magazines, and smokes. "Say buddy," began James. "Can you watch out for me? I think I'm being followed. If you see the same thing, will you call the cops? I'm headed over to the Big Four Railroad Bridge for a smoke. I'll cross the street and back again to make it easier for you." James gave the man a dollar tip.

"Sure, buddy. For a dollar, I'll be your guardian angel."

***

James's body was found the next morning downstream near the old Fontaine Ferry pier. He had a gash on the back of his head.

Gangsters in Chicago gunned down Wolf Sullowald in 1932 as he was on his way to the World's Fair.

Niall Mullins choked to death on a piece of steak at a restaurant in Columbus, Ohio in 1937.

PART TWO

CHAPTER SEVEN

Oh Krishna, what satisfaction could we find in killing?
Chapter One, *Bhagavad Gita**

The news of the day: Japan wars on U.S. and Britain; makes sudden attack on Hawaii; heavy fighting at sea reported –Guam Bombarded; army ship is sunk.

Japanese force lands in Malta.

Lewis wins captive mine fight; arbitrators grant union shop.
The New York Times, Front page for December 8, 1941.

ANDREW O'Neil was in trouble. He had been talking to Moira about their fate. So much had been put on hold in the past: Moira's degree and his law school dreams. Events had not gone smoothly, but now they had saved enough for their aspirations to finally be realized. Andrew had drawn up a plan for next year, the fall of 1942, which made it all possible. All their waiting and working—first to get married, and second to realize their dreams and ambitions they nurtured at Macalester College. He was so full of his conversation that he didn't notice that he was almost out of gas! He knew the roads around Menomonie, Wisconsin well. After all, he was a traveling salesman. He knew of a station on Stout Road, but he wasn't sure he'd make it.

---

* *The Bhagavad Gita,* tr. Eknath Easwaran, (Tomales, CA: Nilgigi Press, 1985).

Luck was with him. He saw the trapezoid sign with the red letters: *Sinclair* and underneath, a little green brontosaurs. The '36 Willys Coup glided up to the slender gasoline pump that resembled an exotic dancer. Andrew parked his car and started pumping his gas. He could hear a loud radio in the office. Against his will he listened to the news:

The Japanese have bombed Pearl Harbor in a surprise and dastardly attack. The evil Japs have sunk at least nine American ships, including the Arizona. Thousands are presumed to be dead. It is the worst sneak attack ever against America by a foreign power. President Roosevelt is reportedly asking Congress for a declaration of war!

Andrew was riveted. He spilled some gasoline on the ground as he overfilled his tank. Then he acted in mechanical sequential order: (a) look at the cost, (b) get out your wallet, and (c) walk to the office.

The man in the office was a fat Norwegian with two weeks of beard on his face and a shirt that showed circular yellow-brown stains under the armpits. "It was a little over fifteen-gallons," said Andrew.

"Buck sixty-five," said the man as he set his stogie down on a derelict car mirror that served as his ashtray.

Andrew paid and left.

"What's the matter?" asked Moira when Andrew returned to the car.

Andrew turned to his wife of almost eighteen months: "It's a catastrophe, darling. They've bombed Pearl Harbor. They'll be calling to me to war—just like they called my brother, James. I'm going to war, and I'll probably be killed."

Moira burst into tears and hugged her husband to death.

***

There was a long silence as they drove back into Menomonie. Moira's gaze was to the right. Andrew was having trouble looking at anything. When they were almost home Moira asked Andrew, "By the way, where is Pearl Harbor?"

"Hawaii."

"But that's not in America."

"Colony."

"We're going to war over a colony?"

"U.S. warships were sunk. Many hundreds—maybe thousands of service men's lives have been lost. I predict war within a day. They already have a draft. I'm registered. They'll call me up, ship me off, and send me home in a box."

Moira began crying again. This time Andrew did, too.

***

When they arrived at their six-room rented house across from Wilson Park on 7th street, their Scottie dog, Chiltren, ran to greet them. There weren't many words spoken on the short trip from the gas station. Chiltren hopped up in the air, indicating that he wanted to be held. It was Moira that picked him up and gave him a kiss on his wet nose. They went inside and fed the dog. Neither Andrew nor Moira was hungry. They went to bed to read their books. After almost an hour, Andrew put down his book. He looked over to his wife with desire. He remembered when he had met Moira at Macalester College. Andrew had been a senior and Moira was a freshman. Andrew was the captain of the debating team and president of the pre-law society, NOMOS. They officially met at a university dance. It was a Saturday night in the fall term near harvest time in October, the last Saturday of the month. The dance was a mixer in which most people came without partners; *stag* they used to call it. The dance was held in the gym whose interior was built as a square. The square could be described this way: one side of the square had the doors; opposite the doors was the stage where the band was playing; perpendicular to this plane was the side of the gymnasium where the women stood in their full dresses and on the other side were the men dressed in dark suits and ties. There was no smoking in the gym. The band was playing "Cheek to Cheek" and the boys started advancing to the opposite wall.

Andrew saw the rail-thin girl who had read at the poetry reading. She had a pure expression on her face that reminded him of his departed sister, Doris. He immediately picked up his pace and asked her to dance. Their first dance was "Begin the Beguine." Andrew was a very imaginative dancer—though he had had no training. Moira was very agile and could make up for Andrew's excesses. In short, they both had a good time. They danced every number until the notes of the closing song, "Blue Moon," had been sent into the night.

After the dance, they went to a coffee shop for some java and an ice cream cone.

They finished their desserts around midnight, but continued talking until closing time at two. Andrew walked Moira back to her dormitory. "I'm going to get detention points for being out after one on a weekend, but I don't care a single bit," said Moira.

Andrew smiled, opened the door and watched his date report in to the dorm monitor.

***

Andrew couldn't wait until he could ask Moira out again. The system at the college was that young men could write notes to young women in a dormitory via the dorm monitor who sat at a large desk at the entrance to the dorm. The monitors had a cubbyhole system for all residents so that when a note was left, it was put into the cubbyhole. When the resident came back to the dorm, she could ask if she had any messages. This was an easy retrieval process. In addition, the residents could write a reply and the beau in reverse fashion could retrieve it: by asking whether a Moira Smith might have written a note to Andrew O'Neil. It was a high stakes affair that left such exchanges very public—especially since the dorm monitors were other students who took the position as *work contract* to lower the amount of tuition they owed to the university.

In this case, Andrew left a note for Moira.

Had a great time at the dance. Are you free next Friday to go to Hamlet? I love Shakespeare.
Andrew O'Neil

The Macalester Drama Club was putting on a production of *Hamlet*. There was no cost for students. Andrew really wanted to invite Moira to watch him lead the debate team against Carleton College on the question of whether Social Security should become law. It was a pivotal question that was a controversial issue of the time. Andrew was dead set against it. He came from a family that had lost its breadwinner when he was ten. He lived in an unheated attic in St. Paul that often became a torture zone that was only marginally warmer than the outside temperature of twenty degrees below zero, Fahrenheit. This required a heap of blankets that covered head and feet—no air holes. He got his first job when he was eleven working at a carnival, and pushed himself to work before and after school at St. Luke's. This often put him over the edge. He was a growing boy living on four or five hours of sleep (sometimes less when there was lots of homework). He would doze off in class and Sister Benedict would walk over to him and slap him on his ear to wake him up. She sometimes hit him so hard that his ear bled. Andrew grew to hate all nuns.

Little-by-little, the jobs that Andrew got paid him more money. All funds had to be turned in to his mother, Frederica. She ran the household. She railed against her dead husband who she said brought shame upon the whole family because of the bankruptcy of the family business: a general store/pharmacy.

Because Andrew came home after midnight, there was no food left for him to eat. His older sister, Ellen, would save half of her dinner in her apron and take it to her room to give to her brother when he came home after work. One day when Andrew came home after an eight-hour shift at a brewery, Ellen came out of her room and led him into the kitchen (normally they went up to the attic so that Frederica wouldn't discover that she was covertly feeding Andrew). But on this night she took him to the kitchen and gave him some meatloaf and bread. Andrew sat down and first drank some milk—his favorite beverage. It was not homogenized. Ellen took pains to open a new pint bottle for Andrew so that he might get the cream at the top.

After his meal that was downed within minutes, Ellen took a scrap of paper from her blouse. "I found this today while I was doing some cleaning. It's one of Doris' poems. I knew that you would want it":

My voice is gone, I cannot talk

My strength is gone, I cannot walk

The bumps under my skin
They won't go away
But merge with the bumps atop.

A rash inflames my joints

I cannot but ask-----why?

My brother's hope keeps me alive
I love my brother as I now die.

12/20/28

Andrew took the bit of paper and religiously put it into his wallet. He would later insert it into his scrapbook that he would keep until the day he died. The book had fifty pages and he'd already filled twenty by the time he was sixteen—the same age as Doris was when she caught rheumatic fever and died (she was two years older than Andrew). When Doris left, Ellen stepped in to save him. But there was no one like Doris.

Life in the twenties for the O'Neil family was tough. Each child had to go out and earn his and her share of money. All money went to Frederica without deduction. Frederica also received a black envelope each month with no return address. No one was allowed to look at it. The postmark said Louisville. The mother became a recluse. She occasionally went away from the family for weeks at a time without explanation. Gradually, Frederica began speaking German around the family. No one understood a word she said.

The bond between Ellen and Andrew carried each of them through. Ellen was plain and was not interested in boys except her little brother. Andrew persevered. He shared with her nun horror stories from his school, generally revolving around the corporal punishment to his left-ear because he fell asleep during class. When talking to Ellen, he often lifted his hand to his left ear—the one the nuns often slapped—because it was ringing.

There were few priests at Andrew's school. Once when he was trying out for the running team, he collapsed after a mile. The coach, a kindly priest, picked up Andrew and gave him some water and a chocolate bar. Andrew had no quarrel with priests.

Then in 1930 his cousin, Julia, was born from Ruth and Otto. There was quite a fête. Unfortunately, Andrew had to work that day: Sunday.

Andrew became the second O'Neil to graduate from high school. He was also the first to go to college. The process was difficult. His mother thought it was an extreme arrogance to go to college. "Do you know that my uncle Wolf never passed through what they call in Amerika the third-grade? He came to Amerika and could barely speak English, but taught himself so that his accent went away within a decade. And now do you know how many stores he runs?

A dozen! And he has a factory in New Orleans, too. He is what Amerika is all about. And he didn't need any college!"

"If he's so successful, then why doesn't he help us? After all, we're family, aren't we?"

Frederica opened a drawer and took out the rolling pin. Then she slowly walked forward toward her son. Andrew got up from his chair, kept his hands to his side, and clenched his fists. "Come on, mama, beat up on me just like you used to beat up on Dà. I can take it. The nuns have taught me how to accept physical punishment. But don't keep on about your uncle, Wolf, as if he's anything but trash. He has no living family but us, but does he help us? Has he ever helped us? Or is he the Devil in our midst?"

Frederica suddenly became terrified of her youngest child. She dropped the rolling pin and ran away. Andrew watched her escape. It was Sunday, and he didn't have to work this day. But he had filled up his pen with ink and gotten three sheets of paper and a blotter to write out his application for university work. A week later he was hired as assistant recruiter for the college. The job paid room, board, and tuition. And he only had to work forty hours a week! Andrew was free at last.

Andrew moved out of the house on August 1st, 1932. He began classes in September and his life went on smoothly until he was suddenly arrested by Moira Smith. He could remember the date. It was Thursday, October 17th, 1935. He had just finished a mock debate for the upcoming series against Carleton College. Andrew was tired, but he was somehow lured into a poetry reading by a hand-written sign that also sported the likeness of a female deer. (Drawing doodles of deer during class lectures was one of Andrew's pastimes.) There were seven students sitting in front of the room. There was also a wooden lectern. Each student would read three poems and then sit down so that the succeeding student would have their chance. All the poets were females. Andrew sat down near the back. Andrew's entrance made the number of those in the audience equal to the number of presenters.

Moira was the last to speak. She was medium tall and very thin. She wore dark-framed glasses. Moira's poems were about growing up next to an Indian Reservation in Wolf Point, Montana. Moira was poised and read fluently.

After the reading, Andrew went up to Moira and said, "I really liked your poem about eating rattlesnake. I couldn't imagine doing that." Moira smiled and tilted her head. "You'd be surprised what you can do if you have no other choice."

Andrew laughed and made a mental note to see this girl again. The Saturday next he had his wish at the dance. Then when he went back to her dorm to see whether she wanted to see Hamlet, he was given a positive response. He would pick her up at her dorm and walk her over to the theater. Andrew carefully folded the slip of paper and vowed to put it into his scrapbook.

***

On the night of the play, Andrew resolved to talk to Moira about politics. He would tell her about his being captain of the debating team and how he was against the Social Security Bill because he had made it through tough circumstances and doggonit, if he could do it, then so should everyone else. There should be no handouts—even to old people!

But Andrew never got the chance to talk politics. All the way Moira talked about her interpretation of various key themes in *Hamlet*. Though Andrew was no intellectual slouch, he was no match for Moira concerning *Hamlet*. "What are you, an English major?" asked Andrew.

Moira smiled. "I intend to be, but I'm just a freshman."

"I'm pre-law. That means I take courses in philosophy, economics, and politics."

"Ah, a well-rounded person. Maybe that's why the other girls say you're a BMOC." BMOC meant 'big man on campus.' It was an epithet that was much sought after.

Andrew responded with a broad smile.

The play and post-play coffee went very well. Andrew and Moira became a couple. One day in April, 1936, after they were walking back from Sunday services at the Baptist Church, Andrew proposed that they have lunch together at a sit-down place. Moira had some studying to do, but she consented. The place Andrew chose was Roy's Diner. It wasn't fancy, but the food was good and the prices were low. The couple got a booth by the window. Andrew ordered coffee and meatloaf while Moira ordered tea and vegetable soup. "You know, Moira, these past six months with you have been the happiest of my whole life."

Moira broke her bread and buttered it thinly.

"In May, I'm going to graduate. I hope to work a couple of years to get money to go to law school. I know I'd have a good future in law."

Moira smiled, nodded her head, and took a bite of bread.

"Well, with you being a freshman and all. Well, I know that this might be the end of us as a couple—what with you being in school and me working a job or two to get my law school stake."

Moira pursed her lips.

"That's how things will work out, if we *don't* do something. But I'm a man who intends to take his fortune into his own two hands. I don't want to lose you, Moira. That's why I want to marry you. What do you say?"

"About your going to law school?"

Andrew scowled.

"About marriage? Well, I'm only a freshman in college. I've got three years to go. I couldn't be a student and be married. We couldn't afford the tuition. My father certainly wouldn't support me for a degree if I were married. And then with your law school tuition, we could never pay our bills. It doesn't seem very practical."

"Bother the practicality! Would you like to be my wife?"

"Well, hypothetically, if I were to *bother the practicality* as you say, I could very well imagine being your wife. I am very fond of you."

Andrew smiled and reached for her hand—but then the meatloaf and soup came.

***

Nothing was decided at the lunch except that Andrew and Moira would continue to be a couple—only this time a pre-engaged couple who knew that dreams just didn't *happen,* they had to be founded upon practical reality or else they were doomed to fail.

***

It was June when Moira came home to her parents' apartment on 15ᵗʰ near Grand & Nicolet. Moira was coming home from her job as a secretary at the law offices of Swenson, Peterson, & Johansson. She landed a good summer job because of her shorthand skills and her typing speed (100 words per minute with nary a mistake). She could also correct grammar and didn't take a lunch break. It was around seven o'clock in the evening when Moira walked the three blocks from the streetcar stop to their third-floor apartment. It was a nice building with a self-service elevator. Moira pulled back the bronze metal safety fencing and got in the elevator; shut it again and pulled a waist high handle attached to a semi-circular device that had six positions for the six stops in the building (including the basement). The elevator always made a terrific racket when it went into operation, but the racket was nothing like she was about to hear from her father.

"I just got a letter from the college telling me that you declared a major in English!" Malcolm (Mac) Smith was sixty-one. He was completely bald. His voice was raspy. Mac sat his daughter down on the green sofa with the little white flower pattern. The room was light because they used blinds that were pulled up.

Moira put her purse down, "Yes, Father, that is correct."

"Are you suffering from amnesia?" Mac was pacing on their multi-colored rag rug. "I sent you to that rich kids' school in order that you could get your two years in before medical school or nursing college. This year you got two 'A's in biology, one in math, and a third in Latin. This is all medical school is about. You forget, I almost made it through medical school but for a nervous breakdown. Your success was what I was counting on to make my life complete."

"But Dad, you are a very successful man." She wanted to remind him about her three 'As' in English Literature and a 'B' in philosophy—but she held her speech.

"That has nothing to do with it, young lady. Of course I'm successful, and one of the reasons is that I always finish what I start. I've always done that—except ah," he cleared his throat, "— with medicine. That's why I want *you* to go to medical school."

"But Father, my heart isn't into medicine. Besides, do you know how many women they accept to medical school? One or two per class. They are the oddities."

Mac got up and started pacing. "So they're oddities, are they? They had a woman in my medical school class. They're women in medicine." Mac was walking away. His voice was getting very soft. He stopped at the window and looked out at the city. It was his city now. He was a manager in Minneapolis for *Great Northern*, one of the hubs in its railroad empire. Mac lingered at the window and then suddenly spun around and walked toward his daughter, "And when *haven't* you been an oddity, my dear? Look at you, you're skinny as a rail. No man would ever have you. A career is what you need—a career in medicine." Then Mac sat right next to his daughter. He was only inches away from her and he gazed at her with a forceful stare. "You have the opportunity to make *right* a lot of the *wrong* that happened to me. *You* can do it. You've got the brains that your soldier brother never had. You're as smart as a man. You could make it as a doctor, even if you're the only female in the goddamn class!"

Moira looked down. "I'll think about it, Dad."

And she did. Moira went to the University of Minnesota to visit the Alpha Epsilon Iota women's medical fraternity. She talked to various medical students who were enrolled in the University of Minnesota School of Medicine. What she came away with were many stories that were similar to what her father had said: there were opportunities for women in medicine, but it wasn't easy. At the turn of the century there were more women physicians, but many of them were spinster career women driven by their devotion to help others (and to be independent of men). But then there came a demographic change as more women tried a model that balanced a traditional life along with medicine. This resulted in a drop in females who entered and graduated from medical school.

Still there was the question: did Totem-pole Smith (as she was sometimes called, derisively) want to remain an outsider? This was the little girl who played with the Indians at Wolf Point (and who was challenged to fights because of it by her Norwegian girlfriends), and who always worked long hours at the Baptist Church suppers and Sunday evening church while the men just came and went. Moira was always an outsider. Did she want to be one forever? That's how she saw her choice before her.

Moira chose not to pursue medicine. This meant that her father ceased paying her tuition, and he made her get her own place to live. It also meant that she and Andrew could now formulate a financial goal that they would have to meet in order to be married. The model that Moira argued for was that they would have to have six months' expenses up front and the basics in housewares: pots & pans, glassware, silverware, and china. They also wanted expenses for a week to honeymoon. Everything would be put off until that goal was met.

This steep requirement necessitated that they both work full time for four years. On June 26th, 1940, they were wed. On their honeymoon at a cottage in the lake resort of Sherwood Forest,

Minnesota they discovered a mutual interest in card games: cribbage, honeymoon-bridge, gin rummy, and two-hand poker. As they played, they planned their future; they both would go back to school and have a two-story house with four children.

***

"I'm not going to wait to be drafted," said Andrew as they were doing dishes. Chiltren was climbing up Andrew's leg for *his* dinner. Andrew decided to stop and feed Lord Chiltren (their pet's nickname) so that he could talk to Moira.

***

Andrew decided that he could cut a better deal if he enlisted than if he waited to be drafted. On May 1st, 1942, Andrew O'Neil enlisted in the Marines. He went to boot camp one month later. In the interval, Andrew and Moira made an unsaid pact. The diaphragm stayed in the drawer. Nothing was said. Should he die, there must be something tangible that would live after him. And so it came to pass.

CHAPTER EIGHT

To protect men of virtue . . . I appear in age after age
Bhagavad-Gita, Fourth Teaching[*]

The News of the Day: BOMBERS BLAST COLOGNE, Britain strikes with air fleet of 1,250 planes, Germans admit to great damage.

British tanks and airplanes gain in desert. Tide of battle in Libya turned in five-day fight. Trap was set for Germans.

Senator Josiah W. Bailey's margin over Richard T. Fountain gained steadily today as additional returns were reported from yesterday's Democratic Primary for the United States Senate.

Food riots broke out today in Vichy (unoccupied France), Two policemen killed. Laval urges Nazi cooperation.

Enemy U-Boats sink U.S. Ships.

Japs' Midget Subs Attack Sydney Harbor

Nazi Henchman kills 20 Czechs in retaliation. Nazi firing squads in the old Czech capital of Prague executed 20 more persons today in connection with the Gestapos sweeping reprisals for the attack last Wednesday upon the German leader Reinhard Heydrich.

[Small comic insert of an African American male with a white surgical mask covering his nose and mouth looking into a mirror] Just a little marriage/ to liven up the gloom/ We got a baby carriage/ All we needs a broom.
The Charlotte Observer, front page for 6/1/1942

AFTER he enlisted, Andrew was sent to Marine boot camp at Cherry Point, North Carolina. Cherry Point was a training ground for the Pacific Theater—where the Marines played an especially important

---

[*] *The Bhagavad Gita*, tr. Eknath Easwaran, (Tomales, CA: Nilgigi Press, 1985).

role. Boot camp was no trouble for Andrew. He had endured lots of long hours and hard work He was twenty-eight, older than most of the other enlistees. But he didn't mind because he had been a man by himself most of his life. Andrew was one of the few recruits who actually liked military food and didn't complain about sleeping on a pallet bed.

When his drill sergeant would yell to them, "Get out of bed, you goddamn jarheads!" Andrew took it calmly in stride. *In some ways*, he semi-consciously said to himself, *these drill sergeants have nothing on the nuns at St. Luke's. If you want to win the war, you should get the nuns together and send them to run boot camp.* Andrew didn't like what he was hearing about the Japanese. The Marines characterized them as dedicated warriors who saw their emperor as a god. How could anyone defeat an army fighting for god? No one saw Franklin Roosevelt as a god—even those lousy Democrats who voted for him three times! Andrew had hoped that Lucky Lindy would have decided to run in 1940. If he'd won, American would not be in the war now.

American First: no involvement in foreign wars. It was Washington's legacy. Lindbergh knew airplanes and would have stopped Pearl Harbor. As for Hitler, Lindbergh could have persuaded him to stop his game plan concerning the states that bordered Germany. Those states were probably fair game, given European history over the past nine hundred years. Going beyond that was the Napoleon fallacy. It doesn't work in the modern world. There was only one Roman Empire. It happened once and every effort thereafter by the Roman Catholic Church to put it back together again was like saving the glow from lightning bugs captured in a jar. It couldn't happen. Lindbergh would have been just the man to have convinced Hitler of his folly and kept everything in check. Hitler respected Lindbergh—after all, Hitler had awarded Lindbergh a prize: they knew each other's souls.

Instead, they had this rich guy: Roosevelt (who some said was crippled). Why did America need a crippled leader in war? Was someone missing an important element there? Andrew thought so. He had to get himself out of the regular path to death. He was not going to ship out as a private, aka cannon fodder. He had to take his fate into his own hands.

His first choice was submarine duty. American submarines were so well built that they could withstand most attacks. Also, there were long intervals in which there would be no attacking at all.

In stealth, they moved unseen toward a target. Then in secret they sent out their torpedoes from a considerable distance. They were rarely attacked and the death rate was low.

Andrew's unit was scheduled to deploy on July 15th for the South Pacific by way of New Zealand. On July 12th, Andrew was accepted for an extended try-out at submarine school. This separated him from his unit. The school lasted two weeks. His unit went away without him. He would later find out that over half of the unit never came back from the war alive.

But after ten days, Andrew was turned down for submarine duty because he had an overbite and could not properly use the rescue oxygen units necessary if the sub was hit. Andrew was assigned to another unit that was targeted for a major offensive against the Japanese in Guadalcanal, an island in the Solomon's—South Pacific. It was set to be the first major offensive against the Japanese, who were in control. The mission would protect Australia against attacks and give a strategic position for the Allies to get to Indo-China.

Andrew didn't like it. He didn't know why. But he instantly applied to officer's candidate school. He took a test. The unit was set to deploy on August 1, 1942. His score was set to come in on Friday, July 31st. But there was a glitch. When he went to the post office there was no notice. The scores had been delayed because of some *circumstances*. But Andrew didn't want to be a victim of circumstances. That evening, he checked into the infirmary with blood coming out of his rectum: *a hemorrhoid* was the official report. But it delayed Andrew's departure with his unit that was going to the Solomon's. On Monday, August 2nd Andrew received his letter that he had been accepted into officer training school. Weeks later, Andrew learned that his entire unit—down to the man—had been killed at Guadalcanal in the battle of Tenaru.

Rifleman Andrew O'Neil had risen to second lieutenant, and because of his legal expertise was assigned to the Adjutant Generals Corps. He saw no action in the South Pacific. He served his country doing what he loved most: practicing the law. His only casualty was a loss of hearing in his left ear due to military exercises in which the explosion of a dummy grenade came too close to his damaged ear. Andrew never blamed the military, but instead focused his bitterness upon Sister Benedict.

CHAPTER NINE

Krishna, you praise renunciation of actions and then discipline.
  *Bhagavad Gita, The Fifth Teaching**

The news of the Day: The War in Europe is ended! Surrender is unconditional; V-E will be proclaimed today; Our troops on Okinawa gain; Surrender of criminals required.
  The New York Times Front page for May 8, 1945.

Japan Surrenders, End of the War! Emperor accepts Allied rule; M'Arthur supreme commander; our manpower curbs voided.
  The New York Times, Front page for August 15, 1945.

DYLAN Evans excitedly wrote down the un-coded message: "Japan has surrendered!" His ship had been lying just outside Shanghai for two weeks. During this last interval, ashore near Shanghai, they had been granted two shore liberties. On the first, Dylan joined a group who had been invited by the president of St. John's University and was living in the west side of Shanghai. He had asked some seamen to a dinner at his considerable house. He arranged for rickshaw rides to the campus. The group arrived in the early afternoon and played softball with students till the late afternoon. The president, his wife, and their two little girls sat at the head of the table that was set out on the lawn. The head table looked out to six other tables that fanned out geometrically. Everyone said that it reminded them of the sun and its extended rays, but the president tried to hush such talk.

The dinner was all so luxurious—especially in wartime. The group was served egg drop soup and pork-filled dumplings, along with the main course of beef teriyaki. For dessert they had ice cream. It was a feast such as the sailors had not tasted in years. [Later, Dylan learned that the luxuries came at a cost. To live

* *The Bhagavad Gita,* tr. Eknath Easwaran, (Tomales, CA: Nilgigi Press, 1985).

comfortably, the president had bargained with the Japanese. In 1951, the president's entire family was herded into the French Quarter to the British racetrack along with hundreds of others and gunned down by the Red Chinese for collaborating with the Japanese.]

Dylan and a few mates went ashore one more time for a brief walk around the streets: soaking up the cultural trappings of a society so totally foreign to America. It was all so terrifically exotic to a nineteen-year-old boy who had never been out of Newark, New Jersey. His Welsh parents, Eluned and Glyn, were first generation immigrants from south Wales near Cardiff. Glyn hated the work in the coalmines because he was asthmatic and the coal dust gave him coughing fits. He thought he'd die like his father if he remained, so he and his wife left via Ireland where passage for work was easier to come by.

Dylan grew up in Newark, New Jersey. He was a gentle soul being raised by a coal miner who became a welder in the Newark shipyards. There were many fights as Glyn sought to make his boy a rugby star (or at least the American equivalent, football). But Dylan wasn't interested. He liked reading poetry.

"You're a goddamn fairy, you are," yelled his father.

Dylan was silent.

Then his father grabbed Dylan's shoulders and shook him. Dylan broke free and set his fist to strike back, but he stopped. His father saw his action and struck first and knocked his son out with one blow.

Afterwards, the father was all apologies. Eluned told her son that he had to turn a cold eye on it all. "Life in south Wales is very brutal. The English think we're scum. They treat us like that. The only way to survive is to fight back and fight back again."

Dylan didn't like that deal. He knew that he was the lucky one who made it to be a teenager (unlike his older sister, Catherine, who died at three months of some infection that made her cough a lot). Dylan got very good grades in school. His teachers would remark to his mother that Dylan was one of the brightest students to attend Central High School. But that didn't satisfy Glyn. He wanted to raise a *real* man who could win most any fight he got into.

"That's the only way you win *respect*, Dylan. That's something you got to think about—especially being a 'four eyes' kid. If the other blokes know that you can break their noses, then they'll leave you alone. No more jokes about your glasses. That's all that any man wants: to be left alone."

Dylan nodded and went through the fight training with his father. But Dylan's heart wasn't in it. His mind started drifting to Wilfred Owen's writings on World War I and Yeats's poem on the death of Lady Gregory's son. Slam. Then there was a pain in his right shoulder as Glyn put Dylan into a full-Nelson after taking him to the ground by attacking his knees.

Glyn relented. "Boy, you've got to guard your knees. That's the surest way to take a guy down and once you're down in the mud, they will have their way with you. Nothing you can do except eye-gouge."

"I would never gouge your eyes, Father."

Glyn laughed in glee and slapped his son on the shoulder that was strained. A sharp pain resulted and Dylan fell to the ground. Glyn laughed again derisively and spat to the side. "You'll never win a fight that way, boy. You've got to grow some balls to get respect."

At Sunday evening church, Dylan and Eluned knelt down to pray. Glyn never went to Sunday evening church and rarely went to Sunday morning church. He said that he didn't like the sound of American English in church. It didn't sound holy enough for him. Besides, he knew the Church of England, Low Church service well enough, but didn't get on with the long sermons in the Presbyterian Church that his wife insisted that they attend. As Dylan knelt in prayer, he felt his underwear was twisted around his genitals. It was uncomfortable, but Dylan did not adjust things. It made him mindful.

***

Dylan graduated from high school at the top of his class of seven hundred. He was thinking about college since all his teachers had recommended it. But Glyn made it very clear that he wasn't going to pay a nickel for any college education. Glyn had made due with almost no formal education (since the school system in Wales was run by the English who paddled your behind for speaking Welsh during recess). Glyn knew that he couldn't go too far in that system before he'd fight back and probably kill one of his English bastard teachers. It was providential that he went into the mines at twelve.

With no prospect in continuing education, Dylan decided to join the Navy. He passed a test and as a result was sent to radio school in Maryland. When he graduated he followed a route from the Solomons where Dylan boarded his ship, the Sierra, in Leyte Bay where MacArthur *returned*. The battle was over when Dylan arrived, but there was still "clean-up" to do. The Sierra was part of the Seventh Fleet and had an admiral flag aboard. On a good day it could do twenty-six knots.

The USS Sierra was in the heavy cruiser class of navy vessels with about 1,100 in the crew. It was the length of a football field with three decks and a bridge topside and four decks below. Eight-inch and five-inch guns were mounted fore and aft main. Twenty and forty millimeter belts fed guns that were mounted on side decks. When those guns were firing, it was almost impossible to hear the Morse code coming in. Dylan's glasses would fog up with his perspiration. The communications team (radio, flags, lights, and radar) was located on the bridge deck with a radio shack and an adjacent decoding room. Dylan spent most of his time in the radio shack decoding Morse code messages. He was part of a communications team that translated incoming messages and then typed them up for the commanding officers. It was vital work that took a quick mind and a fast pencil. Information, the Navy preached, was the way to win the war. Men's lives depended upon how complete and accurate they (the communication team) were. Dylan was one of the best.

While they were still in Leyte Bay for the clean-up action, Dylan walked out of the radio shack and smelled a strange toxic odor unlike any he had experienced before. Dylan was trying to figure it out when ensign McLaughlin confronted him.

"Whatcha sniffin, Evans? Jap perfume?"

Dylan stood up straight, "Yes, sir."

McLaughlin laughed. "You don't even know what I'm talking about, do you son?"

"No, sir."

"Well, you know we've won this goddamn thing, the island is ours. But there are Japs hung in there still. They've got them scattered in caves in the hills. Well, our guys are out there tonight with flame-throwers and frying those sons-of-bitches in their caves until they're crisp. The night breezes waft the perfumes our way; it's the smell of victory, son." Then the ensign walked away.

Dylan returned to the radio shack. He swore to himself that he'd never forget the perfume of charred flesh. But the tap-tap of the Morse code was enough to captivate one's mind. Dylan worked past his shift that night.

Iwo Jima was the next venue to etch its terrors into Dylan's mind. The U.S.S. Sierra stood back in the assault (perhaps because they bore an admiral flag?). A group of destroyers (called "tin cans") diverted the Japanese shore batteries to fire at them while the real invasion of LST and LSMs brought marines and infantry on a delayed schedule from a different sight line. The tin cans darted in and out with the mission of drawing fire and avoiding being sunk. It was treacherous business. One of the tin cans that had been hit pulled alongside the Sierra and off-loaded its casualties. Then they turned around and entered the shadow of death once more.

The sound of 8" shells resounding out against the enemy batteries produced so much noise that Dylan could no longer hear the messages coming in. He went outside of the radio shack and watched the panorama of it all. Approaching the Sierra was another tin can that had been hit badly. It was limping along to try to reach the Sierra. When it arrived, a tall, slender, baby-faced captain with blond wispy hair (only 22 years old) was pacing the deck in irregular patterns, muttering to himself. When the vessel had been towed alongside the Sierra, there was a mass exodus of crewman—the injured first. As the evacuation began, the captain screamed something out and jumped overboard. No one ever saw him again.

During a military engagement, there were no resources to revive those who were sore in spirit. Dylan returned to his place in the Radio Shack. The meaningless staccato of non-rhythmic sounds was better than the viewing of the process of warfare. Soon it would be over and *meaningful* taps would reign once more.

When his shift ended, Dylan went down to his bunk. His was the second one up in a string of five hung bunk beds that provided no privacy: visually everything was in view and the smell of male sweat was pervasive and challenged Dylan.

Dylan mounted to the second bunk and reached under his pillow for his Bible. It was a ratty book with ripped cloth-covered boards and a spine that was split and taped together. It appeared to be ready to fall apart at any moment. Dylan swung into his bunk, holding onto the rope ladder with one hand and his Bible with the other. The light wasn't very good, but adequate for reading. Tonight, it was difficult to hold the Book still. He turned to Psalm 88:

Oh Lord, my God, by day I call for help,

By night I cry aloud in thy presence.
Let my prayer come before thee,
Hear my loud lament;
For I have had my fill of woes,
And they have brought me to the threshold of Sheol.

Dylan let his Bible fall onto his chest. He closed his eyes. Then he opened them and cleaned his glasses. In the bunk above Dylan, Ned Jackson said, "Why don't you just let that fall apart? You know it's not so nice for us to see you reading your stupid Bible down there. Holy shit, Evans, why do you read that stuff anyway?"

Harold Cohen from bunk two said, "Shut the fuck up, Jackson. I'm trying to get some sleep down here."

Jackson replied, "Oh sure, Cohen. I've seen you reading the Book too. Only you Jew boys do it on the sly."

"Shut up, Jackson. You don't know what you're talking about," replied Cohen.

"What's the problem?" asked Dylan.

Jackson was silent for a moment. Then he down shifted. "Well, at least you're not like Doyle who gets down on his knees in all the filth of the quarters and prays out loud with his hands held together! Holy shit, I don't know what this mumbo jumbo is about. We're in a war here—don't you know? We're about killing. What's to pray about that?"

Then there was silence. Dylan finished the psalm. He turned over on his right side and hugged his Bible, much as a child might hug his teddy bear. He still felt the terror of the young captain jumping overboard to his death. He hugged his Bible tighter. He would be on duty in five hours.

Later, the Sierra was part of a massive build-up of ships off the west coast of Japan in spring and summer of 1945. But then, inexplicably, they pulled back in August to Inchon, Korea and then across the China Sea to Tsingtao.

The Japanese had withdrawn and the Sierra moved forward cautiously. The big navy cruiser moored quietly alongside the giant sized black boulders lining the harbor. The next day at dawn, when Dylan was just getting off his shift, the rosy-fingered dawn illumined a scene of tragic proportions. He would have normally gone directly below to get a few hours of sleep, but his progress was arrested. Before him he saw something askew. The black rocks were different—but how? Wildlife? He took off and cleaned his glasses. Then he squinted to see more clearly. What Dylan saw was an army of children standing atop the rocks closest to the bay. There were hundreds of these little wretches: boys and girls standing naked or covered by a loincloth. They were grouped into gangs. Many also had a knife in mouth or hand. Their eyes were hollow and the faces were blank. It struck Dylan as a vision out of Hell.

They came at dawn because it was then that the Sierra dumped its daily garbage over the fantail into the harbor. The harbor was a cesspool of old sewage, rotting fruit and vegetables, bobbing bits of plastic and metallic junk and a few decomposing human corpses barely visible as part of the black scum. It was all topped off by a thin layer of diesel fuel that graciously covered the water and mixed with everything.

When the day's garbage was tossed overboard, the gang leaders signaled the go-ahead. Instantly, two or three from each gang (boys and girls) dove into the cesspool toward the cruiser's fantail. They were gathering food for their gang. But there were more of them than there was of even this thin fare. As the hunters scavenged, there was savage competition. The knives came out and flashed red in the early morning sun as shrieks pierced the air and more children dove in to protect their own. Several died in the skirmish.

More often than not, though, the wounded made it back to the rocks and hoped that someone in their gang would have gotten them something to eat. When it was over, the gangs divided the food that kept them alive.

Some of the officers and crew of the Sierra viewed the morning warfare as good sport. They would bet and cheer for one group or individual making it to some food or being foiled. Sometimes they upped the ante by tossing oranges or candy bars into the harbor and betting on who would get to them first. A package of cigarettes got even more attention since it could be sold on the streets of Tsingtao and feed a family for a week.

Then Dylan took a message from fleet command that the Sierra was to leave the next morning at 0600. The ship dumped its morning garbage in its usual manner. Dylan looked outside at the forgotten children of Tsingtao, waiting for their last meal as the Sierra made its way to its next destination.

***

It was then that the message of the bombing of Hiroshima came. The message came with special coding that had to be sent next door. Just before the end of his shift, Frank Hertzman (from the code room) visited Dylan.

Frank was a short, dark-haired genius. His glasses were bigger and thicker than Dylan's. It was midnight. Frank pulled up a metal chair so that he could talk privately. "You know, that bomb they dropped today in Hiroshima was really something."

"That so? Knock out a munitions plant?"

"No munitions plants in Hiroshima."

"That so? Why did they bomb it?" Dylan took off his glasses.

"To wipe out the whole town."

"No shit."

"Yeah. The whole city, 150,000 people. The new bomb—they call it the 'little boy'—killed the lot of them."

"That's impossible. You must have gotten some bad information." Dylan cleaned his glasses on his shirt sleeve and put them on again.

"That's what was in the message you gave me once I decoded it—a top secret one, that was. If we didn't have an admiral aboard, we'd never have gotten it."

Dylan smiled and shook Frank's hand. His shift was over and Michael was there to take over. He made his way to the sleeping quarters. There had to be a Psalm that would cover this. King David knew the depths of human depravity—he contributed to it. How was the Lord to be understood in all of this? Dylan read and read the Psalms, but he kept returning to the words, 'My God, my God, why hast thou forsaken me?"

Dylan felt alternately like a worm and as an outcast with his bones out of joint. He decided to turn to his diary that he had been a very irregular contributor to. This is because Dylan wasn't keen on recording the facts of his life as opposed to setting out a meaning to it all.

'The Code of the Line' by Dylan Evans.*

The life in the Navy is all about lines. First of all, there are the lines you have to wait in. These are many. You wait in line in boot camp to get shots. You wait in line to get your gear. You wait in some sort of fatalistic line to await your assignment. This is a

---

* I put this in over the objection of Boylan. He thought I wasn't being straight with you. But then we got that out of the way at the beginning.

blind line. Once assigned to the combat zone, there are even more lines: chow lines, mail lines, headlines, canteen lines, movie lines, medic lines, boarding lines, de-boarding lines, barber lines, and then there were the artificial lines of group formation.

Lines are the worldview mentality of naval operations. They govern rank in vertical lines. They govern daily life in horizontal lines: roll call lines, battle call lines, special details lines, etc. (Sometimes I think the lines turn back on themselves and become circles—but this is heresy!) This linear mentality of the Navy is drummed into the skulls of everyone from admiral to seaman. Naval ships that are armored and capable of attack are called line ships (in contrast to service and supply ships). Ships in fleet formation are called "ships of the line" meaning that to sail in formation is to keep your place in line: you are 'holding the line.' In the United States Navy, the line must be kept at all costs. This is the shared community worldview of the Navy.

Even the way of recognizing the personnel of the ship is designated not in terms of functional capability such as doctor, lawyer, chaplain, but rather as a 'line officer.'

Every sailor knows what it is to 'fall in line' or to 'fall out of line' or to 'line up' or 'count off by line' or to 'march by line' or to 'follow the line, ship-shape, mister.' Orders are given by word or by signal: calls of the pipe, bugle, or loudspeaker: each has a direct cause-effect linear mechanism. (Pipe, bugle, loudspeaker = stimulus condition)=> conditioned response. This is just like Pavlov's dogs. The line from stimulus to response must be exact and without exception. To be out of line is to be exiled from the community of the ship. And the community of the ship is the dedicated mission (at least nominally) for which we all have signed on (the dotted line).

This dedication to the code of the line, I believe, is why some of the sailors criticize those of us who read our Bible. How can the Bible stand up against the Line? (I wonder if Jesus ever made his disciples stand in line? I rather doubt it. I think lines would annoy him.)

The code of the line is exact. There is no mercy. When I was in basic training I had a small reading light. I admit that I was reading a novel and not the Holy Book, but because I fell asleep and left my light on past "lights out" I had to perform a 72 hour KP detail (day and night continuously) of picking up garbage and putting it into containers to be removed by garbage trucks. Even simple violations of the code of the line were treated harshly.

What I don't understand is how there can be a rule and not-a-rule. If we live by the line and we all accept it (what choice do we have), then what should be the problem? The rule of the line says to do such and such and then there is no more conversation. After all, we are at war! We should follow the dictates of the Navy. The Navy defines our community. The Navy says how we are to win this war to save our families and sweethearts. And the Navy says it begins and ends with a line.

But what does it mean to stay in a line? I think that it means that we must accept that the line chain of command is something that we will agree to obey—unto our own death. We do this for some other purpose. But the line is a secular sacred. We cannot question the dogma or else everything falls apart. I believe in the line. I believe that it allows the United States of America to fulfill its vision of goodness against the godless forces of evil. I want to be a positive agent of change. How do I do it in a radio shack?

By following the lines.

***

The Sierra left for another venue. But the events of Hiroshima still resonated with Dylan. But then he heard about the 'fat man bomb' and Nagasaki. Another 80,000 civilians were killed. Frank Hertzman again delivered the news to Dylan. It was more than he could endure. Dylan left the room and ran towards the toilet but he didn't make it soon enough before he vomited. Killing so many civilians wasn't the way of the line. It wasn't Navy. What was happening?

When Dylan left the head, musical notes told him it was mess time. He went into line. What sort of line did the *fat man* stand in? And what lines did the exploding civilian bodies fall into? In the end, the dead all form in a line: horizontal at rigor mortis.

The chow line was very long. It snaked around several passageways, inching its way toward the chow hall. Most sailors in the line were mute. It wasn't pleasant to stand for what would be an hour or more just to receive a scoop of mystery delight next to some potatoes and holy vegetables (that is, vegetables that had had the hell cooked out of them—tasteless, vitamin-less, shells of vegetable fiber). It was all washed down with god-awful coffee.

It was this slim fare of institutional nutrition for which the men waited.

A minority of sailors in line engaged in self-deception so that they chatted as if they were somewhere else. Still others took the occasion to re-read letters from home, or books, or magazines. Some had just come off assignment, and some were ready to go on. All trudged forward to their place in line.

Up ahead of Dylan there were two burly boatswains walking down the line toward the rear, but then they stopped abruptly to talk to a small guy in line who had been reading quietly. It was obvious to all of the sailors who were in visual contact with the situation that the two boatswains wanted to cut in line and were pressuring the little guy to let them in. It was the oldest kind of extortion: the strong against the weak.

The small man held his ground but was still engaged with the anarchists. Soon the tired, apathetic group of seamen started to take notice. This was the group directly behind the meek little man. After all, they were involved, too. Who knows what *extra* stops might be involved in letting a couple of guys in *just here*? Maybe it's at that time that they run out of mystery meat? Or perhaps there's no more coffee and they have to drink water until they make more? Or perhaps they just have to wait a few more minutes in line?

Or perhaps there was more to it than that? The fifteen or twenty behind the meek targeted weak link had been in line for forty-five minutes. They were exhausted from getting off of shift or a bit grumpy for being about to go onto shift. But they were agitated that some sailors were going to forgo what they just went through just because *they couldn't be bothered*. Those in front of the little sailor were bothered to. Those eight or nine who were paying attention were thinking to themselves that something was wrong about this. They weren't as adamant as those behind because they would not be disadvantaged by the action. But still, it was very uncomfortable. One of the men thought that if that had happened just in front of him that he would deck these loud mouth boatswains.

But then the proximate group heard the voice of the meek sailor. He was talking to the bullies.

"Comrades. We are roughly of the same military rank. We are all non-coms here; you do not out-rank me. There is one mess line and you want to get in near the front. You realize that I've been waiting here forty-five minutes or more already."

Then one of the boatswains slugged the little man and laid him out. His nose was bleeding. He didn't move for a moment. The men just in front and behind bowed to his aid. But the little man was wiry. He lifted himself up. He took out a handkerchief and wiped his nose. His mates in line were clenching their fists at these two boatswains. If they wanted a fight, they'd get pummeled.

The little man frowned at both men and then aggressively pointed his finger at them. "I am sorry for you two. I'm going to do something that will teach you a lesson."

The two boatswains moved to their haunches as they prepared for the attack.

Then the meek seaman said, "Justice must be served in the line and in the war. I voluntarily let you in but to compensate to the others behind me I will go to the back of the line. You must think about this. If you don't, it is to your own peril."

And so he left the line and moved to the very back. The jug heads inserted themselves in line. Whether they thought about the significance of this event or not is unclear. But there were many who did. The witnesses recorded a first-hand account of what happened, and passed along to others what they had seen. These jughead interlopers were marked men. The meek little man took on a special aura that was never verbally expressed but generally understood. The incident became another narrative that shaped the community worldview of the ship. And few sailors thereafter tried to flagrantly cut in line.

***

It was only a week or so before the Japanese surrendered.

CHAPTER TEN

The kinds of faith express themselves in the habits of those who hold them: in the food they like, the work they do, the disciplines they practice and the gifts they give.
     Chapter 17, *The Bhagavad Gita**

The news of the day: Merchants and Clerks Settle: Stores to Reopen Monday. Agree on 40 hour work week; 6 day store operation. Accord climaxes 13 hours of continuous negotiation.

Vast changes are planned for the Red Cross. The American Red Cross will undergo important and far reaching changes in its organizational structure after Congress reconvenes.

Strike Ends Plant May not be Reopened. An eight day old strike at the Pointer Willamette Truck Trailer Plant ended today as members of Local 662 Machinists Union, AFL, voted to return to work but plant officials indicated operations might not be resumed.

Half of U.S. Farms are now Electrified.

Where you go to Church in Great Falls this Morning. First Church of Christ Scientist, First Avenue North and Thirteenth Streets. "Matter" 11a.m. Sunday School 11 a.m.
     Great Falls Tribune, Front Page for September 22, 1946

ANDREW O'Neil took a series of trains that eventually landed him in Great Falls, Montana. The Chicago, Milwaukee, St. Paul, and Pacific Railroad tower caught Andrew's attention as he exited the terminal. He studied the tower for a moment. Something looked wrong. Then he had it. There was no 'Pacific' listed on the tower. Andrew scratched his head and moved on.

---

* *The Bhagavad Gita*, tr. Eknath Easwaran (Tomales, CA: Nilgiri Press, 1985).

Andrew had the address of Malcolm Smith on a small scrap of paper. At the train station, he asked a woman selling flowers whether she knew where 9th and 5th was. She said she didn't. Then there was a vendor selling hot dogs. He was also ignorant. Andrew felt frustrated.

Train travel via coach was very boring. He was most aware of the ride from New York to Chicago on the Cardinal. The trip took a little over a day. In the car were four ex-servicemen who were cutting up something awful.

The tall blonde guy fancied himself to be the showman. He would go on with impersonations of Jack Benny and his cast of characters. When he came to Rochester, Jack Benny's black servant, the corporal (for he was still wearing his uniform), would hop around and dance in the way he thought 'colored' people did. His traveling companions (all dressed in uniform and none above corporal) were quite amused and boisterously communicated their approval. There were no black people in the rail carriage.

But the comedy routine would so exhaust the tall blonde guy that he would take a swig at the common bottle of booze (that was tended by the Italian soldier with short-cropped black hair, light skin, and a huge nose) and sit down with his mates. The war dogs had swiveled the seats around so that on each side of the aisle the seats were facing each other: four places to sit—one was for the blonde comedian, one was now asleep, one was taken up by a soldier staring out the window as if he were a zombie, and the fourth was occupied by the Italian (all by himself, holding the bottle). When the tall blonde guy hit his seat, he passed out. In fifteen minutes or so, the phoenix would rise again for another show. There was always a quiet smile on the Italian's face.

The other two men were of mixed ethnic origin—probably some German/Scandinavian mixture. One was engaged and the other kept falling asleep. They definitely weren't up for center stage. They would support their clown by clapping, drinking, and occasionally spontaneously breaking into song.

The other people in the compartment were demur. They were being entertained by gods (albeit drunken gods—perhaps Bacchus and his retinue?). Andrew traveled in civilian clothes. They were the same clothes that he had worn on the train down to North Carolina for his induction. He sat in the last seat of the compartment on the left. In the seat in front of him (that was also swiveled around by the magic levers that turned the seats so that they faced themselves) was a taciturn collection that appeared to be two grandparents traveling with two grandchildren. Something seemed to be amiss because they rarely spoke or engaged in any activity.

Andrew leaned back and beheld the spectacle. But try as he might, the experience exhausted him. His saving grace was a pack of Lucky Strikes. When he decided to smoke, he walked back and opened the door that led between cars. There he stood on the metal coupling platforms that connected the cars. The platforms were semi-circles atop each other with silver studs that stood bright above the grease and grime. To the sides were tough metal-lined curtains that blocked out the light but not the loud sound of the train's wheels bounding over the rails. Here he was alone. Here Andrew had a Lucky Strike.

One of the things that *strikes* you when you exit Pittsburgh to points west is that the cadence of the 'clickity-clack' alters. From New York to Pittsburgh, the shorter rails were regular 4/4 time. But after Pittsburgh they altered to syncopated 5/6 time because of the many modifications in the Ohio rail beds. When Andrew was between cars, he tried to think. So much of the last four years had been a nightmare. All his hard work, and all his plans: everything had been altered by the war. He had come from so little. He had worked so hard. He had gone to college. He had accumulated money so he could get married. He was ready to go back to school to study law and work toward his ambition to run for Congress and shape America in his Jeffersonian vision of what the country should be: a haven for the free with few fetters that would stop an ordinary man like himself from rising from nothing to the pinnacle of success, the United States Congress.

What validated these hyperbolic dreams? The country itself. The promise was that *anyone* who was smart enough and willing to work hard enough could rise to the top in one generation. And before the bombing of Pearl Harbor, Andrew was well on his way to his dream. But then there was the goddamn War: Roosevelt's war. Why hadn't they nominated Lindbergh instead of the insipid Willkie? Why, he was just a Democrat in Republican clothing. Why else would Roosevelt bring Wilkie into the camp and support his 'one world' shenanigans? Andrew didn't shed a tear when heard about his death.

But Lucky Lindy would have kept the United States out of the War. Lindy knew Hitler and was awarded a medal by Hermann

Göring. The America First movement would have kept the United States out of war. Andrew wished they had succeeded. Roosevelt and his Social Security and alphabet-soup programs were just the stuff of a rich guy with some sort of zany conscience. The whole thing made Andrew angry. He finished his smoke and ground out the butt on the silver studs atop the swiveling platform on which he was standing. He returned to his seat.

Then the tall blonde guy (Andrew named him 'Fritz') started another routine.

***

When the train arrived in Great Falls, it was already dark. Andrew had never been to the city and he felt a vague sense of apprehension. He got his duffel bag from baggage claim and started out of the terminal. After his vain attempts at directions, his attention was arrested by, "Shoe shine, boss?"

Andrew looked around and saw the supplicant: an aged African American male. The man had something familiar about him. Andrew decided on a shine. He got onto the chair that was elevated by a small wooden platform and put his left shoe on the slanted pine box.

As the man worked, Andrew thought about where he was going this time of evening. He didn't have a clue. Andrew looked down at the man shining his shoes. He was very efficient and moved with decisive direction.

"Excuse me, mister, but do you know this town well?"

The man stopped shining Andrew's shoes. He put the shoe rag over his shoulder and looked up at the younger white man. "Well, sir, dat depends upon what youse means by 'know.'"

Andrew nodded and reached into his pocket and brought out a piece of paper with Moira's address on it: 510 9th Street/Avenue North, apt #42.

"Well sir, I does know where that is. But you have to understand that in this city we separate 'streets' and 'avenues.' I no idea why. I'm just a shoe shine so I don't know."

Andrew looked down at the man who was shining his civilian shoes that hadn't been shined in four years. Montana didn't strike Andrew as the sort of magnet that would attract black people, but maybe it was because it was an important Western railroad town and that the railroads were one of the few national companies that hired black people—porters, cooks, waiters, etc. It started to make sense to him.

Andrew took out his piece of paper again. He hadn't read it correctly. The words 'street' and 'avenue' were clearly separate. "Well, mister—" Andrew paused. "Say, I don't think I ever caught your name."

"John, sir. My name is John." The man was around fifty (though Andrew couldn't be very sure—he might be ten or fifteen years younger or older). He was light skinned and had a scar on his left temple. His skin was scattered with dark spots.

"Well, John, my name is Andrew. And I'm just back from the war, coming home to my wife and young son. I don't know anything about this place. I'd appreciate your advice."

John finished the buffing of Andrew's shoes. John had been kneeling on a rolled up blue towel while he did his job. As John arose, Andrew witnessed a body that was stiff and slow in straightening. John flashed a smile of very white teeth with one canine tooth missing. "Well, sir, if youse give me dat paper dere again, I'll try to help youse."

Andrew complied, and John had it all figured out very quickly. He decided that 'street' was correct and not 'avenue.' In less than five minutes Andrew was on his way, and John had a quarter for his work and a seventy-five-cent tip.

***

When Andrew got to the apartment building he paused at the mailboxes to see where the Smiths resided: 510 Ninth *Street*, #42— top floor. The elevator was straight ahead. Andrew started forward, and then sensed another presence. This was a skill indoctrinated in the Marines. He paused as a resident in a hurry rushed past him to the elevator. Andrew was in an accommodating mood. He turned aside and decided to take the stairs. The stair case ran right next to the elevator. The elevator ran so slowly that he decided to race the elevator to the top floor.

***

When Andrew had left for induction in May of 1942, they had been living in Wisconsin. But Andrew's pay as a traveling salesman for Procter and Gamble had been $50 a week plus expenses and a company car. This was enough to rent a two-bedroom house and eat meat four days a week. In the Marines, Andrew's pay was $50 a month (plus room and board for himself). Andrew kept $5 a month and sent $45 on regular allotment to Moira. But this was not enough to pay expenses the way they had been living, so Moira wrote to her mother to see whether she could move back home. Then she divided all their worldly goods into three piles: (a) must keep with me, (b) must keep but may be sent by the mail, (c) must sell. With the money from (c) Moira bought a one-way train ticket and packed two suitcases and four cardboard boxes.

This was all she could do. She held the yard sale and had as her goal that everything must go. The merchandise was priced to move, but at the end of the day, Moira would give things away rather than assign them to the garbage. Her upbringing near the Indian Reservation gave her a great respect for keeping the flow of goods moving. So long as it was useful to someone, any knickknack was better in a person's hands than it was in a garbage dump.

Moira believed in traveling light: her silver, china, and some linen went into the boxes. Her clothes and family mementoes went into the suitcase. She only kept two books: her Bible that had been given to her by her mother and the 1936 Macalister yearbook. She was two months pregnant, and had not begun to show. She was nauseous some but rarely vomited more than once a day. Moira was a tough one. She had been sick before but had always come out of it victorious.

Moira's mother took three weeks before responding. It was a short letter.

> *Dear Moira,*
>
> *So sad to hear that Andrew had to go to war, but I suppose that everyone is these days. I talked to your father about your staying here and he agreed (after much cajoling under the following conditions: (a) you sleep with the baby once he is born in the main room on the floor, and (b) you accept a job at Great Northern in the secretarial pool at a salary of $85 a month that you will turn over to your father to offset any extra expenses). I will look after the baby while you are at work.*
>
> *If this is acceptable to you, then let me know and I will expect you shortly thereafter. I do look forward to seeing you again.*

Love,
Mother

p.s. Your brother also enlisted and is working with the U.S.O. He is using his work as a trumpet player (just like his father) to present shows for the servicemen.

Upon receipt of this letter, Moira had her sale, bought a one-way ticket, sent a letter to her mother, and in less than a week was on her way. Of course, she went through Great Northern instead of cobbling together another route on other lines. In principle, her father, Mac, had a lifetime pass for himself and his children to ride free on the Great Northern. But Mac only used the pass himself for business, and later only allowed his wife, Flo, to visit her daughter twice when she lived in the Chicago area. Whenever his son Mac or his daughter Moira visited him in Montana, they had to pay full fare.

Moira rode coach class. There were three levels of accommodation on the Great Northern in 1942: coach, sleeper, and private room. In coach class one sat in a reserved or unreserved seat (according to one's ticket). Each coach car had an aisle in the center and a row of moveable bench seats on each side. In one configuration, all the benches could be centered in one direction (especially desirable to singles or couples). In another configuration, the seats could be swiveled so that four people might face each other (designed for families or groups traveling together). Sleeper class was only viable at night. By day, people with these tickets sat in unreserved coach. By night they retired to their reserved bunk. It constituted a single bed on one of two levels (lower and upper). There was fresh linen on the beds and a heavy curtain that could be pulled for privacy. There was also a porter who would be dedicated to supervising two sleeper cars all night long.

Those with private rooms were at the top of the pecking order (superseded only by the ultra-rich who would have their own private car attached to the train). Those with private rooms had a personal compartment that could seat four people. In the night, the porter would fold the seats into four single beds. There was also a small private toilet and shower. The entire bathroom had the floor space of a normal executive desk. Though the accommodations were cramped, it was considered to be high luxury to ride in a private compartment. Most patrons who had this class of ticket rarely sat in coach.

At five o'clock, the porter would stop by to reserve seats for dinner in the dining car. Most people in the train would put down for a time (though the poorest would make do with food they brought aboard). Moira brought her food with her. She ate her cheese and bread once most of the people in her car had departed for dinner.

At ten o'clock the porter would announce the evening call. This meant that those in sleepers should retire there and those who wished to change for sleep could head to the public toilet located at the end of the car. Moira did have a robe in one of her brown cardboard suitcases with metal rims. But when she saw that there were three nuns heading toward the toilet, she decided just to sleep in her clothes. It had been Moira's experience that the nuns locked the door to the toilet and took a long time because their habits were multi-layered. Moira also wondered whether the nuns held a prayer service in the toilet—because it was private. Baptists would never think of such a thing. Imagine taking the Bible into the toilet! Moira shut her eyes and fell asleep as she pictured the scene of a group of nuns holding a prayer service in the common bathroom.

The next day the train arrived. Florence, Moira's mother, was waiting at the end of the train platform for her daughter—just beyond the black wrought iron gate. Standing at the gate was a man in a company uniform checking tickets one last time.

Moira was wearing a dark brown, thin cotton dress that had a high button-down neckline and smooth lines to the high empire waist. Then the lines flowed out, forming an "A" line. Because she had slept in her clothes, they were rather wrinkled and smelled a little. Moira's shoes were black single-strap with a very small heel. The eyehole on the strap of the left shoe was about to merge with its lower cousin. This made her left shoe feel loose.

Moira wondered how she would find a way home. The family had moved since she had gotten married. Then she saw her mother. Moira stopped. She set down her two suitcases and her heavy cloth coat that she carried over her arm. It was summer, but winters in Montana were fierce. Florence hadn't found her daughter yet. Both mother and daughter were short sighted. The distance was a mere twenty-five yards filled with travelers determined to exit.

Florence was standing there, wearing a green hat with some tattered mesh atop. Her permed light brown hair was losing a little of its hold. She wore a straight-line ivory dress that came to the middle of her tibia and was slightly stained at the hem. As Florence surveyed the crowd, she got up on her tiptoes to get a better view. She deftly twisted to move her fifty-two-year-old body back and forth. And then she found her daughter. At that moment Florence froze.

Moira ran to her mother. In the last four yards, she lost her left shoe. Moira didn't stop until she was in the arms of her mother. "Oh, Mommy!"

Florence was unable to say a word.

The two remained together in a world that contained only them, when an index finger touched Moira's right shoulder accompanied by, "Excuse me, ma'am. Excuse me."

Moira loosened her hold and twisted her head around to see a middle-aged man with a balding pate and a smile on his face holding her two suitcases and her missing left shoe.

Then it all came back to Moira: the events before she had left the real world. Immediately, she broke her embrace and turned to the man to retrieve her cargo, "Oh, thank you. I'm so sorry."

"No need, ma'am. You're welcome."

"Let me help you with those, dear," said Florence. "It's not too long a walk, but in your condition, ah," Florence cleared her throat. "We have to talk about a few things before we get home." Moira smiled and picked-up the heavier suitcase. Florence took the lighter one and the winter coat. They were headed for home.

Luckily, the route to the apartment that hot summer day was along tree-lined streets. The shade made the temperature bearable. "I must tell you a few things, dear," began Florence after they had left the throng of the terminal.

"You're looking healthy, Mom," replied Moira.

Florence smiled. "I think we can still wear the same clothes. That will come in handy in the time to come."

"Oh mother, I wouldn't—"

"You have to be practical, girl. This is a terrible war. Who knows if your Andrew will ever come home?"

"Mother!"

"You've got to be practical, girl. This is a terrible war. Who knows whether we will even win it? The Japs might run this country. How would that be? Them and their slanty eyes!"

"Mother!"

"And your father's drinking again."

Moira pursed her lips.

"He had to give up his spot in the Union band. He couldn't hack it anymore."

"But father and music—"

"It's who he is. But he's also 67. Most men are dead by 67—after all, you get Social Security at 65 just in time to die—" Florence's diatribe was cut short by a horse-drawn cart that almost ran them down. Moira pulled her mother back as she tripped and fell. As Moira helped her mother to her feet the matriarch said, "Damn horses! I wish we'd get rid of the lot of them. I've heard on the radio that in the East it's all automobiles. That's the way it should be here, too. Them automobiles have horns that warn a person that they're coming—just like railroad engines."

"Do you want me to take that suitcase now, Mother?"

"He couldn't keep up with the rhythm; arthritis in his hands. When you play the trumpet you've got to keep a beat. He's lost it. And now he's drinking himself to death."

The two didn't talk anymore until they got home.

The Smith's apartment was on the fourth floor. This meant a long walk up or an adventure on a self-service elevator (that was even more antiquated than the one the Smith's had when they lived in the Twin Cities). When Florence moved the lever to the fourth position (the top floor) the machine violently jerked. Moira grabbed the side of the elevator car to stabilize herself. Florence moved to protect her daughter. "Don't worry, dear. It's a bit primitive, but you remember how we lived in Wolf Point? We had the only car for miles around us. Everything then was like in pre-historic times. At least this old lizzy works and we only pay $45 a month for rent. Who can complain?"

They arrived at apartment 42. It was a one-bedroom corner apartment with a kitchen and a large living room that also housed the dining table. The room was full of windows and was bright. On the inner wall were a sofa and low table. Next to the sofa near the large picture window was a large cardboard box. Moira walked into the room to inspect everything. "You will sleep on the sofa, Moira. You can put your things into the box there and when the child is born we will rig something out for it on the floor next to you. Everything will be just fine."

Moira thought about her two-bedroom house in Menomonie Falls: solid brick and with a half-attic. They even had a yard. Lord Chiltren loved to run after balls thrown by herself and Andrew there. Sometimes Moira would trick the dog and pretend to throw, but not let go of the ball! The dog was so confused. His lordship didn't appreciate jokes. It was sad at the end when she had to give away Lord Chiltren in the last flurry to simplify. "So, has Papa gotten me a job yet?"

Florence moved her daughter to the table and sat her down. Then she put on water for tea. They had an electric stove that had a "hot" burner that went on more efficiently than the others. When the teakettle sang, Florence fixed her concoction: sugar, tea, and ground chicory root.

"You know, Moira, that you have very important talents in the office. You can type like the dickens, take shorthand, and write letters. You're a college girl with a head on your shoulders who could have been anything she wanted in the world!"

As she talked, Florence looked up to the ceiling as if she were addressing God Himself. Moira followed her mother's invocation with rapt attention. "Oh, mother, really."

"I'm serious. You could have gone to medical school. You could have been a reporter. You could have written a radio show. I believe it."

Moira moved forward and hugged her mother. But her mother would have none of it. "I'm serious!" she proclaimed. "This isn't just some mother talking. You *are* first rate."

Moira moved back and took a sip of tea. "The tea is just as I remember it, Mom. You haven't lost your touch."

Florence smiled and turned her gaze modestly downward. There was an awkward silence while the two women cast their eyes about before resuming contact.

"You're starting Monday at the office. You'll earn $88 a month after taxes. There's also Union health insurance that will pay for the baby. Daddy wants all of your paycheck for himself."

"All of it? You just told me that the rent is $45. I'm one third of that—or one-half once the baby is born. I wouldn't eat more $10 a month. Make that $14 once the baby is born. That's only $37. Even if he cut my paycheck in half it wouldn't equal that!"

Florence started stirring her tea vigorously with a teaspoon. Then she lifted the spoon out of the teacup and dropped it on the table. The spoon dropped awkwardly and fell over so that it projected a convex posture. Then she looked her daughter in the eye before looking out the window as she talked to her. "His idea is this: you are coming here. You will disrupt his life. He has gotten you a job in the midst of hard times because of his union position. You should be thankful that you *can* pay him back."

Florence began to cry. She suppressed it almost immediately. "Of course, anything that Andrew sends you is *yours*." She looked her daughter in the eye. Then she smiled and grimaced. "That is, so long as he stays alive."

This time it was Moira's turn to cry.

***

When Mac came home he yelled out, "Is Suzy here?" Suzy was a pet name that Mac used with his daughter when she was very young. Florence came out of the kitchen as Moira got up and meandered down the hall to her father. Mac beamed and ran to meet his little girl. "Suzy, how are you? And how's the little stranger? Heard from Andy recently?"

"Mac, you've just asked a thousand questions. Your daughter just got off the train. She's tired."

Mac gave his Suzy a hug and walked her into the living room. Florence followed and sat herself at the dining room table while father and daughter sat on the sofa that would be Moira's bed. Mac started several sentences before he found one he liked, "Your room here, has Flo talked to you about it?"

"Yes, father, she's gone through all the details—except one: will I be paying you directly or will you simply garnish my paychecks?"

Mac frowned. "*Garnish*. I don't much like that word, Suzy. That's a word they use for debtors."

"But aren't I a *debtor* to you?"

Mac smiled again. "Oh Suzy, you're no debtor. You're family. There's always a place for you here with your folks."

Moira smiled and kissed her father on the cheek. Mac responded with a hug and then sprang up to pour himself a drink and read the newspaper. "What's for dinner, Flo?"

"Bass from the Park," was the reply from the kitchen. The park in question was Glacier National Park that had some of the best fish and game in the area. It was always very dear because of the transport costs.

"Bass from the Park, eh? I like it. Where'd you get the money? I haven't paid you your allowance yet."

"My sewing money. You've always said that I can do with that as I like because I earn it."

Mac opened the newspaper and nodded. "Damn right. Everything a person makes belongs to them and to them alone. That's what it means to live in a free country."

Moira got up to help her mother in the kitchen.

***

Florence Moe Smith was well known as a baker. She sometimes sold her baked goods to a shop a few blocks away when her sewing business was light (she generally repaired clothes, but could also create a wedding dress from a picture in the newspaper). Florence sewed on an old Singer machine that used to have a foot pump, but was now fully electric. It was heavy, black cast iron with bright gold letters that were worn around the edges.

Tonight Florence, the baker, would be serving her famous cinnamon buns along with the fish cooked with leeks. Every dinner for Florence was half dessert. She had quite a sweet tooth. And yet at five feet-five inches she had gained nary a pound in twenty years: 125 on the bathroom scale in her underwear.

***

Moira went to work two days later. She had a bit of an uphill battle among the office pool. People saw her as having gotten her job through the influence of some unknown male manager. The Depression was still very real in central Montana. The war effort hadn't picked things up in Great Falls. The women who sat in the typing pool also resented the fact that Moira was granted an aisle seat (very valuable because one could get to the bathroom quicker), and there was open air on one side.

After a week on the job, a redheaded woman who sat near Moira in the typing pool asked, "So what did you have to do to get this job, doll face?"

It was lunchtime. One third of the pool went to the lunchroom at the same time and sat together. The lunchroom was a dour room painted in pea soup green. Square wooden tables that could seat eight were often pulled together to seat twelve. There was giggling after the question.

"What do you mean by your question?" replied Moira. The women were all eating food brought from home, usually wrapped in oilcloth. Moira was eating some carrots and cheese.

"What do you mean? 'What do you mean?'" The crowd tittered once more. The redhead took off a big bite of beef jerky. She had buckteeth and muscular biceps. "You know what I'm talking about, sweetheart. Who did you have to lay down to get your job?"

There was a murmur and a titter among the hoi polloi. Moira put down her food. "You have a very insulting way about you. What did I do to deserve your cruel un-Christian treatment?"

Redhead didn't blink, "Lookee here, my Christian nun, these jobs in the typing pool are hard to get. You have to pass a test after you've worked at filing or the mailroom for a few years. You just dance in here and go right to the top. Just like that." Redhead snapped her fingers. "Things like that don't just happen. There has to be a reason, and I'm sure yours is no good."

Moira grimaced. She looked around to her gallery. "Well, ladies, I am willing to tell you my story. I hope that you, also, will do the same with me. I am not a secretive person. I am a college-educated woman—and I don't mean business college. My father wanted me to continue to medical school. My husband just volunteered for the Marines. He will be leaving shortly for the Pacific to fight the Japanese. I don't know if I'll ever see him again. My father, Malcolm Smith, helped me get this job. I am very well qualified for the situation. I was valedictorian of my high school class—first in a class of four hundred. I can read Latin, French, and Spanish. I can type 100 words a minute and take short hand. I can also correct the grammar of the letters I send out. I sit on the end of the aisle because I'm three months pregnant with my husband's child—a child he may never have the chance to meet.

"I am sorry if I have done anything to offend any of you. That is not my intention. I know the world is very difficult just now. I hope our country will pull through." Then Moira extended her hand to the redhead. The crowd was silent while the redhead pondered the event. She scratched the back of her head through the medium length straight greasy hair. Then she nodded her head. "Well, missy, I guess I didn't have you figured right. I'm sorry. It's just that we don't take to strangers much here."

Then redhead shook Moira's hand. "What's your name?" asked Moira.

"Bella."

"Well, Bella, if it would make things easier, I'm not really a stranger either. I was born near an Indian Reservation in Wolf Point, Montana. I'm a native."

This was the cincher. After that, Moira was one of the girls.

***

As time went by, Moira and Bella became the titular leaders of the typing pool. When management made unreasonable demands, the two women would go to the supervisor together with their complaint. If that didn't work, they went straight to Malcolm Smith, the head union leader of the branch.

When Mac was on the job he was all business—that is unless he was giving someone *the business*. Mac could use his gift of humor to disarm an opponent. Because of his doubly powerful position as a high-ranking employee and top union representative, he was not a man to be dismissed. When Mac told a joke, everyone laughed—even if they didn't *get it*.

One time Moira and Bella came into Mac's corner office with a grievance. Mac sat behind a partner's desk. It was his opinion that a union organizer ought to be a social chap. He had pictures on the wall of various bands he'd played in—including one taken on a Mississippi paddle wheel back in the day. There was even a picture of him shaking hands with Harry Truman at a big Great Northern event at which the band played. Mac had just stepped down as bandleader, but he was still known for his rousing trumpet solos. Also on his wall was his famed trumpet. He hadn't touched it in two years.

Out of view in his desk were two items of import. The first was a letter written by his father, Cedric, as he lay dying in the flu epidemic of 1918. Two features of the letter stuck in Mac's consciousness: (a) Cedric said he was proud of Mac's musical career, and (b) Cedric bemoaned that Mac had never become a doctor so that his son might save him in these last days. Cedric Smith was 75 years old when he died.

The second item of import was a bottle of single malt Scotch whiskey. Though the Smythe family of New England always claimed allegiance to Grand Britannia, rebel Cedric had identified as a Scott or Scott-Irish. It was only the faction of detractors who morphed that term to *Scotch-Irish.*

Opposite the partner's desk were four white oak chairs with solid backs and a carved decoration near the top on each side (just at the right place to hit your shoulder blades and cause discomfort—though this was not his intent). Mac, himself, sat in an oak chair that was stained black so that the seal of the Great Northern could be displayed. In the center of the desk at the front was a painted wooden mascot of the company: a full-fleeced mountain goat climbing upwards (towards a summit?).

"How can I help you girls today?" Mac had a smile on his face. He was all business. He motioned for them to sit down.

Moira and Bella sat down. Then Moira scooted her chair right up into the opposite side of the partner's desk. Bella followed her lead. "Here's our complaint. We come to you as our Union representative, but we also hope that your management position might also come in handy," began Moira.

Mac smiled, "What is the problem?"

"We work ten-hour shifts with only a half-hour for lunch. Often our supervisors give us an unreasonable amount of work to do so that we end up working eleven to twelve hours—the last two without pay because they say we should have been able to finish up in ten."

Bella nodded her head. Both women sat bolt upright.

Mac leaned and tilted his chair backwards. "So, you're upset because you're working twelve hours?"

"But they don't pay us for twelve hours," put Bella, she started to lean forward.

Moira nodded but remained bolt upright.

Mac smiled. "Then you're upset that they don't pay you for twelve hours when you've done ten hours work?"

Both women frowned. Outside a crow flew into the window of Mac's corner office and tumbled to his death four stories down.

Mac turned his head, got up and walked over to the window. "Bird brains." He chuckled and then turned back to the secretaries. "I'll talk to your supervisor and see what he has to say about this. I am your union representative and I will look after your interests." Mac extended his hand. Moira took it, but Bella turned and left before an offer could be extended to her. As Bella left, she said loudly with her back to Mac and her face to the open office door, "We work by the hour. This isn't a piece-work operation. *We're* not on salary."

The declaration was heard by other secretaries around the office door (none of whom altered their demeanor in the slightest).

Moira left feeling that their fate would be that of the dead crow. She was wrong. Mac created work rules for the typing pool that when they worked over ten hours, they would be paid time and a half.

The typing pool (including Moira and Bella) were ecstatic. The two were held in high regard. Mac Smith (who garnished his daughter's wages) was also ten dollars richer each month.

***

When Liam O'Neil was born in the middle of the winter (February 15, 1943), things changed. Mac had contacted the family physician, Samuel Price, about the situation when Moira was in her eighth month. He agreed to perform the delivery for $85 (more if there were complications). Mac said that Moira had to save Andrew's $45 monthly army allotment to pay the fee.

The delivery was divine. The bag of waters broke at six o'clock in the morning, a half-hour after Moira woke-up. The doctor was called after some last minute deliberations by Mac about whether his medical training might qualify him to perform the task himself. It certainly would be cheaper (though whether the savings would be passed along was still an issue in Mac's mind). But if there were any problems, Mac didn't want to be the one who was blamed. Dr. Price was called and after a six-hour labor, Liam was born. There were no complications.

***

Later that day, Florence came upon her daughter who was attempting to nurse her child. Florence leaned over and stroked her daughter's hair. The boy was a bouncing, red-skinned chubby child.

"What made you think of calling him Liam?" asked Florence. "It's such a strange name."

Moira smiled. "When Andrew left for the War and I suspected I was pregnant, I went to the library to look up Irish first names. When I came upon 'Liam' it said that it was really 'William.' 'William' is the name of the Norman conqueror of Britain."

Florence cocked her head. She was out of her ken.

"'William the Conqueror: instigator of the Norman Conquest—you know, 1066 and all that.' I wanted my boy to be special."

Florence laughed heartily and hugged her daughter. "He'll always be special because he's *your* son. I don't care if you name him Norman."

***

Moira was allowed two weeks off after birth using acquired leave time and part of her annual vacation. When she left for work on that first day back, she handed over Liam to her mother. The nursing wasn't going well, so they invested in four glass feeding bottles and eight rubber nipples. It was no longer necessary for a woman to biologically feed her child, claimed Mac. Modern science had come up with a new remedy just like it had with the clothes washing machine. No longer did women have to spend hours a day doing laundry. The washing machine allowed the housewife to throw the clothes into the metal tub, put in some soap, and turn on the proper setting. Within an hour, the machine had done it all!

Now, also, women no longer had to breast feed their children! That was very primitive—like those women in *National Geographic Magazine* from Africa or the South Pacific who walk around with uncovered breasts. The modern woman purchased specially formulated powder that could be mixed into water and placed into a sterile glass bottle with sterile rubber nipples. Not only was the mother relieved of a time-consuming task, but the infant was actually being more nutritionally fed! It was a miracle of modern science.

Moira wasn't so sure. She listened to her father's lectures on the subject. They carried some weight because of his medical background. But Moira wasn't confident that science had all the answers to things. She had grown up very simply at Wolf Point and Havre. The only medical care they ever received was from Mac. He had a few herbal remedies, but he mostly relied upon his theory about the intestines. Mac believed that all health arose from balancing intestine health. This was achieved via putting hot water into rubber bags and laying them against the skin. His other sure-fire remedy was the enema. The enema cleaned out the blockages in the intestines and would thus promote broad general health. Mac would claim to quote Galen about digestion and its relation to the liver and to the heart. The single book that Mac possessed from his early years was a one-volume compilation of the works of Galen applicable to modern medicine.

When anyone was sick in the family, they had to take the herbal remedy and several enemas. Mac swore by his treatments. Remarkably, few family members ever reported being sick—especially past ten years old. Moira had once snuck away to a friend when she was eleven because she was coughing and spitting up blood. Her friend put Moira up in a cabin the family owned in the hills. It was summer and Moira stayed away for a month. It wasn't until years later when Moira had a physical for college that required a chest x-ray that she learned that she had had tuberculosis. There was no known treatment for the disease at the time. Enemas were of no value.

***

When it came time for Moira to return to work, she placed Liam in her mother's care. Moira had written out several lists about feeding times, how to sterilize the bottles and nipples, and the best way to mix formula. These were rather like kitchen chores, so Florence tacked the papers onto her recipe cork board. She was good at kitchen work.

What Moira didn't instruct her mother in was how she, Moira, wanted her mother to raise Liam. Because Moira basically raised herself as a child, she really didn't give much thought to it. But when she came home on the first day back she found Liam all pushed up in the corner of his crib (a dresser drawer lined with a blanket). She instantly ran to him, fearing the worst.

Liam was listless. Mommy Moira kissed his blue lips and gave him a smack on the rump. The result was a spillage of feces out of Liam's diaper and loosely fitted rubber pants. The splatter was mostly on the floor but also on Moira's skirt (one of six that she owned). But the spanking worked. Liam started bawling with powerful lungs. Moira kissed her child over and over again as she took her son to the far corner of the room to a towel on the floor that was the changing area.

When Moira was almost done, Florence came out of the kitchen and declared, "Tonight, sweetie, we're having corn and my cinnamon rolls. I've been working on them since lunch."

Moira looked up to her mother who stood at the entrance to the kitchen in her white and red checked apron, holding a wooden spoon and grinning ear to ear.

"Thank you, Mother," she replied as she finished changing Liam, adding oil on his bottom to help with his diaper rash and then putting him back into his drawer with a new diaper and rubber pants. Then it was on to the toilet to rinse out his dirty underthings and deposit them into the makeshift hamper (a metal pail with a board that sat on top to keep the smell down).

Moira then went back to her son and picked him up and sang to him. She didn't realize that his little left foot that was kicking to the music was also rubbing the errant feces into his mother's skirt.

***

When Liam was six months old, Moira stopped into a bookstore. She had intended on buying herself a mystery novel to help her get to sleep each night. Moira had saved a dollar for this luxury. She got directions to the mystery section and picked up a Dorothy Sayers novel. On her way to the cash register, she saw a new series of books that she had never before beheld: Golden Books. There were ten volumes in the display case and each cost twenty-five cents. Moira was fascinated. She put down her book and picked up *Mother Goose*. The rhymes were beautiful. Moira had never read any of these before. She had heard references to Mother Goose in high school English classes, but she had never read any of the rhymes herself. But here before her in a simple cardboard binding with a gold colored spine were colored pictures and children's poetry. "There lived an old lady who lived in a shoe who had so many children she didn't know what to do . . ." Poet Moira rewrote the lines in her head, "There lived a young woman who lived on a sofa, she had a single child who lived in a drawer, and she didn't know what to do!" Moira picked up book after book in the display. She settled on: *Mother Goose, The Three Kittens, The Little Red Hen,* and *Prayers for Children.* Christmas was set. Ready or not, she would read these books to Liam over and over again until he understood them, and then until he could read them himself.

***

"You know I'm Jewish." Moira turned her head to look at Sarah again. Sarah didn't look Jewish to her. But then Moira had not known more than a handful of Jews in her life.

"I didn't know. You don't resemble the few Jews that I have known."

Sarah laughed. "Yeah, we're good at being invisible. You know in Great Falls, we meet in an apartment of a man named Jacob who pretends to be our rabbi, but he never even finished college. In his day job he works for the post office as a letter carrier."

"College is overrated," replied Moira. The two were eating in the lunchroom. Both had to eat late because they were involved in a desperate typing project that had to meet the 2pm mail.

"Oh, I like him and everything, but you know, Moira," Sarah paused and grabbed Moira's hand in her own, "My faith teaches me that I am among the chosen people of God. But then here am I in Great Falls, Montana, and all I see about me are Baptist Christians."

Moira squeezed Sarah's hand. "You know, Jesus was a Jew. Christians and Jews aren't that far apart, really." Then she looked up to her co-worker. "I think at the end of the day—at the end of time—that we have to look after each other. You've looked after me, and I will look after you. After all, there is only one God above us all. How we think about Him and how we structure our reactions to Him create differences. But why should those differences separate people who work together and trust each other?"

Sarah hugged Moira and wouldn't let go. It was time to go back to work.

***

Sarah, Moira, and Bella became the leaders of the typing pool. They arranged the seating order so that they could sit in the front with each other on the aisle. Sarah was in the middle. The new topic of the day was Jacob (de-linked from his rabbi role). Jacob was thirty. Sarah was twenty-five. Within this threesome, Jacob was merely identified as a letter carrier for the post office.

At lunch one day Sarah said, "You know, I read in the paper the other day that if a girl isn't married by twenty-five then she's more likely to be killed by being hit by a meteor from outer space than to ever be married."

Bella slapped Sarah on the shoulder blade as she chewed her baloney sandwich. "Don't believe a word of it, girl." Bella was spitting out bits of food on the table in front of her. She picked up a glass of water to wash down her mouthful. Then she shook her head as if she were shaking off water from her hair. "Sure, *I* was married when I was seventeen. Dropped out of high school and married the star football quarterback who was two years older and had a steady job at his dad's insurance business. I thought I was set. But you know the insurance business is cyclical—like the stock market. His pay depended upon commissions and people don't much like spending money on insurance unless they have to. When times is tight, the first thing to go is insurance."

"I was twenty-three when I married," returned Moira. "And I knew girls who didn't get married until they were almost thirty—"

"—Almost thirty?" chimed in Bella in a skeptical tone.

"Sure," returned Moira still looking at Sarah. "When the right guy comes around—like your letter carrier, Jacob, I think you should help nature take its course."

Sarah smiled and blushed.

Whap! Another blow to the shoulder blade with the open hand of Bella. "That's right, Sara, you've gotta get a guy's attention. Sure every guy thinks he's the football quarterback, but you have to show him that you're the head cheerleader. Take an interest in his job. Take an interest in his hobbies—he *does* have hobbies, right?" Bella took another big bite of her sandwich.

Sarah smiled, "Yes, he likes to collect stamps. He buys them in blocks of four on the first day issue so that they have the cancellation mark with the date. You should see his albums. He has two volumes so far."

Then the buzzer sounded. The half-hour was over: back to work. On the way, Moira said to Sarah, "You know, there's a coin and stamp shop near to where I live. When we get off work, why don't we go over there to learn a few things?"

Sarah gave a full smile, showing her rather large front teeth and the one crooked canine tooth. Then she reflexively pulled her lips back together and nodded her head. Moira gave a light rub to Sara's shoulder. In her left hand, Moira carried her half-eaten lunch in a brown paper bag.

***

After work, the two headed toward Moira's home. They found the shop, which looked dark. They decided to try the door. When the two women opened the door, a little bell positioned at the top rang to signal their entry. This was followed by the click of a light switch and the sound of shoes shuffling on the floor. In a manner of moments they beheld a small, thin man without any hair save for two inches on the bottom of the hair line—almost like a high fur cranial collar. "Can I help you, ladies?" The man's voice was high and squeaky.

"Well, we were interested in whether you had some inexpensive stamps in a block of four that isn't too recent?" Moira took charge.

"Well you know ladies, that stamps have eternal value. They never go down. They are like gold: they hold their value." As he talked, the man took the wire rimmed glasses off of his nose and began to polish them on the sleeve of his shirt.

"That may be, but it doesn't answer my question," returned Moira. Sarah had drifted over to a shelf that displayed cases of stamps.

The stamp man walked over to where Sarah was standing to supervise her activities. Sarah was looking at some blue stamps. Sarah was partial to blue. "How much are these, mister?"

The little man looked back to Sarah without a pause, "Those are 1917 commemoratives that were issued when we went to war. I could sell them to you for twenty-five dollars—even though they are worth half again as much."

Sarah began to cough repeatedly. Moira moved to her aid, patting her gently upon the back. "I'm sorry, mister--?"

"Boyle. My name is Boyle. I'm a born American."

Boyle moved back when Moira moved up. The twilight sun was making the shop rather dark. The two side electric lights had low wattage bulbs.

"Well, Mr. Boyle, we are not Rockefellers. We need something more in the price range of two dollars. What can you sell us? After all, a stamp at the post office is only three cents. That's quite a mark-up!"

Mr. Boyle began rubbing his bald head with his left hand. He pursed his lips and then lifted his right hand with the index finger extended. "I've got it! There's a rather nice block of sixteen Susan B. Anthony commemorative stamps with first day cover that I could sell you for a dollar fifty. What do you say?"

"Done!" said Moira. Sarah came up with the dollar and Moira pitched in the fifty cents.

Mister Boyle wrapped the stamps (that were sealed between two thin square glass plates) with brown paper against a cardboard backing and put on two pieces of cellophane tape. Everything looked very official. The women thanked Mr. Boyle, but before they could go the proprietor got their attention and pointed to a little sign that was on the side wall. "You ladies want to learn more about stamps, you should go to the Philatelic meeting at Jefferson High School next Saturday at 7:00pm." Moira made eye contact and smiled. Then the two women left.

"This is wonderful, Moira," said Sarah as she was holding her package close to her heart as if it were a baby. "But how should I present this to Jacob?"

"Let's sit on that bench over there, Sarah."

The bench was situated on a very small park across the street. Moira put her hand on Sara's shoulder. It was mid-November and the weather was getting cold. "We've got to be quick about this, Sarah, but I think that you should suggest to Jacob that you go to that stamp show and then afterwards you can give him the stamps." Moira smiled as a sign that the deal was closed.

Sarah didn't return the smile. "Moira, the show is on Saturday. That's our holy day. I couldn't ask a rabbi out on the Sabbath."

Moira erased her smile and nodded her head. "Please forgive me, Sarah. I'm not too knowledgeable about Judaism. But am I wrong to surmise that the Sabbath begins at 5pm on Friday and goes to 4:59 on Saturday? If that's so, then you could go to something at 7pm without a problem."

Sarah seemed perplexed. It seemed to make sense to her but she wasn't sure it was that simple. But she'd have to ask Jacob if it was correct. She stood up and shook Moira's hand. "I'll let you know what happens."

***

When Moira got home, she kissed her mother and went to Liam, who was lying in his dresser drawer and kicking a piece of string that Florence had hung over his space from a rack that she normally used to dry clothes. Liam seemed to love to kick the string as he rolled a bit from side-to-side. Moira picked up her child and held him in her arms as she told him one of the rhymes from the still-hidden Golden Books. "There was an old woman who lived in a shoe who had so many children that she didn't know what to do!"

At the end of the phrase, Moira raised her pitch and began laughing as she started tickling her baby. A moment later, it was time for diaper changing.

***

Sarah got married in March. Moira and Bella came for the event. Jacob had to train a lay person to perform the proceedings (since there were no other rabbis in Great Falls—to their knowledge). The Chupah was constructed with four pine dowels that supported a white bed sheet. The Sheva Brachot was read in an English translation from the Yiddish that Jacob had done. They had a small cup of wine and Jacob could only afford a brass ring, but when they broke the glass and when they moved outside for the veiling, everything seemed magical.

Moira was very moved by the ceremony. Bella was anxious to get back to her bowling league.

***

In April, Liam took his first steps. It was a Sunday, April 9th— Easter. The snow outside hadn't melted yet so the Baptist church the Smiths attended had their Easter egg hunt in the church basement among the Sunday School rooms. Moira and Florence brought Liam downstairs to observe the older children. Mac stayed upstairs with his cronies, drinking coffee and munching on sugar cookies.

The basement of the church was rather plain. The floor was concrete and the walls were painted cinderblock. None of the classrooms had doors, but each was carpeted and had a cast iron hot water heater that came from the boiler room down the hall. The Sunday school teachers had decorated their rooms with crepe paper and colorful pictures. They had also hidden marshmallows, jelly beans, and a few chocolate eggs in clean areas around the four classrooms (0-4; 5-8; 9-12; teens). Liam was very stimulated. He uttered happy sounds and kicked his feet. Moira often wished that she had a dictionary of baby talk. She so wanted to understand what her child was saying. Liam squirmed so hard that he almost fell out of Moira's arms.

Moira decided to set her child down on the carpet and pulled up his little white sailor-suit pants that Florence had sewn for her grandchild. Liam looked at the other toddlers and started crawling toward them. When he got to a small wooden chair that had been pulled into the center of the room by one of the older children, he stopped. It was an unfinished pine chair that had been well sanded so that it had no splinters. Liam grabbed at the chair and pulled himself up. He saw the other youngsters walking about. There were no other crawling children in the room. Liam didn't look back at his mother, but resolutely took two steps forward before falling forward onto his face. Moira rushed forward and stopped. Liam had already righted himself and crawled back to the chair. Moira retreated as Liam moved forward and this time took three steps before he fell.

On the fourth try, Liam was walking like a duck, moving side to side. This time Moira could not restrain herself. She left her mother and flew to her baby. She lifted her ambulatory child and plied his face with kisses. Another mother came over and handed Moira a yellow jelly bean. Moira smiled and rewarded her child's achievement. But the real reward came a moment later when after a few more athletic feats the child said, "Ma ma. Ma ma." The words were loud and clear. There was no need for a dictionary now.

It was an historic Easter.

***

In the summer, Moira decided to move her child to solid foods. She mushed up vegetables with a fork first and then with a potato whisk. Then she filled his drinking cup with apple juice. Liam took to solids—though he was a very messy eater.

Liam loved his Golden Books. He loved them so much that he took the crayons that Moira bought him and enhanced his tomes. The first time he did this was one evening in early summer. Mac had gotten home late. He had been at a union meeting. There had been a great deal of drinking and singing of union songs. When he made his entrance to the apartment he was singing "Pat works on the Railway."

Moira was in the bathroom getting ready for bed. Florence was already asleep. Liam was sitting on a little chair that they had borrowed from church. He had his Golden Book, *The Little Red Hen*. Liam thought that it would be a good idea to draw more red hens on every page. He was making happy sounds at a low volume as he drew his masterpieces.

When Mac came in, he delivered the final refrain and looked around for his audience. They were not to be found. He marched forward to the living/dining room. The only person he could see was young Liam. Mac strode forward and began singing again. Liam did not respond. He was busy in his creative endeavor. Mac stopped singing. He marched over and picked up the child. "Well my little selfish brat," he began as he turned the child, crayon in hand, so that he had to look at him. "You must learn to show respect for the master of the house! It's me who pays your way in the world, you know, so you should pay me proper respect when I come home!"

Liam was not making eye contact with his grandfather. He flailed his arms in the air and kicked his legs. In the process of this random movement, Liam hit Mac's nose with the red crayon.

"Damnation, you brat," declared Mac as he transferred his charge to his left hand and formed his right hand into a fist. Mac paused, shook his head, and dropped the child onto the floor. Liam fell on his bottom and rolled instinctively to his side.

The toilet flushed. Moira was out in her nightgown. "Father, what's wrong?"

Mac was looking at Liam, who was crawling away from him and drawing a red line on the floor (as he had not relinquished his crayon). "Look at this!" yelled Mac as he dove down and grabbed the crayon out of Liam's hands and then, while he was on the floor he screamed, "This brat is a menace. He's drawing all over the floor and all over this book I got him for Christmas." Mac, still on the floor on his side, picked up the Golden Book. He inspected the decorated pages and then spit on one of them and ripped the book in half at the spine. Then he threw the two parts against the wall.

Mac looked up at his daughter and clenched his fists again. Moira stood firm. Then Mac shut his eyes, shook his head, raised himself up and walked toward the bedroom. He was met there by his wife who stood with her arms crossed. Mac said, "Paugh" and pushed his wife against the wall. He waddled into his room, took off his clothes, and fell into bed. In five minutes, he was asleep.

Moira went to her son and picked him up. Liam was anxious. Florence went over and retrieved the two halves of the book and rejoined them with a strip of cloth that she had from her sewing and some horse glue. Within a few minutes, she presented it to her daughter who proceeded to read the book to Liam and to exclaim over each and every drawing he made. Within an hour, Liam was quiet and Moira put him in his dresser drawer to go to sleep. Moira lay next to him on the floor so that her mother could sleep on the couch.

***

Malcolm was right about one thing. He had presented Liam that book at Christmas last. The reason was that he had bought no gift for Liam and had prohibited his wife from doing so either. Moira thought that Liam should be remembered by all the family. So she wrapped the gift that she had purchased with her meager funds and gave it to her father to present on Christmas morning. The remainder of Moira's purchase went to her child from her own hand. It was more than Moira had ever had at Christmas when she was a child.

***

Moira found herself searching through the trash at the typing pool. There were so many perfectly good pages of paper that were being thrown away just because they had an uncorrectable typing error on them. Moira wanted the pages for Liam. She would gather them in a shoulder bag that she now carried in addition to her purse. When she got home, she would put the iron on the stove and take out the ironing board. After covering the paper with a pillow case (to prevent scorching) she flattened the paper for her artist son. He always had half a ream of paper at his disposal and he made use of most of it. Liam now had a pencil, which he used to sketch his design before he colored it all in.

Liam especially liked drawing characters from his Golden Books. Liam would reconstruct them and make up his own stories. Moira would collect his books and fasten them with three staples along the edges. At the front was a blank page. She wanted to teach Liam to write his name. The task was made easier because the child had only four letters to his name. The "I" was the easiest, then the "L." The "A" took some doing because of the coordination of the three strokes. But it was the "M" that gave Liam fits. His efforts were generally three to five humped letters. No worries. Both mother and child were very proud of his efforts.

Every day, Liam would read a story to his mother after she read a story to him. It was a wonderful moment of shared intimacy that would stay with Moira forever.

***

In the newspaper, Moira read that on the Fourth of July there would be a display of children's art at the park near the river. She collected some of the most promising pieces (books and single drawings) and went to the grocery store to get some cardboard boxes that she could cut up and make flat with some wood braces in the back. These would be the displays of her child's art.

Then she arranged with her supervisor at work that she could come in early and stay late one day in order to be able to get several hours off the next day to travel to the Third Presbyterian Church to fill out the registration form and get information on when and how the set-up would proceed.

When the Fourth of July rolled along, Moira arose before 7am with Liam's art and walked two miles to the riverfront site. She was not the first one there. It was already past 8. There were several mothers who were scrambling to get the best spots on the various cork-covered plywood walls that had been hastily constructed for the event (all costs had been defrayed by the $1 application fee— "highway robbery" was what Moira thought when she forked over the money). She thought, "I'll bet it would have been lower had I been a Presbyterian!"

Nonetheless, she attached Liam's work with pushpins and proudly wrote out his name on the identification card. Moira could hardly wait to get home. She'd bought a roll of film for her Kodak camera and was ready to shoot the whole roll on Liam's show (12 pictures in all).

When she got home, she found her mother cooking bacon and eggs for Mac, who was dressed in his pajama pants and a thin-strapped t-shirt, smoking a thick cigar while he read the morning paper. In front of him was a very large cup of black coffee.

"Hello mother!" chimed Moira.

Before Florence could reply, Mac barked out, "Where have you been, Suzy? The little scooter was screaming his head off so that Flo had to get out of bed to go feed him! What kind of mother are you, anyway?" Mac then sneezed very loudly and blew his nose on the bottom of his t-shirt.

Moira forced a smile, and went to her mother to assist in Mac's breakfast. She saw that it was about time to put in the toast and she removed the butter from the ice box. Mac went back to his paper and began singing *You Always Hurt the One You Love*. Within three minutes, the master was served and the women retreated to young Liam. Moira wanted to tell her mother what she had done.

"That's wonderful, Moira. We just have to go see it. How long will it be up?"

Moira tilted her head. "It's just today, Mother. I have to pick up everything at five. I'd really like it if you and dad could come and see it."

"Where is the exhibition?" asked Florence as she took off her glasses and rubbed her eyes with her left hand.

"Gibson Park."

"Why that's almost a two-mile walk!" Florence dropped her glasses and quickly picked them up from the floor.

"You can do it, Mother. I did it today in less than an hour."

"But two miles, dear. That's quite a jaunt at my age." Florence was shaking her head and pulling back her hair with both hands. She never had it permed (like her daughter did from a kit from the drug store) but kept it straight and tied it with a cloth covered band in the back.

"Oh, mother, don't talk that way. We can leave earlier and stop frequently and sit on the benches. I want to take Liam in the pram."

Florence continued to shake her head. "That pram was loaned to us in order to take Liam to church. It wasn't for gallivanting around town!"

Moira leaned over to hug her mother. Then Liam began cry out just moments after Mac started singing *The Washington Post March* (Mac was the trumpet).

Florence stood bolt upright. "The parade. We've forgotten about the parade. We can't go anywhere today except to the parade."

Moira half expected her mother to salute an imaginary flag in her pique of patriotic enthusiasm. Moira turned and picked up her toddler. She wanted to cry, but couldn't.

***

In the end, Moira and Liam went to the parade and then departed for the art exhibit alone. Moira remembered to take her camera.

She enlisted a parent to hold up Liam in front of his artwork. Then she snapped up a storm.

When they got home, she had Liam tell her (such as he could) the stories he had written. After each one, Moira would cover her son with kisses. Liam responded with a roaring smile punctuated by his fat, pink cheeks.

***

When September rolled around, Moira received Andrew's letter. He had been discharged and was about to buy his ticket West. He hadn't given her his date or time of arrival. He merely said, "sometime this month." Well, September in Great Falls was a month of changes. One went from hot weather with all windows open and the fans strategically placed to cool the house to the opposite: the reviving up of the boiler and putting on the heat for the first time—a forerunner of the sub-zero winters.

It was Wednesday, and Wednesday was when the Smith household often ran out of food money for the week. Florence generally went shopping for two days at a time with a somewhat larger haul on Friday when Malcolm paid her for the family expenses. Moira often bought some fruit or vegetables, along with Zwieback out of her scant funds from Andrew so that Liam wouldn't be without. On several occasions when Moira was delayed at work, she would come home and find that only Mac had had a real meal of leftovers. Florence was nibbling on one of her stale cinnamon buns with some tea, and Liam was given some milk and water mixed together in a cup along with his pacifier.

"He's no longer a baby!" was Moira's complaint. "This boy's brain is growing the fastest it ever will. I will not let him starve!"

Florence evinced a pained expression while Mac finished his meal with his third beer and belched.

Moira resolved that on Wednesday and Thursday she would stop and buy supplementary food for her child. Well, it was Wednesday and she was only able to buy a banana and Zwieback. She was in a cranky mood. Sarah had had a fight with Jacob. He called her a *Shabbos goy* because she worked late last Friday night and missed his celebration of *Shabbat*. For this offence, he refused to talk to her except for practical details for one week: no hugging, no kissing, nothing—for one entire week!

"If it weren't for you, Moira, I'd never have married him. You're to blame for the whole thing. You've made me a *Shabbos goy*. I'm so unhappy!"

Moira tried to comfort her, but was interrupted by Bella, who had tickets to the boxing match.

"I really can't, Bella. This is Wednesday and I've got to feed Liam."

"Ah, can't you get your mom to do it?"

"I wish I could. But she doesn't have much nutritional sense—" Moira stopped herself. She was about to say that her mother didn't have anything beyond a sixth-grade education, but then Moira instantly remembered that neither did Bella. Moira responded with a smile and reached over to put her arm around Sarah's shoulder, but Sarah was gone. Moira tried to see whether she was still in the room. When she turned back to respond to Bella, she found that she was gone, too. Moira slumped back into a chair for a moment to catch her breath and figure out what had happened.

Just then Ted Stevens came by and said, "Oh, I'm so glad I caught you. All the other girls have left. We've got an important packet we need typed so that we can messenger it tonight."

Moira looked up.

"Don't give me that, missy. This is a business here. It will only take a few minutes."

An hour later, Moira left—just in time to be able to buy some food for her son. She was angry. She opened the front door to her apartment building. She had to push past some idiot who didn't seem to know where he was going. Immediately she raced for the elevator. It was on the ground floor. She wasn't sure what she thought of the stranger. The iron door opened, and she opened the mesh screen door and shut it again quickly. Then she turned the lever to the fourth floor. The aged engine kicked in and gradually raised up the heavy metal cage.

Because the cage was open-mesh on the sides above four feet, Moira could see that a figure was running up the steps at a pace better than the elevator. The man was carrying a duffle bag over his shoulder. Moira felt afraid. Her parent's apartment was sixty or more paces from the elevator: plenty of time to be attacked. Moira plotted what she would do. The man was already at the top level when the elevator was only at the third level. All Moira had were her purse and the food bag for Liam. She couldn't waste the food bag. She could scream, but the two apartments closest to the elevator were occupied by old people who kept the radio loud almost all day, listening to soap operas.

She would just have to do something extraordinary. She set down the food bag and grabbed the straps of her purse with two hands. Her slight 125-pound frame would not carry a big clout, but that is what she intended to do and then improvise the rest.

Then the elevator stopped. Moira crouched low in order to deliver the hardest blow. The steel doors opened, and through the metal cross-hatched inner door she could see the menacing man before her: it was Andrew! Moira gasped. Andrew exclaimed, "Moira!"

The couple stood stunned as the heavy metal doors began to close, Moira still inside the lift. The elevator was being summoned by an importuning patron below. Andrew dropped his duffle and started down the stairs—two at a time—so that he could arrive at the destination before the iron cage. Andrew falsely assumed that the elevator was going to the ground floor when it really was going to the second floor. He realized this when he was already at the bottom of the stairs, and the loud engine stopped for a moment. The ex-Marine decided instinctively to climb the stairs yet again to the second floor. After four steps, Andrew came to his senses and stopped. The elevator was engaged again and was making its descent. Andrew laughed and waved at Moira as the carriage made its way to its destination.

The second-floor caller, a middle-aged woman with a Scottie dog, got out and made an indignant sound. Andrew paid no heed. He rushed into the elevator to his wife and kissed her while Moira pulled the lever forward to #4 and closed the mesh door deftly with her right foot. The ancient contraption began again with a jolt that caused Andrew to lift his bride into the air and almost hit her head on the top of the cage. The couple was giddy.

When the rattling contraption reached its destination, it was Moira who opened the metal screen door and marshaled her husband toward the apartment.

Moira put her key into the lock and opened the door. Andrew followed his wife inside the apartment. He had never been there before. They walked down the entry hall—everything opened on the left. First, there was the bedroom of Malcolm and Florence. Then there was the bathroom. Then they came to the opening for the kitchen, (also on the left)—when they heard a crash of broken glass.

"You damned brat! Now look what you've done!"

"Oh Mac, that's nothing. It's just a cheap vase."

Then there was the sound of a slap. "You dumb animal. That was my anniversary gift to you. I gave it to you with flowers in it, remember?"

Florence and Liam began to cry. Andrew pushed past Moira and ran to his son. The boy was standing up and holding his hand, which was bleeding from a splinter of glass in the fleshy part of his right hand. Andrew scooped up his son, removed the shard, and tried to examine the damage while Mac made after the intruder with his walking stick. With one swift movement of his left elbow, Andrew struck Mac in the sternum and stunned the older man. Then Andrew followed up by snatching the stick and confronting his adversary. Mac realized he was outmanned. "Who the hell are *you* coming in here like that?"

"I'm the child's father, back from the War. Do you want to make something of it? With two hands, I'm even more destructive."

Mac froze. He had had a bit too much to drink. It had skewed his basic sense of survival. He knew that he held a bad position— both physically and socially. He shut his eyes.

The two women stood frozen in utter confusion. This was not the way a homecoming was supposed to be. Andrew took out his handkerchief and applied some pressure to the wound.

Mac took a deep breath and stepped forward. "Andrew?" he said insouciantly.

Andrew cocked his head. "Malcolm?"

"No other, you leatherneck. Welcome back from the War." Malcolm reached out his hand and Andrew took it. Then Moira snatched the child to take him to the bathroom for repair, and Florence began picking up the glass while the two men retired to the kitchen to have a beer.

***

That night Andrew held his son in his arms as he slept on the floor covered by a blanket from his duffle. Two days later, the family of three were on a train headed for St. Paul.

CHAPTER ELEVEN

May my word be one with my thought, and my thought
Be one with my word. Oh Lord of Love.
The Aitareya Upanishad[2]

The news of the day: Truman Warns Soviet; U.S. Planes in Action: 500
pound bombs loosed upon invaders. Rocket carrying jets also sent on
Truman's orders

Harry (Chink) Meltzer, Detroit hoodlum and Purple Gang alumnus,
drew 20 years in prison and fines totaling $30,000 for counterfeiting.

The Tigers boosted their American League lead to 4 ½ games over the
New York Yankees with a 9-3 win over the Chicago White Sox behind
southpaw Ted Gray's 5-hit pitching
Detroit Free Press, Front Page June 28, 1950

DYLAN Evans had never been to an Inter-Varsity meeting before. It
was a social group of Protestants Christians. They met in Angell
Hall where Dylan had had several English Literature classes. He
had applied to Rutgers for a year before his service, he had been
intent on being an architect. He had wanted to be the one to design
the next New York City skyscraper. It had been his dream to create
an emblem to America's special place in world history. How better
to do so than via steel, cement, and glass? But his dad would not
support his dream. Then there had been the events of the war—such
as Tsingtao and the dropping of the a-bombs. Dylan made a retreat
to literature. He loved the British Victorian era. It was today's
America, only a century before. All the problems were the same to
Dylan: new industrialization, traditional values displaced, a rise in
atheism, the impoverishment of the working class, and the
emergence of a gilded class who seemed to exist outside normal

---

[2] From *The Upanishads*, translated by Eknath Easwaran (Tomales, CA:
Nilgiri Press, 1987).

laws and conventionality. That was why he chose an English Literature major.

The party was in a regular classroom with all the desks pushed to the side and refreshments on the table normally reserved for the lecturer. The oblong table was covered in a white table cloth, set with three plates of various cookies and a punch bowl filled with fruit juice. At the far end of the table was a portable record player with Bing Crosby singing, "San Fernando Valley." Dylan moved to the cookies. He especially liked chocolate macaroons. He took one and ate it in two bites. Dylan then picked up a napkin and piled three more into his hand.

"Careful there, sailor, too much ballast can sink a ship!" The speaker was a very tall girl with curly medium-light brown hair. The woman had a broad smile with perfect white teeth and deep sunken dark eyes and dark eyebrows that were perfectly sculpted. She wore light gray tortoise shell glasses that tilted up at the sides. Immediately, Dylan thought of "owl-eyed" Minerva, goddess of poetry, medicine, and wisdom. He tried to stretch out his lips into a smile but he was afraid to show his teeth.

"There's still plenty there," he began stammering. "You know, ah the apostle Paul—"

"The apostle Paul never ate chocolate macaroons. If he had, then the weak flesh that he is so explicit about would have totally collapsed!"

Dylan looked perplexed and put down his cache of cookies.

Minerva tilted her head and smiled. She reached out and lifted the napkin with its spoils to the mysterious stranger. "I was just teasing. Remember, 'this is the day that the Lord has made, let us rejoice and be glad in it.' My name is Wilma Hart. I'm a freshman math major; I intend to go onto primary school education."

Dylan was confronted by two objects: the macaroons and this mysterious woman who seemed to be effortlessly in control. It was just too good. Wilma poured herself a glass of punch and the pair walked toward the center of the room.

"So how did you know I was in the Navy?"

Wilma smiled and took a drink of punch. "Well, you know I'm no Miss Marple and this room is neither a vicarage nor a library! But your navy tie clip is a rather telling clue, don't you think?"

Dylan looked down at his metal tie clip with the navy emblem emblazoned upon it. Then he looked back at Wilma. "I guess that is a giveaway." He then downed another cookie in one bite.

"So where did you serve in the War?"

"The Pacific. Not much action really. We were in a supporting role."

"What did you do?"

"I worked in communications. You know, the radio shack and all that."

"So you know Morse Code?"

"I'm fluent in it. Do you think that Michigan will let me use that for my foreign language?"

Wilma laughed and finished her drink.

"So, what's your major?" she asked as Dylan was in the process of finishing his last cookie.

Dylan's mouth went into overdrive as he attempted to masticate and down his sweet. With determination, he was able to respond with only a short delay. "Well, you know, before the War, I applied to Rutgers."

"Rutgers? Isn't that in New Jersey?"

"New Jersey. Yes. My family lived there and then they moved during the war. My dad had to find work."

"Lots of people have had to shift about looking for work. They say the Depression is over, but I'm not so sure. Things have been tough for most of the country."

"But not in Michigan. Along with Pennsylvania and Ohio you have the manufacturing capitals of the country. That's why my dad moved."

"So naturally, your choice of state schools changed with your family."

Dylan nodded. "I wanted to be an architect, but now I'm thinking something else—"

Just then the head of Inter-Varsity got the attention of the group by clinking his spoon on an empty glass.

"Ladies and gentlemen, I hope you are all having a good time. I just have a couple of announcements to make before I let you return to your reveries. First, the Bible Study Group will be reading Paul's letter to the Romans in this room next Monday from 9:00-10:30pm. Please bring your Bibles with you. And the Social Action Group will meet at the First Presbyterian Church on Washtenaw Avenue between Hill Street and South University Avenue on Thursday just around five. They will be manning a soup kitchen. If you haven't had a chance to sign in, please do so. Relax and enjoy the evening."

The record player went on again with Frankie Carle crooning, "Oh What it Seems to Be."

"Do you go to any of those groups?" asked Wilma.

"This is my first IV event. I just saw a poster for it and decided to come by."

"Does that mean you're not sure you're IV or you're not sure you're a Christian?"

Dylan looked down and licked his lips. Then he looked back up at Wilma. "I'm not sure that's a question one person can ask another. I mean, isn't there only one Being who can make that determination? It's not that I'm resentful or anything. Far from it. In fact, I'm glad to have had a chance to meet and talk to you. But I just don't think that words are what's called for."

Dylan looked down again at his shoes. He hadn't polished them the way he did in the Navy. His head was spinning. When he looked up, Wilma was turning to walk away. Dylan stepped forward and grabbed her arm. "Say, why don't you and I meet again at the Bible Study on Monday. Then you might find out more about the way I think. I'm just stumbling around right now. This isn't a fair test."

Wilma stopped, tilted her head, and smiled. "Well, I was planning to go anyway. I don't care if we sit next to each other. I'm happy to discover what you think."

***

Well, not only did Wilma sit next to Dylan at the Bible Study Group, but they became such a regular fixture at the IV meetings thereafter that they were elected co-presidents a year later: Dylan headed up the Bible Study Group and Wilma headed the Social Action Group. One day in April 1948, the Social Action headed to Detroit on a mission to deliver clothes, food, and basic living supplies to the unemployed. The group rode on a Great Lakes Greyhound bus and stowed their hoard in the luggage compartment of the coach. When they got to Missionary Baptist Church there was already a sizeable crowd milling around. Dylan, Harry Brinkman, and Sandy Johansson unloaded the heavy bags from the bus and started for the Church. The women took lighter parcels (smaller boxes filled with fruit and canned goods). There were around seventy-five people in a crowd outside the church. The people formed an impasse. The three men tried to clear the way to the church some thirty feet away, but the going was difficult; hands were groping the young missionaries. People were expressing their various personal verbal petitions all at the same time. Then there was a scream. It was Wilma. Dylan knew it immediately and dropped his bag and pushed his way backward. A young man in his late teens had pushed her to the ground and snatched her box. As he was making his escape, the crowd parted for him. Dylan was there in seven steps and grabbed the man by the shoulder and wrestled him to the ground. The man fell head first and Dylan sat on his back with his forearm against the back of the other's neck, keeping his face against the pavement.

"You've got to show some respect there, mister. That's my woman there. She's your sister in Christ and you better get that through your skull before I bash it in. I'm a Navy veteran, and I know how to do it."

Then there was a click. A hand grabbed Dylan's long black hair and yanked his head back. Against his throat, Dylan felt the cold of metal. The man underneath flipped over as the holder of the switchblade knife said, "No more of that, white boy. You ain't no goddamn hero come to save the colored folk. You just a common cracker—"

Suddenly the feeling of the knife was gone. The crowd became quiet in an instant. There was the sound of a slap. Dylan twisted his head up and saw a full-bodied middle-aged black woman in a brown dress pointing her finger at the young man who had held the knife to Dylan's throat. As the attention was on the knife holder, the man who had been underneath Dylan started to scamper up. In a flash, the woman turned her head. "Not so fast, LeRoy. Get back here."

The crowd blocked LeRoy's progress. A couple of men grabbed the teen. LeRoy turned back to the lady in the brown dress. "What you be wanting me for, Sister Denise?"

"What did you say? The two of you is rascals, you are. Why I have half a mind to—"

Just then Denise was interrupted by a tall man dressed all in black. He wore a bright green stole around his neck. "What's all the rumble about?" intoned the pastor with a deep baritone voice. The two young men just grinned. "Get over here Charles and LeRoy." The two came as ordered. The tall man reached out and put one hand on the shoulder of Charles and his other on the shoulder of LeRoy. Then he frowned. "Now you tell me what happened."

LeRoy began. "Well, Pastor Richards, we were all gathered around here for the stuff and all—and I just saw the way that girl was holding her box out on the side. And the box was marked FOOD. Well, you know how things have been at home. I just wanted to snatch it away. After all, they brought it for us so I'm not stealing or anything."

Pastor Richards nodded and then turned to Charles. "And how do *you* fit into this story?"

Charles looked down. "Well, it's just like LeRoy said, Pastor Richards. And then this white boy comes out of nowhere and tackles LeRoy to the ground. So naturally I intervened to help LeRoy."

"Yes, and he did it with this," Sister Denise produced the switch blade and opened it with a loud click.

Pastor Richards took the knife and retracted the blade. "You pulled a knife on our Christian brother who was bringing us charity?"

"Well, he took LeRoy to the ground. What was I supposed to do?"

"And why did he take LeRoy to the ground?"

Charles was silent. Denise filled the gap. "It's because LeRoy pushed the girl to the ground and she screamed. The man was one of our Christian brothers. He dropped the bag he was carrying to look after the girl. He said she was *his* girl. He took LeRoy down when Charles pulled the knife."

"Does anyone here question Sister Denise's account of events?" asked Pastor Richards to the crowd. There was a little murmuring, but no one came forward.

"Well, here's what we're going to do here. LeRoy, I want you to assist the young lady you pushed down. Stick by her and help her distribute the food.

"Charles, you do the same to the young man you pulled the knife on. We are members of the holy body of Jesus Christ. We turn anger into love. By the end of this afternoon each of you will have one more friend."

***

On the ride back in the bus, Wilma turned to Dylan, "I know that we're supposed to be peaceful, but I really like the way you came to my aid." Wilma reached out her hand and grabbed Dylan's arm.

"I probably over did it a bit there. The whole Navy thing was a bit much."

"I liked it. I especially liked it when you said I was your woman."

Dylan smiled. "Well we have been steadily dating. I wouldn't want anything to—"

"I know, dear." Wilma turned and gave Dylan a soft kiss on the lips. Dylan pulled Wilma to his shoulder and looked out the back bus window onto the world they were leaving.

**

Wilma and Dylan were married soon after Wilma graduated from college and Dylan had finished his masters' degree in English Literature. They decided to combine a honeymoon and moving trip to the West Coast, in a car that someone wanted driven to L.A. while he took the relaxing train. All Wilma and Dylan had to do was pay for the gas and repair the car should it break down or get a flat tire. Thankfully for Wilma and Dylan, the trip was a breeze. They drove nearly four hundred miles a day on route 66 that they picked up outside of Chicago. As they drove along Will Roger's Highway (as it was also called), they wondered what life would bring them when they reached Los Angeles and Fuller Theological Seminary where Dylan had been accepted to study for the ministry.

Route 66 was a two-lane road (one in each direction). It went through small and large towns along the way. Often on each side of the town were small motor hotels where people could stay for a couple dollars a night. However, the Evans were pinching their pennies. They had only $200 for their move and early expenses in Pasadena. It would be a ten-day trip out there and then they would have to put money down on an apartment. They figured that it would be around eight dollars a day, with $6 going for gas. That didn't allow any money for hotels (fancy or otherwise). So what they generally did was pull over onto the shoulder, open the windows, and go to sleep.

One evening when Dylan was very tired, they were between Rolla and Springfield, Missouri. It was a hot summer night and there were no reflectors on the road to help the driver stay on the pavement. Dylan decided it was time to pull over. There was hardly any shoulder, so he pulled slightly into a hay field. Wilma was already asleep, but awoke for a moment when they stopped.

"What's the matter?" she asked.

"Nothing," replied Dylan. "Go back to sleep now."

His wife didn't need any convincing. There wasn't any water around, but there were lots of bugs. The little creatures were like furies and kept waking Dylan up. Then in the middle of the night there was a hot-rodder who must have been going eighty on the straight Missouri road. Once again, Dylan was awakened. This time he opened the door, as if on command from the radio shack. Dylan got out and stretched his arms. When he got to his senses, he realized that he was not in the South Pacific. He was in a wheat field in Missouri. Suddenly he felt disoriented: without purpose and direction. Only the half-moon provided any light, and Dylan felt as if he were in a netherworld. Then he turned his head noticed their car from the outside. This prompted him to look inside. There he saw his bride, oblivious to the bugs, noise, and heat. Her very presence brough him around. It would be all right. He got back into the car and fell into a deep sleep.

Then he felt the metal against his throat. Dylan opened his eyes and saw a short, scrawny farmer just outside the car holding a pitchfork that was stationed just next to Dylan's neck.

Dylan raised his right arm to grab the tine touching his neck.

"What you doin' on my field?"

"What does it look like? We drove until we had to get sleep."

"You've run over some of my crop here."

Dylan grimaced, "Do you mind if I get out of my car?"

"Why?"

"I want to assess any damage I've done."

The farmer grunted as he started to move his pitch fork, but Dylan had a good grip on the outer tine. The two men eyeballed each other for what seemed to be an eternity. Then the farmer pulled back his pitch fork. "Go ahead and get out."

Dylan got out of his car and put his two hands against the small of his back and tried to stretch. As he did this, he let out a short cry of pain.

"What you doing, boy?" asked the farmer.

Dylan turned and looked at the farmer. He was a small, thin man—no more than five-foot-three or so. He had on a very large straw hat that sported a very wavy brim. His hair was gray and his skin looked like leather. By the way he was nervously moving his lower chin in and out, it was apparent that he was playing with his dentures. The man still held his pitch fork forward with a menacing stance.

"Well, father, I'm just a little sore. We haven't been in a real bed since the day we were married—ten days ago up in Michigan."

The farmer lowered his pitch fork. "You on your honeymoon?"

"Yes, sir. Pretty poor honeymoon: all day driving; living on sandwiches and soda."

"Whatcha doing that for? That's no kind of honeymoon."

"Your right, father. It's no kind of honeymoon. But we have to cross the country in a hurry on two hundred dollars."

"Two hundred dollars. Why, you'd almost spend that on gas." The farmer placed his pitch fork handle on the ground and grabbed it under the tines. Dylan thought it was one-half of 'American Gothic.'

"You're right there. It's a car we're driving for a fella who wanted to take the train across country."

"T'ain't even your own car?"

"No, sir." Dylan felt his hair falling onto his face. He grasped his forehead with both hands and pulled his hair back.

The farmer scratched his chin with his free left hand. Then he squinted and peered hard at Dylan. Again, he moved his jaw about and pulled his dentures back and forth with his tongue. "Tell me this, boy. Why are you doing this stupid thing? Driving across country with you bride on no money; almost like a hobo."

"I'm going to seminary in Los Angeles."

"Cemetery?"

"No, *seminary*. I'm studying to be a minister of Jesus Christ."

"Jesus H. Christ?"

"Yes, sir. I'm called to the ministry. Remember, Jesus didn't have much money either."

The farmer frowned and looked at the ground. Then he shook his head and looked up again. "You're studying to be a preacher?"

"Yes."

"But our preacher here is just the postman. He ain't got no schooling."

"Well, I'm a Presbyterian. They require all their ministers to attend four years of college and then two years of seminary training."

"What for?"

"Well, I've got to learn about the languages the Bible was written in and all the great men who have written about the message of our

Savior. Fuller Seminary says that the passion for the Holy Spirit has to be matched by school learning. And I'm going to do it."

The old farmer shook his head and dropped his pitch fork to the ground. "Tarnation, I had you all wrong." The old farmer approached Dylan.

Dylan nodded his head and said, "Now let's see how much damage I've done and what I can do to pay you back." The young man stepped forward, but the old man grabbed him.

"You'll do nothing of the kind. We're going back to my house and my wife is going to bake you and yours a country breakfast."

"Oh, no, I couldn't—"

The old farmer put his hand in the air and gestured with his index finger. "If you haven't found out by now, pastor, I'm not a man to be crossed. You and your misses are a coming with me." Dylan looked the farmer square in the eye. They crossed eye-beams for a spell, then Dylan broke the moment as he lifted his hands and set them on the farmer's shoulders.

"We would be honored to eat breakfast with you, kind sir. I will wake my wife directly."

Dylan walked over to the passenger's side of the car and opened the door. Wilma was snoring. Dylan kissed his bride lightly on the lips. She awoke clear headed. "Where are we?"

"We've met a fellow Christian who has invited us to breakfast."

Wilma smiled. "How wonderful! Breakfast is my favorite meal of the day."

Dylan introduced the farmer (whose name was John Brown) and they walked with enthusiasm toward a morning feast.

The car was left unlocked with the keys still in the ignition. The right tires were six inches to the side of the last wheat row. No damage had been done.

***

Dylan and Wilma arrived in Pasadena a week later. Dylan's first port of call was the bursars' office. He picked up his living stipend check (paid for by the GI-Bill). They established a bank account and Dylan and Wilma realized a standard of living that was modest but comfortable.

The next year, Dylan finished his program and was given a degree that certified his skill in language and scholarship in the Bible and relevant theology. The problem was, how to find a job.

Dylan had been working part time at The University of Southern California, teaching a course or two each term in English Literature to earn some money. When Dylan had finished his program, he had two advanced degrees: a Masters in English at the University of Michigan and a Masters of Divinity from Fuller Theological Seminary. But initially he had no job offers when he completed his second degree.

Then the University of Southern California offered him a three-year full-time job. It was not on the tenure track, but it paid like it was. Dylan couldn't turn it down. In the second year of his three-year contract, Dylan and Wilma had a child: Lynn Evans. They elected infant baptism and christened the child Lynn Marie. Wilma didn't try breast feeding her child. She was a math major and very inclined to science. Therefore, she was taken over by the bottle method. Everything sounded so precise: powder mixed precisely with all the vitamins a child could need, a sanitary system of sterilizing the nipples and bottles, and the reliability of delivery. Wilma had talked to several other seminary wives (since they still lived in the same neighborhood) who had been tense and could not produce milk. What mother would want to starve her child to death just to save a few dollars on baby formula and equipment? Their little rented duplex—a one-bedroom flat with a living room, a bath (with no shower), and a small kitchen—was overflowing. They used a dresser drawer that was set down on the floor for a crib.

**

Lynn Marie used to play in the postage stamp back yard that was a hangout for many of the local lizards. Lynn liked to crawl around in the yard. It was enclosed with a chain link fence so Wilma felt as if she could let Lynn have some time by herself. Mother would set her daughter down and then sit in a chair from the kitchen as she read her book, *The Good Earth*.

So Lynn would move about on her hands and knees with her cloth diaper and cover pants, creating a rather prominent posterior. The ground was spotted with tufts of grass that Dylan only occasionally cut with his neighbor's push mower. Today the tufts were especially high. This gave the salamanders a place to hide. When Lynn got close to one of their hiding places, a crafty lizard exited with a burst of energy! This surprised Lynn so that she rolled backwards onto her bottom. She began laughing and waving her hands. Wilma looked up from her book and smiled. Soon, Lynn was back on the dirt, moving for another salamander oasis. It was a symbiotic relationship: she didn't bother them and they didn't attack her. But to find even a barren backyard so full of animal playmates delighted the child.

There was also a mechanical swing in the backyard. Wilma would lift Lynn Marie and set her in the seat. The crank went for five turns and then it would swing the infant back and forth for six or seven minutes. Lynn loved her swing and would show her joy by kicking her little legs up and down. There was also a musical effect of the worn spring mechanism that would creak loudly (the swing was a hand-me-down from a Fuller couple who had gotten a job in Texas and didn't want to move much stuff).

***

As Dylan and Wilma were doing the dishes they returned to the topic of jobs. "I just don't understand why I can't get a church. Everybody else seems to be set, and Fuller's one of the best in the country," said Dylan (who did the drying).

"Well dear, you have narrowed your sights quite a bit. The other students will take jobs at any protestant church—Baptist, Methodist, Lutheran, United Church of Christ, United Brethren, Presbyterian main line, Non-denominational, and probably a half-dozen more that I forget. But you have your eyes set only on Reformed Presbyterian."

"It's what I believe to be the truest. How could I effectively lead a congregation if I didn't think that they represented the Gospel of our Lord in the most correct confession of faith?"

"But dear, surely these other congregations could come around to the way you saw things?"

"I'd be a fraud. I'd be no better than that Elmer Gantry character that Sinclair Lewis wrote about."

Wilma stopped for a moment and hugged her husband with her wet, sudsy hands. "Dylan, you'd never be an Elmer Gantry. He was an evil man and was totally against the gospel he was preaching."
Dylan looked at his wife squarely in the eye. "That's why I must have the highest standards. If I don't get a church, then it is the will of God. And I must follow His directive and go into teaching English."
The two stood there in a frieze for what seemed to be an eternity: Wilma hugging Dylan and looking up at his face; Dylan with his

hands at his side and staring right back at his wife. Then there was a crashing of broken glass and a scream. Lynn Marie had just broken one of two lamps that they owned.

The parent rescue team was there in a flash. Dylan picked up Lynn Marie with one deft movement. He was yelling at the top of his voice and the infant was crying with equal decibel strength. Wilma ran to get the broom and dustpan.

When Wilma had cleaned up all the shards and even the tiniest pieces of glass, she returned and finished the dishes. When she returned to the bedroom she found her husband asleep on the bed, holding his sleeping daughter on his chest.

***

When the USC contract was not extended, Dylan applied for and was accepted for a tenure track position at Wheaton College in Wheaton, Illinois (just west of Chicago). They prepared for their long journey with more resources than they had before. For one thing, they owned their own car and for another they had money for motels for two-thirds of the nights. It was (by comparison) a sojourn of luxury.

CHAPTER TWELVE

Before the world was created, the Self
Alone existed; nothing whatever stirred.
Then the Self thought "Let me create the world."
He brought forth all the worlds out of himself.
    The Aitareya Upanishad[3]

The news of the day: Santa makes his calls to countries in Europe: Yanks help bring cheer in West Germany. In Germany, home of the Christmas tree Santa Claus never has so many helpers. No refugee, no cripple, no elderly nor ill person has been forgotten. The United States Army of Occupation, the American Air Force and civilian personnel have worked hand in hand with German mayors, religious, welfare, religious, and women's groups in the arrangement of parties and preparation of gifts.

    Gifts to Yanks bring Cheer on the Korean Front: GIs delighted by box contents
    The Chicago Tribune, Front Page December 25, 1952

MOIRA O'Neil rushed to the telephone. It was late afternoon on Christmas Eve. Her bag of waters had just burst in the bathroom. She waddled into the bedroom and put on a robe. She had to get Andrew on the phone; she was going into labor.

"Hel-loooo?" was the greeting by a male voice from the sales room at Standard Register. There was a positive lilt to the voice as if the person at the other end was waiting for a sale to close.

"This is an emergency!" screamed Moira into the phone. "You've got to get Andrew O'Neil on the line." While she stood there shaking, little Liam ran up to her and began to cry, "Mommy, what's wrong? Mommy?"

"O'Neil? Hmm. Let me look around the office. You just hang tight," the voice sounded disappointed but resolute. After what seemed to be an eternity and one contraction later: "He isn't here. He's out on a big sales call: Marshall Fields." The man's voice was

---

[3] From *The Upanishads*, translated by Eknath Easwaran (Tomales, CA: Nilgiri Press, 1987).

from the mid-South—probably around Tennessee. He elongated his words a bit which gave his voice a patient cadence. The problem was that patience was the enemy of an emergency!

"Well, you get someone in the office to let him know that I'm calling a taxi. Tell him his wife is going into labor at St. Francis hospital in Evanston."

Then the man from Tennessee was a little rattled. He began stuttering. He couldn't bring forth a coherent sentence before hanging up.

Twenty minutes later, the taxi delivered Moira and Liam to the emergency admitting area just off Ridge Road. Moira was put in a wheel chair. An orderly took Liam's hand and the squad rushed forward to the obstetrics ward. Moira was wheeled to a bed in a room that had twenty beds—each with a flat curtain that separated each bed on the sides. At the head of the bed was a wall, and the foot of the bed was open to the room. Just before entering the ward, the orderly took Liam away.

"Where are you taking my boy?" Moira's voice was high-pitched and cracking.

"Just to the waiting room. There are plenty of magazines there and other waiting children. He'll be just fine," intoned Nurse McGuire, a middle-aged woman about five-foot-two and slightly overweight. Her naturally black hair was already streaked with lines of gray.

"Someone there will look out for him, right?"

"Dunna you worry about that, luv. It will be just fine. When your husband gets here, he'll entertain him."

Moira thought about the Tennessee stutterer. It was getting rather too much for her. They stopped the wheelchair at the bed, and Nurse McGuire undressed Moira and put her into a gown. Moira's eyes rolled. In a normal situation she would have tried to maneuver for her privacy (since one side of rectilinear space was open to the ward), but this was hardly normal. Rules were different here. Then came another contraction. They were getting stronger and longer. Plus, they were causing nausea and a tightness in her throat and upper chest.

Nurse McGuire put her into bed, and then she left.

Moira didn't like this. She felt an urge to pant. The overhead lights were very bright. They hurt Moira's eyes. She heard voices of women screaming. This was very different from when Liam had been born. Was this an obstetrics ward or the torture chamber in a

Nazi Stalag?   Some screams were of a pure and continuous tone while others seemed to modulate in a vibrato.   The recognition of this cacophony coincided with the end of the contraction.   All was better, but she had to pant.

Then Nurse McGuire returned.   It was time to shave Moira and take vitals.

"Have you called Doctor Marx?"

The question was not answered.   Nurse McGuire was into her routine.   Then came another contraction.   The nurse stopped what she was doing and put her hands forcefully upon Moira's shoulders. "Dunna think about that, luv.   In a few minutes we'll have you hooked-up."

Moira was in the midst of pain.   It was her only reality.   The surge seemed to have a pattern.   It was like an athletic event.   Her body was being pressed to the brink.   Then it held steady: a pulsating pain.   Then, suddenly, it was over. She was sweating heavily now. "How dilated am I?" managed a gasping Moira.

"Almost three inches, luv.   Hang on.   We call the doctor at three."

This was not good news for Moira.   She started gnashing her teeth.

Nurse McGuire delivered a wash cloth to Moira.   "Dunna do that, luv. It will loosen your fillings. Bite down on this instead."

Moira screwed up her face as another wave of nausea hit her. She didn't have any cavities—nary a filling in her mouth.   What about that anesthetic?   Was that offered to her with Liam?   Then came another contraction.   This one was even stronger.   Find a point on the ceiling, her mother had told her.   Concentrate.   Don't lose it. Make that point your haven. Leave your body to inhabit the point.

Moira found her point.   She focused with all her spirit.   And then the contraction abated. "Roll over now, luv. Relief is here."

And it was.   Before the next contraction was over.   Discomfort and irritation: yes, still there.   But that searing athletic testing of her body just beyond endurance had ceased.   Four and a half hours later, Dr. Wilhelm Marx arrived. She was 3.3 inches and well into third-stage labor. Within an hour the child was born. There was one nurse and the doctor in attendance.   The umbilical cord was clamped and cut.   The doctor held the baby and stroked his back. He cried right away.

Nurse McGuire declared, "Darlin', it's a boy!"

Then the doctor presented the baby to the mother and took out a clipboard to run the cutting edge newborn test that Dr. Virginia Apgar had created: **A**ppearance, **P**ulse, **G**rimace, **A**ctivity, and **R**espiration. The newborn scored a perfect ten.

Moira was only looking at her baby. She was in such awe. What a gift from heaven. Though she had been hoping in the back of her mind that it might be a girl and balance the children, she was ecstatic to be holding the living being she had been carrying around for such a long time. The emotion was too much. Still she had the wherewithal to count the fingers and toes.

"Put him on your breast, mum," suggested Nurse McGuire.

Moira complied. Though she had not been successful in nursing Liam; it didn't matter. This was her baby now, and it was suckling at her breast! Moira looked at her baby; she watched him rooting. She felt his very essence: it was heaven.

***

Sometime later (was it a minute? was it a half-hour? could it have been more?) Andrew came in with Liam, hand-in-hand. Andrew was very circumspect about entering the maternity ward with all the open fourth sides of the rectangles. He responded by looking down at his shoes so that he did not violate anyone's privacy as he was led by Nurse McGuire (who happily noted the demeanor of Andrew).

Then they arrived at Moira's bed. Andrew's jaw dropped. He had not been present at Liam's birth. Before him was his wife with their baby at her breast. This whole presentation was foreign to him (even though he came from a large family—still he had been the youngest). This was unlike anything he had ever experienced.

He dropped Liam's hand and ran to his wife. "Moira, is everything okay?"

Moira looked up, "Andy, it's a boy!"

Andrew skipped a beat, and then replied, "Wonderful!" Then he tiptoed forward and put his hand forward, paused, and looked back to Nurse McGuire, "May I touch him?"

Nurse McGuire moved forward on the other side of the bed. She inserted her finger at the side of the baby's mouth and pulled slightly to remove the child from Moira's teat. Then she lifted the baby while deftly covering the skin with a thin towel and handed the bundle to the father.

The new father accepted his charge and held it close to him. He tried several times to say something, but couldn't.

"Daddy?"

Andrew was deaf to all noise at that moment.

"Daddy?"

Liam pulled sharply on his father's pants. Andrew looked down to his nine-year-old boy. "Daddy, can I hold it, too?"

"Liam, it's not an 'it' but a boy baby—just like you."

"I'm no baby. I'm a big boy."

Andrew smiled. "Of course you are. But babies are very fragile. You must be very careful." Then Andrew panicked internally. How could this be done safely? Andrew looked to Nurse McGuire who effortlessly moved in and let Liam hold his brother while sitting in her lap. By all accounts it was a miraculous moment.

***

Moira stayed a week in the hospital. On the ride home, Andrew thought about how their lives were forming themselves. It seemed like only yesterday that they had come home on the train from Great Falls, Montana to St. Paul. Andrew remembering coming home with his three-year old son: the seats had been moved by the lever on the floor that allowed them to swivel so that four seats could be facing each other (instead of all looking in one direction).

While they rode through the Badlands in eastern Montana Moira said, "This is where I came from. Wolf Point is not too far from here. This is sacred Indian land."

"Yes," replied Andrew vacantly.

"You know that my mother would check my head for lice at least once a week. She thought that all the Indian children at my reservation school were very dirty."

"But they weren't, were they?" Andrew was looking outside the windows at the high buttes that created such stark architecture against the big sky.

"What? They *weren't* dirty? Every child is dirty. Children love dirt." Moira pulled the hair away from her face and restrained it with a metal barrette. Then she looked back at her husband who was still captivated by the buttes. "When I was a little girl I used to make my brother, Mac, mud pies and he ate them." Moira laughed. Andrew turned his head but his gaze did not engage Moira's. "I even ate them, too!" Andrew nodded and turned back to the landscape.

Moira leaned forward across the chasm of the adjoining seats and shook him. "Don't you understand, children *are* filthy by nature. It's how they get immersed into life."

Andrew thought about Frederica and how she used to treat Doris. He grimaced and asked, "What tribe was on the reservation? And why did you have to attend that school?"

Moira smiled. She arranged the little blanket around Liam, who was sleeping with his head on her lap. "I had to attend that school or attend no school. Wolf Point was a very small place. I was one of twelve non-Indian children in the area compared to sixty-five of the native children who attended the Fort Peck School."

Andrew turned back to his wife. "What nation were the Indians?"

"Sioux. Fort Peck was for the Sioux Nation."

They traveled another hour with both of them gazing at the buttes and little Liam still asleep. Then Andrew asked, "And how has your connection with the Indians affected you?"

Moira grimaced. "I don't know. I just thought I'd mention it as we traversed this territory. It's very spiritual to me in a way I do not understand."

Andrew didn't know what to say either. And so they spoke no more on the subject and carried on to St. Paul.

***

When they arrived to St. Paul, things were not as they had hoped. There was a housing crisis. Many of the servicemen left from their parents' home only to return aspiring to independent housing. This glut of demand created a shortage and a temporary housing bubble.

When they arrived they went to Andrew's sister, Ruth. She lived in a comfortable five-bedroom house on Snelling Avenue. Otto had retired when his daughter, Julia, was born in 1930. Otto was then thirty-three years old. But the royalties on his patent for the dial telephone paid him handsomely every year—and would continue to do so until the day he died.

The house was a brick colonial. In addition to the five bedrooms, there was a kitchen, dining room, living room, billiards room, library, office for Otto, sewing room for Ruth, workshop for Otto, and laundry room for the maid. Otto and Ruth shared a bedroom. Julia had a bedroom. There was one guest bedroom and two bedrooms were furnished and covered with sheets. The deal was that Andrew and Moira would stay with Ruth and Otto rent free until they could find an apartment and Andrew could find a job.

The Munsons were very generous to the O'Neils.

"Pass the jam, please," said Andrew at the breakfast table. The breakfast room was a part of the kitchen. It was differentiated by having wallpaper instead of painted walls. The patterns of the wallpaper were of scenes from Oberhausen in Northwest Germany (Otto's ancestral home) circa 1700.

Ruth passed the jam.

Andrew layered the jam thickly over the butter and took a bite of the crisp toast.

Otto watched his in-law masticate his food. Otto frowned.

Ruth said, "Otto, you've hardly touched your eggs!"

Otto smiled with one side of his face. He looked at the depiction of the mother on the wallpaper who was scolding her frisky child. "Oh, I'm not so very hungry actually. Why don't you give seconds to Andrew? I'm sure he won't let good food go to waste."

Andrew took another large bite of toast. "No, Otto. Go ahead and eat. It's good for you."

"What's good—" began Otto with animation, but then stopped.

"Yes?" intoned Andrew after a short interval.

"What's good is that wholesome food doesn't go to waste. " Otto smiled broadly and pushed the plate before Andrew. Andrew shrugged his shoulders and started to eat the castaway food.

Otto seemed pleased, "Gutes essen!" Otto's accent in German reminded Andrew of someone else. He paused momentarily and wiped his mouth. Then Andrew looked to Moira, who was only eating plain toast breakfast along with a cup of black coffee.

Moira did not display any emotion. Ruth got up and began doing dishes. Moira sprung up to help (though she hadn't finished either her piece of plain toast or her coffee). Andrew looked down and consumed the two scrambled eggs (his first portion had been one egg scrambled).

"Say, Andy, how's the job hunt going?" Otto leaned back on his chair so that it was only supported by two legs.

"I've been out Monday through Friday for the two weeks we've been here. Don't think that we don't appreciate all your hospitality. When I get a job, I'll pay you back for all your hospitality—"

"Oh, Andy, don't say that," responded Ruth as she was cleaning Julia's breakfast dishes. "You're family. We're rather comfortable, as you can see. Don't think anything of it."

Andrew nodded to his sister, but then turned to Otto. "I'm grateful to you Otto. I will pay you back."

Otto grunted as he got up and left the kitchen.

***

The next week Andrew was hired by Standard Register, a forms management company headquartered in Ohio. Andrew was to be a traveling salesman just as he had been with Proctor and Gamble. They would give him a company car and an *expense account!*

One of the nice things about being on a commission-based compensation system is that everything you make is yours. The company *loans* you money in the form of a draw. This is for the purpose of a level paycheck so that you can meet your expenses. But if the company pays you more than you've brought in (on a rolling three-month system), then you are in debt to the company. This may sound onerous to some, but to Andrew it was freedom. He could come and go as he pleased because ultimately what he got in commissions had already made the company money. So that if he sold a forms processing machine for $100 and it paid a 10% commission, then his $10 did not cost the company a dime. They made $90 dollars in the process. And if he couldn't sell enough, it still didn't cost the company a dime because he was personally responsible for the difference. Pure commission sales contracts conferred freedom upon their recipients. Nothing is for nothing so that what you earn is what you get. How you get there is your own business. Andrew loved this.

***

"So, what law school?" asked Moira the first night in their new apartment. They had moved to Minneapolis near the university. A Marine buddy of Andrew's, Kyle Shrumpt (who was also from St. Paul), had heard about the apartment from his older sister, Helga, (who was in the same parish as Ellen and heard that the O'Neils didn't have a place to live—even though Andrew had a steady job). Kyle worked at a construction company and they had just rehabbed a building. The paint wasn't even dry and almost every room was rented. Kyle put down a deposit for Andy, and then got Helga to tell Ellen.

Ellen had always been Andrew's favorite sister after Doris (who died young).   Ellen had been the one who was trying to keep the family together. She was the only child still at home looking after Frederica (whose health and mind were ailing). Ellen was the sister who had fed her brother during the time that he lived in the unheated attic of their St. Paul family home. After Andrew would come home from work, Ellen fed him purloined food and that which she saved from her own meal for her brother. Even though all of Andrew's money went to his mother, he was cut out of the official food distribution system because he didn't sit down for the family meal (he was at work).

Ellen had tirelessly sought the best career for her younger brother.   She had gathered information brochures from the University of Minnesota Law School on the four-year law degree program for working people. The classes were mostly at night and on the weekend. Plus, Andrew had some flexibility in his sales job since he was only accountable to his sales figures. If he sold enough, the company didn't care how many hours he worked. If he sold too little, then he was history. It was that simple. "That simple" was heaven to Andrew.

It was mid-November when they moved in. To celebrate, Andrew bought two new candles and a rump roast. Moira exclaimed over the meat. "This will feed us for the rest of the week," she said. Andrew beamed and then took out the law school brochures that Ellen had acquired. Andrew had read them several times over. The corners of the three-color coated paper were somewhat devoid of color from fingerprint images of many page turnings, and the pages were no longer flat. These details were not lost on Moira.

"It's the University of Minnesota, Moira.   They have this innovative dean there, Everett Fraser, who has created a *Minnesota Plan* that has various degree options and ways to get there."

"But you've got a job, Andrew. What are we going to do? Live out on the street during the winter?"

But Andrew kept smiling and flipped through the various pages until he found the one he wanted, "See? Look here. They have a program you can do while still holding a full time job."

"But you don't want to jeopardize your job at Proctor—I mean Standard and Register. Good jobs are hard to find. And I *don't* want to move back in with Ruth!"

"Yeah, Otto is a bit of a little Hitler, isn't he?"

"Anyone who retires so young just because he gets lucky with some invention or other is bound to be a monster. It isn't God's plan for people to retire before they can grow a beard."

Andrew moved toward Moira and put his hand on her shoulder, but she pushed it away. "No, don't. I've lived too long in poverty. I want a real home and all that goes with it. I've paid my dues."

"But Moira, it won't interfere with my job. I'll still bring home a good paycheck and when I get to be a lawyer, I'll be doing what I love."

"I love being able to pay my bills."

Andrew stopped and took a step back. It had been terrible having to move in with her parents during the war. She was away from Liam and had to compete with a different class of people. Moira was raised without much money among the Indians and the economically poor, but she had always read. Thanks to the Carnegie library, she had largely educated herself (far beyond what they had offered in school). Moira had been the valedictorian of her high school, but that paled to the sort of work that she completed without anyone's attention—much less mentoring. And then she only attended one year of college because she hadn't agreed to be a doctor. It would have meant a change in schools and a different life. Yet she had chosen *him*. She had suffered. But was it necessary for him to suffer, too?

Andrew decided to lie low for a while.

***

The winters in the Twin Cities are often very cold. This winter was no exception. Moira devoted her days to teaching Liam. Her goal was to get him reading before he started first grade. The Golden Books gave way to A.A. Milne's Winnie the Pooh books (illustrated by E.H. Shepard). The Pooh stories and Milne's own poetry excited Moira's own creative urge. She quickly memorized many of these and then performed a one-person show for her son. When she intoned, "James, James, Morrison's mother seems to have been m-i-s-l-a-i-d! Last seen wandering *vaguely* quite of her own accord.

She tried to get down to the end of the town, forty shillings reward!" Liam would wail in delight.

Andrew worked with Standard Register in their business consulting division. He was learning how the company worked and doing what was expected of him—not too dissimilar to the military. After over a year of small sales and lots of customer service (that didn't pay any premium—except that you get to keep your business), Andrew caught a break in the summer of 1948. Andrew found a family contact (through his sister, Ellen) and he was able to use the contact to get an appointment at the State Capitol in their management services division. Andrew highlighted Standard Register's 'work simplification' business consulting program that the War Department had adopted during WWII. The entire idea was on how to work more efficiently within large organizations with less waste. The bread and butter of forms access and management were a part of the picture, but systems engineering was at the forefront. Andrew understood the process in a fundamental way. This included three significant improvements that he integrated into his proposal (which he forwarded to the home office).

The result was a very big sale to the State of Minnesota. This led, in turn, to large sales to Cargill and Woodcraft. Andrew's innovations were made a permanent part of the management consulting program. By Easter 1949, Andrew had scored some serious commissions and had been admitted to the University of Minnesota's law school on their extended program.

***

When the family went to an Easter egg hunt in the local park after church, Andrew felt that his whole life was finally coming together. He had his pretty wife, Moira, his son, Liam, they had a nice apartment, a nice bank account, and a future he'd always dreamed about: law school. The Easter egg hunt was held in a city park that had few trees (mostly grass and a couple baseball diamonds). This meant that there were few really good hiding places for the eggs. Mostly, the organizers simply dropped the wrapped candy eggs into the grass. All the children (around seventy-five) gathered in the parking lot and then the head blew a whistle and the children had at it. Andrew, Moira, and the other parents followed behind at a slower pace. It was a nice day for mid-April. Minnesota often has erratic springs that vary between warmth and extended snows. The land of 10,000 lakes is also a spawning ground for mosquitoes (sometimes jokingly referred to as the state "bird").

The children were full of energy as they filled their paper sacks with candy eggs. The organizers said there were around ten eggs per child so that children who had gotten ten eggs were encouraged to return to their parents and call it a day. There were also adults stationed at the perimeter of the park to ensure that no child wandered off.

Andrew and Moira walked together with Moira holding Andrew's arm. They didn't speak but simply moved toward their child (who was in the middle of the field). Then Andrew stepped on something that squashed. He stopped and bent down. It was a now flat candy egg. "Well, so much for hiding the eggs in the thoroughfare. I wonder how many will have the same fate?" Moira put on her tight smile. She was getting nervous.

Children were now returning to their parents. There was a lot of yelling and high-pitched noise. It was unclear whether this was excitement, happiness, or complaint. One of the last children to return to his parents was Liam. He approached them with his head low.

"Liam, honey, how did you do?" intoned Moira.

Liam looked up and grimaced.

"What's the matter, honey? Didn't you get the eggs you wanted?" Moira stretched her arms out to her six-year old. Normally, Liam would race to the open arms, but now he simply shuffled forward. Andrew walked toward his son and took the sack. There were two flattened eggs. "Two eggs?" asked the father. "Were some of the kids taking more than their share?"

"Those big boys took the round eggs and then started stepping on the rest."

"Well, for what it's worth, I accidently stepped on an egg near the beginning of the hunt. Here, I kept it for you. At the end of the day, it all gets mixed up in your stomach the same as if it had been round."

Liam looked up at his father. He had nothing to say. Then his mother picked him up in her arms and hugged him, and Liam began to cry. The trio walked back to the car. It had suddenly become overcast and was beginning to rain.

***

After Easter dinner, Andrew and Moira put Liam to bed. Andrew told Liam a story and then Moira read Liam a story. When the parents returned to their own bedroom, Andrew let Moira know about the news.

"I've two wonderful things to tell you. First of all, in my May 1st paycheck there will be bonuses on the three large cases I closed."

"How much?" asked Moira.

"Seventy-five hundred dollars." This was equal to Andrew's annual draw, and it was in addition.

Moira's eyes grew to saucers.

"Yep, and I've got another big lead at Bernicks!"

"Wow. You know, I really like Dr. Pepper. Do you suppose they'll throw in a few cases for the deal?"

"Well, I haven't even made my presentation yet, but I'm on a roll!"

Moira cuddled close to her husband.

"But there's more! I've been accepted into the extended law program at the University of Minnesota that I told you about."

Moira moved back. "I thought we had agreed that your job came first. Our house, our dreams . . ."

"All of those can go forward. This is a program that works around your work schedule. It's for working people, like me."

Moira was silent.

"And besides, I can have dreams for me, too. Right?"

Moira turned away and arranged her pillow for sleep.

Andrew turned off the light. He didn't feel like reading tonight.

***

The Bernicks case was more nuanced than Andrew's other cases. Part of their problem was accounting methodology. Andrew had taken three accounting classes at McAlister. He knew some of the nuts and bolts, but he was also an idea man. He understood how accounting methods could be used to cover up bad business practices. What happened was that Bernicks didn't buy any of the turn-key Standard Register products, but they did hire Andrew to simplify their business practices and how they managed their money flow. [It was well-known that many of the successful commissioned sales force would take this sort of side work and pocket all the money. Andrew insisted that Standard Register should receive half of the money he earned—even though he was not a salaried worker. The very fact that he was on the "draw" meant to him that he owed something to his company.]

By August 1949, Andrew was just finishing his work with Bernicks. His classes at the law school would begin in early September. He was sent a letter about his textbook, and Andrew paid his fall fee for one class on Tuesday and Thursday, 6:00-7:15 p.m.

Andrew opened his text: Benjamin N. Cardozo, *The Nature of the Judicial Process*. His hands shook as he leafed past the title page to the table of contents. This sacred book would be his salvation. On his own over the next week, Andrew read deep into the night and finished the book. It energized him. Sure, most of the class would be the lectures and tests, but he felt that he was one long step there.

***

Then in the middle of September, after he had attended two weeks of classes, Andrew received the following call from the home office of Standard Register.

"Andrew O'Neil?" intoned the voice on the line.

"Yes," he replied. Andrew was sitting at a metal desk that he shared with 15 other commission-only sales personnel.

"You are Andrew O'Neil?"

"Yes."

"Well, I'm glad I finally got you. I've been trying for three days."

"Well, sir, we sales guys need to be out in the field to be doing our jobs. We can't close too many deals sitting at our desks."

"Well said, young man." The man at the other end of the line cleared his throat. "You are a young man, right?"

"Thirty-five, sir. And I served in the Great War."

"Very good. Very good." The man paused on his side of the line and there was a clear sound of the drinking of fluids. "You'll have to excuse me, Andrew. I'm just having lunch."

"Yes sir," replied Andrew.

"Four-fifteen in the afternoon and I'm just having lunch." There was a pause in which more eating and drinking took place. Then the man cleared his throat, "I don't know if I told you who you are talking to?"

"No sir," replied Andrew as he took out his handkerchief and started twisting it tightly.

"I'm John Flanagan, senior vice-president for sales."

"Yes sir. I'm flattered that you called me, sir. I hope I haven't done anything wrong."

"Oh, but you have, O'Neil. You've taken our business simplification turnkey product and you've customized it to every big case you've closed. Is this not correct?"

"Yes sir, but—"

"There are no 'buts' about it, young man. Listen O'Neil, that product was good enough for the Department of War in the Big One."

"Yes sir."

"Then what makes you think that you're so goddamn smart that you can customize it to various clients?"

"I just want the client to get the most out of it, sir. I didn't mean any disrespect. I've gone back to my clients to see how things have been going, and they seem satisfied." Andrew now had the handkerchief in a tight wadded ball that he was squeezing with all of his might. Andrew's colleagues started noticing that all was not necessarily well. They stopped working and started migrating toward Andrew.

"Satisfied? Do you think they're *satisfied?*"

"That's what they tell me, Mr. Flanagan."

"Well that's not what they tell the home office of Standard Register. Do you know what they tell us?"

"No sir, Mr. Flanagan." By now half the office was crowded around Andrew's desk.

"They tell us that your customized program is the best thing they've seen since sliced bread! They rave about all the money they are saving through systems efficiencies. You're goddamn corrections, son, are strokes of genius!"

Andrew started to cough. Someone immediately handed him their soda bottle. Andrew took a swig. Everyone was very tense.

Before Andrew could respond, Vice-president Flanagan followed-up, "Your work is so damn good, that I'm promoting you now to our top sales office in Chicago. You're going to be our new general sales manager of the central region. I'm doubling your salary and setting in a bonus schedule based upon your numbers. We'll pick-up the move and sweeten the deal with a twenty-five hundred dollar bonus. What do you say?"

Andrew's jaw dropped. "What can I say, sir, but 'thank you.'"

"Then it's a deal?"

"Well, I have to talk it over with my wife, but I'm sure that won't be an obstacle. When can I call you back?"

"Tomorrow morning by nine-o'clock. We've got to get the ball rolling. I want you in Chicago in two weeks."

"Yes sir. I'll call you tomorrow at nine."

Then the line went dead. Andrew hung up the phone and stood up. "They've made me general sales manager of the central region. I start in two weeks."

There was a pause and then everyone was moving toward Andrew. He was engulfed in a sea of well-wishers. His back was slapped so many times it was almost raw.

***

When Andrew returned home he was greeted by Liam. "Daddy's home!"

The words put Andrew onto another planet. He lifted his son in his arms and gave him a big kiss. Then he set him down, hung up his coat, and asked Liam about his day at school. Soon Moira came out of the kitchen and sat down to supply emendations to Liam's account along with a bowl of pretzels.

"I don't have to ask what we're having for dinner," began Andrew after Liam's academic review. "I can smell it from here: spam and eggs, one of my favorites."

Liam went into a dance, reciting the words 'spam' and 'eggs.' He was very happy. He loved first grade.

***

It wasn't until Andrew and Moira were in bed that he popped the news. The couple had a double bed with a coiled mattress and box spring. They didn't have a head board or foot board: only a simple metal frame that elevated the mattress from the floor. Two wooden slats kept everything steady. They had coarse cotton sheets, an old blanket that Moira had as a girl, and a comforter that had been designed for a single bed.

On each side of the bed they had little tables that supported reading lamps. Andrew had his law book open and was reflexively reading his assignment for his next class. Moira was in the bathroom brushing her teeth and fixing her hair. On her bedside table was *Middlemarch*.

When Moira came to bed in her red and white checked flannel pajamas, she took one look at her husband reading and gave him a smile. Then she adjusted her pillows and reached over for her book. She was just on the part discussing foreign statues when Andrew set his book down on his thighs and said, "I received a call today from John Flanagan. He's the senior vice-president for sales."

Moira stopped reading and looked at her husband. "Is there anything wrong?"

"No. That's what I thought at first, too. The whole office started gathering around because my answers must have given them the willies." Then Andrew reached over and touched his wife's shoulder. "There's nothing wrong. I've been promoted."

Moira started to smile. "What does that mean? *Promoted.*"

"Well, Standard Register is separated into four regions: Central (the Midwest), East (the Northeast), South, and West. They want to make me general sales manager of the Central region. That means that they would double my salary (no more draw). They'd also give me bonus opportunities on top of that and they'd give me a twenty-five hundred dollar stipend for making the move."

"The move?"

"Yes, the Central Region runs out of Chicago. I'd have a corner office overlooking Lake Michigan. They'd pay for all moving expenses and with the bonus, our savings, and my new salary, we could buy a house!"

"A house? In Chicago? Isn't that really expensive there?"

"Oh, I'm not saying that we could buy it for cash, but we could get a mortgage. They say that all you need is 30% down and they finance the rest over thirty years."

"But we don't know Chicago. We don't know the neighborhoods like we do Minneapolis and St. Paul. In a city, knowing the neighborhoods is *everything.*"

"Yes. That's why we'll probably rent for a few years and then buy where we think is right."

There was a long silence as Moira decided to get up to go to the bathroom. Andrew picked up his law book and began re-reading the last paragraph on torts.

When Moira returned she fixed her pillow again and looked up to the ceiling, "And how far would $15,000 go in Chicago?"

"$15,000 plus bonuses. I talked to our local sales manager who said that bonuses can double your pay on a good year."

"$30,000? I don't know if we could spend that kind of money. If it only costs us $500 to eat a year and $600 on rent and $1,000 on everything else, then what will we do with all that dough?"

"Save it for our house. I don't think we should go on a spending spree just because we have more money. I say, live as we live and save the rest. If we save enough, maybe we won't *need* a mortgage."

Moira looked at her husband, cocked her head, and then scratched her scalp. She then turned and picked up her book. Mrs. Casaubon (formerly Dorothea Brooke) was poised by a statue of a reclining Ariadne (then called Cleopatra) in the Vatican Hall of Statues. Dorothea preferred sculpture to painting, and Will preferred the verbal arts to all the visual arts. Just as Moira began to think about this, Andrew said, "I've got to give them my final answer tomorrow by 9am. They want me down in Chicago in two weeks."

"Two weeks?"

"Yes. Of course, we can work things out more slowly up here. Say a month or so. It's easy to get out of our month-to-month lease."

Moira didn't want mention how hard it had been to get their month-to-month lease. It had required staying with his sister Ruth for almost two months. Even though the Munsons were fabulously rich, they acted as if every crust of bread was sending them to the poor house. It had been humiliating. This apartment had been their salvation. Moira knew they wouldn't live there forever, but to be told 'two weeks'?

"Darling, I know that a month is rather short notice for you. The church women's group, your library volunteering and all that, but it will put us on a much firmer financial footing."

Moira established eye contact with Andrew. They gazed at each other and then began reading their books again.

After an extended interval, Moira said, "All right. We move."

Andrew replied, "All right. We move."

Then they turned to each other. They were at a loss about what to do. Andrew started first by taking his law book off of his lap, closing it, and tossing it onto the floor with a thud. Then he turned off his reading lamp and buried his head into his pillow.

Moira tried to pick up the story once more, but she couldn't. It was five years before she picked up *Middlemarch* again.

PART THREE

CHAPTER THIRTEEN

Y: The sun is our light, for by that light we sit, work, go out, and come back.
J: When the sun sets, what is the light of man?
  Brihadaranyaka Upanishad, ch. 4[*]

The news of the day: Men Walk on Moon: Voice from Moon; "Eagle has landed."

Houston: Roger, Tranquility, we copy you on the ground. You've got a bunch of guys about to turn blue. We're breathing again. Thanks a lot.

A powdery surface is closely explored. Men have landed and walked on the moon. Two American Astronauts of Apollo 11 steered their fragile four-legged lunar module safely and smoothly to the historic landing yesterday at 4:17:40 p.m. Eastern Daylight Time. . . Neil A. Armstrong declared as he placed his foot on the moon, "That's one small step for man, one giant leap for mankind."
  The New York Times, Front page for July 20th 1969

SEÁMUS and his father, Andrew, were sitting in their family room watching the baseball game on television. The Dodgers were playing the Giants in Candlestick Park. Two great pitchers were on the mound: Claude Osteen for the Dodgers and Gaylord Perry for the Giants. As the game was just getting underway, the network news broke in and said that the United States space craft, Apollo 11,

---

[*] Brihadaranyaka Upanishad, ch. 4. Tr. Eknath Easwaran (Tomales, CA: Nilgiri Press, 1987).

had landed on the moon. When they cut back the announcers said that Maury Wills had singled on an infield hit and had been driven in by Manny Mota's triple to right field.

"Aw Dad," began Seámus, "why did they put on that newsbreak? We missed a score!" Seámus got up and went to the refrigerator for a coke. When he returned Len Gabrielson singled to right center, scoring Mota (Parker, who had walked while Seámus was getting his beverage, went only to second). Seámus then watched Tom Haller, the catcher, send a rope to center scoring Wes Parker.

"Doggone it all!" intoned Andrew at the score. It was 3-0 and only the top of the first. Flyouts by Sizemore and Osteen ended the inning. While it was on commercial break, Andrew asked Seámus, "Do you really think they've landed a space ship on the moon?"

"Sure. Don't you ever watch Star Trek?"

Andrew scratched his short-cropped graying hair. "No, I haven't. But what does that have to do with anything? That's just a tv show."

"Dad, don't you know that they base these shows on stuff that really happens or is about to happen?" Seámus took a long swig of Coca-Cola. The thick hourglass bottle seemed custom made for his teenage hand.

"Seámus, a television show is a work of fiction—unless it's a news show or something—and even then," Andrew cleared his throat. "But Star Trek just came out of someone's head. This moon landing really happened. I mean, Seámus, you were a Boy Scout. You did a lot of camping. What did you think about when you looked at the moon in the sky?"

"I don't know. I thought it was a big rock in the sky that the sun shone upon so that when we looked at it on earth that reflection made it look full, half, crescent—you know."

Andrew got up and stood directly in front of his son. "Don't you realize how far away the moon is? Don't you realize what it means to put an American on the moon?"

"Does that mean we own it?" asked Seámus.

"Own the moon?"

"Yeah. In the Age of Discovery when the Europeans went around the world discovering new lands, they planted their flag wherever they went. That meant that they owned it because they discovered it."

Andrew didn't respond.

"I didn't make this up. It's in my history book."

"I believe you. But I don't think anyone can own the moon."

"Why not? The British took over Australia and that's a whole continent."

"I don't know. No one owns Antarctica. Besides, the Moon is an entire planet. I just don't think it makes sense to me."

"Why do you think Kennedy wanted us to get to the moon?"

"I don't know," replied Andrew. "Was it to show the Russians that Capitalism was superior to Communism?"

"Those are economic theories, Dad. They have nothing to do with science. In fact, I think the whole thing is only about building an empire: first the Earth (our world) and then the Moon. Mark my words, Mars is next!"

Andrew decided to pour himself a cup of coffee. The Giants didn't score in the bottom of the first.

Andrew wanted to say something to his son about the 'man in the moon' or of it's being said to be made of 'green cheese' or the perfect aether that could neither be created or destroyed. He didn't know what to say to his son, who was now making *Jiffy Pop* popcorn on the oven-top.

The Giants didn't get on the board until the third. Willie Mays and Willie McCovey got into the act, putting San Francisco on top. Even Gaylord Perry (the notorious spit ball pitcher) hit his first home run in the effort. Everything in the game was surreal for Andrew. Dick Tracey. The Green Hornet. Captain Marvel. *Journey to the Center of the Earth.* Putting a man on the moon. Fiction was becoming real. Seámus was right, but in the wrong way. The final score was 7-3 Giants. Neither team seemed headed for the Pennant. But there had been something magical about the game to Andrew.

***

1969 was also the year that Seámus was heading for his final year of high school. Andrew wanted to talk to him about going to college. Liam had gone to college—several colleges, in fact, before getting his degree at the University of Washington while living at home with his folks in Seattle. He received his master's degree in experimental psychology in June of 1969. That event exhausted his student draft deferment. Liam felt as if he had two choices: wait to be drafted and go in at the lowest level or enlist with his master's degree and try to get into a commission. The advantage of the second option was that it would take longer to get into combat, and when he got there he would be in a leadership role. (Liam didn't know that in World War II low-level officers were often the first to be shot by snipers.) By August, Liam had been commissioned as an Ensign in the U.S. Navy. Because he was going into the Medical Services Corps, he didn't have to report to OCS. Still he had to report to Pensacola, Florida. As a flight human factors expert (because of his psychology background), Liam had to take the emergency training required of anyone who would be up in the air on a regular basis. This included learning how to escape from being enmeshed in a parachute underwater, escaping from a flight cockpit underwater, speed water slides, and other skills that could mean the difference between life and death during an accident or enemy fire. Some of these tests were, themselves, rather dangerous. Many of the flight and para flight personnel used to joke that it was more dangerous to go through training than it was to go through combat.

Liam survived. He didn't have to go into the theater of combat because his job in the great scheme of things was to help assess how user-friendly the flying instruments were in times of distress. Did they make pilots more or less efficient? This meant administering various pen and paper tests with pilots in training in flight simulators, and occasionally in the air with those who were proclaimed fit to die for their country after training.

Liam enjoyed the work. The routine of running tests and writing up the results pleased him. It was solitary work. This pleased him, too. What didn't please Liam was the high testosterone, roughly jocular, hard-drinking lifestyle of the pilots (the group with whom he was most associated).

One night when he was at the *Shoot the Moon Tavern* with some top gun aspirants, he became the object of general interest. "Say, professor. Why don't you move away from beer and drink a real man's drink?"

The man proposing the challenge was a lieutenant junior grade (j.g.). The top gun want-to-be was six-foot and two hundred pounds of muscle. Liam, a short scrawny lad with black horned-rimmed glasses holding thick lenses, tried to force a smile. But the result only prompted laughter. "No, professor, you don't smile at the drink. You send it down the hatch," barked the antagonist. The guys started laughing and one lad with a crew cut out of the early sixties slapped Liam on the back and then lifted the glass to Liam's lips and tried to pour it down his throat.

Liam struggled a little, but that only made the game more humorous for the crew. Liam's glasses fell to the floor. Crew cut retrieved them but held them at a distance. "You have to drink one of your own to get them back." Liam was very near sighted. He could hear the words but beyond that everything was a blur. He felt the drink in his hand and started to sip it.

"Down the hatch! Down the hatch!" the group chanted. Liam was able to finish the shot in two more attempts. The glasses were placed back on his face. There was a huge thumb print on one lens. Liam didn't dare take his glasses off to clean them. He had already had two beers before this onslaught. His vision was getting blurry. Another glass was put into his hand. He started to drink it. The liquor went down quicker this time. Liam looked up after he finished. The group was onto a different subject. No one paid him any attention. Liam wanted to go home. He tried to get up, but felt unsteady. Liam put his head down to try to clear it. Things only got worse. His head was spinning. That was the last thing he remembered.

Liam awoke in his bed the next morning after reveille. He had a headache. He had never been drunk before. He made a vow then and there that he never would be again.

***

When Seámus started his senior year of high school, he was (for the first time) entering the same school for the fourth year. The normal pattern had been to move every two or three years. This odyssey life-style was instigated by his father's success at business.

When Seámus was born, the family had been living in an apartment in Rogers Park on the north side of Chicago. Then when Seámus turned three, the family moved to a suburb that was on the Northwestern Rail Line: Park Ridge. It was the first house that the family had owned. They bought the three-story house (that had been built in 1922). The new price was $14,000: $10,000 down and a $4,000 mortgage.

It was the dawn of the age of network television. The family decided to buy a TV and hired a carpenter to create a pine cabinet for the set in the semi-finished basement (a finished family room and unfinished workshop and laundry room, separated by a sheetrock wall covered by stained-pine quarter-inch paneling). The cabinet also contained book shelves and storage areas. So large was the cabinet that it ran half the gambit of the wall. This created a new, diminished sense of space. There was a large sofa that could fit the family and two side stuffed chairs for guests.

Upstairs they had the family radio that was also contained within its own mahogany cabinet. It was 1955 and the real media attraction was network radio. Such shows as *Gunsmoke, My Little Margie, NBC Radio Theater, Lum and Abner* (re-runs), *The Lone Ranger, Suspense,* and Andrew's two favorites: *Dragnet* and *Perry Mason,* were the staple of family entertainment. That is why the radio was adjacent to the two main level rooms (between the front room and the dining room). After dinner, the boys and Andrew would retreat to the front room to listen to their favorites while Moira did the dishes and then joined them while she did her mending.

But while the family preferred the radio, Seámus was taken with the television. He couldn't very well go downstairs when *Gunsmoke* was on. It would be unsupportive of the family. No. The only two times that he was able to watch the television was on the weekend. The first of these was at 4:30am when Seámus would naturally wake-up. Seámus was an early riser. On weekdays his parents were, too (getting up at 5am). But the parents hated getting up so early. They did it so that Andrew could catch the 7 o'clock train to Chicago so that he might walk through the door before 8. "A manager should always be the first one there and the last one to leave," Andrew used to say. "That's what they pay me for. And I'll be jiggered if I'm ever going to cheat anyone out of a single penny if I can help it." So though Seámus would wake-up at 4:30am every day of the week, it would do no good to sneak downstairs because television did not begin until 5am (when the parents woke up).

But on Saturdays things were different. The parents slept in until 9:30am. Liam always slept until he was awoken. That left a large span of time. Seámus would get out of bed and tip toe downstairs to the main level of the house and into the kitchen. There he would slide a chair over to the refrigerator, open the door, get on the chair so that he could reach the aerosol-charged can of whipped cream. From there he would apply three or four inches of whipped cream to a coffee cup saucer. Armed also with a spoon, he would make his way downstairs to turn on the television. Now, at 4:45am, the only thing on the tv was the test pattern. In this case it was the image of a Native American in headdress enclosed in a circle with a "9" atop the circle. This was WGN, channel 9. At 5am was a half-hour army training film: *The Big Picture*. Seámus would take in the images of heroic army soldiers and normal life in a peacetime army. The host and narrator was Master Sergeant Stewart Queen. After *The Big Picture*, the whipped cream was done and Seámus crept upstairs again and cleared out the dishes from the dishwasher and placed his own used dish inside (with all traces of whipped cream licked off the plate).

Then it was downstairs to watch cartoons until the parents woke up and made breakfast.

The only other time that Seámus watched television was when the Chicago Cubs or Chicago White Sox were in town. WGN televised all their home games. Jack Brickhouse was the play-by-play announcer. The baseball games on the weekend drew the three males together. Moira didn't like baseball and only watched when the White Sox went to the World Series in 1959. Andrew offered to buy his wife a mink stole if the Sox didn't win. Fortunately for Moira, the Sox lost to the new Los Angeles Dodgers in six games.

***

One day in late spring when Seámus was five, he was walking home from morning kindergarten with his cadre of five friends. One chum in the group, Johnny Hansen, suddenly broke away from the group. He raced forward to Seámus' house. The group of five-year-old boys was moving forward very slowly. This was because they were entertaining each other with songs, stories, and performing little dances that included hopping about. It was a procession that would sometimes walk past someone's house before there was recognition of their incremental task.

Today was different.

Johnny ran back to the group yelling, "Seámus, Seámus!"

There was no reply because Johnny was outside of the magic circle. However, when he pierced the sacred space he merely became a part of the general theme of the daily going home ritual. "Seámus!" Johnny grabbed his friend by the shoulders and shook him.

Seámus grabbed Johnny in return.

"You're moving, Seámus!"

"Of course I'm moving, Johnny. How else could I get home?"

The group started a song about moving on the railroad that they had just been taught in school. The cadre sang with emotion as they neared the 1020 N. Hamlin home. When they got close enough, Seámus spun away from the group, twirling like a helicopter maple seed on its way to earth. Then Seámus' foot became entangled and he fell. Falling was not something unusual to Seámus. He did it with some regularity. But this time something was different. The big blue eyes that were adorned with unusually long eyelashes looked up at his tackling antagonist and saw that it was a metal sign that was planted in the ground with two thin metal pipes. The sign was white with striking bold red letters: FOR SALE: D.C.H. Reality.

Then Seámus felt confused. He looked again to his house. It was still there. The sign was on his property. Then he remembered Johnny. Then he got up and started screaming as he ran into the house to confront his mother.

***

After lunch, Seámus decided to go bike riding. Hamlin Street was a low traffic neighborhood. First of all, only about half of the residents owned cars, and second, it was not a convenient by-pass for people who were stuck in traffic on Northwest Highway or Oakton Street (both busy roads).

Seámus got onto his bike and started off toward Marguerite Street where Johnny Hansen and Billy Pinkston lived. These were his two closest friends. They were only two blocks from his house, but Seámus decided to ride his bike. He had gone no more than thirty feet when a stray dog started barking and running at Seámus. Normally, Seámus was not disturbed by dogs. His own dachshund, Stretch, was a great friend. But at this moment, Seámus was rattled and ran his bicycle into a parked car bumper, and Seámus fell to the cement. The dog came up to Seámus and licked the remaining peanut butter and jelly that were still on his face. Seámus didn't get up right away, but the dog stood his ground, guarding the child. The whimpering sounds of the dog made Seámus climb to his feet. He looked down to his pants—sure enough, he'd ripped a hole around his knee again. His mother bought patches by the dozens so that she could repair the consequences of his forays into the world. Seámus then looked at his bike. It was fine, as was the bumper of the car he ran into. Perhaps it would be better to walk to his friends' houses. Seámus dropped his bike in his front yard and proceeded by foot to Marguerite Street.

***

"It's not going to be far away," said Seámus as he turned his spot over to his friend on the tire swing: a large truck tire that was secured by three ropes that attached at triangular points on the tire and was tied to an overhanging tree branch. "Mommy said that they would buy me a bunk bed so that I could have my old friends over for sleep overs."

"Will you still be going to Oakton School?"

It was a good question, but it was one that he hadn't asked. "I don't know."

"Too bad if you don't go to Oakton School."

Then Seámus pushed Johnny out of the tire swing and Johnny fell to the ground crying. Then Seámus ran away. When he got to the street Seámus realized that he was crying, too. Seámus started walking home when he saw an empty soup can lying on its side. He ran up to kick the can as hard as he could, but his timing was off and the can only suffered a glancing blow.

***

It took longer than Seámus had imagined to move into his new home on Cherry Street. The old house wasn't on the market long, but then there was some problem. Some of the neighbors came over to the house after dinner. Seámus' mother told him to go to bed. "But I haven't had my story yet," was his reply.

"You might not get a story tonight, Snuggles. You've got to be a team player."

So Seámus went upstairs: a team player. However, after Seámus had put on his pajamas, he crept to the top of the stairs just beyond the bannister post so that he could hear what was going on. Seámus surmised that his brother wasn't home—or if he was, then he was nowhere in sight. He was riveted by the drama downstairs. Seámus couldn't follow all of it, but the neighbors were mad. First of all, there was that man Hal Matter. He was from the South, and he hated dogs. He once tried to kill the family dog, Stretch, with some steak that was full of rat poison. It was on the O'Neil property just near the fence between the yards. Seámus had found the steak first and took it to his mother. She smelled it and called the police. There was an investigation, but they couldn't prove anything. Anyone could have done it, but since Hal Matter was always calling the police himself about Stretch's barking and his precious nap time, the family was certain that it was him.

Mr. Matter was quiet at first and then started yelling, "Nigger neighbors!" Seámus wasn't sure what a "nigger" was. Maybe it was someone from a foreign country? Seámus wondered if they were angry at his father wanting to sell the house to someone from a foreign country. Mr. Matter and the other neighbors were angry. This confused Seámus because in school they said that all Americans came from foreign countries. So what was the big deal?

Seámus' father started screaming back. He said he was a Marine who fought for our country and he would sell his house to whomever he wanted. This was America: a free country.

There was more yelling. Another man said he had been in the army and that he could take Andrew then and there in his own living room. Then Seámus' dad said that he kept his service revolver in the hall drawer. He walked over to the chest of drawers and put his hand on the handle of the drawer. Then the neighbors decided to leave. Seámus scrambled back to his room as quietly as he could. After a while, he heard his father climb the stairs and walk into his room. Seámus closed his eyes and pretended to be asleep. He didn't want a story that night.

***

Seámus had to change schools when he went to Cherry Street. Within three years, they were in New Jersey. The wheel continued to turn. Moving about was Seámus' fate. It didn't ever stop because then there wouldn't be change. When Liam came home from Vietnam, it was time for Seámus to go to college. Seámus had applied to two schools: Yale and Pembroke (an excellent small college in Minnesota). Seámus got into both. Seámus had been born in the Midwest. Seámus chose Pembroke.

Pembroke College is a small liberal arts college located 45 miles south of Minneapolis-St. Paul. Seámus was keen to revisit his roots in the Midwest, having lived on the two coasts for a time. It was also close to where his mother and father lived. They had met at Macalester College in St. Paul. In fact, Seámus wanted to visit St. Paul to get a sense of where his parents had met.

These are the expectations that Seámus had upon arriving to college. For a city boy, Pembroke was out in the middle of nowhere. Seámus felt a little nervous. He arrived a day early and entered his room. It was smallish and very hot. Seámus took a walk into town and bought a small fan which he placed on a chair next to his bed.

The next morning his roommate arrived, parents in tow. Seámus, who had come in by air the day before to Minneapolis and took a shared van to campus, was intimidated by the presence of the family—especially the mother, who gave Seámus the sort of look that seemed to suggest that Seámus wasn't good enough to room with her son.

Mrs. Teebie also didn't like the way Seámus had arranged the room. Before she left, she instructed the men, including Seámus, to construct the convertible beds into bunks: one atop the other. Then she arranged the one desk so that it was under the window for light and the two dressers next to the small closet. She even declared that her son, Irwin, would have the left-hand side of the closet because they voted Democratic.

Seámus went along with everything.

In the afternoon was the new-student convocation in the Chapel (which was larger than any church that Seámus had ever attended).

The new president of the university (an alumnus of Princeton) spoke in grand tones about his aims for the college. The subject and manner of delivery were white noise to Seámus. Instead, he fixated on the stained-glass arched window behind the President. There was a figure of Jesus with his arms spread and lots of people below him—looking up.

What particularly struck Seámus about the figure of Jesus in the window was what appeared to be a small circular break in the glass around the lower ankle tendon. Seámus wondered why they hadn't fixed it. After all, this was supposed to be a wealthy school.

"Now I want you freshman to look to your right and then to your left. I'll stop for a moment: do it!" The President reached out and pointed his finger at his audience. Seámus didn't like to be ordered about, but he complied on a minimum level (turning his head only a few degrees).

"Now if you all did this—save for those sitting on the aisles, though I suppose you could look across the aisle if you are in the middle—you have a group of three. A group of three. Well, I'll tell you this about Pembroke: we run a tough school here. One of you won't be here to graduate. You'll flunk out either because you're stupid or lazy. I don't care. A diploma from Pembroke means something, and it's only for the elite!"

There was some assorted clapping and a mandatory bar-b-que that they were to attend in order to meet their classmates.

Seámus decided to go back to his room and skip dinner.

CHAPTER FOURTEEN

The Man has a thousand heads, a thousand eyes, a thousand feet. He pervaded the earth on all sides and extended beyond it as far as ten fingers.[*]
The Creation Hymn

The news of the day: Troops and Rioters Battle House-to-House in Belfast,
Detroit Free Press. July 4, 1970.

The top pop song on July 4, 1970 was "Mama Told Me Not to Come" Three Dog Night

AS the summer ran on the corn grew higher. *Knee High by the Fourth of July.* It was an expression that her father and her mother's father used to discuss. "I want waist high—not knee high," said William Hart as he started rocking in his bright red rocking chair on the front porch. The Harts owned a house that William had built with the help of a few farmer friends when he first moved in. The project took eight months. They just beat the cruel Michigan winters.

"But, Dad," began Dylan in the way he liked to address his father-in-law. "Everything I've read says that *knee high* is just fine. *Waist high* is an old myth. You needn't have *waist high* for a good crop." Dylan was sitting on a straight-backed conventional chair. Before them were the 40 acres that William owned with his wife, Madge.

"And how many years have you been in the farming business, Dylan?"

Dylan stretched a smile on his face. This was not a conversation that would have a productive endpoint. But as Dylan let the input cross his brain he finally said, "You know the answer to that, Dad.

---

[*] *The Creation Hymn*, 10.90, from *The Rig Veda*, tr. Wendy O'Flaherty (New York: Penguin, 1981).

But I can read. And after our last visit I went to our college library and read a few things."

William took a cigarette from the pack in his shirt pocket and lit it. He extinguished the flame with his finger before tossing the match away. From where they sat on the porch, they could see 20 acres of the 40-acre farm in rural Michigan. It was a warm July day, but not too humid.

If Dylan and William had been attentive, they would have seen two heads bobbing up and down amongst the short corn stalks. The heads were of Lynn Marie and Dylan Jr. who were playing hide-and-seek in rows between the corn stalks. If they were to play this game near to harvest, it would be next to impossible to catch someone because of the vegetable cover. But now, on the Fourth of July, it was a snap. They had to change the rules so that one wasn't *caught* unless the other physically "tagged" them by a touch on the shoulder or head.

Because it was so difficult to conceal, the game had an added attraction as brother and sister darted around the field. When they had been smaller, it was easier to hide any time. Many teenagers might give up such rural pastimes as they mature, but not Lynn and Dylan, Jr. (sometimes called D-J). There was a magic about the farm.

When they had been younger, Lynn and D-J would climb to the loft in the barn and jump down into the hay pile that fed the small number of cattle that grandpa raised. There was something amazing about jumping down twenty feet in the air. It seemed like a hundred. A half-second seemed like an eternity. The hay gave way and one sunk down until they were almost immersed. Yes, for exurban kids living just west of Chicago, their visits to the farm were akin to going to Disneyland.

It was with this spirit that brother and sister continued their traditional hide-and-seek game.

Then the pair heard giggling in the cornfield that caught their attention. . "Ain't they something?" put William.

Dylan nodded and smiled.

And that was that until Madge called for dinner.

***

Lynn Marie was a blond-haired, thin girl. She was the only blonde in the family. This was often the cause of jokes about blonde milkmen in the 1950s. But on the Evans's side of the family (they lived in a nearby town—New Zeeland, Michigan), grandpa Glyn created a notebook with details on family history. They were farmers in the north of Wales, not too far from Snowdonia. These folk in the north were close to the Scots and the fair-haired Irish. It was perfectly natural, said Glyn, that Lynn Marie would be blonde with pale skin and little body fat. That was her ancestry. And who we *are* has a lot to do with where we *came from*. Or so proclaimed the blunt Glyn.

Even though he was a defender of his granddaughter, Glyn was a habitual teaser of all female kind. There was hardly a moment when he would be still. Once, when Lynn Marie was just 13, the family was visiting her father's parents in Zeeland, Michigan (only a half-hour away from the Hart farm). They were having dinner in a diner.

The waitress came over to give them their menus.

"That was done pretty good, there sweetie," said Glyn with a smile. Eluned frowned at her husband.

"Thank you, sir," said the twenty-five year old waitress. "Is there anything I can get you at this time?"

"How about another grandchild? We like our grandchildren." Glyn smiled broadly at his humor. No one else at the table smiled. Lynn quickly glanced at everyone without moving her head much. The family was breathing audibly and displayed atypical facial expressions.

"I'm sorry sir, we do not have any *grandchildren* on the menu. Might I suggest our hamburgers? They are very popular." The waitress smiled and lifted her paper tablet and pencil so she could take our order.

"I would *not* trade a grandchild for a hamburger," announced Glyn as he took his hand and spanked the waitress.

The waitress put on a forced smile and then exited the scene.

Eluned said, "Oh Glyn, you scamp. You've driven her away. Now how are we to get our dinner?"

Lynn wanted to melt under the table.

***

Lynn favored the Harts over the Evans as grandparents. William Hart and his wife Madge were simple people. They loved their black and white television. William used to sit and watch Detroit Tigers games.   Since he was the only one who liked baseball these television interludes were attended by her father and William. Dylan would be asleep before the end of the first inning.   The children were free to roam about the farm.

Another television favorite of the whole family was *Bonanza*. Everyone in the family would watch the show and then turn off the set and reenact the episode with a few changes.   Mother, Wilma, would often play a man's part because there weren't very many women on the show. (Madge refused to play a man's part.) William often played the "bad guy."   He would light up a corncob pipe and use it to gesture.   Everyone stayed in their chair, but Lynn and D-J would often stand on their chairs because they felt the need to move.

The re-enactment was always better than the show itself.   Then they'd go to sleep and get up and go to church before heading home to Illinois.   In the car, the children would listen carefully to Mom and Dad's recounting of every conversation that came up—along with a commentary.   They also would review the health of the wider clan to see who needed a letter or a card of cheer.

The two Michigan venues were a home-away-from-home that they visited four or five times a year—generally for the weekend only, but in the summer they would spend a week.   That included a trip to the sand dunes.   Running down the dunes until their legs would no longer hold them and they tumbled the rest of the way was pure excitement.   They always finished with a splash in Lake Michigan.

***

The Evans and Hart families were always in close contact.   It wasn't until Lynn's senior year in high school that there was any health difficulty.   That was when William had a stroke.   Dylan and Wilma decided to load up the wood-paneled Ford station wagon to see what they could do.   However, there was one problem: Lynn was the editor of the school yearbook and it was due out first thing Monday morning.   It was Friday.   The crew had scheduled with their faculty advisor a work session that night until ten, and then two twelve-hour days to "put it to bed" on Saturday and Sunday.   It was one of the most important jobs at Wheaton Central High School.   If Lynn went to Michigan, then she would have to resign as editor of the yearbook.   Lynn had put in perhaps 120 hours on the project already: assigning the photo shoots, choosing and cropping pictures, creating copy with the help of her area editors, et al. It had been the most time-consuming task she had ever undertaken.

Her family had supported her, too. They had let her cut down her hours as a waitress at *Around the Clock: A Family Restaurant* (really a diner) in downtown Wheaton. Lynn had to work and turn over her paychecks to her mother to help with family bills. (They also housed two boarding students from Wheaton College where Dylan taught English Literature.) But college teachers were not well paid—especially college teachers at religiously affiliated colleges. When Lynn was in junior high school, her mother (who had a primary school teaching certificate) took a job teaching kindergarten. It was then, for the first time, that they were able to put a little money away.

"Of course you're going to see your grandfather. Why, he might die. Do you want to have that on your conscience, young lady?" asked Wilma to her daughter. The two women were in the kitchen. Wilma had her back to the sink, and Lynn had her back to the entrance to the living room.

"But how could my going make any difference in that? I'm no doctor."

"Well, you want to be," said Wilma, who began wagging her finger at Lynn.

"A child psychiatrist," corrected Lynn.

"Well, that's a doctor. And a doctor has the best interests of his patient always at heart." Wilma walked forward and grabbed her daughter's shoulders.

"Well, I'm not a doctor now, Mother. You don't know what this weekend means to me."

Wilma paused. Her hands were still on her daughter's shoulders. Then she said, "Well, I've always said that these sorts of choices are up to you. I'm not going to force you to see your grandfather on his death bed. He has always been very generous to you; he's always given you a Christmas present."

Lynn nodded. She broke eye contact with her mother and said in a softer voice, "Yes, those three years of Tinker Toys were fun. D-J liked his, too."

This response made Wilma pause again. She cleared her throat and took her arms off her daughter's shoulders. "All right. If you want to disappoint your mother and work on your selfish project at school, then go ahead. You can ride your bike to school; it's only four miles. There's plenty of left-overs in the refrigerator. But I really hope that you don't make that choice. You know on the road of life there are events that test *who we are*. I believe that this is one of those events, missy."

Mother and daughter were in full eye-contact now. Then Wilma squinted at her daughter as if she were peering into her soul. "So this is it: tell me whether you are going with us to see Grandpa in his hour of need?"

Lynn paused, then pursed her lips. "I'm staying here," she said right at her mother. Then she pivoted and left the room. Before she made it to the front door she stopped and turned.

Wilma involuntarily gasped.

"I hope you have a safe trip, Mother, and I hope Grandpa pulls through."

Then Lynn left the house for school.

***

Lynn Evans directed the production of what her faculty advisor said was one of the best yearbooks at Wheaton Central High School in many years.

William Hart recovered and lived five more years before dying at the age of 84 of another stroke.

CHAPTER FIFTEEN

He who is awake in those that sleep,
The Person who fashions desire after desire—
That indeed is the Pure. That is Brahman.
That indeed is called the Immortal.*
  Katha Upanishad

The news of the day: Goggles, Gloves, Go! Mapping the Snowmobile Trails

  RTA eyes 6-county Gasoline Tax

  Carter Plans Tax Rebate: $50 payout tied to size of family.

  Sub-standard tankers roam the high seas: 'Flags of Convenience make controls difficult'

  Racial Mix of Teachers Continues to Improve: Student Integration Continues to Lag

  Iron Workers in Chicago back Bilandic for election.

  Cold snap reaches 30 days.
  The Chicago Tribune. January 26, 1977

IT was a terrible snow storm. It lasted two days. It was one of the worst storms in memory.   Seámus O'Neil lived in a decrepit graduate student housing studio flat on East 57th Street. It was a three-story building with two apartments on each floor: one studio and one single bedroom. Seámus lived in #3-B.

  Seámus didn't talk much to the other residents of the building. He knew that in #3-A was a family from Korea. He didn't know whether they were from the North or the South (though he assumed

---

* "One's Real Person (self), The Same as the World Ground" from *Katha Upanishad* , tr. Robert Hume, *The Thirteen Principal Upanishads* (New York: Oxford University Press, 1921).

the latter). Still, they acted very frightened. This caused Seámus to reflect.

Seámus never had contact with those on floors 1 or 2.

Seámus knew about the storm due to his transistor radio that fit into the palm of his hand. It was powered by two AA batteries. There was a jack for ear phones in case he wanted to listen to music loudly. Seámus occasionally listened to music, but most of all he liked to make his own music. He had a reasonably good voice and could play most sheet music on the clarinet (a B-flat instrument). His other recreation was running. Seámus was a mediocre middle-distance runner who was just good enough to join the graduate track club at Chicago University.

Seámus was attracted to the attitude that Chicago University had about sports. At one time, they were a Division I school (the highest rank in United States college athletics). Then in the mid-1930s they started to re-think their position. As at so many fine schools the new role of college sports created a fork in their journey. One path led to becoming a top sports school in the country. Various schools in the 1930s were heading that way, like Yale, Fordham, Notre Dame, Michigan and several of the southern state schools. Chicago was in a conference called The Big Ten (meaning the schools involved thought themselves pretty big stuff: their title said so).

But Chicago was to go down a different path. They resigned from the Big Ten. Their last star football player, Jay Berwanger, won the first Heisman Trophy (the highest prize for a college football player) but never played professional sports. At the end of the decade, Chicago University decided to leave the Big Ten and tore down their large stadium named for their illustrious football coach, Amos Alonzo Stagg. In its place was a field of grass that later acquired a running track. This was to represent their dedication to education over sports.

But in the late 60s to the early 70s, the field became a drug hang out. Crime arose and threatened the university. The deft administrators acted quickly and put up a 15-foot chain link fence to protect the field. But to no avail. The druggies used wire cutters to gain entrance and created a central station for the drug business on the South Side.

This activity on the campus of Chicago University threatened the safety of the university. What could they do? A higher fence? Armed gunmen ready to kill the drug traffickers?

There was much debate. Enter Ted Haydon. Ted had been the captain of the track and field team in 1933 when they were a powerhouse in the Big Ten. Then he got a Ph.D. in sociology. He also worked with Saul Alinsky. It was time for him to step forward.

For Haydon, the path was clear: you must use your community to help you solve your problems. This was Hyde Park, Chicago. There were more vibrant, positive people in the white, black, and Latino communities than there were druggies. So Haydon got a mandate and took down all the fences. No more fences. At the same time, he used his community organizing skills that he had learned from Alinsky to get neighborhood groups to use the property as recreational space when the University wasn't using it.

Grandmothers and aunts would take their young charges to the long-jump pits to play in the sand. There was also some low-level playground equipment that was set up at the corners. This was a boon for the poor folk in Hyde Park in the day and night time. Grandmothers and their surrogates patrolled the place as a safe haven for youngsters and teens. And soon the drug business and vandalism went elsewhere. Who can compete with grandmothers and aging aunts of all races united? The track and its surrounding field now was now run by the neighborhood.

Though Chicago had only intermural sports, Haydon had another vision: Division III sports (no scholarships, no special treatment for athletes). He also created the track club for graduate students and independent athletes. Haydon was a talented coach. That was why he was named the U.S.A. middle-distance Olympic coach. His athletes would come to the neighborhood track around 4 o'clock each afternoon after finishing their day jobs. This was the era of amateur sports.

Seámus loved to be on the same running track with these talented athletes. Sometimes he could run part of their workouts with them. For example, he once ran a workout with the world record holder in the half-mile who was training for two events in the 1976 Olympics. This athlete wanted to do an interval workout of 10 x 440 at 55 seconds or better. Seámus could run one 440 at that rate. It was his personal record (p.r.). He entered the workout on quarter mile number 3. The athlete took his little competition to run a 48 second quarter. He thanked Seámus afterwards for pushing him. It's so hard to work out when no one is in your class.

Now I wanted to go on further with this story, but my producer, Boylan, said that people weren't so interested in the history of track and field and that I should go on with the snow storm. And so I will. Side note: the 800-meter world record holder lost to Alberto Juantorena from Cuba in the 1976 Montreal Olympics. (Juantorena was technically a member of the military and so had subsidized training).

***

But now we are back in 1977 and the snow storm. Seámus knew the outlook was bad. He also knew that he hadn't been to Mr. G's on 53rd street for a while. He was low on food. Perhaps it would be a good idea to venture out and get some food before it became impossible to walk there.

Because Seámus tried to be at least a semi-rational being, he got dressed-up in his parka, gloves, stocking hat, and his nearly run-down boots. With a strong resolve, he descended the stairs. However, when he got to the first floor, he was arrested by a tenant in 1-A. The doors on the stairwell are set-up with economy of space in mind. If the doors to 1-A and 1-B were to be opened at the same time there would be about four inches of clearance. Now in this case only 1-A was opened, but with the imminent exit of the tenant of 1-A, that more than took up the space available. Thus, Seámus had to stop on the last stair.

The tenant was a 5' 5" woman with blond hair and light skin. It was Lynn Marie Evans. She was about to grab the front door when she noticed that there was a man on the steps who had stopped in order that she might pass. Lynn nodded her head and was out the front door.

Seámus was two steps behind, but turned left adding an extra block to his route because he did not want to appear to be a stalker. It just so happened that the two inhabitants of 910 E. 57th Street were both going to Mr. G's to get some food just in case the snow storm turned out to be as bad as predicted. It had already been snowing for an hour, but the sidewalks were still pretty clear. It was a 6-block walk to the grocery store.

When they got to the deli counter there was a question as to who was next. Seámus motioned to Lynn to go. But she motioned back. "You let me leave the building first, now it is my turn to be polite."

Seámus smiled and ordered his cold cuts and sliced cheese.

When they were at the checkout Lynn waited for Seámus to pay. Then she raised her right hand with her index finger straight up as if she were making the number one. "You know, it's faster if you go to the right. The way you went makes you walk an extra block."

Seámus smiled and said, "I'll follow your lead. Or at least your footprints. The snow is getting worse."

And so they walked back together. Lynn discovered that Seámus was a third year graduate student in ancient Greek history. He was about to take his qualifying test that would allow him to begin his dissertation. Seámus discovered that Lynn was a second year student in English Literature specializing in the English Victorian Novel. She was gearing up for her "seventy-five book exam."

"I've heard that is one of the toughest tests ever," said Seámus.

"Oh, I don't know," returned Lynn. "You just have to create a list of seventy-five books that covers all genres and types along with critics. And then you have to be able to answer detailed questions on any of the books."

They both laughed.

When they reached 910 E. 57th Street, they parted ways, with Seámus going up to 3-B and Lynn taking 1-A.

Twenty-four hours later the snow was so high that no one could exit by the front door; it was blocked by snow that went half-way up. However, there were still the fire escapes. At the back of the building was an old wooden fire escape that was painted light blue. The construction style of the fire escape meant it was covered with a roof all the way down. There was still snow that had blown on the steps, but it was considerably less than on the sidewalks and streets.

Seámus decided that he would take it upon himself to sweep the snow off the steps all the way down. When he got to the bottom he saw Lynn, who tapped on the window. She was mouthing something that Seámus could not fathom.

Then she opened her back door, "What are you doing?" she asked.

"Well, I'm on the top floor and the thought of this becoming impassable was making me nervous. So I thought I'd give us all an escape route in case we needed it."

Lynn nodded her head abruptly. "That's rather neighborly of you. Now it's my turn to return the good deed. Would you like some hot chocolate?"

Seámus smiled. "I'd be delighted." And so Seámus kicked off the snow from his boots and entered Lynn's kitchen.

The apartments in 910 E. 57th were semi-furnished. That is, the studios contained a table in the kitchen, a sofa and a desk and chair in the large room, and a Murphy pull-down bed in the same room. The only thing that separated the ground floor apartments from the other two floors were all the bars on the windows. Though this was Hyde Park, it abutted a high crime area only three blocks south.

Seámus commented on the similarity in the apartments. Lynn said that she didn't mind about the similarity but that she could lose the bars on the windows in a minute. She said that it made her feel as if she were in jail. The snow accentuated this.

"Well, I must say that you are very tolerant then."

"Oh, I don't know about that. But it's nice to be living away from home. I lived with my parents when I went to college."

The two were sitting at the kitchen table sipping the hot chocolate.

"That must have been rough."

"Yeah, it was the only way my parents could swing it. My dad is an English professor at Wheaton College. By going to Wheaton, I could make good on the tuition-benefit to faculty."

"And by living at home you wouldn't cost them anything, either."

"Exactly."

Seámus finished his cup. Lynn poured him another.

"I went to Pembroke College in Minnesota. My parents were living in Seattle at the time. The only time they saw the college was when I graduated. They drove cross-country."

"I've heard of Pembroke. That's really hard to get into."

"Yeah. I don't know. I may have had a regional advantage in admission. They try to get students from as many states as possible. Washington State is a long ways away. If I'd been from Minnesota I probably wouldn't have gotten in."

"Well, you never know?"

Then Seámus got up to leave. "Wheaton College is a Protestant Christian school, right?"

Lynn first shrugged her shoulders and then nodded her head. "Yes it is. A little too strict about what students can and cannot do for my taste. But it was free and I got my B.A. without any debt. That was fine."

"And after the first year here at Chicago, everything's paid for by a research assistantship or some grant or other."

"Yeah. That's nice."

"Well, I gotta go. Nice meeting you, Lynn."

"Likewise, Seámus. I wonder how long we will be snowed in."

"Well, I'll sweeping the stairs again tomorrow if it's impassable outside."

"My box of chocolate is only half-way down."

***

There were two more days of chocolate reward. The pair planned a date to the international film night that they held each Wednesday in Cobb Hall. The movie was free. The school even provided popcorn.

Soon Seámus was going to English Department events and Lynn was attending events in History and in Classics. At Chicago University, there were lots of interdisciplinary concentrations. Seámus was studying ancient Greek History. Therefore, he had to have both a background in History and take courses in the Classics—especially ancient Greek.

After a year, they decided to get married. They announced the news to Dylan and Wilma by phone and to Andrew and Moira by letter. Dylan and Wilma wanted to invite Seámus to a dinner—rather a grilling, and not hamburgers.

"So, you're a Catholic?" asked Dylan nervously as he sat with Seámus in their living room, munching on some peanuts and lemonade before dinner.

"Well, kind of," returned Seámus as he took in a small handful of peanuts and started to gag.

"Kind of?"

Seámus took a drink to clear his throat. "Yes, my father was raised Catholic. But the nuns used to box his ears at school so that he's partially deaf in one ear. He stopped going to mass when he became independent. And then my mother is Baptist."

"Ah, Baptist," said Dylan as he nodded his head and smiled.

"Yes. So they compromised and became Methodist."

"Methodist? And that's a compromise?"

"Well, I'm no expert on these issues, myself. But as a history buff I know that the Anglican Church—called Episcopal in America—was built on the notion of divorce. Otherwise it was just the Catholic Church with the King or Queen as the head. So if the Methodist Church was an off-shoot of the Anglo-Catholic Church, then it is a nod toward a sort of compromise, I guess."

Dylan took a deep breath. "I don't know if you are aware of the fact, young man, that I went to seminary—one of the best in the country—and so know quite a bit about these matters. I would hardly call the mainline Methodist Church as Catholic in *any* sense."

"Yes sir. I was speaking historically only."

"Well, I'm not sure you're right about that either." Dylan leaned forward in his chair. Seámus grabbed his hands together and pulled up his shoulders. This wasn't going well. It was time for another handful of peanuts. This time Seámus intended to eat them one at a time.

Dylan peered at Seámus above the lenses of his horn-rimmed glasses. Seámus thought he was in a court of law looking up at the judge. All that was missing was the black robe.

"It seems to me, young man—Seámus—that you are very confused about the role of our Lord Jesus Christ in your life."

Seámus gagged again. This time it took the last of the lemonade to cure him. "I've never gone to seminary, sir. I've told you my background. Lynn seems fine with it. We've attended a Lutheran Church on occasion in Hyde Park."

Dylan began shaking his head. "I think it's time we go into the kitchen. We don't want to keep the women waiting."

***

Seámus O'Neil and Lynn Marie Evans married in Wheaton, Illinois in a private chapel within the Episcopal Church. There were a dozen people present, including Andrew and Moira O'Neil who came by jet plane all the way from their new home in San Diego to see their son get married. The newlywed couple spent the weekend at a Holiday Inn and then went back to 910 E. 57th Street apartment 3-B.

Seámus and Lynn were working on their dissertations at the same time. Seámus was a teaching adjunct at two area colleges and Lynn worked at the cheese shop on the 4th floor of the building called *Classics*. All told they just covered expenses. Since they were only two blocks from the main library, they established certain working areas there so that the other could locate their mate—where else could they be except in the library, at their job, or in the apartment?

Seámus continued his A.A.U. running. He said that it helped him concentrate.

***

After more than a year of this schedule, Seámus got an additional job of typing dissertations for other students. Seámus was ¾ done on his and was working at a steady rate. Lynn worked rather differently. She would assemble a compendium of notes and then when the moment was right would dive in and write for two days straight, crash, and then start a new pile of notes.

Oddly enough, Seámus' typing skills made his dissertation typing the highest per hour job he had. He got paid a dollar per page and he could type 10 pages per hour. He could charge more if he had to proofread. Even more if translation was involved: Seámus read French, German, Latin, and Greek (in addition to English, of course).

Seámus dedicated all of the dissertation typing to a special bank account that was for savings and paid a higher interest rate.

In the end, they both got degrees. In a perfect world they would have found university teaching jobs at the same school. But that's not what happened.

CHAPTER SIXTEEN

I cannot see what could dispel my grief, [this] parching of the senses*
   Chapter 2, Bhagavad Gita

The news of the day: DePaul loses to Boston College in the NCAA Tournament

   Egypt's Mubarak calls off his state visit to Israel

   Haig to Russia: Join the Latin Talk: Secretary of State Alexander Haig called for talks with the Soviet Union to ease tensions in Central America.

   Floods in Ft. Wayne force 2,500 to evacuate

   Hottest book in Japan details WWII atrocities.
The Chicago Tribune, Front page March 15, 1982

IT was the *Ides of March*. Seámus commented at their kitchen table that a change was about to occur.

"Certainly not the death of Caesar," commented Lynn.

"D'accord," replied Seámus.

The couple still lived in 910 E. 57th St. But that would have to change. Lynn had defended her dissertation and they would have to move by early June. That meant that they would have to become gainfully employed (as opposed to putting together many small part-time jobs to pay the bills).

There is a tide in the time of men . . . .

This had to be the tide.

"So my job prospects are nil for the full-time tenure track positions," said Seámus. "I always get several interviews at good places but then just a few on-campus interviews and no offers."

"I haven't really tried yet because I took longer than you did to write the damned dissertation. What I suggest is that I look at high school jobs since the MLA jobs are already taken. I could teach a

---

* *Hindu Scriptures,* tr. R.C. Zaehner (New York: Dutton, 1966): II.8.

couple of years and then try to publish a few of my chapters of my dissertation as articles in journals. If they look good, then maybe I could get a tenure track job."

The couple was in the kitchen around the standard-issue table and chairs. They were having breakfast: black coffee for Lynn and granola on yogurt with coffee for Seámus.

"That sounds like a plan. If my memory is correct, the middle of March is when most high school districts have to let faculty know if they are riffed (fired)."

The couple didn't say a word further until they had finished their portion. Then they hurried over to the library along with a new legal pad of paper to copy down the names of high school districts that they were willing to move to. The list included the western and northern suburbs of Chicago. They had fifty-five prospects.

Then, together they created a "file." This included a resume, a statement of teaching philosophy, teaching evaluations for the four courses Lynn had taught as a teaching assistant at Chicago University, an abstract of her dissertation, and the address of the place where they could request letters of recommendation from her dissertation committee.

Much of the file could be typed once. Seámus did this. He then went to one of the new "photo copy stores" on the near north side to make their copies at 10 cents a page.

The application letters had to be typed one-at-a-time. Seámus did this.

***

Lynn was successful. She was hired at a prestigious high school in Milwaukee, Wisconsin. This was fortunate, but it created a new problem. Milwaukee had a good bus system, but it wasn't as comprehensive as the Chicago Transit Authority. They needed a car. Lynn's job was in a rich area in the upper East Side. They could only afford to live on the West Side. They needed a car.

Seámus called Andrew about this situation. Andrew noted the various points at stake and then took a couple of weeks to think about it. In the end, Andrew offered to give Seámus their twelve-year-old Buick Skylark if he could come out and get it.

It would be a stretch, but Seámus had created an emergency savings account and this sounded like an emergency. They would accept the job. They would put their goods into the Evans's house until after they flew to the O'Neil's (who were now in Santa Barbara, California), and after a short visit they would drive the car across country to Milwaukee and their new home.

**

It all worked. They found an upper duplex two-bedroom for rent. It was near a park where Seámus could exercise. Seámus connected with Marquette University as a tutor in Greek, History, and Mathematics. This money stream was light, but it allowed them to pay their bills with a small amount left over.

Lynn drove the car to her work. Seámus bought a bicycle from The Lighthouse for the Blind's thrift store for $10. He eventually put 15,000 miles on that bike before they moved again.

Seámus and Lynn were in an interesting historical bubble. And they weren't alone. After the war (the Big One, WWII) the United States passed the most extensive G.I. Bill for educational benefits ever. There was a tremendous investment in human capital in the form of grants to cover college tuition and living expenses, both at the undergraduate and graduate levels. A G.I. could go *anywhere* in the United States, from Pottsville U. to Harvard. In fact, as careful readers of this account may remember, Dylan Evans took advantage of these provisions in order to finish up his B.A. degree at the University of Michigan and then get an M.A. degree in English Literature, also at the University of Michigan. Finally, he received a D. Div. from Fuller Theological Seminary. Altogether, the government of the United States paid for 7 years of schooling for his 3 years of military service.

This may seem overly generous on the government's part, but I have been told by Boylan (who is more up on these facts than I am) that in the subsequent 30 years, the public investment in human capital was actually paid back due to the recipients getting higher paying jobs that necessitated paying higher taxes. The government recovered its original investment with interest!

Andrew O'Neil did not go back to school to get his law degree.

At any rate, the surge in people enrolling in public and private colleges and universities during the late 40s and 50s under the G.I. Bill created a big demand for faculty. The minimum requirement to teach at the tertiary level was supposed to be a master's degree. But the demand was so high that those with bachelor's degrees and some other outstanding feature were often hired, as well.

The 1960s played this out in a big way. M.A. and Ph.D. programs swelled. Demand for qualified teachers was high. Lots of people received degrees and got good jobs. But then there was a moment of diminishing returns. By the mid-70s the tide was turning. And then a few years later, the mandatory retirement of tenured faculty was overturned by an Act of Congress. It was considered *age discrimination*. This had a dramatic effect. The unemployment rate for Ph.D.s in all areas within the academy began to soar (some people can work in business outside the academy—especially scientists).

Seámus and Lynn hit the job market at this time. Where only a few years before there had been only 5-6 applicants for every tenure track job, now there were 200! As they say in real estate, timing is *everything*.

Lynn's plan was to try and publish chapters of her dissertation and so improve her chances among the 200. Seámus's plan was to publish his dissertation, whole, and write a few new articles on the side.

Both of them tried to execute their plans. Seámus couldn't publish his dissertation, but did get an article accepted for publication. Lynn also got an article accepted for publication. Nonetheless, the result was that all of their limited resources were devoted to going to the national conventions in their disciplines for one or two nights for interviews and then to come home and scrimp for several months waiting to be invited to an on-campus interview. Unfortunately, these never came.

Seámus got a big part-time job at the Milwaukee Natural History Museum. Seámus was not a scientist, but he did have a degree in History and so he could segue to *public history*. And popular history is what museums are all about. This move gave the couple a bump in pay. They decided to have a baby—to be born in the summer when Lynn didn't work.

Toward the middle of May, Lynn was at 7 months and getting bigger. Her health was fine. Often she felt better than at any time in her life. There was one drawback; she was getting tired of teaching high school.

"Why don't you talk to folk at the museum about becoming full time? Then I could quit my job and be with my baby." It was the beginning of a conversation that repeated itself daily. Seámus talked to his boss and found that there *might* be an opening, but the pay would be less than their two jobs together. Seámus asked his boss to let him know when and if the full-time job opened up.

Seámus wanted to be supportive, but was a little disappointed, too. They had scrimped for so long together and were finally with a little breathing room and now they'd be down for the count again. However, it was true that the baby would need looking after. Daycare was too expensive and there was no relative in town to watch the child. The couple went through numerous discussions on the matter—many of which ended up in yelling.

***

It was the 11th day of June when Seámus drove his bicycle up to their duplex. He had a spring to his step. He unlocked the side door and bounced up the stairs two at a time. Lynn heard her husband and walked over to the staircase.

"Hello?" She said, though in a moment Seámus was there and giving her a hug.

Seámus took off his bicycle backpack and undid the top flap. With one smooth motion he took out a white rose that he had bought her.

"What's the occasion?" asked Lynn.

"The end of your school year?" put Seámus.

"That was Friday."

"Your birthday?"

"Try again."

"How about a job in Washington, D.C.?"

Lynn tipped her head to the right. "Come again?"

"You'd better sit down."

The couple moved over to their sofa (a hand-me-down from a thrift store covered with a red throw rug). It almost seemed chic next to their red carpet remnant and re-finished coffee table (Seámus thought he had some talent in woodworking—though he was quite alone in that judgment). "Well, do you ever remember me telling you about Jorge Diaz?"

"The guy who tore apart your paper at the History meeting a couple of years ago?"

"Yeah, he hated my methodology. Didn't have much to say about my conclusions if you accepted the way I was going about things, but yes that's the guy."

"What about him? Did he have an accident or something?"

Seámus laughed. "No way. I mean, not a bad accident."

"Is there such a thing as a *good* accident?" Lynn touched her belly as the baby began kicking.

"Well, as a matter of fact, there is. They call it a research grant. Professor Diaz has gotten a three-year grant at the Free University in Berlin to work on their Pergamum artifacts. They are doing a permanent exhibit at the Staatliche Museum and Diaz will get a book publication out of the whole thing."

Lynn tilted her head the other way. "That's very nice for Señor Diaz, but what has this to do with us?"

"Only this: I went to check my mail at Marquette. There in my mail cubby was a letter from Notre Dame-Loyola of Washington, D.C., and Diaz had put his last name below the printed return address. Well, the letter was short. He wanted me to phone him. I got permission from Marquette to call from the bull-pen adjuncts office."

"And did you get through?"

"Oddly enough, I did. You know university professors are generally only in their offices for the three hours of posted time a week. They are notoriously hard to contact by phone."

Lynn straightened up her head and began stroking her belly.

"So I got through. He was quite the gentleman. Apparently, in his home country of Chile, it is a great compliment to tear someone apart at an academic conference. He didn't think badly of me at all. In fact, he was sympathetic that I've never had a full time academic position."

"Easy for him to say," put in Lynn.

"Not so fast. It gets better for us. They are going to offer me a three-year non-tenure track position teaching ancient Greek History in the History Department. Then I mentioned you and wondered whether there might be something for you—after a year or two, according to how you are doing."

"A term appointment for me, too?"

"Yes. That's what I asked for. I told him about the baby and how you wanted to be at home for at least the child's first year—but maybe the first two years. He entirely understood and said he'd look into it."

"What's the pay?"

"Well, that's the good part. Since Diaz is well paid and since the grant will entirely cover his salary, the University is prepared to be very generous on his recommendation. We will make a little more than we are right now counting your high school salary, my museum pay, and my Marquette pay."

Lynn leaned over and gave her husband a hug. "This is wonderful news, but what will we do about the baby?"

"Well, the university will pay for our move. We can do it before you deliver or after. We'll have to consult your doctor about which is best for the health of all concerned."

Then there was some silence. Seámus got up to hang up his things and take off his shoes. As he was engaged in putting away his things Lynn chimed, "Notre Dame-Loyola, isn't that a basketball school?"

"Well, they are in a transition period," said Seámus with a grimace.

Then the baby started kicking hard.

***

Though Lynn was very tired of teaching high school English and had determined to give up her job so that she could be with her baby for a few years, she was not keen on having things shoved down her throat. She didn't like it that it was now all revolving around Seámus. He had never held a full-time job in his life. He was always putting together various combinations of part time jobs. It was she who had done the heavy lifting that allowed the marriage to be financially solvent. This was the way it had always been. What would happen next? Would the credit cards start showing *his* name instead of *hers*?

The job came through. It would be a three-year job with no possibility of a fourth year. But by then, they would be in Washington, D.C. and well-positioned to find something for their next leg in life.

Lynn decided that she wanted at least two years at home with their baby and would decide by March of the second year whether she would accept a one-year position on top of Seámus' third year.

The obstetrician and Wilma Evans determined that the baby should be born in Milwaukee and then brought down to Wheaton for two months. This was because the first two months of life were the most dangerous for the child. Wilma related countless cases of injury and death in the early months of life. "When the child is six months old, he or she will have reached a significant milestone."

And Wilma as a certified kindergarten teacher knew quite a lot about young lads and lasses.

Whenever the birth would happen (sometime in July) Seámus would have until mid-August before he had to drive to Washington, D.C. He would stay with a family friend of the Evans's, who used to live in Wheaton and taught with Dylan. From there, Seámus would go on a hunt for an apartment. He would check in by phone each night (though rather quickly as it was a long-distance phone call).

And so it happened. When Lynn's bag of waters broke, Seámus drove her to the hospital. The labor was long: 19 hours. The nurses waited until 17 hours before calling the obstetrician. She came in a flash and Bridget O'Neil was born at 5:00 am on July 12, 1984. She was 21 inches and 7.5 pounds. Mother and father were captivated by the miracle. Sure, they had both taken classes in biology in college. They were not stupid people. But who could be prepared for the presentation of an entirely new life: screaming and kicking her way into the world. Bridget was already making her mark.

***

With the consent of the landlord, they altered their plan some. The new parents found a moving company who would store their things until September 27th and then deliver them to the "to-be-decided" location in Washington, D.C. On July 30th the movers came in and on the next day Seámus took his wife and daughter down to Wheaton, Illinois for a couple of weeks.

Dylan was very happy to have his new grandchild in the house, but he also wanted to make a couple of things perfectly clear with Seámus.

"You know, Wilma and I are very happy for your child. We welcome her into the world and we want to support your move. In 35 years we have only moved twice."

"You certainly have been very stable," replied Seámus. The two men sat at the kitchen table sipping some tap water without ice.

"Yes. Stability is a virtue. We should all strive to cultivate virtue."

Seámus nodded and finished his glass of water.

"Now, you will be here for two weeks and Lynn will be with us for another six weeks."

"It is very generous of you. We thank you."

Dylan peered at his son-in-law over his glasses. Seámus was getting a little uncomfortable at the silence. "We are almost flat broke, or I'd pay you rent for the time."

Dylan nodded his head, "Humph."

"If you'd like, we could work-up a loan contract for the rent we should be paying you for my two weeks and Lynn and the baby's two months."

Dylan started strumming the brown Formica-topped table with his fingers. "We'd never charge the baby. She's not taking any food; she's nursing. But I could work out something for you and Lynn. No rush, just pay us when you can."

"Whatever you say is fine with us. We don't have many options."

"Not now you don't."

Seámus was not quite sure what that meant. Did that mean that they should have never gotten married unless they had a strong financial footing? Did it mean that they should have not gotten pregnant? Did it mean that they should have stayed in Milwaukee? Did Dylan know that Lynn was going to quit her job teaching high school? It was a decision she made after becoming pregnant. At that time they did seem fiscally solvent: Lynn had a full time job. Seámus had an adjunct teaching job, some tutoring, and the part-time job at the museum. If Lynn earned a dollar, then Seámus earned fifty cents. They were more than able to pay their bills. It was not a financially irresponsible thing to do at the time. After all, it was not an unknown phenomenon in the history of humankind for married couples to have children. And for Reform-minded Presbyterian Dylan, Seámus might have noted that Mary and Joseph weren't the most fiscally solid parents, and that was with the consent of God Almighty!

Seámus said none of this but replied, "And of course for my two weeks here I will be happy to take on your chores: mowing the lawn, minor repairs, taking out the garbage . . . "

Dylan stood up, prompting Seámus to stand up. Dylan extended his hand to his son-in-law, "I'm happy that you have taken this attitude, Seámus. It's in keeping with the way I've always seen you."

"Thank you, Mr. Evans."

Seámus turned to exit the kitchen when Dylan said, "And by the way, you can go over the back yard for dog droppings from our beagle, Prince. The shovel is by the garage door."

***

And so it was. Seámus drove to the east coast in the old Buick Skylark. The car had 120,000 miles on it and sometimes overheated when in heavy traffic. Fortunately, there wasn't any heavy traffic along the route which Seámus drove in one stint— around 18 hours.

Seámus arrived in the Washington, D.C. neighborhood of Tenleytown. The family friends of the Evans's (who used to live a few doors down from them in Wheaton), the Crows, were very hospitable—despite the fact that they were going through severe marital difficulties that in five months would end in divorce.

Seámus parked his car on the street. The Crows lived four blocks from the Tenleytown Redline Metro Stop. There were food stores, a movie theater, and a Sears Department Store all within the same walking distance. The location seemed like heaven to Seámus. Also, because Washington, D.C. was predominantly African American, and because real estate prices are often driven by racism, rents were reasonable.

Seámus' roles were twofold. First he had to check in at Notre Dame-Loyola so that they knew he had arrived. He also wanted to get signed up for payroll (health and dental insurance, TIAA/CREF retirement plan, and reimbursement on his moving expenses— including the drive east). Details, details . . . a horror for most, but Seámus was not a man who despised details. His academic work in History was all about details: a codex for an ancient manuscript, all the variant interpretations of crucial passages that were essential to building some overarching vision to explain what it was all about. And that, after all, was the purpose that people were put on earth.

Second, Seámus had to get a list of three properties that he felt confident about and then get on the phone with Lynn to discuss them.

Money was very limited but Notre Dame-Loyola's pay system gave him his first paycheck two weeks after arrival. This allowed Seámus to make use of the new technology of direct deposit. No more having to get your check and take it to the bank and wait three days before being able to use the funds. No. If one were to be paid on the 30th of the month, with direct deposit one could start using the money after 8am on the 30th of the month—a savings of almost a week over the old system!

***

Seámus got through the detail work with ease. He had a shared office with three other term-appointment History instructors. The campus of Notre Dame-Loyola was situated in the historic section of Washington called Georgetown. The front part of the campus was splendid in a mixture of Gothic/medieval-revival and brick Federalist architecture.

The first weekend after his arrival, he had to travel by university bus to their retreat house on the eastern shore of Maryland. On the retreat for new faculty at the university, he met a poet, Anthony Hecht. Seámus knew the poet who had come to D.C. on his being named *Consultant to the Library of Congress,* a title that was soon changed to *Poet Laureate of the United States.*

He also met a few other individuals who were on the tenure track and so were going through the ritual with a different sort of expectation than Seámus had. Still, Seámus loved to dream. In his wildest fantasies, he would do such a good job in his three years that they would promote him to a tenure track position. After all, the fairly new president, Father Healey, spoke at the retreat on how he was going to change Notre Dame-Loyola from a 150th place school in the United States to a top 20 school.

This would mean that there would be lots of encouraged retirements (encouraged by financial incentives). Thus it was not irrational to think there might be opportunity for Seámus and for his wife, Lynn. How wonderful that would be!

***

Though Seámus searched far and wide for a rental opportunity in the Washington, D.C. area, there always seemed to be something wrong when Seámus talked to Lynn by phone. The Crows were very generous in allowing Seámus to use their phone for a 10-minute long-distance call. Though Seámus offered, they never took reimbursement.

Cara Crow even went the mile further by looking in their neighborhood for rentals. She found one just three doors down that was from a foreign service person who had just been posted to Mongolia for five years. It wasn't forever, but because everyone knew each other, the deal was done at an affordable price. In fact, Cara had the crew over for dinner to seal the deal.

Lynn was very happy about this. It was only the second property she said she was willing to move into.

On October 1, 1984 the three O'Neils moved into a small house in Tenlytown, Washington, D.C.

***

The first thing the O'Neils noticed about moving to Washington, D.C. was that the normal cost of living was much higher than in Milwaukee. This was particularly true with food. In Milwaukee, they bought fresh fruit and vegetables at a store two blocks away, and name brand groceries at a big store. Now in D.C., they bought few fresh fruits and vegetables and went to a bargain grocery store to buy generic goods, and still their bill was 50% higher!

"How can they take farm food from Mexico or Chile and sell it for so much more? The shipping distance is comparable," said Seámus when they loaded up their car and drove home. It was a standard tirade which only changed with the countries involved. It was also one of the few instances each week in which they used a car. Washington, D.C. was not friendly to bicycles, so Seámus gave up riding the streets. He'd rather be inconvenienced than dead.

Instead, Seámus walked to the Tenleytown Metro station and took the Red Line to Dupont Circle, and from there took the free shuttle that Notre Dame-Loyola provided for its students, staff, and faculty. The whole trip took around an hour one-way (a good deal of that time was waiting).

But despite the strain of a higher cost of living, the O'Neils made good use of their location. Washington, D.C. in this era had many free venues. For any age, there were the art museums (the National Gallery, the Freer, and the Hirshorn), the Smithsonian Museums of American History, Natural History, the Castle, and the popular Air and Space Museum, and the national monuments. None of these cost a cent. Then there were the free dramatic productions on Saturday morning at the National Theater and the Kennedy Center. And everything was very accessible by Metro.

Lynn became the grand scheduler. Aside from the three days a week that Seámus had to be at the college, she created weekly adventures. These also included children's bookshops like *The Cheshire Cat* that was partly owned by the famous poet, Linda Pastan. They would host readings by famous writers and housed it all in a child-friendly space. These bookstores were located far and wide—from Alexandria to Reston to Baltimore: this meant the car.

It was a very happy time for the O'Neils. Young Bridget was very stimulated and her development went apace. She walked at a year (one day after her first birthday party in which other neighborhood children six months to a year older were walking). The parents noted that Bridget was a competitive lass.

When they had been there a year and a half, Lynn came forward for her one-year position starting in September. Everything worked out as planned. Lynn was welcomed into the English Department. It was especially good timing as their Victorian-Modernist person was going on sabbatical. No muss, no fuss.

Lynn got an office of her own. It had a view of the back side of the campus: the Jesuit graveyard and the sports stadium. Because of the flexibility of class scheduling, they were able to arrange their schedules so that when Lynn taught, Seámus was at home with Bridget and vice versa. Everyone was a winner. Life was grand!

The couple took a Fall outing to Skyline Drive in Virginia. It was so beautiful in autumn that there was a back-up. This started getting Seámus very worried. Their Buick was approaching 150,000 miles. The couple kept it up-to-date as best they could at a local service station that didn't try to rip them off. Now and again they had talked about getting another car—either a new one or a used one. Right now, things were in the black. They had a new income to live on. They felt giddy. But Seámus was a cautious sort of person who had convinced his wife to put their extra money into a *house fund*. It would be the down payment on the future house they wanted to own. After all, owning a house is part of the American Dream. You haven't made it until you could buy a house.

The O'Neils made it to the park all right. It was raw, natural beauty. The fall foliage was intense. So many primary colors all created via the natural rhythms that inhabit time. The park was set up for either a slow drive through, or one could stop and get out and walk a bit. The O'Neils chose the slow drive through. Lynn would exclaim to Bridget, "Look at that yellow tree! Look at that fox over there. Look at the hawk in the sky."

Occasionally Seámus would become so entranced with Lynn's commentary that he would take a look and almost rear-end the car in front of him.

However, on exiting the park in the stop-and-go stream, steam started rising from the hood. Seámus looked at the temperature gauge and it was on red. Seámus pulled over at a rest area. He knew the danger of opening up the radiator cap too soon. He did not aspire to have second and third degree burns over his face, hands, and arms. So they waited two hours for the engine block to cool.

Lynn and Bridget took the opportunity to engage in a game on some playground equipment while Seámus sat back and watched. After about forty-five minutes, the parents switched roles. Lynn and Seámus approached play with their daughter rather differently. Lynn wanted to see what Bridget could do on the playground equipment. She encouraged her daughter to stretch her physical prowess. Always an attentive mother, Lynn was there to catch Bridget when she let go of the monkey bars.

Seámus rather preferred playing *make believe* games based upon stories that he told her when she would go to sleep each night. Some of these were fantasy and some were based upon Ancient Greek History (another form of fantasy). In these games, father and daughter would assume some dramatic role and play it out with imaginary swords, horses, and costume.

Between the two, young Bridget was thoroughly challenged: *mens sana in corpore sano.*

After Athens had won the Peloponnesian War (because they listened to Socrates over the *hoi polloi*), it was time for Seámus to fill up the radiator with water. He went to the latrine and filled their two large soda cups with water and took them to the car. Seámus used a towel to open the radiator cap (there was no steam) and dumped it in. He had no idea how much water it would take. It looked like close to a gallon. That meant four trips.

Then Seámus tried the engine and it turned over and the temperature gauge was within normal limits.

Though the couple had recently joined the American Automobile Association (AAA) for just such situations, they didn't need a tow. Instead, they made it back to Tenleytown in one piece.

Two weeks later they purchased a new Ford Taurus station wagon. They dipped into their house fund for the down payment. They knew that they could make the monthly payments easily with their new financial arrangement.

In order to celebrate their new car, the three O'Neils took a day trip to Baltimore to visit the Inner Harbor and then go to the Lexington Market for a pick-up dinner.

Baltimore was a city in transition. It had become one of the most depressed cities in the Mid-Atlantic region once the big industries of the 40s-70s started drying up big time in the 1980s.

This put thousands of middle class factory workers out of a job. The houses they had purchased as part of the American Dream were now being foreclosed. Most of these poor souls were African American. Though the percentage of African Americans in Baltimore and D.C. at that time were comparable, still there was more work in D.C. because of the supporting jobs associated with the Federal Government: jobs in the cafeteria, jobs in landscaping, jobs in maintenance of the Mall, and jobs in the Smithsonian, etc. Baltimore's answer to combat unemployment was the construction of a tourist attraction: the Inner Harbor and then a new baseball stadium that was in the plans.

Seámus tried to put these events into a context. What historical trends were occurring in Baltimore and the upper-Midwest? Were they similar since both were manufacturing jobs? It was as if someone were trying to re-define America. But who would hire these individuals skilled in an economy that seemed to be traveling to Japan or China? Could you really blame a manufacturer for moving the plant somewhere else where the workforce would do the job for pennies a day?

Well, probably not if profit for shareholders was the sole aim of business. It didn't have to be. It wasn't in Scandinavia. These issues bothered Seámus a lot as he tried to make sense of everything.

Because things were going so well in their own personal lives, Lynn did not like to enter into conversations about these topics. Instead, she cajoled Seámus to be a *team player* and extol over the Baltimore Aquarium and his sandwich from the Lexington Market.

***

"So what's wrong with being happy?" asked Lynn to her husband as they lay in bed together.

"Nothing. Aristotle says in both Books 1 and 10 of the *Nicomachean Ethics* that happiness is the only thing that people seek for its own sake and not for the sake of something else."

"Exactly. And I know you like Aristotle. I like Aristotle. At Chicago University, he was revered as the foundation of literary criticism."

"So that means we are on the same side, once again." Seámus leaned over and kissed his wife. She returned his advances. Life was good right now.

Forty-five days later, the Walgreens' pregnancy test had a dot inside the circle.

***

Christmas in 1987 was joyous at the O'Neil household. Seámus had a chance to think about how many students of his had expressed gratitude in the way he presented material in his classes, and he was directing two undergraduate theses and one M.A. thesis. These were students who were excited by the way he presented his lectures. Seámus found ways of making the events in the Ancient World seem relevant to their lives today. Along the way, he had a theory of how history progressed and then regressed, according to economic status, military conquest, and the role of religion.

Seámus was not original, but he combined the work of several others into a unique way one might confront what was going on before them. Without being a positivist, he believed in certain verities of historical inquiry. He thought that the essential quest of humankind was to separate the wheat from the chaff. What is it all about, anyway? And how can we get there?

***

Lynn was also doing splendid in her teaching. They had just finished the fall term of her one-year contract. In her three-class load of 60 students, she had inspired 6 to become English majors. She was a passionate advocate of her vision of destiny as set out by Thomas Hardy in *Hap*.

> If but some vengeful god would call to me
> From up the sky and laugh: "Thou suffering thing,
> Know that thy sorrow is my ecstasy:
> That thy love's loss is my hate's profiting!"
>
> Then I would bear it, clench myself, and die,
> Steeled by the sense of ire unmerited:
> Half-eased in that a Powerfuller than I
> Had willed and meted me the tears I shed.
> But not so. How arrives it joy lies slain,
> And why unblooms the best hope ever sown?
> —Crass Casualty obstructs the sun and rain,

And dicing Time for Gladness casts a moan . . .
These purblind Doomsters had as readily strown
Blisses about my pilgrimage as pain.

Though Hardy went to his local parish for services, he did not buy into a Divine Plan. Instead, he saw the dross of everyday life, the maya, as randomly forming the environment we are forced to live in. Right now, things seemed fine. They had a three-year-old baby girl who was a joy. They had paid off the note to her father for the rent incurred before their move, and they had even put a down payment on a new car. It was the first new car they ever had together. Even the sale of the old car went well, though the Ford dealer would not give them anything for the 1968 Buick Skylark with high mileage. "If *you* give me $100 I'll take it off your hands for you," declared the salesman.

Seámus had demurred. He put up some post cards on bulletin boards at Notre Dame-Loyola and someone working in maintenance called in two days. Selling price was $200, cash: "as is." Seámus drove the deal. Lynn was amazed at the way her husband could negotiate with someone who was so different and yet be on a fair and level plane with him. Like many of Irish heritage, Seámus was loquacious and had an exact vocabulary. The buyer was also a mechanic and had carefully looked under the hood and said with assurance, "I can get another hundred thousand easily out of this baby." Seámus smiled. They shook hands, and exchanged money and title. The deal was complete.

Despite their new car, the O'Neils didn't change their routine much. They only used it for shopping and for destinations outside the city. Inside the city, there were the Metro and city busses. It was a rather schizophrenic approach to the transportation worldview. In his heart, Seámus wished he could still ride his bike. But with narrow streets and hypercompetitive drivers, the risk was too high. He had two people who needed him and one on the way.

***

It was Thursday March 17th, St. Patrick's Day, that both of the O'Neils received letters from Notre Dame-Loyola. Lynne had prepared corned beef, cabbage, and soda bread for dinner as a celebration meal. Even Bridget had agreed to eat it (though she hadn't last year).

Lynn had chosen a flat cut of the corned beef. She used nine inch-wide strips of beef, a spoonful of brown sugar, a spoonful of clover fed honey, a clove of garlic, and a head of cabbage cut into ½ inch wide strips. In her own special way (as opposed to the recipe) she added two carrots cut into 1 ½ inch strips julienne. She would boil the meat, fat-side up for a couple of minutes, drain the water, then get a new bit of water going and repeat—up to three times. This got the salt out of the meat and made it easy to separate the fat from the meat. Then on the oven in a saucepan she would brown the rest and then add the beef strips, coating it with the honey and brown sugar, finally covering the saucepan at low heat for ten minutes. At the end, there was a concoction that was sweet and moist. The dry soda bread and creamery butter made a good combination. It was all served with a pint of Guinness for the adults and root beer for Bridget.

The dinner was celebratory. Seámus read a story to the family about the Red Branch. He and Bridget had already prepared a dramatic presentation to come after dinner. Lynn was a great audience. A good time was had by all.

After Seámus had finished with the dishes, he took his little girl to bed to read her a story and sing a few songs together. Lynn had already had her play time with Bridget while Seámus was doing the dishes.

As Seámus and Lynn headed to bed, Lynn asked, "Have you read the mail today?"

"No, I'm pretty tired. Let's look at it tomorrow."

"D'accord," responded his wife.

***

The next morning over breakfast, the two opened their letters. It was no real surprise in one sense. Bad news. They would both be out of a job when the spring term ended. In one sense, this shouldn't have been a surprise as they had both signed term contracts for teaching. Seámus' had been for three years, and Lynn's had been for one year. However, this was not what was primary in their minds. They both expected that since they had performed at the highest level, then they might be kept on. Wouldn't that make sense for a university that wanted to be highly ranked?

"I was one of three nominated for teaching honors among the entire faculty of 26. I also got more students to declare English majors than any other: tenure track or otherwise. I know we signed a contract, but I exceeded my expectations by a mile. I'm doing better than anyone in my teaching, and wasn't it Father Healy's idea that Notre Dame-Loyola would take a different track than other aspiring national universities? Instead of creating a powerhouse group of publishing scholars, it would emphasize undergraduate teaching. Well, goddamn it, that's me. I made it in high school teaching. If you can make it there, you've got what it takes," Lynn got up and started circling the room. It was her turn to go to class. Seámus would watch Bridget.

Then, Seámus got up and hugged his wife. After a moment, he pulled away slightly so that he could look her in the eyes, "Let's see if we can fight this."

"How?"

"Let's start with the department chair and then go the academic vice president. We may not win this one, but we owe it to ourselves to try."

Lynn looked back with a thoughtful expression of her own. There was a silence and then she kissed her husband.

***

When Lynn left, Seámus woke up Bridget. His little girl was a good sleeper. So many people complain when they have a baby that they take a year or two away from sleeping uninterrupted. That had rarely been the case with Bridget. Her morning routine was breakfast (some Irish oatmeal with some brown sugar atop and orange juice) and then some puzzles to get the mind moving. After that, Bridget would curl up next to her daddy and they would both look at their books. Bridget was not a reader yet, but was steadily incorporating more words into her consciousness.

At the end of the morning they would take a walk to the neighborhood playground and indulge in make-believe games using the playground equipment as props: airplanes, rocket ships, ladders over molten lava, etc. Then it was off to home for lunch.

After lunch, Seámus read Bridget a story and then she played dress-up in her room while Seámus went back to work. It was a peaceful existence. This had to be the way of life for Seámus and

Lynn. Seámus was sure of it. Sure, they had a roadblock ahead: they were both to become unemployed. But this was noise.

He was mindful of Tennyson's take on the *Odyssey:*

> The lights begin to twinkle from the rocks;
> The long day wanes; the slow moon climbs; the deep
> Moans round with many voices. Come my friends,
> 'T is not too late to seek a newer world.
> Push off, and sitting well in order smite
> The sounding furrows; for my purpose holds
> To sail beyond the sunset and the baths
> Of all the western stars, until I die . . .
> To strive, to seek, to find, and not to yield.

For Seámus, the mission was clear. The details and distractions of life's vicissitudes (maya) should not cause one to stray from his natural mission. It was clear, certain, and God-given. And Seámus was determined to keep on course.

***

As expected, both Seámus and Lynn were turned down for an extension of their teaching contracts. They had signed legal documents that were perfectly clear in their language. It did not matter how well or poorly they had done. A contract is a contract.

On the bright side was the fact that they finished teaching in early May and they continued to receive paychecks until July 31st. That gave them two months to shift about. If that didn't work, there was always unemployment insurance that would extend their pay (albeit at a lower level) for six more months. These facts lightened the blow for Seámus. They weren't relevant to Lynn. After all, their paychecks ended on July 31st and their baby was due on August 15th! What could be worse? And after July 31st they would no longer have health insurance!

Lynn went into depression. Seámus started buying the newspaper to look for a new job.

CHAPTER SEVENTEEN

To give up works dictated by desire,
Wise men allow this to be renunciation;
Surrender of all the fruits [that accrue] to works
Discerning men call self-surrender.
    Bhagavad Gita, XVIII.1*

The news of the day: Navy Missile Downs Iranian Jetliner. A U.S. Warship fighting gunboats in the Persian Gulf yesterday mistook an Iranian civilian jetliner for an attacking Iranian F14 fighter plane and blew it out of the hazy sky with a heat-seeking missile, the Pentagon announced 290 persons aboard the European made A300 Airbus and that all had perished.
    The Washington Post July 4, 1988

SEÁMUS O'Neil was perplexed. Most of the jobs that he had applied for in his life had been part-time jobs. Part-time jobs were so much easier to get than full-time jobs. He had several deal points. First, he had to make enough to pay his rent, buy groceries, and pay utilities. Second, he needed health insurance. His policy with Notre Dame-Loyola would run out on July 31—less than a month away. Lynn was due in mid-August.

All other things being equal, Seámus would prefer to work at a museum in the capacity of an historian. After all, his Ph.D. was in History and he had worked both at the university level and at the public museum in Milwaukee. When Seámus started his search, he was very optimistic. Washington, D.C. and environs had a number of museums that featured History. Shouldn't that make getting a job a snap?

Unfortunately not. Many people majored, got masters, or Ph.D.s in History for that very reason: the existence of jobs outside the academy. This meant that every job was filled with a considerable waiting list in the event a job would open up. In the

---

* R.C. Zaehner, tr. *Hindu Scriptures* (New York: Dutton, 1966).

long scheme of things, if Seámus had applied right now, he might hear back on something in three years or so. Three years! Why hadn't he done that when he accepted his term appointment? Probably he'd be in a job right now. But he had trusted in a principle that if one were good at a job and went the extra mile that no one would turn him away. How could they? Wasn't there a principle of fairness at stake? Weren't the universities created on the principle that they were artificial communities in which fairness was valued more than in the outside society?

Seámus felt like a sucker. He was down to the wire. Now he was looking at every job that met his minimum requirements of salary and health insurance. Then his eyes hit upon a listing:

Young executive training program: People's Insurance, competitive salary plus benefits.

Seámus liked the words "competitive salary" and "benefits." He copied down the number and called on Tuesday July 5th at 9:00am.

"Yes, I read your advertisement in the newspaper about a young executive training program. Is that still open?"

"It is right now," said the man on the other end. His voice had a lilting quality.

"Can I come by to talk to you about it?"

"You want an interview?" said the man as the pitch rose to a higher register.

"Yes. I can come whenever you want."

"Where do you live?"

"Tenleytown, D.C."

"D.C., eh?" The man snorted. "Well, we're in Maryland. Bethesda. If you take the Metro we are two blocks from the Bethesda Metro stop. From where you are that's a 5-minute ride. Can you be here in one-half hour?"

"Absolutely. Ah, by the way, what's your address?"

***

Seámus arrived 5 minutes early to the interview. The interview went well. By 10:30 he was hired and he had filled out all the appropriate forms. He would start immediately and the benefits would begin August 1st. There would be no break in coverage.

***

"Well, what do you think about it?" asked Lynn when he returned at six o'clock.

"It's money. They will pay me for one year guaranteed the same that I was making at Notre Dame-Loyola." The couple was sitting at their kitchen table. Seámus was tired, but it was his turn to make the meal. He kept squinting his eyes and scrunching his nose.

It was lasagna night. Seámus followed a recipe from a family that lived across the street from his birth family when they lived in New Jersey. Lasagna is a dish that most people slaughter because they do not know how to balance the cheeses, the amount of tomatoes, and the layering of ingredients.

But it was a favorite with Seámus. This was especially true since at the time of Bridget's birth it was the last meal that Lynn consumed before she went into labor. The family called this Bridget's "birth food."

Now they were having it around the date of another important birth event.

"It will take some adjusting. I'm not my father, I've never been in the sales business," said Seámus as he started taking the skin off the five garlic cloves that went with the one small sweet onion that was the initial stage of the process. Two tablespoons of olive oil at a medium heat started a process that required patience.

"You are a good salesman," said Lynn.

"Oh really?" said Seámus with a smile.

"Absolutely. You got me, right?"

"Yes, but that's the *high end* market. I'm not sure that *People's Insurance* is doing business there." Seámus wiped his hands on a hand towel and then gave his wife a kiss on the lips.

"So what's ahead?"

"Well, for starters, they have given me two weeks to study for and pass the state insurance examination in D.C. (because that's where we live)."

"Is that hard to do?" Lynn leaned back in her chair and put both hands upon her pronounced belly.

"I don't know. They gave me two study guides. I've taken tests before. But never with this kind of importance; if I don't pass, we're screwed. We'll have to move in with your folks and get a loan for the pregnancy—and these days that's as much as we spent for a year of college."

Lynn kissed the palm of her hand and threw a kiss to her husband as he worked at his signature dish on the stove.

Seámus took to his task with earnestness. There would be tremendous consequences if he could not pass his two-hour state insurance examination. The test was a combination of business practice and law. Therefore, there were many questions that did not make logical sense. They only made sense within the acquired law of the insurance industry which hadn't really got its professional stance together until the 1920s.

Seámus studied in the same fashion that he had at Pembroke and Chicago University. Soon he began to see the driving principles of "transference of risk," "fiduciary responsibility," "indemnity," "the principle of claims," "twisting," "rebating," etc. It was a tale of law, justice, and profitable business practice all rolled into one. It had always been Seámus' policy to try to construct a conception of the whole in order to understand the proper order of the parts.

Because Seámus' father, Andrew, had been in business and had talked at length with Seámus about various cases he had been on first at Standard Register, then at Diebold, and then in his own company, Seámus was not a neophyte for this sort of worldview. The world of business had its own public rules, and also its secret practices.

It was in this latter category that Seámus was on less solid ground. This was because Andrew was a straight-up guy. That could be a problem in planning a business career. Seámus remembered in great clarity an event in his childhood. They were living at Cherry Street right after selling the house at 1020 N. Hamlin. Seámus was seven years old and they were entertaining the executive vice-president of sales at Diebold (a Fortune 500 company). It was the appetizer course. Moira had made some crème puffs and the party was drinking grape juice. Moira was a bit behind the curve in time management (vis-à-vis the main dinner) so she asked Seámus to carry a tray with the appetizers and the grape juice to the party at hand (Andrew and Jack Evans, the senior v.p. of sales). Jack was a man just a few years older than Andrew. He had pale skin and black hair and brown eyes. He stood a couple inches shorter than the five-foot eleven-inch O'Neil. The men were talking shop in the living room, which consisted of a beige couch that could seat three, two straight-back chairs, and an antique rocking chair. In front of the couch was a table atop a white area rug that was four feet by ten feet. Behind the couch was a picture window onto the street. The window had a gold top valence and side curtains.

The men saw young Seámus coming in, trying to be a suave waiter. The men understood the intent of young Seámus so they started clapping as if to show the boy their gratitude at his fine service. The clapping started to disorient Seámus so that when he approached the fine white carpet upon which the tray table sat, Seámus stumbled and fell.

And down it went: child, tray, and all! It was a spectacular failure. Red grape juice staining the white rug and the crème puffs falling every which way. Seámus hit his head, but he was up in a flash, trying to pick up everything. None of the glasses was broken, thanks to the carpet. But then he saw the stain. He stood up and with tears in his eyes he said, "I'm so sorry. I'm so sorry. I don't know how this happened. I'm so sorry." And then he ran into the kitchen to get cleaning supplies. Moira met her boy and scurried for cleaning supplies. And in a flash mother and son were attacking the grape juice stain.

Of course, the carpet was ruined. But they attacked it with ferocity while the men on the couch told the pair to stop. But Moira and Seámus worked for about five minutes on the stain before returning to the kitchen to insure that the dinner wouldn't also be ruined.

The dinner was fine.

After dinner, Moira was cleaning off the dishes from the table. Andrew excused himself to go to the bathroom and Jack Evans took Seámus aside in the front room where all the trouble had occurred. The pair walked in front of the large plate-glass window that looked out at the cul-de-sac upon which the O'Neil house was one of five. In the center was a round tuft of grass that was bordered with curb-shaped cement. "Seámus," began Jack as he put his hand on the boy's shoulder and they looked out at the street. "You shouldn't feel bad about tripping. Sometimes we want to do the very best things, and that desire gets in the way of execution."

Seámus didn't quite understand what Mr. Evans was saying, but he felt by his soft tone and the hand on his shoulder in a supportive fashion that the intent was kind.

"You know, Seámus, that trying to do the right thing is very important in life. There are so many people who have different agendas. I see them all the time in my job. Then I see men like you and your dad. You are very special because you want to do the *right* thing." Jack Evans coughed and took out his handkerchief.

"You should be very proud of your family. They are special. I've never known a man like your dad. He is as honest as the day is long. You should be proud of him. The man has talent, but then there are a lot of men with talent. Your dad has the talent to be the president of a company, but his values are so high that they will always get in the way of that." Jack took off his glasses and cleaned them with his handkerchief and then he wiped his eyes as well. "Things at the top are often dirty. It can make life tough for a man like me. But when I know there are men like your dad, it gives me hope."

Then Jack Evans looked into Seámus' eyes. "Do you know what I mean?"

"I'm not sure, sir. But it's something nice about my dad."

Jack smiled and gave Seámus a hug. "Yes, Seámus, it's very good. Your dad is a rare man in the high level of business; he's got values. He will never compromise them. And that's something to be proud of, boy. It's something to be proud of."

Then the pair was called into the dining room for dessert.

***

Seámus had not thought about that conversation for a long time. But now as he was about to enter the world of business, it all came back to him. How many claims would there be on his integrity? Would he be up to the challenge? What made his father an honest man? Where was Diogenes? It was time to for him to extinguish his lamp and converse with Andrew O'Neil.

***

Seámus was notified that he passed his test one day before Lynn went into labor. The family had health insurance due to Seámus' provisional job status. The couple had gone to Lamaze classes for childbirth. Seámus wanted to be there as a coach to his wife. The first labor had been so long and painful that the couple—especially Lynn—hoped it would be quicker (if not less painful this time).

Since Lynn wanted the birth to be natural as it was with Bridget (no epidural, no drugs), it was rather like running a marathon: an athletic event. Lynn was the focused athlete. She had her concentration points and three levels of breathing down. Most of all, she had in her mind the expectation of pain and how she would confront it. After all, she had been there before.

Lynn's bag of waters broke at 9 pm on August 19th. She alerted Seámus to retrieve the packed overnight bag and her purse and get her to the hospital directly. Seámus was an efficient helper. He did as he was told and how they had practiced. He transported his wife to the hospital by 9:45pm. Lynn found her focal point. Then she had a cleansing breath and waited. Bridget waited in a special room for young siblings. As the next contraction started, Lynn went through the hard short breathing. It was painful, but she was on top of the pain. She knew her companion and she knew how to react.

Seámus went through his pre-instructed coaching routine. He was in awe of his wife.

The baby was in the world at 1 am, August 20th, 1988. Seámus was ecstatic. There were no complications. This was something that the couple did well; Lynn was the director, the baby was the star, and Seámus was lighting and props director.

Within minutes of having the umbilical cord cut, the baby was being placed upon Lynn's breast to stimulate the colostrum that was even now ready for the little boy who they had pre-decided to name Rory (if it had been a boy).

And now they had both! They had a boy and a girl. How could they be happier?

***

Seámus took his wife and son home two days later. Bridget was very keen on being a part of the process. After all, she was already four years old and was about to start pre-school. Bridget was not entirely sure of her role. Should she react to Rory as a surrogate mother or as a playmate? It was very complicated. How could one be a playmate to a chap in diapers? And yet, how could she be the mother when she had to move a chair in the kitchen to climb up to the counter for a glass or plate?

Lynn was in her element. She found ways of bringing Bridget into the picture. Lynn was a born teacher and parent. The triad was together constantly—even more than constantly because Rory (unlike Bridget) did not sleep through the night. Luckily for Lynn, Seámus was able to pop up and walk his son rather quickly. This was because Seámus could go to sleep quickly, wake-up and walk

Rory, and then go back to sleep quickly. Lynn said he was a "push-button" husband: on and off.

***

At work, Seámus was initially clueless. His contract with Peoples Insurance was only guaranteed for a year. After that, he'd go onto straight commission. This was a big jump. Seámus had to figure out how to manage his career. In the office, there were three types of agents. First were the debit life agents. This was the biggest group. Peoples Insurance had a lot of business with lower middle class and poor people. Seámus was surprised at how many parents bought life insurance policies on their children. Existence was tough in poverty areas and one way to balance the death of a child by homicide or illness was to have life insurance on them. And since life insurance on children was very low and would not rise (depending upon the policy), there would be a payday if their child came home in a bag.

The debit agents would go around to lower middle class and poor neighborhoods in Maryland and the District to collect the monthly premiums. This was not necessarily a safe job. It was one thing for a poor person to get enough money for the first monthly premium, but it was another to keep it up among the vicissitudes of life. The bill collector could be the source of anger and violence.

All of the debit agents were male and many of them carried concealed weapons.

The second sort of agent was one who was middle class. He would try to sell life insurance to everyone he knew. Because he knew his clients, his cases would *stick*. (Unlike the debit agents who took over business already written by other debit agents no longer with the company: debit agents had a 75% annual attrition rate.)

This second group tended to stay around longer. They had only a 40% attrition rate. They also had higher education. The debit agents had high school education (or less). The career life agents often had a year of community college. This gave them an *attitude* among those in the office.

Then there was the third group of agents who could also write property and casualty insurance so that they were *full line agents*. These individuals went to special classes (at their own expense) on the weekends to get the extended insurance license. The individuals in this group often had a community college degree, an AA (two years beyond high school)—one even had a 4-year degree, a B.A.

Seámus had put his full education on his application for employment and had been accepted for employment. But he did not intend to discuss it. He wanted to fit into the office so that he might stay employed and be able to pay the bills for his family.

"So, what do you aim to do in insurance?" asked Jimmy Purdham, a debit agent who also played country music on the weekends in up county. Jimmy was about fifty and a great admirer of Ronald Reagan. He stood about five-foot-nine and weighed 200 pounds. He also had a beer belly.

"I don't know for sure. I just passed my life/health test and I thought I'd go for property and casualty, too. I understand there is a class that runs for a month and begins in mid-September."

"Well, you got to be careful about that." Purdham paused to blow his nose. "Say, you want to go to the seven-eleven for some lunch?"

"Ok," replied Seámus. And the pair went over and got chili dogs and a big gulp soda. It was standard gourmet fare for people trying to stay afloat.

When they situated themselves outside the upper level of the Bethesda Metro Station courtyard, Jimmy tried to help Seámus understand what the insurance business was all about.

"You've got to understand, Seámus. If you go the debit route, you've got a sure thing. It's like with my band. We try to get about six or seven places that like us and we rotate every week or so."

"How do they pay you?" asked Seámus.

"Not like they do Bruce Springsteen." Jimmy laughed and spilled some chili on his pant leg.

Seámus pulled one of the twenty paper napkins he had taken for just such an occasion. (It was Lynn who had taught him such insights.) Jimmy gave Seámus a head nod to recognize his help. Seámus nodded back.

"Well, the way the bars think about it, they make so much each night, right? Say they get some more when we come and play. We split that extra money 50-50. In addition, they guarantee us $10 each just for showing up. That's $40 even if the place is empty."

"Yep. And we have a good time, to boot." Jimmy took off his cowboy hat that he liked to wear and ran his fingers through his thick, curly dark brown hair.

"Must be nice," said Seámus. "I can't even hold a tune."

Jimmy laughed. "You know you shouldn't quit. I couldn't neither until I started drinkin' lots of beer. I think there is something about getting drunk that helps people with their musical abilities. Why, I don't never try to play the gee-tar unless I've had at least three rounds in my gut." Jimmy laughed again and slapped Seámus on the shoulder. And Seámus slapped Jimmy back.

Seámus had passed his initiation.

***

So Seámus became an all-lines agent. This had several advantages. For one thing, debit agents often had to work at night or odd hours when poor folk were home so that they could collect the monthly premium. An all-lines agent never had to collect anything except for the initial premium when the policy was written. After that, *collections* became the business of the company.

One of the activities that Seámus enjoyed the least was *cold calling*. Since Seámus had decided that he wanted to work the business market and not the individual market, he could do his cold calling during the day when businesses were generally open and ready for business. Statistics said that if you called 100 businesses about health insurance or commercial vehicle insurance or liability insurance or a BOP (small business office policy), and if you had a decent product and if you were reasonably proficient at verbal communications, then you would get 5 prospects and close 2 of them. Now that was a lot of work. Especially since the insurance company didn't help you in any way. You had to get your own sources via the local newspapers and the yellow pages.

One good thing about calling on businesses is that they wouldn't curse you or slam the phone down and so make a noise that hurt your ear drum. No, small businesses were in the same dilemma themselves: how to stay in business and avoid bankruptcy. It was a zero-sum live-or-die in the jungle worldview.

Seámus generally chose the small town "give-away" papers instead of the *Washington Post* for his leads. This was because they were closer to where he was in life: living on the edge.

Seámus knew he only had twelve months before he was on straight commission. He had two kids and the family had one income. Seámus was not going to let them down.

***

After five months, Seámus had closed twenty health insurance cases (that paid monthly and on which he made 5% commission) and seven forms of business insurance (generally a package that also paid 3% monthly on the liability, property, and business auto insurance).

Then Seámus went to a local conference on environmental insurance. It was a theme he believed in. After all, when the family lived in Milwaukee, he had gone everywhere on his bicycle. Suddenly, Seámus thought that wouldn't it be nice if he could sell insurance in a market that resonated with who he was?

Seámus went for a car ride with his sales manager, John Stang.

Earlier Seámus had told John that they almost had the same name. "No way José. 'John' does not sound like 'Seámus.'"

"Yes, *way* --almost. 'John' is an English name and 'Seán' is the exact Irish equivalent, but 'Seámus' is a poetic cousin. Technically its English counterpart is 'James,'" replied Seámus.

"Well, 'John' is not the same as 'James,'" replied John.

"True," returned Seámus. "But they are closer in Gaelic."

John cleared his throat.

John drove a Ford Crown Victoria. "It's the next thing to the 'Continental,'" John would say. Seámus thought to himself that it reminded him of a police car. Who knows, John might have gotten it used on those county sales that occur each month in Montgomery County. Though the sales office was in Bethesda, most of their business was up-county in Maryland.

"Damn, I never knew that. You've got some education. Everybody talks about it."

"I'm sorry. I shouldn't have said anything."

"No way, dumb-ass. I just mean that you know what you're talking about. No one's saying that your being high and mighty. That's not what I meant. You're a straight guy. I like you." The pair was driving to a destination in *Darnestown* (upper Montgomery County).

John drove them north on highway I-270. It was then that he continued his ongoing story of the Vietnam War. "You know the first time that I thought that I might die was in a fire-fight with the VC and me being a medic with the red cross on my helmet made me a target. They try and kill you first because then you can't care for your platoon. When guys go down it's pivotal. They need for someone to be there because the mantra is that 'we leave no American behind.' And they mean it."

John tried changing lanes and almost hit a big truck. "No harm. No foul," laughed John as he started playing with his thin black moustache that just barely drooped down. When they turned off the freeway, John began again about Vietnam. "They really mean it. And if you are a medic you are probably the most likely to die in the field of fire."

"Then why did you volunteer to be a medic? Why not be a grunt with a gun?" asked Seámus.

"One simple reason: I wanted to become a doctor. That was my life's dream."

"What made you choose that as your goal?"

"Don't know. I like helping people. My whole family likes helping people. We have a family plumbing business. I could have been set." Now John was rubbing his left hand through his jet black hair that was thinning at the temples.

"You don't like plumbing?"

John laughed. "Who in their right mind would choose a career of wrestling with turds when you could be a doctor? You know how much respect people show you when you tell them you're a doctor?"

"No," said Seámus. "I guess I never thought about it."

"It's amazing. It's fucking amazing. And if I could have made it; that would have been mine, too."

"I'm sorry. How far did you get?"

They pulled into a strip mall and John parked the car. "I did a year of community college, but couldn't pass the damn biology. Can't be a doctor if you can't pull the grades. Simple as that." John was now looking directly at Seámus. Seámus was very uncomfortable. Seámus nodded.

Then John slapped Seámus on the shoulder. "Don't think about it. Let's get some lunch here at the Sung Toy Restaurant—they've got a buffet bar: $5 all you can eat. It even includes tea!"

The two insurance agents sat down to their Asian fusion meals. It was a dark restaurant. Formica tables. No chopsticks. When they were done, they went over to an auto parts dealer two doors down. They had an appointment. John was going to talk to one of the two brothers who owned the place about a buy-sell continuation plan that was funded with life and disability insurance. Seámus talked to the other brother about changing their health plan.

After about 45 minutes, Seámus had a sale, and John had a definite *maybe*.

Because John was Seámus' sales manager, John got an over on Seámus' commission. For a health case, Seámus got 5% anu John 2.5%. So it was a successful trip.

When they got back to the office in Bethesda, John saw Pete Peterson, another agent who had a demeanor that Seámus took as being haughty. Pete cut his hair short on the side and spiked it into a crew cut on top. Pete was also a Vietnam vet. Like John, Pete was married with a daughter. Pete had a photo of his wife and daughter on his cubicle wall.

"Yeah, we closed the health case and will probably close the buy-sell. That's the one with the real bucks. And no one can run a business with a partner and not have a buy-sell." John said these words as Seámus disappeared into his cubicle to start filling in the forms for the general contract and then the health forms for each employee for medical underwriting.

Pete floated over to watch Seámus do the paperwork. Pete had a high, hoarse-sounding voice. "You know, if you sign those forms for the employees it will go a lot faster. You get paid and they get their insurance." Pete leaned over Seámus and put his hand on Seámus' back.

"Thanks for the advice," said Seámus as he gathered up the papers into a file folder and put the folder into his brief case. As Seámus stood up, Pete had a sneer on his face. Seámus smiled and exited the office.

***

When Seámus got home, he mentioned to Lynn how he had closed a health insurance case.

Lynn was playing with Rory and Bridget. They were a beautiful trio to behold. "So how much will that bring us?"

"An extra $250 a month if all goes right."

"Sounds great," replied Lynn. "Do you want to join our game?" She didn't have to ask twice.

***

Over time, Seámus spent the most of his time with John Stang. Pete Peterson seemed to be antagonistic. He was always suggesting ways to bend the rules. Well, really *bend* is too kind. They were actually actions which would break the law and if found out could cost Seámus his insurance license at the minimum.

Seámus didn't believe in *office gossip* so he kept this all to himself. One day, however, Pete got into Seámus' face over countersigning a document that Pete had obviously forged. It was a health record. The one the client filled out showed several conditions that would probably nix the deal: hypertension and an abnormal EKG. Peterson was redoing the paperwork and needed a counter signature.

"I'm sorry Pete, but that's not my style." Seámus was sitting in his cubicle making cold calls on commercial health insurance. Peterson was hovering over O'Neil and put his hand on Seámus' shoulder blade.

"Are we a unit here or not?" put Peterson.

"We work in the same office," replied Seámus.

"But we're a team here, right; all for one and one for all."

"Sure. But if you are changing some forms, then you need to go back to the insured and do it by the book."

"The guy lives in Chinatown. A man could get hurt there."

"I don't know much about it. Maybe you could carry a gun?"

"I do that all the time. It's my safety blanket, but that's not what I meant. And you know it." Then Peterson lowered his head so that he was at the level of Seámus' ear. The former Marine whispered, "Have you ever heard of *friendly fire*?"

Seámus shook his head.

"Didn't think so. You're one of those draft-dodging pricks who used to march against the War, weren't you?"

"No, I wasn't. I had a legal college deferment. When school was over, then so was the War."

Peterson grunted, "Damned lucky. Be damned, you." Then Pete stood up, spit on the floor, and walked away.

***

Seámus was more determined than ever to get out of Peoples Insurance. On the side, he was attending seminars in commercial environmental insurance: auto and liability. It seemed to Seámus that there was a great future there. He wanted to get in on the ground floor to help shape the way things would progress. This created a potential difficulty with Peoples Insurance. As an employee at Peoples, Seámus was a *captive agent*. This meant that all business he wrote belonged to Peoples. The only way that Seámus could break free would be to sever ties with Peoples. But that was the problem. Peoples was paying the bills. None of the commissions he was receiving on top of his salary would be his were he to leave Peoples.

Seámus decided to have a talk with the branch manager, Win Gibson. Win was a fat man of fifty-five. He always dressed casually with his belt tightly drawn just below his considerable belly. Win was bald on top with hair on the two sides of the head. He always had a smile on his face even when he fired agents who were not performing. (There was a lot of firing in the office.)

Win's office had a big desk and a chair for Win that allowed him to lean so far back that he was almost lying down. When Seámus came in, Win gave him a hearty handshake and then lay back again.

"What I wanted to talk to you about, Mr. Gibson, was whether it was ethical for me to represent insurance products that Peoples does not handle?"

"Go on."

"Well, I have a possibility of representing some larger commercial cases. At present, we only have products that are set for very small businesses, the B.O.P. policies."

"That's because our core business is life insurance. When we write a B.O.P., the stage is set for a *key-man* policy or a *buy-sell* agreement. That's what we're all about." Win took out a cigarette and lit it.

"I understand, sir. So just to be certain, if I represented a product that was not in competition with any of Peoples' products I would not be violating either the letter or the spirit of my contract?"

Win started to laugh. "Seámus, you have to be the goddamnest most straight-shooter I've ever met."

"I take that as a compliment, sir."

"Damn straight it's a compliment. Everybody is doing stuff on the side. I don't care what you do so long as you make your sales goals." As he uttered these words, Win exhaled a stream of smoke.

"Yes sir. I want to be perfectly clear that if I represent products that are *not* in competition with Peoples that I am not breaking the letter or spirit of my contract."

"I'm not sure you hear very well, young man. I just said so, didn't I?"

"Yes sir. Thank you sir. I just didn't want there to be any misunderstanding."

***

So with that informal assurance, Seámus created a relationship as an insurance broker at a large insurance agency: *Best Insurance.* Because Seámus was now also a broker, he worked for the interest of the client (legally) and he owned the business he wrote—he could take it with him wherever he went. The freedom of this relationship made Seámus happy. It had the word *future* written all over it. Seámus' goal was to continue at Peoples until the end of the contract year and then see whether he might be in a position to leave.

***

At the end of the contract year, Seámus lost his guarantee. He was now on straight commission. That meant a 25% drop in pay. However, during the same time, he had written quite a bit of commercial property and casualty as a broker, and that made up for the 25% with an additional 15%. Thus he was now 15% better than he was when he first started writing insurance. He was also closer to his goal of independence.

Seámus had worked two and a half years at Peoples. They recognized his leaving at the weekly sales meeting on Friday at noon. After they went over the week's production, Win signed off with these words: "This will be the last sales meeting with our friend Seámus O'Neil. He has been a stalwart worker and has always demonstrated a positive attitude. We wish you good luck, Seámus, in your future endeavors." There was light applause. Seámus looked around at the dozen or so agents. Jimmy was smiling, as was John. Seámus couldn't see Pete.

As they exited, Seámus shook the hands of his two comrades in the office. But he had to satisfy his curiosity about where Pete Peterson was.

John Stang frowned and started pulling at his moustache. "Tough thing about that, Seámus. I don't want to sour your leaving, but you asked the question." John cleared his throat. "Pete's wife up and left him with her boss at the bail bondsmen office where she worked."

Seámus shook his head. "I'm so sorry for him."

"Well you don't have to be too sorry for him because he *isn't* no more. Last night Pete took his service revolver and blew his brains out. That's the end of that."

CHAPTER EIGHTEEN

Wherever Krishna, the Lord of Yoga, is
Wherever Arjuna Pritha's son [is]
There is good fortune, victory, success.
Sound policy assured. This I believe.
The Bhagavad Gita, 18. 78[4]

The news of the day: Terrorists Hijack 4 Airlines, Destroy World Trade Center, Hit Pentagon, Hundreds Dead.

In a grim address to the nation last night, President Bush denounced the attacks as a failed attempt to frighten the United States, and promised to hunt down those responsible. "We will make no distinction," he said, "between the terrorists who committed these acts and those who harbor them."

Bush vowed that America would continue to function "without interruption," and federal offices and Congress are scheduled to be open today. But the New York Stock Exchange and Nasdaq Stock Market will remain closed, along with most businesses in lower Manhattan. And yesterday was a day of extraordinary interruptions — for the president, for federal Washington and for the country.

Bush was in a classroom in Florida yesterday morning when the attacks began and spent the day on the move for security reasons, flying to military bases in Louisiana and then Nebraska before returning to Washington in the evening. At one point at Barksdale Air Force Base in Louisiana, the president rode in a camouflaged, armored Humvee, guarded by machine gun-toting soldiers in fatigues.

Vice President Cheney and first lady Laura Bush were whisked away to undisclosed locations in the morning, and congressional leaders were temporarily moved to a secure facility 75 miles west of Washington. The White House, the Capitol, the Supreme Court, the State Department and the Treasury Department were evacuated, along with federal buildings nationwide and the United Nations in New York.

Washington Post September 12, 2001.

---

4 R.C. Zaehner, tr. *Hindu Scriptures* (New York: Dutton, 1966).

WHEN the terrorists hit the World Trade Center, Seámus had just gotten to work at *Best Insurance Agency* whose office was on H Street, not far from Metro Center. The office was just as it always was, except for Gloria Freeman who had been glued to her computer on a site not sanctioned by the company. She was watching live coverage of the scene in New York City. Gloria called her office mates over to her cubicle to see for themselves. Seámus came, too.

The announcer was rather frantic. It seemed that there was a mass evacuation of the World Trade Center. Two planes had hit the World Trade Center. Seámus went back to his corner office. This was bizarre. But there had been hijackings before.

In a half-hour or so, Gloria announced that another plane had hit the Pentagon. One of the younger brokers cried out, "It's an attack. We are being attacked! They're going to kill us all."

This caused some considerable confusion. Jeanne Streeter, the sales manager, came out of her office and declared to the assembled company that they were shutting down for the day. Everyone was to go home. *Best Insurance* had a branch in the World Trade Center. It was being evacuated. All branches on the East Coast were shutting down *right now*.

All of a sudden Seámus thought about his kids. Bridget was at a private high school on Wisconsin Avenue, *Sidwell Friends*. Rory and Michael were in separate public schools. Seámus got on the phone to Lynn and they created an evacuation plan. They divided up the responsibility of retrieving the children. They had to get them home because America was under attack.

Both parents executed their tasks efficiently. There were many others with the same goals. When they were all together in their home (that they now owned as the foreign service family who had rented it to them had retired to their favorite foreign venue) the family watched the video replay over and over. They observed in dismay the collisions with the World Trade Center and the collapse of one of the most expensive commercial properties in the world. Stories were pouring in about heroic actions by first responders (fire and police) and private citizens. There were even some tales of maintenance workers who risked and/or lost their lives in heroic bravery.

When they got up for a respite there was some confusion.

"Why did these people do this?" asked thirteen-year old Rory. Rory was a boy who his teachers did not understand because he did not fit into traditional molds. He was an athlete on the school basketball team. He was also an artist who loved to paint, play his saxophone in the band, and create movies with the new digital camera his father had purchased for the family.

"There is no proper explanation," replied Lynn. "People make choices, but the *reason* for those choices is often obscure."

"History is full of violent events that come forth all by themselves. They change the way things go afterwards," was Seámus' response.

Rory and Bridget decided to go downstairs to talk about it. They would set out their theories at the dinner table.

Michael wanted to play a game. Lynn started with him and then Seámus took over.

At dinner, seven-going on eight-year-old Michael asked whether it might be the case that the terrorist attacks might just be *bad luck.*

"What do you mean by *luck?*" asked Bridget.

"You know, like skinning your knee when you're playing a game." Michael was blonde haired like his mother. He loved dinner-time discussions.

"Okay," put Bridget. "That is *luck* in one way. You didn't plan for it to happen. That might be like falling down because you didn't tie your shoe laces. But it might not be luck in another way since if you tied your shoe laces, you might not have fallen down."

"I tie my laces!" remonstrated Michael.

"Of course you do," put in Rory. "Bridget is only trying to make a point. You know about *making a point,* right?"

Michael took a long drink of iced water. He did it in dramatic fashion so as to lengthen his time to respond. "Well, okay: so what about if I fall down even if I've tied my shoe laces and everything. I just fall."

"That's different," said Bridget. "I agree that sometimes accidents happen. That's just fate."

"I'm not sure I believe in fate," replied Rory. "We read in school about the Calvinists who believed that when you are born everything is set down for you: one is either the *elect* or he isn't. Tough toenails. I don't like that theory."

"Well, we aren't Calvinists. We're Anglo-Catholics. We believe in free will. That means that there is no overriding fate that captures us. We are free to make our lot in life." Bridget liked to hold the position of authority both among her siblings and at school.

Everyone ate a few bites of leftover chicken and rice. Then Michael said, "I'm not as grown-up as you, but I still think that if I've had my laces tied and I skin my knee, it's *bad luck*."

"Okay. It's bad luck," replied Bridget.

"Bad luck," chimed Rory.

"Those people today who died. They didn't forget to tie their shoes. It just happened to them. They *died*. It's bad luck. Really bad luck. Why does Jesus allow that to happen? Jesus isn't for *bad luck*," returned Michael.

Bridget and Rory started eating again. Lynn and Seámus looked at each other. Lynn nodded to her husband. "These are great questions. I expect that you will discuss some of these in school within a pluralistic religious setting. What might be good is that when we go through our bedtime ritual that you express your thoughts to Mommy and me before you go to sleep." Then Seámus took a drink of beer. "It is important to work these things out. Life is complicated."

Lynn nodded. "We need to accept that the world is a dangerous place. That is why we try to make our lives as safe as possible. This Saturday I've got tickets to see *Peter and the Wolf* at Adventure Theater. That might be another venue to think about *bad luck, tragedy,* and *evil*."

The children nodded and their thoughts moved towards dessert.

***

In a week or so, all the special emergency measures for day-to-day people were rescinded. The government was determined to restructure so that this would not happen again. But in the insurance business, it was a profitable time for every company who did not cover either the airplanes or the World Trade Center's property policies. (Of course, there is a standard 'act of war' exclusion in most property policies. But there was some disagreement whether terrorist actions constituted a criminal act [covered] or an act of war [not covered]. Lots of money was in the balance.)

Seámus was at a different point in his life. He now had three children. Michael had been born in 1993. Bridget was ready to do the college tour (something that neither Lynn nor Seámus had ever done, but was now the *de rigeur* for attentive parents). Time seemed to be moving at a very fast pace. What would happen if he blinked?

***

Seámus loved his family. He was intrigued by each of them separately. First there was his wife, Lynn. She was a born teacher and really put in the time with her children. She structured activities that would help each child separately to explore various parts of themselves: Self-knowledge linked with self-actualization. Seámus would follow suit in his own way. Since he didn't have as many Monday through Friday hours to be with the children as Lynn did, he treasured each moment with his children when he got home each night at 6 o'clock. He would bring one of the children into the kitchen with him to talk about their day while he made dinner. Then at dinner he would try to grill another child on their day. After he had done the dishes, he worked with homework along with Lynn (in separate parts of the house). Each utilized their pedagogical skills with the children as they tried to make sure their children were really learning for themselves. They were not *doing* the homework, but re-teaching it. Lynn liked to say that she could teach her children everything they needed to know pre-college and that the schools were a bonus.

Seámus seconded his wife's theory. Then starting around 9 o'clock it was bedtime, starting with Michael first (since he was the youngest). They each got around twenty minutes with Seámus reading them a story (according to the *reading list* that Seámus and Lynn had agreed upon for their children pre-college). Seámus would read a passage. Then there was a brief discussion. Then there was a story from ancient history from Seámus. And finally, a song that would make the journey to dreamland easier.

***

Lynn and Seámus thought of themselves as a team. They generally supported what the other thought about things, but they had their own particular spin on things and there was never a requirement on uniformity. As they prepared Bridget for the most engaging college she might fit into, they also tried as best they could to move each of their brood to reach excellence in all that they did—especially when it came to concern for the fate of others less fortunate than themselves. They did regular shifts among different contingents at homeless shelters and food kitchens. Both parents felt that this was an important part of their children's education (a view not shared by their peer group).

***

Bridget was heading toward college, Rory was heading toward high school, and Michael was heading toward 4th grade. It was quite a span. Each child took her or his own course. This created a great feeling of uncertainty among the O'Neils. Shouldn't there be a *set path* upon which all children walked? After all, hadn't Bridget and Seámus created a syllabus of books to be read aloud to each of their children for their first 12 years of life? It was what they thought their children should be exposed to. It represented a factual and normative synthesis of what a child should know going forth into secondary education (high school).

But their children were different. Bridget tended toward science while Rory and Michael seemed at the moment toward the undecided. They were still trying everything. The factor of the unknown was rather difficult for the parents to handle. Shouldn't it be the case with Bridget, for example, that she should be able to attend whatever college or university she wanted to since she was a well-rounded person with high skills in science?

Certainly Lynn and Seámus thought so. But the college application process seemed to be so filled with random parameters that unfair outcomes seemed very possible. Somehow they muddled through it all. Bridget was accepted at several colleges and Rory seemed prepared for high school and Michael was in trepidation about the 4th grade. The older two children seemed as if they were more independent and barely needed their parents. Even Michael seemed to be on a path he could handle better than his siblings at that age. All of a sudden, it seemed as if parent-work was entering a different mode. This both excited and troubled Lynn and Seámus.

Lynn's response was to re-apply to the colleges in the area to see whether she could get a term appointment. At present, her job was at home with the children. Seámus applied again to the Smithsonian museums that might have some use for a man trained in history. (Seámus played down the fact that his specialty was Ancient Greek history.)

Lynn was unable to get a full-time temporary position and accepted a course-by-course adjunct position at George Washington University. Seámus failed to land a position over an eighteen-month job search. It was fortunate that his environmental insurance sales were steady. They could make their mortgage payments and even pay for Bridget's college tuition. Money was not the driving concern in their lives. They were well-to-do but not rich.

After a couple of years teaching as an adjunct, Lynn made some contacts with book reviewers at a conference she attended in New York. She enjoyed the camaraderie and thought that she would try that out for a year while teaching and then make a decision on what she wanted to do next.

Seámus got his inspiration on how to move forward from a funeral he attended. It was a man he had worked with at the Environmental Protection Agency. The deceased had sought Seámus' help to create new industrial liability regulations to try to reward lower polluters and lessen carbon output through the incentive of their insurance policies. Seámus worked out some unique rating tables using supplements on top of standard ISO ratings to create this discount program. The EPA official, Fred Tot, was equally far minded. At the ceremony, which was held in a funeral home near Crystal City, Seámus met Mrs. Frieda Tot. She told Seámus about a project that had engaged her husband during the last years of his life: he had started a family history project that was more than just who-married-whom. "Fred was really trying to understand his family's history. It was for him a project that gave his life meaning at the end. Do you know what I am talking about?" Frieda was a woman just under 60 (close to the age that Seámus estimated for Fred) with light brown hair. Her face was unlined and she spoke with an even tone with few modulations.

"I'm not sure," responded Seámus. "but I think that is a wonderful project. How far along did he get?"

"Hard to say. When he would make a *find* he would tell it to me. Sometimes he would e-mail it to our son in California. He was really about finding little stories and linking them all so that they might shine together. What he was really after was some large overarching theme that might combine the little scenes into a whole—like the thread upon which one strings the beads of a necklace."

Seámus was taken with this. After he went home he told Lynn about the funeral and the project that his colleague, Fred, had been engaged in. Lynn nodded. She was reading her first novel for review, *The Corrections*, by Jonathan Franzen.

Seámus was off and running and so was Lynn.

***

There are certainly a number of ways to understand events from an historical vantage point. At one end are the chroniclers. They just set down a series of happenings: A then B then C . . . Such historians place great emphasis upon physical records of human life: births, marriages, property exchange, political change, funerals. The *Anglo-Saxon Chronicles* commissioned by King Alfred is a classic example of this sort of history.

Certainly some concentration upon sources is essential to doing proper history. When Seámus was working on his Ph.D. in ancient Greek History—particularly upon the fall of democracy in Athens following their loss in the Peloponnesian War—there were not a lot of documents to choose from. Papyrus under normal conditions falls apart in around 200 years. Parchment is much more durable, but also much more expensive. Sometimes, an historian has to work with the sources he or she has and look for internal contradictions and then make educated guesses.

The second key concern of historians is *giving a causal account of what has happened*. This is very dicey. This is because it relies upon the worldview of the historian and will reflect his or her prejudices. For example, if one were a Marxist then everything would be about economic oppression and the struggle of the working class to get a fair shake. Likewise, if one were a Feminist, then everything would be explained by reference to the oppression of women and their struggle for freedom and equality. If one were immersed in religion, then the account given would mirror that religion's view about the end of time and our current progress report.

Every historian is [at least] concerned with these two dimensions of approaching the past. So it was, also, with Seámus. What he wanted to study was his family history. His family history had always been of interest to him, but after the funeral of his colleague at the EPA, the notion took on new significance. Might some understanding of where he came from enlighten him about who he was today? Is it possible that one could be ignorant of various factors that might be at play even today as he lived his life as son, husband, father, and general individual trying to make a living in the world? Might it have more general implications about the Irish-American experience?

It is within this context that Seámus set out.

First, he needed to examine his sources and get the most reliable data possible. Seámus knew that his father, Andrew, came from a large family. With new internet ancestry sources, he was able to determine Andrew's siblings and where they were born: Marie was born in Philadelphia in 1890, James, Jr. was born in Philadelphia in 1892, Catherine was born in Louisville in 1895, Mollie was born in Louisville in 1898, Ruth was born in Louisville in 1901, Ellen was born in Louisville in 1905, Jeanette was born in Louisville in 1908, Gertrude was born in Louisville in 1910, Doris was born in Louisville in 1912, and Andrew was born in St. Paul in 1914. There were ten children born to James O'Neil and Frederica Sullowald. The children were born in a 24-year period. The second and the last were male and all the rest were female.

Seámus then went after Frederica and found that she had come from Oberhausen, Germany, which was a Baptist stronghold, and had a legal partnership with Wolf Sullowald, who Seámus discovered was her uncle. These seemed to be the main players in the family tree.

The next major question to ask in the fact-finding part of the project is when the Sullowalds and the O'Neils came to the United States from Europe. This sort of research used to be a rather tedious. But in 2003 the internet access to public records was immense. Seámus was able to find out that Seán and Mary O'Neil were processed at Castle Garden, New York in 1862, along with their two sons: Tommy and James. Seán was Seámus' great-grandfather. James was Seámus' grandfather. It was not clear from the records where they lived initially, but in the 1870 census there was a Seán O'Neil living in Philadelphia with his sons Tommy and James. What happened to Mary was unclear (if indeed this was the same family). After all, Seán was a common Irish name. Seámus had kept a diary when he was a young man. Perhaps he had made entries on this. But first Seámus had to go to the attic and find the diaries.

Public records cover marriages, deaths, and certain commercial transactions. But the deaths of poor people often slipped through the cracks—especially those of immigrants. Mary O'Neil's fate could not be determined by the public records available to Seámus.

In addition to his diaries, Seámus needed to visit the two living people who might be able to tell him what was not available in public records: his mother Moira and his aunt Gertrude (who was in ill health). Seámus' mother was 86. Gertrude was in her early nineties. Perhaps Seámus could plan a summer family trip to California to visit his mother, let the kids play in Disneyland, and pop in on Gertrude at her apartment.

Lynn had no objection to visiting a grandparent. They had each lost one parent and so were both down to one: Moira on Seámus' side and Dylan on Lynn's side. Living testimony was slipping away. And the children liked going to the original Disneyland—and not just 9-year-old Michael.

Visiting aging parents can be tricky. Modern medicine keeps people alive for extended periods of time. However, it is often the case that their quality of life does *not* keep pace. Because of the confidential nature of the narrative, Seámus arranged a time in which he could talk to his mother alone, while Lynn and the children went to the Santa Barbara beach.

Seámus took his mother to a park just outside the Santa Barbara arboretum. There was a hill across the street that sported a little path with benches strategically situated. On one of those benches, Seámus sat with his mother.

"It was so nice of you to plan a visit," said Moira. "It's been five years since you last came."

Seámus nodded. "It's difficult for us to be living on opposite coasts."

"Yes, but Santa Barbara is a nice place. Though, it's changing rapidly, you know. When we first moved here there was not the huge wealth that is now developing. You know Fess Parker has had a better career as a real estate developer for the rich than he ever had in the movies."

Moira loved the movies. If she had never gotten married, she could have easily imagined herself on the silver screen. She looked away for a moment at the foliage and tree canopy.

Then Moira turned back to her younger son, "Well, it's nice that your brother, Liam, is in Los Angeles. He's only 90 minutes away in case I need him."

Seámus felt the pinch.

From their perch on the hill they saw the magnificent arboretum that mixed indigenous desert flora with foreign implants from the Midwest and East. When one looked over the scene, one's eyes were arrested by the single redwood tree. The redwood tree is a hallmark of California. Though they are more numerous near San Francisco in Muir Woods, still, the historian's mind is blown away gazing at a living thing that is 2,000 years old.

Then there were the families with their young children scurrying about in an entirely different time frame. It was in this context that Seámus asked his mother, "I'm doing a family history. You know I've always been keen on history."

Moira smiled.

"And I know that you talked with many of Dad's sisters. And maybe his mother?"

Moira's face changed. "No. I never talked with Frederica. She did not come to our marriage. And everything that I've ever heard about her is that she was a she-devil."

"A she-devil?"

"The devil in the form of a woman. We all know that Satan is a man. The root of evil begins with men." Moira was staring out again at the arboretum. Then she cocked her head and looked at her son, "Present company excepted, of course." Moira smiled. It lightened her visage. When she had been talking about Frederica, she had a sternness that made her face transform to a leathery hardness.

"What made her so bad?"

"She was a driven woman who only wanted money. She put money above her husband's happiness. Do you call that a good wife?"

Seámus thought about it for a second, but did not want to go down that road.

"Her uncle, Wolf, was a big crook. He tried to rule James's family. Wolf had no family of his own so he adopted James's and Frederica's."

"And adoption is bad?"

"When it's done without consent it is." Moira turned back and looked her son in the eyes. "That man tried to take everything away from James: his wife and his children. He was a viper whose venom poisoned the family. Only three survived: your father, Doris (who died young), and Ellen (who looked after your father). All three are now dead, of course. Only I live to tell the tale." Then Moira turned her gaze to the sky. The afternoon was beginning to wane.

"Then there was the partner who stole from James. I don't remember his name, but he ran the books and then left town in a hurry for Louisville (where the family had lived under Wolf's thumb for a number of years). That scalawag took the heart out from your grandfather. He went to Louisville to get his money back, but couldn't find the miscreant.

"I'm not surprised. Wolf probably put him up to it. Wolf never liked your father and wanted to destroy him."

Then Moira got up to walk up the hill some more. They got all the way to the top, which was clear of trees and had only grass, a little abstract statue, and four benches. There was nobody else there. It was a private space. Moira sat down, winded. Seámus gave her some space to recover.

"So what happened to grandpa after he went to Louisville after his money?"

Moira stood up and walked about on the grass before sitting down again. "What happened? That's the million dollar question." Moira looked down to her hands which were folded. She was shaking her head back and forth. It wasn't a tremor.

Seámus put his hand on his mother's shoulder. "Is it too painful?"

Moira turned her head and looked her son in the eyes. "I thought I'd never tell you this. It's because I didn't want you to think that it was in *our blood*. You know that all of us go through tough times that test our souls." Then Moira stopped and began to cry. Seámus slid closer and hugged his aged mother. Her body was shaking. Seámus didn't say another word.

After some time he asked, "Is there something more you want to tell me?"

"Yes." Moira straightened herself and rubbed her eyes clear. "James O'Neil, your grandfather, got on top of some big bridge there in Louisville and jumped to his death." Moira paused again. "He killed himself."

Moira sat bolt upright and looked her son in the eyes. "You don't know how long I have wanted to tell you this. But I thought that if you knew that there was suicide in the family that you might take that route when the going got bad."

Seámus hugged his mother again and proceeded on their descent from their promontory.

That night, the family took Moira out to dinner at a fish restaurant, *Moby Dick,* which was attached to the main pier in Santa Barbara. They had a table that faced the sea. Moira took a seat that allowed her to gaze out at the Pacific Ocean. Her grandchildren had their backs to the water, but they didn't mind. They speculated that they might never see this family member again. And they were right.

***

After Seámus left his mother, he drove down to the Englewood district of Los Angeles. It was a changing neighborhood. It had been once solidly middle class when the sisters all left St. Paul in the early 1950s for Los Angeles. Frederica led the crew. It was also when they, in mass (aside from Marie), left the Roman Catholic Church for various Protestant options—especially Christian Science. Seámus wanted his wife and children to meet the only living relative besides his mother on his side of the family.

Seámus and Lynn had agreed that they would take 93-year-old Gertrude to lunch with everyone and then Lynn would drive their rented car to drop Seámus and Gertrude back at Gertrude's apartment to talk about family secrets while she took the kids to the art museum.

Gertrude lived in a two-story rental apartment that looked like a motel from the road. It was essentially a one-bedroom place. There was a space that had a small sitting area and the kitchen. In the middle of the sitting area was a coffee table which serviced Gertrude as a place to eat. There was one more small table that housed an ancient television. Seámus grimaced as he entered the apartment that stank of urine and rotting food. Gertrude's daughter, Sylvia, had become a prosperous lawyer in San Francisco and had (as an associate) married a senior partner, Sydney Chapelstone, in 1975. They had two children, Peter (1981) and Mary (1983). It was a very prosperous family in one of the highest cost-of-living cities in the United States. And yet, Gertrude was living in filth.

Gertrude's husband, Bill Blogett, who she married in 1934, had died in 1967 in a car accident. She had worked the minimum years for social security and that was it. She was also on Medicaid for housing allowance.

Seámus' first instinct was to request that they take a walk outside. But he re-thought that idea. He wanted to talk to Gertrude where she was at: comfortable in the stench of her own making.

"It is so nice of you, James, to come here and talk to me." Gertrude had poured herself a glass of tap water into a vessel that appeared not to have been cleaned for some time.

"*Seámus*, Aunt Gertrude. I'm *Seámus*."

"Yes, of course, James. You so remind me of your son, Andrew. He's got a real future ahead of him. You can bet on it."

"Yes, Gertrude. I think you are right about that." Seámus tried to think about how he could get authentic testimony. He decided to get up and walk to the large plate-glass window that was on the back wall. It was a sunny day and the window revealed a small courtyard in the center of the apartment complex. "It's a beautiful little park you have here. Do you ever go and sit on one of those benches?"

Gertrude began to cough. "Damn Mexicans live here. I don't want to get raped or mugged. No siree. I stay inside except when I go out to buy food." Seámus decided to turn to his aunt with the large window as the backdrop. He was a black silhouette to the 93-year-old relative.

"Aunt Gertrude. What do you know about Wolf Sullowald?"

Instantly, Gertrude grimaced and grunted. "That man was from hell. He raped my mother and murdered my father. I know he got gunned down at the Chicago World's Fair. I know that and I said to myself—good riddance. He was the central source of pain to the family. He made our mother crazy. You know she was at heart a decent German girl, but then she was overturned by Wolf. Your father, James, couldn't do anything about it, Andrew."

Seámus only smiled.

"Wolf enabled that son-of-a-bitch Niall Mullins. He put him into our pharmacy in St. Paul. He was Wolf's spy. He was also selling illegal drugs on the side. Your father, James, wanted to be a real pharmacist just like he had been taught in Philadelphia by one of the best in town, a Quaker man." This time it was Gertrude's turn to get up and stroll to the window. As she walked, she pulled back her stiff hair with her fingers. Seámus wondered when she had last showered.

"Niall was the cat's paw of the Devil. He ran off with James's money. In my opinion, when James went after him in Louisville, Niall killed him when James was walking back to his hotel across some big bridge they have there. Yes, siree. James was found dead with a gash across the back of his skull. He was murdered. But because Wolf was so rich and corrupt he could pass around some money that would give Niall a get-out-of-jail-free card."

Then Gertrude reached out for Seámus' hand and walked him back to the two chairs that were in the apartment. "Andrew, your father was murdered. And no one ever went to jail for it. That's the real truth. I'm sorry, but that's the way it is. The whole thing devastated our mother. It's partly why we all left the Church and went to California for redemption. Most of us became Christian Scientists. It's a personal religion. You don't even have to go to church services.

"I just bought pamphlets by Billy Graham."

Seámus smiled. "Yes, I remember. You sent them as gifts at Christmas."

"No better Christmas gift for a young man."

"Yes, Gertrude."

Then Seámus walked his aunt to the small neighborhood store and bought her some prepared food that she could keep in her refrigerator. He also bought some cleaning supplies. They went back and Seámus cleaned out her refrigerator and cleaned the kitchen and bathroom.

When he had finished, Lynn had returned from the art museum sojourn. They offered to take Gertrude out to dinner, but she declined. She didn't like all the Mexicans in her neighborhood.

***

On the plane back, Lynn suggested that they pay for a private duty nurse to look after Gertrude a couple hours a day. Seámus concurred, but knew that the logistics from the east coast would be difficult. There was a possibility of further Medicaid funding, too. Seámus got right on it when they returned home at the end of August. Unfortunately, just when everything was due to begin, Gertrude O'Neil died of arterial sclerosis on October 8, 2003.

***

Lynn O'Neil's renown as a book reviewer increased. She always got her copy in on time and according to the exact word limit. She wrote from a quirky point of view as a scholar of the English Victorian novel and its transition to Modernism. She was also keen on photography and the visual art world of the time. This allowed her to possess a unique voice that the top national newspapers lapped up. She turned out 12 book reviews a year.

And she liked it.

Bridget graduated from college in 2005, the same year that Seámus took on a part time gig at the new Smithsonian National

Museum of the American Indian. He was hired to review the historiography of a big special exhibit and offer any suggestions for change. He did this on the side. He was still full-time in environmental insurance work. Rory O'Neil was ready for his college visitation summer and Michael was about to enter middle school.

After everyone was asleep, Seámus went to his project of first preference, the O'Neil Family History in America: Maya—An Irish-American History. He would write it all out on the computer and then he planned to print copies for himself and his children on their home computer—perhaps he would have them bound? That depended upon how happy he was with it. He wasn't sure whether he would give a copy to his brother, Liam, because he was worried about what he might think about all the blood and carnage of the family O'Neil.

As Seámus commenced writing all alone, late at night, he began to become confused. He was dealing with testimony (Moira's and Gertrude's), with public records that he had assembled, and his own personal memories both from his current recall and from the two diaries he had found and re-read. These anecdotal accounts from his memory, now recently stimulated and from his diaries, created a consistent understanding of family history from his parents and aunts when he was growing up. This latter twist was most unusual. In some ways it seemed unprofessional. He had a personal interest in the way this was recorded and ultimately interpreted. Perhaps he could get around this by explicitly denying that the history was to be understood as factual? What if the history were really about the larger points of the Irish-American experience in America using situated personal experience that was as truthful as possible, but not accurate to the standard of modern historiography? Maybe he could also introduce an interpretative device that explicitly dealt with fate and human freedom—like the philosophy of Hinduism? He chose Hinduism because it seemed to be so immersed in the context of one's life experience and was such an ancient philosophy. Seámus was comfortable with ancient worldviews. This further frame might thus act in such a way that it created a distance for general historical truth to stand forth? This satisfied Seámus.

Seámus then thought about his sojourn last night to the exhibit he was professionally reviewing. It was on the "Trail of Tears." The museum has as part of its mission to not overly proselytize from the Native American perspective. They want to let the facts speak for themselves. But the facts never just *speak for themselves* because there is no clear demarcation between facts and values (judgments about those facts from a personal worldview perspective).

Between 1838-1839, Andrew Jackson sought to enforce the *Indian Removal Act of 1830* so that the Cherokee, Muscogee, Seminole, Chickasaw, and Choctaw nations (east of the Mississippi) were forced out of their historic homesteads in an exodus far away to what is present-day Oklahoma. Thirty percent of the people who were forcibly evicted died on the trail. Estimates range from 4-6 thousand people perishing.

Seámus thought about his own family's history. In 1838, Mary Hennessey was born in County Cork, Ireland. In ten years her family was to die in the potato famine that was a result of greed-driven public policy by British businessmen who wanted to keep exports level, even when the output had drastically dropped. It was an instance of who is going to take the pain: the bank accounts of rich men who lived in another country, or the hard-working farmers who produced the crop. Since the Irish were viewed as semi-human, it was an easy decision.

Mary was taken in by a relative. She married Seán O'Neil in 1855 but the famine was still killing multitudes. They left for America in 1862, going steerage. Roughly 20% of the travelers on those crowded, unsanitary boat conditions died in the passage

Then Seámus thought about his grandfather, James, who was one of Seán's and Mary's two sons. He worked for a time in the same unhealthy factory as his da. The other son, Tommy, became a cop in New York and died trying to break-up the powerful Five-Points Gang. The other child, Lucy, died of measles when she was three. Mary, the mother, died giving birth to Lucy.

These were terrible times for immigrants (like the Irish) and for natives (like the Cherokee). [There was also, of course, the human genocide known as African slavery—but that was not a part of this museum's exhibit. Perhaps, he could get a job in the newest museum on the drawing board: The African American History Museum.] As Seámus had tried creating his rubric to evaluate the exhibit, he wanted to separate two sorts of pain. There was a real sense that the Irish immigrants were voluntarily leaving a terrible death trap for some chance at survival. If they stayed in Ireland they had a big chance to die. If they left, there was a manageable risk of dying in passage and another manageable risk of not being able to make it in the new country. At least they spoke the language (since Gaelic was a forbidden tongue).

The Native Americans were in *their own place*. Some aggressors were bullying them out for their own advantage. This was involuntary. Was it in any way similar to the English occupation of Ireland? Yes and no. Certainly Seán and Mary made their own choice to leave. The Native Americans were *forced out*. Seámus tried to imagine himself as a Cherokee (the largest nation) and how he would feel. The analogue experience helped him create some notes that perhaps would make the exhibit more effective from its own perspective.

Then Seámus tried to particularize his inquiry to the fate of Seán's son, James. Because James was his grandfather, it seemed to Seámus that the pharmacist's fate was crucial to his getting the interpretation of the family history correct.

The key players were: 1. James O'Neil, 2. Frederica O'Neil (born Sullowald), 3. Niall Mullins (James's business partner in St. Paul), 4. Wolf Sullowald (the German gangster who broke many laws in order to acquire money and power), 5. The St. Paul pharmacy that was a two-tiered operation (a real pharmacy run by James and a drug-running operation run by Niall Mullins), 6. The 10 O'Neil children who had to grow up in the midst of this turbulence. Seámus also wanted to add: 7. The United States of America in which immigrants could freely come at their peril in order to reset their lives.

What Seámus was keen to find out was why James chose to leave his benefactor, Charles Quincy's, pharmacy to set up operations with Wolf? This seemed to be an irrational move. Only a couple of times when he was in the presence of Aunt Ellen was the name Charles Quincy, a Quaker, brought up. Seámus had made a couple notes on this in one of his diaries. As he searched his memory of the entry, he could get nothing more than: Charles Quincy was a pharmacist who was teaching James to be a pharmacist. Charles Quincy was a Quaker and an honest man. James left the business to go out on his own under the wing of Wolf Sullowald and his niece, Frederica. Was it love or passion that made him leave? What would be the most likely scenario? This was something Seámus would have to work out.

Seámus leaned over his computer and contemplated whether he should start writing again. It was past midnight. Seámus decided to go for a walk. He wanted to stroll to the Tenleytown Metro. The

Metro stopped running at midnight, but he wanted to get out into the city where people lived—even though now there would be few people out in this neighborhood. On the way, he stopped and looked at the dark local library. The library closed at 10pm. People in the neighborhood had been complaining about it being too small, so there was an on-going petition to get a new building. The library had always been fine for Bridget, Rory, and Michael. They were able to check out books for free. All they had to do was bring them back in the period specified by the library. Instead of complaining, Seámus thought his neighbors should be happy for the opportunity. After all, isn't the library a relative value-free ticket upward for literate people with ambition? This, at least, was Seámus' opinion. There weren't free public libraries for most of American or Irish history.

As he walked on the mostly deserted streets, Seámus started thinking about people he had known in his life. He had had an upbringing that was similar to "army kids." Andrew had moved the family every three or four years according to his job. That is often the lot of those in upper management within the business world. But this meant that Seámus had many ghosts in his own history. Occasionally on their own accord, these ghosts would appear and present themselves either as they *had been* when Seámus was young or in a *revised form* according to Seámus' knowledge of them via Christmas cards or the new technology of e-mail. When this happened, there was always the tendency to think that Marcia or Paul had *always* been that way, but that Seámus had been too blind to see it.

However, at least on this night, Seámus wanted to change his opinion. He wanted to think about people moving *forward for a future* that they had planned for themselves. He wanted to think that when bad things happened, they were the result of exterior forces that were either good or bad—but beyond personal desert. As Seámus started out, he felt a few rain sprinkles. But it wasn't supposed to rain tonight. Lynn always read the weather forecast to him as they had breakfast coffee. He felt sure that it would pass over.

Then he stopped just in front of the Metro. He knew where this was taking him. He had the ending of the beginning of the O'Neil family history: James had been murdered by Niall Mullins as James was crossing the Ohio River over the Big Four Railroad Bridge. James had been out for a late night ramble, just like Seámus' own late night sojourn this night. Sometimes a person just has to start his thinking when much of the community is asleep. So it was with Seámus tonight as he thought about how to frame his history. *In his way, James had been trying to find out where to go: would he go after the thief, Niall? or his overlord, Wolf? James was searching for a strategy. The only problem with this approach was that James wasn't alone. He had been shadowed by Niall, who wanted to put an end to his machinations. With a blow to the back of the head, James's options were limited. His fate was now utterly determined.*

With that, he descended into the Ohio River with little chance of survival. His destiny overcame him.

Seámus looked up to the still illumined Metro Sign for Tenleytown. He thought about himself, and he thought about his family. Was he, too, turning in a widening gyre he could not control? What if the centre did not hold? Seámus decided to be hopeful. He walked back home, alone, in the rain.

Other Novels by Michael Boylan

Rainbow Curve (2014) Fans of baseball's history will appreciate this compelling tale about race, politics, and corrupting power and one's man's courage to stand-up. *De Anima #1*

The Extinction of Desire (2007) What would you do if you suddenly became rich? *De Anima #2*

To the Promised Land (2015) Are there limits to forgiveness: personal, corporate, and political? *De Anima #3*

Naked Reverse (2016) There is a backdoor to the ivory tower. Find out what happens to one college professor who escapes. *Archē #1*

Georgia: Part One (2106), *Part Two* (2017), *Part Three* (2017) A novel told in three parts. Explore racial identity and themes of social justice through a murder mystery set in the early 20ᵗʰ century. *Archē #2, 3, 4*

T-Rx: The History of a Radical Leader (forthcoming) An epistolary novel about radicalization in the Vietnam-era. What are and what are *not* legitimate tactics for social/political change? *Archē #5*

The Long Fall of the Ball from the Wall (forthcoming) A novel set in the investigation of the JFK assassination that connects this event to larger social phenomena. *Archē #6*

Made in the USA
Middletown, DE
18 May 2020